# RADIOFLASH

# MARK J. HIPP

Black Rose Writing | Texas

ISBN: 978-1-68433-566-4
PUBLISHED BY BLACK ROSE WRITING
www.blackrosewriting.com

Printed in the United States of America
Suggested Retail Price (SRP) $21.95

*Radioflash* is printed in Calluna

# ACKNOWLEDGEMENTS

This book is dedicated to the men and woman of the law enforcement, security, intelligence, military and foreign affairs communities who take the following oath of office (5 U.S.C. § 3331):

> *"I, (name), do solemnly swear (or affirm) that I will support and defend the Constitution of the United States against all enemies, foreign and domestic; that I will bear true faith and allegiance to the same; that I take this obligation freely, without any mental reservation or purpose of evasion; and that I will well and faithfully discharge the duties of the office on which I am about to enter. So help me God."*

We owe a debt of gratitude to the brave Americans who volunteered to serve in harm's way and paid the ultimate price for keeping America safe, secure, and just. Their selfless sacrifice preserves the Constitution and allows this great nation to be a beacon of hope for others to emulate. I have traveled to more than 70 countries during my career as a special agent of the Diplomatic Security Service and I always thanked my good fortunes every time I returned to the U.S. for the opportunities and freedoms it afforded me. Our founding fathers were trailblazers and visionaries, and we should not only live by their example and by the foundation they provided but also strive to enhance their vision.

An America marred by partisan politics, incivility, intransigence, and intolerance devalues the dedicated few who take such an important oath and work to preserve the American way of life, whether it be in a third world country, on a foreign battlefield, behind enemy lines, in the backstreets of an American city, or on the border. Perhaps more importantly, it weakens the security of a great nation, emboldens our enemies, and threatens our way of life. The threats posed by nuclear proliferation, terrorism, hostile intelligence, regional conflict, crime, drugs, political violence, and climate change are continuous, real, daunting, and dangerous. People need to put aside their political differences and work together to conquer these constant threats. For when we work together, we can achieve great things. Our politicians must put America above their own political ambitions, or reelection desires. In the immortal words of President John F. Kennedy, "ask not what your country can do for you, ask what you can do for your country."

This book, albeit fiction, melds current day themes, agencies/organizations, and threats into a fast-paced plot that reflects how ingenuity and forward thinking can be used against our core values and destabilize America and world peace. This book is meant to entertain its reader while providing a look into the origins and plausibility of one of America's true nightmare scenarios involving an electromagnetic pulse.

I did not realize the amount of work, research, and creativity that goes into writing a book. This book could not have been accomplished without the support, thoughts, guidance, and encouragement of a special quorum of people led by my close friends and former colleagues Fred Ketchem and Scot Folensbee, as well as Bob Rosenblatt, Dick Sherman, Debbie Hipp, and Oliver Hurtin. I would also like to say a special thanks to Fred Burton, Sam Katz, and Robert Booth who provided me great insight into the back end of the book world from social media strategies to marketing to website development and much more. Lastly, I would like to call out those wonderful people at Black Rose Writing, to include Reagan Rothe and his team of professionals who were instrumental in getting this book into its final form and to market.

# RADIOFLASH

"*According to the EMP Commission somewhere in the range between 2/3 and 90% of the US population would perish in the first year after an EMP attack, caused by an attacker detonating a nuclear weapon (even a small and simple one) above the earth in low-earth orbit, or by some type of solar coronal mass ejection. It is easy to see how the losses could be so high, since the US has some eighteen critical infrastructures – food, water, telecommunications, finance, medical, transportation etc. All seventeen of the others depend on one: electricity. Without it we are vulnerable to starvation, thirst, disease and social chaos. So if the electric grid is out, not just for hours or days, but for weeks to months, we are faced with the need to obtain the basics of life as was done before the creation of the electric grid. We would be thrust back, not just to the 1980's pre-web, but rather to the 1880's pre-grid. And few of us are prepared to function without being able to obtain life's basic needs in the ways we obtain them today.*"

– Former CIA Director James Woolsey,<br>Post-Hearing Questions for the Record

"*An electromagnetic pulse, or EMP, occurs when a relatively small but carefully designed nuclear warhead is detonated in the atmosphere. The explosion causes what can best be described as a massive power surge, which can damage or disable electrical devices for hundreds of miles on the ground below. As I told the Senate Committee, such an attack would be catastrophic to the United States because we are an electricity-dependent nation and our grid is ill-prepared to handle it. These blackouts could encompass entire regions. Without proper preparation, the grid disruption (and destruction) caused by an EMP could take months to years to repair. Non-perishable foods would spoil from lack of refrigeration. Hospitals would run out of life-saving, temperature-controlled medications within days. Dialysis and other medical devices would stop working. Water systems that rely on electricity would stop pumping water and pipes would burst from the weight and pressure. The cascade of consequences of a protracted regional power outage would be devastating.*"

– Newt Gingrich, Former Speaker of the House

*"The cost of freedom is always high, but Americans have always paid it. And one path we shall never choose, and that is the path of surrender, or submission."*

– President John F. Kennedy

*"The nation whose population depends on the explosively compressed headline service of television news can expect to be exploited by the demagogues and dictators who prey upon the semi-informed."*

– Walter Cronkite

# CHAPTER 1: PHANTOM STRIKE

*North Caucasus, Chechnya*

An eerie loneliness trailed the two shadowy figures as they stepped off the helicopter's skids and into the Stygian night, yet darkness remained their greatest ally. Kneeling behind a layer of dense pine trees, the two eyed their maps and northwesterly bearing on their GPS watches. Springing to their feet, they darted across an open pasture. Northerly wind squalls suddenly appeared; a frigid arctic chill gripped the lush valley. Millions of diamond-like stars shimmered in the cinereous sky, while dawn lingered due to the moon's low orbital path and the nearby mountains that eclipsed its crescent shape. Their dilated eyes scanned the marshland from left to right, unmindful of the landscape's rugged beauty.

The howling wind masked their hurried footsteps as their night vision goggles illuminated the otherwise dark terrain. Careful of their footing, they glided over patches of black ice, skirting a small half-frozen pond. Edging the thick tree line near the base of a foothill, the two agents crouched behind a fallen tree; its millions of needles spewing a subtle pine fragrance into the air. They removed their night vision goggles, exposing their black balaclavas and craggy sphinxlike faces.

The two operatives lifted their thermal imagers to their penetrating eyes and scanned the grassland surrounding the safe house. Over a dozen heavily armed men appeared as nebulous red-yellow silhouettes. Powerful motion lights triggered as a four-man patrol rounded the dwelling. The team leader panned away from the house to the perimeter; black triangular signs with white skull and crossbones indicated a functioning minefield. Microwave sensors and a barbwire fence formed the outermost layer of security. It would be virtually impossible to penetrate the concentric rings of security, let alone get close enough to the legendary rebel leader without detection. Ingenuity – not brawn – would be required for a successful outcome. Extraordinary rendition was not an option.

The team leader eyed the patrol's route as he assembled his Russian-made SV-98 sniper rifle, opening its tripod, tightening its flash suppressor, and dialing in the 7X power scope. He inserted a ten-round clip into its magazine bay, tugging on the magazine to ensure its fit. The rifle's 7.62 caliber round laced with shellfish toxin guaranteed death to its recipient. The wind howled as branch limbs cracked and danced erratically in the morning twilight. Tapping his handheld wind meter, his face sank at the twenty-five mile per hour gusting crosswinds. "Nothing's easy," he muttered as he peered through his scope and centered its crosshairs on the front door.

Meanwhile, the other agent unzipped a bulging black backpack and withdrew a miniature metallic object known as the silver widow. Seven appendages protruded from its softball-sized core; three extended vertically and formed its legs, while four others extended horizontally and led to four separate brushless motors that powered its rotors. The operator nimbly unfolded and snapped the appendages into their extended position. The silvery drone resembled four toy helicopters joined at their tails.

The two agents traded turns watching the five-thousand square foot rambler while waiting for daybreak. The intermittent sleet and steady doses of adrenaline thwarted any rest. The success of their mission hinged on their heightened senses. The latest signals intelligence indicated that the Ghost, aka Moussa Rahman, would depart at dawn to inspect a high-tech Chechen weapon's lab meticulously chiseled out of a nearby mountain. Their mission, like most covert operations, depended on timing, opportunity, and a bit of luck.

The two observed three navy blue Toyota Land Cruisers inching towards the front of the house as the sun crested the mountaintop. A light fog ascended from the ground, casting shadowy beams as the sun's rays pierced an old windmill. The sniper crawled low and parallel to a fallen pine tree and up a slope to a large gray boulder. Stretching his rifle forward, he stabilized its tripod by rocking it back and forth in the dirt. Peering through his rangefinder, its lower screen vacillated between 985 and 995 yards to the front door. He glanced right and eyed the thirty-five mile per hour wind gusts on his meter.

The former Spetsnaz sharpshooter anticipated just seconds to identify the target and squeeze the trigger. Unfazed, he could shoot the eye out of a rat at four-hundred yards. His breathing slowed as his field of vision narrowed to the front porch; his finger relaxed upon the trigger. Time decelerated as he waited once again to prove his shooting prowess.

Inserting the small metallic blasting cap into the two pounds of American-made C-4 high explosive attached to the drone's underbelly, the ten-year veteran of the Federal Security Service (FSB) ran a diagnostic check on an iPad-like controller. The operator tapped the computer's touch-screen interface; the drone's four rotors hummed to life. The agent's finger slid upward on the screen, as the rotors spun faster; the silver widow shot above the tree line and hovered seconds later. Even the gale-force winds did little to jolt its stability. The drone's high-tech lightweight batteries increased its airborne time to thirty minutes. The operator piloted the drone to five-hundred feet and then toward the safe house using the touch-screen. The silver widow streaked toward its target at sixty miles per hour.

The FSB operator tapped the screen; the drone's built-in digital camera aperture sprung open and relayed the ground below to a ten-by-eight inch touch-screen monitor. Zooming in on one of the guard towers situated at each corner of the property, machine guns, grenade launchers, and sniper rifles appeared. The drone's grayish color, small signature, and aerial acrobatics evaded the guards' detection. Facing overwhelming odds, their survival depended upon the element of surprise and a hasty retreat.

The front door snapped open; a brawny man dressed in olive green military fatigues emerged wearing a white winter parka and a gray scarf that covered his neck, chin, and a portion of his lower mouth. The sniper swept his scope upward to his target's face. His black shark-like pupils and a two-inch facial scar along his cheekbone sealed his fate and his tombstone. He clicked off the rifle's safety.

The seasoned sniper squeezed the trigger; a severe side wind emerged, causing him to compensate while compressing the trigger to the rear. A muffled shot rang out. The bullet ripped through the center of the parka; its force propelled the man backward as he disappeared below the vehicle's roofline. The agent whispered, "He's wearing body armor. It's up to you. Take him."

"Watch this move Yuri," mumbled the operator with a playful grin.

The drone's digital camera zoomed in on the vehicle's backseat as a bodyguard covered Rahman. Pressing the touch-screen, the operator sent the drone into a steep dive as the Land Cruiser rolled forward. A bodyguard standing next to the car snapped his eyes and the barrel of his assault rifle skyward and fired; a barrage of bullets whizzed by the streaking silver widow.

A split-second later, whitish-orange flames and gray smoke billowed skyward as the Land Cruiser's roof exploded. Smoldering metallic fragments ripped through its compartment, slicing the throat of the driver and showering down on Rahman and his bodyguard. The car fishtailed and crashed into a nearby hundred-year-old oak tree; the engine's compartment crumpled. The driver's body slumped forward, resting on the horn; its steady blare echoed throughout the valley and summoned an army of reinforcements to the area.

With their eyes bulging while taking short, fast breaths, two of the four tower guards frantically fired their machine guns in the direction of the agents; hundreds of rounds peppered the log and shredded its shell as bark fragments showered the area. Muscles relaxed, the stoic sniper took an easy breath, centered his scope to the tower nearest him and fired a single shot; the guard slammed back against the wall before dropping to its cold cement floor.

"Get moving to the rally point," barked Yuri, turning towards his partner with a twinkle in his eye and a faint grin. "I'll cover you."

"What about you?"

"I'll be right behind you. Now move. That's an order." The sniper swept his rifle to the left, aimed, and squeezed the trigger. The guard's head snapped back as blood spattered the wall.

The FSB agent listened for a lull in the gunfire, crawled down a small incline, and ran hugging the tree line. A barrage of mortar rounds peppered the pasture, splattering dirt and a plume of gray smoke with each impact. The deafening blasts reverberated throughout the valley.

The operator's mind raced. I can make it. It's only another half mile to the rendezvous point. I can't leave Yuri. I have to get to the other side of the field.

Upon clearing the pasture, the agent stood behind a large spruce tree while the FSB sniper darted across the pasture under a hail of gunfire. The agent raised an AK-47 assault rifle and fired over Yuri's head, lighting up the far tree line. Seconds later, the drone operator reloaded and continued firing. The fleeing sniper zigzagged repeatedly to evade a barrage of rounds. Making it to the tree line, blood trickled from his lower thigh and left shoulder. They glanced at one another before turning away from their hunters.

The two agents sprinted through the dense forest, not peering back. Dodging a stream of trees and shrubs that encroached upon them, they embraced the foliage's concealment from the trailing rebels. Tracking hounds doggedly pursued them; their steadily increasing, high-pitched barks boomed throughout the nearby hills. The sniper glanced over his shoulder as his strides increased. Approaching the rally point, Yuri staggered as blood oozed from his shoulder. His heartbeat quickened as adrenaline flooded his extremities. Gritting his teeth, he soldiered on to the next clearing.

Peering through the limbs of several pine trees, their wide glowing eyes tracked the approaching Kamov KA-60 Kasatka, aka Killer Whale, helicopter. Their sagging postures straightened as warmth radiated throughout their bodies. The sniper thrust his fist skyward.

The pilot swooped into the tiny clearing; its four circulating blades blowing and twisting the nearby treetops. The helicopter leveled off at twenty feet above the ground and pivoted ninety degrees to face the tree line. A one-piece transverse boom through the cabin to rear of its doors provided suspension for two seven-round 80mm rocket pods and two 7.62mm gun pods. The craft's streamlined shape and armament intimidated adversaries. The uneven terrain, abundant mix of small trees and dense shrubbery precluded the skilled pilot from landing. The gusts of wind did little to affect the hovering of the modern marvel.

The two agents emerged from the woodland and darted for the helicopter's dangling cables. They traversed the thirty yards in seconds and snapped their C-clamps imbedded on their web gear to the cables. Rounds fired from the tree line struck all around them, splattering dirt upward like a hard rain rebounding off the pavement. The Killer Whale's pilot flipped the safety off his machine guns and strafed the tree line with hundreds of rounds in seconds. A sudden lull descended over the field, but the veteran pilot knew it was temporary and scanned the woodline in anticipation of his next salvo.

Yuri raised his thumb to the crew chief. The pilot launched three volleys of two of its rockets. Six distinct fireballs exploded in the woods. A dozen insurgents lay dead; their twisted and burnt bodies lay lifelessly strewn across the moss-covered ground. Pulling up on the collective control, the pilot increased power and blade pitch of the craft's four rotors to generate additional lift. He used the pedals and the cyclic control to maneuver the craft away from the impending danger and up over the trees, careful not to drag his cargo into the pines below. Seconds later, the crew chief hoisted the two agents into the helicopter. Once they cleared the passenger door, the crew chief swung them inside and guided them into their seats. The Killer Whale sped off for their homeland, accelerating to its cruise speed of one-hundred and seventy-one miles per hour.

The sniper tore his balaclava off his head while the medic hurriedly treated his leg and shoulder wound. An intimidating figure, Yuri's six-foot four inch frame supported pure muscle. His two wounds were little more than an annoyance to him. He would certainly live to carry out other covert missions for Russia. He glanced at his partner, who sat quietly in the cold breeze.

"We didn't exactly shoe a flea," Yuri said as the medic finished cleaning and bandaging his shoulder wound.

"Nothing's easy, but we finally nailed that bastard," replied the drone operator, removing her balaclava. She shook her head from side to side, releasing her long flowing blonde hair into the wind. "The scumbag got off too easy."

"That crosswind sucked." Yuri flinched as the medic stitched him up. "I know I hit him."

"I wish that shellfish toxin had time to do its job," said the five-foot, seven inch Russian bombshell. "I can't believe our government recruited him. No wonder he scares our leaders. Governments have fallen for less. We risked our lives to clean up their mess. This operation was a suicide mission." Her defiant crystal blue eyes sparkled in the low light.

"It's ironic, isn't it?" Yuri shook his head. "He used our training to rally Islamic extremists against us. I wish I'd killed him, but your drone finished him. No one could've survived that blast. We should've filmed the operation. You'd be famous Svetlana. Your grandfather's smiling down upon you."

She waived him off. "Fame's overrated. I'm just glad he's dead."

"How can I get one of those drones? My son's birthday is coming up. Are you okay?" He patted her shoulder. "How does it feel getting your first kill?"

"I'm both elated and down." She lowered her head. "I keep seeing his face. He's there, cowering and pleading for his life. I take it. May God forgive me." Her hands covered her face as her stomach stirred.

"The world's better off; you can be proud of that. I'll sleep better tonight. I've sniped over one-hundred people; their faces disappear in time. Show no mercy Svetlana; they'd slit your throat without any remorse."

Andropov stared pensively out the helicopter's window. The slight tremor in her left hand subsided as the pilot announced their safe return to Russian air space. She finally could relax; her adrenaline plunged to normal. She had trained rigorously for the mission for the past couple of months, and its anticlimactic conclusion surprised her. In the upcoming days, she would rest and prepare for her next mission, whatever or wherever it would be.

# CHAPTER 2: REVELATION

*Two Weeks Later*

The wind wailed as nimbostratus clouds blanketed the pinkish-orange hues of dawn. Peering over his shoulder at the three-story brick complex behind him, Diplomatic Security (DS) Special Agent Matt James scanned the service entrance.

"How did they breach the embassy?" He pressed the receiver to his ear. His brows rose before morphing to a frown. "This group is no J-V team. Can't believe they missed this plot. Leave it to the politicians to dismantle the CIA as the world crumbles," the gritty team leader muttered, before scowling and slamming down the receiver to his classified satellite telephone. He turned to his team, who all eyed him.

"T-I-A (Threat Investigations and Analysis) informs that four terrorists have taken our ambassador and his special assistant hostage in the embassy," James reported, surveying his team. "They've threatened to blow it up in an hour unless the press arrives soon or if they see any police. The bastards want to put our ambassador on trial for blasphemy. No doubt she'll be convicted and then beheaded or burned alive." His fists tightened. "Not on my watch. We need to show strength, and I'll be damned if I'm going to let her kids or anyone else see this trial on television. I'd rather die than let this travesty happen." His face reddened as he loosened his collar.

Special Agent Sean O'Donnell shook his head while rubbing his forehead. "This is Delta Force's mission. They're trained for hostage rescue."

James tugged his collar. "We're out of time. They're six hours out. The ambassador will be dead in an hour. We need to strike now. Are you guys in?

There's no dishonor if you bow out, but I can't sit by and let the ambassador die when we could've stopped it in its tracks."

O'Donnell grimaced, as did the four other agents. "You know we'd follow you to hell and back, but this operation is a suicide mission. These terrorists are professionals; they slaughtered five highly trained Marines to take over our embassy. Besides, the director ordered us to stand down and gather more information for Delta."

"Screw the director." James lowered his head and spit on the ground; his eyes turned cold. "He's a paper-pushing, ass-kissing bureaucrat who only cares about his own damn career. Gear up. It's time to settle a score and deliver America a victory."

Jack Thomas snapped his head around; his eyes widened at his team leader's portrayal of the director. They all recognized he sold out the service for the top job, yet few had the balls to state it so openly and risk his wrath. None of them desired an assignment to West or East Africa for their candor.

"Okay, listen up." James raised his hand. "This assault is as deadly as it gets. Our mission is simple. We're going to rescue the hostages and neutralize the terrorists. Are there any questions?"

"What do we know about the bomb?" O'Donnell leaned in and eyed his teammates.

James growled and coughed. "They reportedly have a suitcase full of explosives, which could drop the building if affixed to the right structure. We'll need to operate silently and catch them with their pants down." He placed a stun grenade into his front vest pouch. "We believe the bomb is time activated, but for all we know it could be detonated by a dead-man's switch."

"This op sounds like my kind of fun," Dutch Wagner enthused. "Let's get some. Time's wasting."

James let out a grunt. "Wagner's right. We'll use the sewer system to approach the back entrance and then breach the door, climb a flight of stairs, traverse two corridors, and then hit the suite. Any concerns?" James tilted back his head as his hands formed a steeple.

"Where's George?" Thomas asked, charging his assault rifle.

"He's gathering intel. We'll need to neutralize the threat and, if possible, isolate, contain, and arrest the four terrorists. Don't take any unnecessary risks. They won't give up without a fight. We must prevent that bomb from detonating. Now let's move." James strapped on his ballistic helmet, savoring his forty-sixty odds.

Wagner slid the cast-iron circular lid aside. Its scraping against the asphalt reverberated throughout the block.

"Could you make any more noise, Dutch? James grumbled, shaking his head. "You should just tell them we're coming."

Wagner shrugged before descending into the bowels of the city. A burst of methane gas vented skyward, awaking his olfactory senses. "Damn, it smells like O'Donnell's breath."

"You ought to feel like a pig in shit Dutch, and right at home." James descended the steel ladder with the rest of his team in succession. Trudging through an inch of greenish-brown sludge, the agents dodged a surfeit of cobwebs that reflected the tunnel's lack of use. Bats awoke and scurried past them, breaking the sound of trickling water and the tunnel's otherwise eerie silence. Flashlights mounted to their weapons illuminated their path as hundreds of rats scurried for cracks and adjoining pipes. The drone of their steady screeching sent shivers down James' spine.

"I hate bats and rats." James' voice shook. His jaw clenched as he kicked a cat-sized rat to the side. It shrieked in protest, glared back at him, and then wandered away. "These things only spread disease. The world would be better without them."

"Yeah, we need to kill the four rats in the ambassador's suite first," said Wagner, climbing the latter. He lifted the manhole cover six inches and scanned left to right. A partially concealed masked man squatted behind a dumpster; his rifle covered the building's rear entrance. Balancing the sewage cover with his head, he extended his arm and silenced pistol outside, aimed, and squeezed the trigger twice. The terrorist fell to the ground. He pushed the manhole cover aside and jimmied his body and equipment through its opening. Raising his assault rifle, he turned back to the opening and swept his hand across his body. "Let's move. It's clear."

Exiting the manhole, James dropped to a knee and aimed his rifle at the second-floor windows. One by one, his team piled out of the manhole and darted to the rear entrance. O'Donnell inserted a key override into the door and unlocked it; the team funneled through the entrance seconds later.

James directed his team's actions with a mix of hand signals. They entered the stairwell and darted to the second floor in under a minute. With their Colt M-4 assault rifles pointed in the direction of their movement, they paused behind the corner of an adjoining hall. O'Donnell kneeled, opened his telescoping mirror, and peered around the corner, angling a small silver-dollar sized mirror from side to side. The smoke-filled corridor appeared empty, so the six-person team rounded the corner in unison and glided towards the ambassador's office.

Donning their night vision goggles with thermal adaptors, the team plowed through the wafting gray smoke. Sweat poured from their foreheads as flames roared around them. A piney, gaseous, and metallic stench permeated the air as the fire consumed desks, chairs, and walls. Their skin reddened as they passed a fire-engulfed suite; its searing heat flooded the hallway. Dark silt attached to their faces.

Analyzing the floor-to-ceiling black smoke spewing out of the adjoining rooms, James recognized his team's limitations in the toxic environment without rebreathers. His mouth and throat dried from the five-hundred degree heat and thick black smoke. Maintaining radio silence, he advanced his team toward the end of the hall. His left hand shot skyward, making a fist. His team froze in their positions while their eyes scanned their designated sectors.

Squatting, James' knees cracked, breaking the eerie silence except for the buzzing of the overhead fluorescent lights that flickered periodically. He scrutinized a piece of monofilament fishing line extending across the hall. His fingers slid across it to the pin of an American-made fragmentary grenade hidden behind a doorjamb. Removing his combat knife from his waist belt, he slashed the line to separate the grenade's pin from it. He stood quickly, pointing his index and middle finger at his eyes and then directing them down the hallway. They moved in unison with members peeling off to cover open doors and then rejoining the surging train-like team as the last man passed.

Nearing the executive suite, the team stacked evenly on each side of the door, careful not to cast their shadows through the door slightly ajar. James pointed to O'Donnell and then to his own eyes before sweeping his hand across the doorjamb. O'Donnell nodded and sidestepped deliberately to increase his field of vision within the suite. Raising his left hand, O'Donnell crossed his index and middle finger. The team observed as he pointed to the location of each of the four intruders within the room.

The team's concentration waned from O'Donnell to listen to the voice emanating on their earpieces. Their eyes enlarged as T-1-A informed them that the terrorists possessed a Soviet-era tactical nuclear weapon. Their stomachs cringed at the news while James appreciated the increased challenge and risk.

The team's decisive moment loomed in the scorching heat. James alone would shoulder any blame for a botched operation. He seldom experienced disappointment and never quit. Not that it mattered. He and millions of others would be incinerated in the blink of an eye.

They remained in position, knees slightly bent and ready to spring forward. James double clicked his push-to-talk button on his radio, indicating his readiness for his second team to initiate their assault. He pulled the pin on a stun grenade and lobbed it into the center of the room. *Bam!* A brilliant yellow flash spiked the room as the grenade's percussion rattled the suite. He squeezed O'Donnell's shoulder. "GO."

Dangling on top of the office's main window by a rope strung from the roof of the embassy, Special Agent George Atwell descended another five feet to straddle the window. He squeezed the trigger twice on his silenced pistol; a terrorist manning the suitcase fell lifeless to the ground. His eyes searched for other targets.

O'Donnell shouldered the door open, veered left, and darted to cover the far corner of the room. Shots rang out as he cleared the door's threshold. James, only a split-second behind him, tracked in on the muzzle flash through the wafting smoke and shot twice into the intruder at center-mass. The terrorist fell lifeless to the ground. Wagner and O'Donnell pivoted at opposite corners in the room to cover the center area; both agents fired multiple shots. Two other extremists fell lifeless to the ground as the front of their shirts turned dark red.

The team visually cleared the room in seconds by checking under the desks, pulling the curtains back, and inspecting a small coat closet. Wagner and O'Donnell's pistols remained pointed at the four fallen intruders, while Thomas checked each one for a pulse. Thomas approached the last terrorist and touched the side of the man's throat. He whipped his fingertips across his neck.

"Clear," James barked. "Get the ambassador out of here." He approached the suitcase and glanced down at the clock affixed to the top of it; its timer flashed red numbers in one-second intervals: "thirty-five, thirty-four, thirty-three..."

James closed his eyes, sighed, and then glanced at his teammates; his face solemn. He placed both of his clammy hands on his tepid face. A fiery mushroom cloud supplanted his thoughts as the words from the Book of Revelation sounded in his head. "The fourth angel poured his vial on the sun, and power was given to him to scorch men with fire. And men were scorched with great heat."

For the first time in James' life, failure gripped him. His stomach churned, as he understood all too well the gravity of the situation. His failure would affect many and could threaten another war. He examined the clock, looking for a way to stop its countdown.

. . . . .

Meanwhile, on a country road, DS Special Agents' Doug Smith and Dave Steele drove the speed limit in their dark blue four-door Chevy sedan. Smith's hands remained relaxed on the steering wheel at the ten and two position while Steele rode shotgun and reviewed a map on his GPS. Neither agent understood the content or value of the Top Secret documents they carried; the materials covered the latest trends and predictions regarding nuclear proliferation. The two twelve year veterans only knew their mission involved protecting three orange diplomatic pouches stuffed into the trunk of their vehicle and transporting them across the border to the embassy; and they both remained savvy enough to avoid any further questions than their mission required.

The rolling green hills intermixed with fields reminded Smith of the Wales countryside. The recently tilled cornfields and freshly cut pastures diffused fine debris that made his eyes water while unleashing a green mildew smell that rivaled fresh cut wet grass. Cows and horses roamed freely while a throng of sparrows left the shelter of nearby oak and pine trees to fly above the fields to scavenge for a smorgasbord of flying insects. The sun rested high in the sky and evaporated the last remnants of a morning rain that left the air clear and fresh.

Smith clasped his fingers together in his lap while his eyes darted between a meandering brook and a family of deer. Inhaling the crisp air, he closed his eyes and struggled to forget all of the carnage he had witnessed the previous year in Iraq. His new assignment allowed him to travel to six continents and experience firsthand myriad cultures, people, food, art, and history. He relished finishing today's mission, so he could forego his high protein, body building diet to taste the rich food of his German heritage at a nearby establishment.

A Remington 870 shotgun rested in the center console, reminding him that his trip required work. Smith looked at his oversized teddy bear partner, who gazed fleetingly out the window until he eyed him.

"You drive slower than my eighty-five-year-old grandmother. I'd like to get there today." Steele smirked.

His eyebrow raised; he required no prodding to drive fast and take chances. "Hold on to your seat. I'm taking us to warp drive." He stomped on the accelerator and felt the surge of the engine's V-8 roar, jerking the car forward as he unleashed the vehicle's horsepower.

Steele gripped the armrest; his face tightened. Smith reveled in his partner's trepidation, so he pushed the laws of physics even further while rounding a hairpin corner; his car wheels screeched to maintain their rubber on the road. Accelerating out of the corner, he floored the gas pedal as he hit a straight patch of road.

Smith glanced into his rearview mirror and noticed two cars approaching. He peered over at his partner. "Dave, we've got company. They're not ours. Keep an eye on them."

Steele looked over his shoulder just as the first car, a red sedan with three Middle Eastern-looking passengers approached the two agents on the outside lane. Their empty stares suggested trouble as their sedan darted ahead. Smith's gut churned as the hairs on the back of his neck straightened; chills tingled down his spine as the passing car slowed.

Smith glanced at his partner; his wide eyes and stiffened face indicated he had the same bad vibes. "Saddle up. It's about to get rough." Smith's eyebrows drew together.

Smith glanced at his speedometer as the front car decelerated. He pulled up on the rear quarter panel and turned into the red sedan, causing its back wheels to slide sideways. The sedan flew off the road and spun out in a field of grass hitting an embankment; its hood sprung up from the impact.

"Nice," Steele said, pivoting to spot the other car pulling alongside. "Let's ditch the other A-holes." He reached for his Sig Sauer 9mm pistol tucked under his thigh.

Smith's peripheral vision caught the glint of the second vehicle pulling even to his car. His eyes caught the barrels of Israeli-made Uzi submachine guns protruding from both passenger windows. He slammed down on the brake pedal as gunfire erupted; his tires screeched as orange flashes streaked by the front windshield. The attacker's car flew by as the agent's vehicle jerked to a stop. Burnt rubber and grayish smoke drifted in the light breeze.

Realizing the lurking danger, Smith slammed the gear selector into reverse. Stomping on the gas pedal, he accelerated to twenty-five miles per hour. Removing his foot off the gas pedal, he cranked the steering wheel hard to the right. The vehicle spun one-hundred eighty degrees and faced in the opposite direction. He shifted into drive and accelerated away from the attackers.

Incessant beeps from their smartphones broke their focus. Steele glanced at his phone and recognized the number that appeared on it. They both scanned the area for a secondary attack and a safe way out of the kill zone.

Steele glanced up into the light blue sky; a dozen turkey vultures circled overhead. "We better get moving or they might come after us." They drove up a small incline and headed back to their office.

# CHAPTER 3: DARK DAYS

Syria's ancient and disputed history distinguished it from others. Long known for its strategic location along the eastern edges of the Mediterranean and at the crossroads to the Middle East and Asia, it remained disputed land for endless centuries. The Egyptian, Roman, and Ottoman empires had all tried to conquer and maintain this strategic area. Yet, the resilience of its people and the abundant mix of cultures gave the country a unique and exotic flair.

Known as the fragrant city for its profusion of the revered jasmine flower, Damascus captivated many as the oldest continuously inhabited city on the planet. Many in the region believed it to be the most important political and cultural center in the Arab world, and their beliefs were well founded; the people of the region had contributed greatly to the fields of science, art, culture, politics, commerce and industry from the earliest of times. It made sense that such a glorious and ambitious plan would crystalize in this venerated metropolitan oasis now plagued by civil war.

Peering over his shoulder, the cagey man's eyes twitched as perspiration pooled on his forehead. He contemplated turning around, but instead stepped downward into the unknown while wiping his forehead with a white handkerchief. Upon entering the grimy basement of the dirty stucco house in old Damascus, a combination of stale tobacco smoke, Turkish coffee and thousand-year old mold overpowered his olfactory senses. The man sensed the atmosphere shift from one of fear to relief tinged with anger. Seven taut faces glared up at him as he descended the stairs into the safe house. Despite their unified appearance, he recognized their individual isolation by their folded arms and their backs tucked up against the nearest walls. This behavior did not disturb him. He preferred they kept their distance. He surveyed the room and exchanged glances with the leaders of the highly secretive and deadly Khorasan Group.

The man stopped at the head of a seventeenth century walnut rectangular table and welcomed each of the seven leaders. He first shook hands with Khalil Moumad, who formerly led the operational arm of Al-Qaeda in the Islamic Maghreb. Moumad's rapid rise to the top of the North African franchise and subsequent recruitment into the Khorasan Group seemed logical given his ten-year-old acquaintanceship with the merciless killer. He admired Moumad's ability to disguise, outfit, and detonate a bomb by a hundred different means. He pitied the explosive technicians that had to match wits with the zealot.

"Did you increase the bubonic plague's virulence?" The man asked sneering. "Don't need another careless accident killing our fighters, like that fiasco at your base in eastern Algeria. We need a breakthrough in our biological weapons capability. The specialist sheikh demands results sooner than later."

"That accident cost us forty of our best warriors. We've mutated the plague to increase its virulence; it will devastate the infidels and make the fourteenth century bubonic strain look like nothing more than a common cold and that plague culled a third of Europe's population." Moumad pressed his lips together into a thin line.

"Good, I'm glad we've got that straight." The man licked his lips, smiling wryly. "For a minute, you seemed to be softening. Only this type of determination can defeat our enemies."

Shuffling around the table, he greeted Faisal Ahkmat, a former military commander and bomb-making expert with Al-Qaeda in the Arab Peninsula (AQAP). Ahkmat's fanaticism and skill troubled him, as did his excessive ambition. He anticipated Ahkmat openly challenging his authority; something he wished to avoid. His concealable chemical explosives advances made him a living legend.

"Thanks to Ahkmat's leadership, AQAP has taken the fight to our greatest enemy and is the tip of the spear against the West. The Christmas day bomber sparked great fear in America, forcing them to adopt new airport screening technology. AQAP's ingenious work in Dubai and London on the cargo planes triggered further panic. If Saudi traitors hadn't interfered, then the toner cartridges would've detonated over America. His liquid explosive has already defeated the latest screening equipment on trial runs," the man said, grinning.

"They won't be so lucky next time. We'll strike fear in the belly of the beast itself." Ahkmat ran his hand through his hair. "This is Allah's will."

Sidestepping right, the man embraced his new confidant, Moussa Rahman, who led the military wing of Al-Qaeda in the Caucasus. A former Chechen military commander, his suicide bombings, kidnappings, and rocket attacks propelled him to the top of Russia's hit list. His tenacity, harsh intimidation tactics, and resilience bolstered his reputation well beyond his native home in the Republic of Georgia. Both his friends and his foes saw him as an unstoppable force with nine lives. Most kept their distance from him.

The man bowed. "Moussa, you cheated death recently. Someone wants you dead."

"They almost got me," Rahman said as his fingers touched his parted lips. "Not only did they snipe me, they defeated my security and attacked me with a drone. The FSB agents killed my driver and best bodyguard. The bastards blew up my new armored car. I'll get even with Russia. Mark my words."

"I'm glad you survived. You can seek revenge after our watershed mission." The man glanced to his right.

Continuing his salutations, he embraced Moustafa Yousef, the second in command of the notorious al-Shabaab. He feared the cold-blooded butcher but valued his vision and ingenuity. Yousef built a six-thousand strong force and liberated large swaths of territory throughout Somalia and in its capital. The man withheld his disgust of the Somali, whose lawlessness and corruption oozed from his soul. He enlisted Yousef for his European and American recruits, who could defeat airport screening measures.

"Yousef, your group's external reach is floundering in recent months."

"You're forgetting our successful university attack in Kenya," he barked. "The CIA's mercenaries are hunting me. Their drones are decimating my top lieutenants. I'm growing tired of sleeping in a new location every night. It's a good thing I've multiple wives to keep me company." He lit a cigarette and snickered.

The man returned a short laugh. "Let's turn the tables on the CIA. You'll do so soon as part of the Khorasan Group. I promise you."

"I look forward to that day." Yousef gently bit his lip.

The man glanced at the next in line. "It's been too long Hassan. What have you been doing these past years?"

Nidal shook his head. "Surviving, like my fellow warriors, the Israelis have been chasing me around the region. They almost caught up with me on several occasions. The Mossad put a bounty on my head."

A strategic planner for Al-Qaeda in Palestine, Nidal espoused the total liberation of Palestine through an armed struggle, while opposing any negotiated settlement of the Palestinian-Israeli issue. Known as the terrorist's terrorist, Nidal favored well-publicized attacks on civilian targets and had been instrumental in the successful missile attacks on many of Israel's southern towns. He favored spectacular attacks and publicized beheadings.

The man finished the ritual with his two last conspirators. He greeted Muhammad Ayud with a wry smile. Ayud led the operational wing of Al-Qaeda in Iraq (AQI) before the group pledged its allegiance to ISIS. Ayud disavowed their brutal tactics and slaughter of countless fellow Muslims. He wanted no part in the killing of innocent men, women, and children, so ISIS vowed to slay him for his disloyalty.

"How's the jihad going in Iraq? ISIS is fighting the infidels and their puppet government." The man probed knowing that a good portion of AQI had morphed into ISIS. The crusaders had left the Iraqi government with a formidable counterterrorist force, one that doggedly pursued AQI and now ISIS to purge them from the planet.

"This will be a long war, but we're a patient group." Ayud paused and cleared his throat. "Iran's Quds Force is still feeding us money, explosives, and training. Yet it's becoming increasingly difficult to defeat the traitorous Iraqi government. ISIS will preoccupy them for many years, so we can concentrate on our plans against the West. Even with ISIS' rise in the region, this fight's a coin toss, so we must unite against the infidels."

The man nodded in agreement, recognizing the importance of keeping his friends close, but his enemies even closer. His skepticism of Ayud remained hidden. AQI certainly had talent. In past years, the group carried out numerous suicide bombings, assaults, car bombings and several spectacular assassinations in Baghdad and throughout the country. The man planned to harness Ayud's enthusiasm, energy, and bomb-making prowess to target western interests.

Looping the table, he finished by greeting Abdul Ramzi, a young and dedicated chemist recruited from al-Qaeda core.

"Mahaba Abdul. How's the specialist sheikh?"

"He's in good health and extends his greetings, wishing you great success in your vital mission. He'd never divulge this defeat openly. Privately he admits that the crusaders are thwarting our glorious cause, disrupting our finances, eliminating key tacticians, and limiting our area of operations. Their effective high-tech war is decentralizing al-Qaeda. This disruption is the chief reason that we must pool our best minds to attack America. The stakes are great, but they're even greater if we fail. The Khorasan Group must succeed if we're to defeat the infidels, surpass ISIS, and reestablish an enduring Islamic caliphate."

"I'm glad you're still thinking big. We all should. Only by taking great risks can we expect to succeed. It's not going to be easy, but then what is? Wouldn't you all agree?" The man sat at the head of the table. The seven venerable Khorasan leaders waited anxiously for the reasons behind the urgent meeting.

This was a deadly group, without a doubt. And they were not at all pleased with him at the moment. Raising a hand to forestall any talk, the man swung his gaze around the room. "My tardiness was unavoidable. I've new information. The Americans, fearing a threat to their plans for a meeting between the Palestinian president, the Syrian president and the Israeli prime minister, have advanced their plans by a day and will be maintaining a total blackout on all activities. The meeting will take place in two-and-a-half days in Ramallah at 3:00 pm. This change doesn't give us much time to finalize our arrangements."

· · · · ·

*WASHINGTON, DC*

Jim Cummings, the Director of the Diplomatic Security Service (DSS) for the U.S. Department of State, was reaching for the phone when his special assistant burst into his office.

"Sir, you'd better have a look at this. It just came in 'FLASH' from our Embassy in Jerusalem – classified TOP SECRET."

The director looked up, startled, his irritation at the sudden intrusion changing to concern. "FLASH," he mused, "I've been in government for thirty years, and I've only seen a handful of these. The last one occurred when the Taliban breached our consulate's perimeter in Herat."

His face grave, he glanced at his assistant before returning his gaze to the sheet of paper before him. "John, can you ask my office manager to hold all calls until she hears from me? It's going to be another long day. You'd better stay close. We've got an emergency to tackle. Thanks."

The director opened the envelope, and as he read the first line, his stomach churned.

```
//DS CHANNEL//TOP SECRET JERUSALEM 0776
VZCZCLBI
OO RUEHMV
DE RUEHLB #0776 130
ZNY CCCCC ZZH
Z 101204Z APRIL 21
FM AMEMBASSY JERUSALEM
SECSTATE WASHDC 0001
BT

TOP SECRET JERUSALEM 00776
DS CHANNEL
E.O. 12356: DECL: OADR
TAGS: ASEC

SUBJECT: TERRORIST THREAT TO SECSTATE

1. USE OF ACRONYM PRECLUDES DOWNGRADING.
2. TOP SECRET - ENTIRE TEXT.
3. The CIA advises that the U.S. secretary of state
will be the target of an assassination attempt
during his visit to the West Bank for the upcoming
Middle East peace talks. Khorasan terrorists
uncovered the security revisions and incorporated
scheduling changes into their plan. Logistics for
the group are being provided by Iranian's Quds
Force.

4. Source is deemed completely reliable and holds
the highest possible validation rating. Source
advises that the Khorasan Group is fully capable of
fulfilling its mission in an effective manner. The
attack will utilize both explosives and automatic
weapons. The location of the attack is unknown at
this time, but it is anticipated that it will take
place prior to the meeting and most likely near the
Presidential Palace.

5. Please advise on the appropriate course of
action. There is very little Post can do to ensure
the safety of the secretary. Post strongly
recommends that the secretary cancel his meeting or,
at a minimum, reschedule his visit to the West Bank.

WILLIAMS ##
```

The director shook his head in disgust, cleared his throat, and pushed the button on the speakerphone. "John, get Gina Jackson in here pronto.

And call Jack Henderson with the Office of Mobile Security Deployments (MSD) and tell him to put a team together on emergency standby. Tell Henderson I want the best possible team assembled, regardless of their current mission assignments. When you're finished, come and join me. But first, stop by Margaret's desk and get me two Alka Seltzer. Thanks."

The director started making a few notes concerning his options when he heard a knock at the door. "Come in, I'm glad you're here. Thanks for coming Gina."

He motioned the Deputy Assistant Secretary for International Programs to a chair. "We just received FLASH traffic from Jerusalem. CIA reports that terrorists will take a crack at the secretary on his upcoming trip. The source is deemed absolutely reliable."

"We've kept the secretary's trip quiet, even from most government officials. How could they know about our schedule revisions?" Jackson clutched her hands as her stomach churned.

The director shook his head. "They must have an inside source. They know we've revised our security plan, so we need to make further security enhancements. The secretary will not alter his plans and be swayed by this group."

Gina grimaced. "This is the Khorasan Group. They're sophisticated and have assembled the most dangerous minds into a small dedicated group. We should ask the secretary to reconsider." She rubbed her eyelid.

The director glanced out his window toward the Washington Monument. "We did and he ordered us to make this visit happen. So that's what we're going to do."

· · · · ·

*Austria – Twenty Miles East of Vienna*
Pierre Lafonte, or so he called himself today, repositioned himself in the passenger's side of a French-made heavy duty truck carrying two fully loaded containers of cargo. His lower back ached from the lack of motion and a minor dose of arthritis. It had been a long night; they had made excellent time as they neared Vienna. Fatigue and sleepiness now surfaced. He and his driving partner had departed Kiev nineteen hours ago.

His gold Rolex watch read four in the morning, signaling his turn at the helm. He dreaded his pending shift, as they both looked for a suitable area to pull over. Rounding a sharp, ninety-degree corner, he observed a three-car accident that blocked most of the two-lane roadway. His partner downshifted while pressing his brakes.

Pierre gazed forward. His guarded nature, derived from both nurture and trade, had kept him alive on many occasions over the years. He scrutinized the mishap and suspected something more. A second later, a barrage of bullets whizzed by, slicing through the thick cool air and confirming his suspicion.

Lafonte turned to his partner. "Ram them! We must keep moving. Don't stop for anything." He jerked his head back.

The driver struggled to shift gears; a round ripped through his forehead. His eyes rolled back before he slumped over the wheel. Lafonte dove to the floor, as a salvo of high-caliber rounds shattered the windshield and tore through the truck's passenger compartment. Glass shards scattered throughout its confines. His heart palpitated.

Lafonte impulsively gripped his Glock .45-caliber pistol tucked in his waistbelt to return fire. He instead laid there and listened as his colleagues scurried to the right side of the truck; they took up tactical positions among the tree line and in the adjacent ditch. They returned fire with the familiar sound of Russian AK-74s that made a deafening commotion.

A Rocket Propelled Grenade whistled by and found its mark with a roaring impact. The front foremost blocking sedan exploded into a thousand pieces as shrapnel ripped through all in its path. Four attackers died and the others fled without looking back. Only Lafonte's driver and one security member perished in the brazen assault. His cargo remained intact.

The robbery attempt did not surprise him. Its black market value exceeded twenty million dollars, but this cargo already had a buyer who waited for his goods. He recognized the steep price of betrayal, given the buyer's global criminal and terrorist connections.

Lafonte and his team quickly covered their tracks. They realized the upheaval would summon Austrian police to the scene. He could not afford to answer questions or have his cargo inspected. He hurriedly dumped the bodies of his two fallen comrades and four adversaries into the trunks of the cars. The team pushed the vehicles off the road and watched them tumble down into a small ravine, crashing at its base.

Lafonte's mind wandered as the gravity of the inescapable situation pressed down on him. He recognized that loose ends required cleansing and feared for his life following the delivery of his merchandise. Grabbing a rag and wrapping it around his hand, he brushed off the glass fragments from the truck's floor and front seat. After peering back into the woods, he leaped into the front driver's side of the truck and turned the key in the ignition. The powerful engine roared, echoing throughout the nearby evergreen-covered hills. His foot floored the accelerator as thoughts raced through his head. He glanced down at his left hand on the steering wheel. It was still shaking, almost uncontrollably. He contemplated his options. None of them seemed too appealing, but any one of them would be better than dead.

# CHAPTER 4: GEARING UP

James glanced up and the three-story glass facility in suburban Virginia; it mirrored the two others in the three-building complex. The American flag crackled in the light breeze; its stars and stripes backlit in the sunny blue sky. His eyes turned bright while his nerve endings tingled. He closed his eyes as the Star-Spangled Banner sounded in his head. Shaking off his reverie, he walked through a set of double glass doors at the Diplomatic Security Training Center. He scuttled up three flights of stairs and swiped his badge on a card reader. The door's locking mechanism triggered, so he pulled on the handle and strutted into the Office of Mobile Security Deployments (MSD). Agents darted through the reception area giving him only a cursory nod. World news blared in the background as a teleprompter flashed three temporary closings in the Middle East. Phones rang incessantly while an office manager struggled to field and route them.

He walked by the special weapons vault and met Special Agent Don Mattson who peered around the corner. "I heard T-1-A threw you a last-minute wrench into your hostage rescue exercise. There's nothing like inserting a nuke into your scenario to brighten your day." Mattson grinned.

James snickered. "I like a challenge, but thirty-five seconds to disarm a nuke might even tax my superman abilities. Luckily, I doused the clock and its batteries with liquid nitrogen to stop it until explosive technicians could arrive and render the mock device safe."

"You piss the boss off? Your scenario sucked compared to Steele and Smith's anti-terrorism driving exercises. At least you all passed your proficiency tests." Mattson tapped his finger on the counter.

"I'm not here to make friends." James shrugged. "It's only a matter of time before terrorists grab a nuke with Iran joining the club. We must train for the worst-case scenario to prevent a nuke from detonating on our soil."

Mattson canted his head. "Armageddon can wait. You're launching to the Middle East to protect the secretary of state. I've packed your gear and equipment."

"We probably have enough gear to topple a small government. Not sure how you do it. You could find a snow shovel in the Egyptian desert. Remember in Liberia when you combed the countryside and found us parts to fix that Harley." James patted Mattson on the back.

"I enjoyed building that bike from scratch. You nicknamed me Mr. Gadget after that." Mattson eyebrows wiggled. "Here's the list of equipment."

James studied the two-page list: five Colt Commando assault rifles, four MP-5K submachine guns, one SR-25 sniper rifle, twelve hundred rounds of ammunition, fifty magazines, six night vision devices, two sets of binoculars, two hand-held thermal imagers, two cameras, etc.

"This list looks great Don. Thanks for organizing it."

"Watch your backs on this one."

"Count on it." James rocked back on his heels and winked. "This is what I live for."

Atwell poked his head around the corner. "James, come on. The briefing is about to start."

"Who's giving it?" His eyes narrowed.

"It's one of the spooks from across the river." Atwell reseated his glasses on his nose.

"That's interesting since their motto is to admit nothing, deny everything, and make counter-accusations." His eyes narrowed.

"This meeting is serious. The director's bringing the briefer here, so I'm guessing we're being thrown into the fire."

"Hey George." James peered over his mentor's shoulder. "The guy must be disguised."

Turning, Atwell's jaw dropped. "Yeah, you're right. I like the CIA's hiring practices. I'm sure she's good at eliciting info."

"Let's head to the conference room." James' eyes glimmered. "I can't miss this briefing. She may be a cougar, but I'd like to be mauled by her."

"It's all relative Matt. She may be a cougar to you, but she's a young chick to me. I'll bet she likes older, more mature men versus young bucks like you." Atwell leaned forward with a gleam in his eye.

"That sounds like a wager. Let's see who can get her digits first." James rubbed his hands together.

"You're on. Don't be disappointed when you lose. Experience generally beats youth," Atwell said, walking with wide steps.

Entering the room, they saw Wagner and O'Donnell standing in the corner discussing their upcoming mission. The four agents sat down at the table with stoic faces. James glanced up to notice his boss, the director and the terrorist expert stride into the room. He skimmed his fingertips along his jaw line as his bright eyes followed the poised and elegant woman into the room. Her white blouse and neatly pressed charcoal suit hugged her svelte figure; her blueblood posture remained erect as she eyed the group.

"Gentleman, you were handpicked for this mission given your outstanding records and proven skills," the director droned.

Wagner's brows rose as he grabbed his crotch. James bumped shoulders with him and whispered behind his hand, "No matter how many times you check, Dutch, you won't find anything there."

"That's original." Wagner's lips flattened.

The director coughed as his fiery eyes pierced the two agents. "What I'm about to tell you doesn't leave this room. It's highly classified and a matter of national security. As you're aware, the secretary will travel to Ramallah to attend peace talks. The CIA has informed us that the Khorasan Group plans to assassinate him in an ambush-style attack. This threat is sanctioned by al-Qaeda's leadership."

"Can't he just cancel his trip? This meeting can't be expected to accomplish much and it isn't worth his life or those around him." James pressed his lips together.

The director's face flushed as a vein in his temple bulged. "The secretary is unwilling to let terrorists interfere with his recent diplomatic advances in the Middle East."

"This peace mission is just great. If I only had a dollar for every time someone touted progress in the Middle East, then I'd be a millionaire," Atwell muttered, lifting a single eyebrow as he folded his arms over his stomach and leaned back in his chair.

"You'll depart immediately to conduct surveillance detection (SD) operations." The director's eyes swept the room. "In carrying out this covert mission, you'll be on your own. You'll have difficulty blending-in; Palestinian government assistance is out of the question, as they may be penetrated by terrorists. Now, when the secretary's plane lands, you'll split the team and deploy a counterassault team while continuing your S-D operation. They already briefed the agent-in-charge and he endorsed your involvement. He's permitting three more MSD agents to travel on the secretary's plane. However, he's requested that you take orders directly from him."

The director inhaled deeply. "Now gentleman, I know this reporting chain isn't protocol, but I'd ask you to at least keep him apprised of any developments. Do you have any questions or concerns?"

Wagner raised his hand. "I've got one. What are our rules of engagement?"

The director's chin rose. "If you see any threat to yourselves or FALCON (referring to the secretary of state by his call sign), then you should take whatever steps necessary to protect yourselves and neutralize the threat, including the use of lethal force. Do I make myself clear?"

The agents chorused, "Yes sir."

"With that in mind, I'd like to introduce you to one of the CIA's top Middle East experts, Katharine Davis." The director sat.

Davis stood. "This information is highly classified and needs to be safeguarded. A source's life is at stake."

Atwell's attentiveness waned as he studied the analyst's sparkling green eyes, petite curvy frame, silky blonde hair and soft but refined facial features.

"It appears that a number of the military wings of at least seven of the more radical al-Qaeda or al-Qaeda-affiliated groups have banded together to fight the West and the Israeli-Palestinian peace talks currently solidifying. This means they're pooling their technological skills, which makes them more capable, dangerous, and likely to succeed in their attacks."

"What groups are we talking about? I'm guessing Al-Qaeda in Palestine, Al-Qaeda in the Maghreb, and Al-Qaeda in the Arabic Peninsula?" Atwell's chin raised as his hands formed a steeple.

"Yes and a few more to include Al-Qaeda in Iraq, Al-Shabaab and several other al-Qaeda-affiliated groups." Her eyes gleamed. "They're calling themselves the Khorasan Group."

O'Donnell raised his hand. "I thought these groups disliked one another?"

She gave an easy nod. "We're decimating their forces with strategic drone strikes while strangling their finances. They're uniting to counter us, our allies, and our influence in the peace process."

She established eye contact with each agent. "The hit on the secretary is both symbolic and a reminder to other countries to quit meddling in the region."

"Excuse me Katharine." Wagner cleared his throat. "Do we know any specifics about the number of attackers and their weapons?" He pressed his lips into a fine line.

She glanced down. "Our information reflects a possible ambush using automatic weapons and explosives. It could take place around the presidential palace, the Canadian ambassador's residence, or from the airport."

"Hopefully, your surveillance operation can identify the most likely attack location." The director nodded.

"Anyone else?" Davis scanned her audience.

"You'll keep us apprised of any new developments?" James beamed.

"Of course I will." She gave him a casual nod. "The base chief will brief you upon your arrival. Thank you for your time. Good luck."

Atwell stood. "On behalf of the team I'd like to thank you for your information and candid answers. I'm sure you'll want a debriefing upon our return. If you give me your card, I'll call you when we return." Atwell shook her hand and passed her MSD's challenge coin.

"Hold on." She reached into her pocket. "Here's my card."

James glanced at Atwell. "Always the diplomat," he mused. "I wonder what she left out. Don't think that business card counts as digits."

"It certainly does. You have the first round tonight. Like I stressed, experience usually beats youth."

James placed his palms together and bowed to his best friend.

The MSD chief instructed the agents to remain seated as the DS director and the CIA expert strolled out of the room.

"This protective operation is more than a C-Y-A mission, isn't it boss?" James scratched his face.

"How many times has the director blessed us with his godly presence and dynamic personality?" The MSD chief shrugged. "Does that answer your question Matt?"

"Absolutely."

"Let's go over your mission." The MSD director checked his watch. "The director ordered me to assemble our best agents for this critical mission. I've chosen you. I don't have to reiterate the gravity of the situation. You all know the stakes. Atwell will lead the team and James will be his deputy on this operation. The mission is simple. Conduct surveillance detection operations and provide a counterassault team for all the secretary's moves. You'll operate independently with limited assistance from the regional security officer (RSO) and the base chief. The counterassault team will be a part of the secretary's protective detail. Mattson has packed your equipment and will get you to the airport. Your diplomatic passports will arrive shortly with your visas. Smith and Steele will be here by fifteen-thirty. You'll need to brief them here or while in route. Get anything else you need, and good luck." The MSD director gave a single nod, before dashing out of the room.

The team filed out of the conference room, silent and serious. James stepped into the elevator and pushed the "B" button. Exiting the elevator, he turned right and opened a glass door to the complex's underground parking area. Strolling to his car, he popped the trunk to his brand new black Dodge Stealth. He reached in and grabbed a black nylon bag with multiple pockets along with a small suitcase. Slamming the lid shut, he grabbed his bags and carried them to a nearby Suburban. The tailgate lay open so he tossed his bags inside, appreciating Mattson's efficiency.

James glanced at his watch and noted they had forty minutes before departing to catch their flight. He turned toward the door and saw Wagner and O'Donnell exiting the elevator with two heavy plastic containers. He trotted over to hold open the glass doors so they could pass unimpeded through them. The three agents loaded the equipment into the Suburban and returned to the third floor to retrieve the other remaining cases. Mattson had most of the gear neatly stacked on a four-wheel cart. They finished harmoniously packing and loading the remaining gear in less than fifteen minutes.

Steele waltzed into the storage vault with his arms crossed while sporting a huge grin. "Hey, what's taking you so long? I've a plane to catch."

"It's about time you got your sorry ass here. I know you didn't get caught in Winchester rush hour traffic. Since you guys missed the real work, how about loading this gear into the Suburban?" James pointed to the carts.

Steele glanced at his partner. "Let's go Doug. Now we know our true purpose on this trip."

"They didn't invite you for your looks." Smith lifted a case onto the cart.

Steele held the door open while Smith pushed the cart into the hallway and toward the elevator. Steele rushed ahead to press the down button. The elevator doors sprung open. Pushing the cart, Smith then struggled to prevent it from hitting Atwell as he emerged from the elevator.

"How's it going?" Atwell rushed by carrying an orange bag marked "Diplomatic Pouch."

Smith wiped his brow. "This load is it and we're ready to roll."

"Excellent. Let's rally in my office for a team briefing while rechecking the equipment list." Atwell felt a lightness in his chest.

Steele raised a thumb in assent as the elevator doors clanged shut.

Atwell greeted James inside the MSD reception area. "What's that awful smell? You forget to shower George?" James' nostrils flared as he observed Atwell's underarm sweat stains.

"These pouches aren't getting any lighter and I'm not getting any younger," Atwell grumbled as he led the way back to his office. He welcomed the inconvenience as it paid him overtime while he feasted and slept in business class.

Entering his office, Atwell scoffed as O'Donnell and Wagner rifled through his desk.

"Make yourselves at home." Atwell nudged O'Donnell aside.

"What do you think I'm doing?" Wagner looked up, slamming the top desk drawer shut. The remnants of three-month-old chocolate-mint Girl Scout cookies nearly spilled out of his mouth.

"What's this for?" O'Donnell seated the stethoscope's plugs into his ear while placing the diaphram on his heart.

Atwell stroked his meticulously groomed beard and pointed at the wall separating his from the director's office. "It's surprising what you can hear through a wall. That's enough screwing around. Let's get down to business."

Mattson ducked into the office and interrupted Atwell's discussion regarding individual duties. "The flight's on time. We should leave now to get you through the airport with all your gear. Besides, I need to hurry home to watch the big game on TV tonight."

"Who's driving the other vehicle?" James cocked his head to one side.

"You're lucky. I got fast Freddy." Mattson covered his eyes.

Wagner crossed his arms. "You think he'll get us there in one piece? The crazy bastard drives worse than a caffeine-crazed Italian on holiday."

"I'll ride shotgun with Mattson. You guys can roll the dice with Freddy, and good luck with that." Atwell gave a purposeful shiver.

"That's messed up." James cringed. "What's life without a little thrill? Let's roll." He sprang to his feet.

Two fully loaded vehicles departed the building in unison, much like a protective detail on a motorcade move. Twenty-two minutes later, they pulled in front of the United Airlines check-in counter at Dulles International Airport. Curious onlookers watched them offload their equipment and personal baggage. A porter trotted over but before he spoke, O'Donnell asked him to retrieve two more coworkers.

Filling their carts, the porters struggled to reach the check-in counter; their carts' wheels buckled from their load's weight. The size, special markings, and the design of the containers piqued the interest of passersby. Disregarding their quizzical stares, the team marched toward the business class counter. O'Donnell rushed to the counter with all the team's tickets and passports. He mentally prepared to negotiate with the unsuspecting flight attendant.

"May I help the next in line?" The attendant motioned, smiling.

O'Donnell tossed the tickets and the passports on the counter. "We have six diplomats with excess baggage traveling to Tel Aviv."

The woman glanced fleetingly at the assorted equipment cases and suitcases; her erect posture suddenly wilted.

Smith stepped forward with an alluring smile. "It looks worse than it appears."

"I think we can get you guys on your way in a few minutes." The attendant eyed Smith's physique and smiled. She beckoned another co-worker for assistance and the team proceeded to the gate ten minutes later.

Atwell approached the security checkpoint and flashed his special agent credentials and badge to the TSA supervisor. Inspecting Atwell's diplomatic courier letter, the guard recorded Atwell's name, badge number and flight information. Atwell signed the logbook, walked through the metal detector, and picked up the pouch.

James glanced at Atwell. "I hope it's a good trip with all our time and effort."

"We get paid either way." Atwell walked with a slow, steady gait. "Let's hope nothing happens and we can add another tack to our world maps."

"I've seen roughly seventy countries on six continents since joining DS." James eyes twinkled. "It's great learning about other countries and their cultures."

"I've visited about eighty countries in thirteen years. I wonder where the last half of our careers will take us, providing we survive them." Atwell stretched his arms out wide.

The team scuttled through the corridor and arrived at the AreoTrain staging area. The train teemed with passengers, but they crowded onboard, ignoring a handful of dirty looks. Their plane's looming departure precluded them from catching the next available train. After the doors closed, the automated announcement listed the stopping sequence at the different concourses.

Wagner nudged the people behind them. "Could you please give us a little room?" Responding without a word, an elderly couple stepped two feet backwards.

"Much obliged." Wagner stepped forward.

Within five minutes of the AeroTrain gliding through the tunnel system, it pulled up to concourse C. The team exited and pressed forward to their departure gate. An announcement over the PA system indicated their flight had begun boarding. Atwell led his team to the check-in line where they pre-boarded with two dozen business travelers and tourists. Arriving at their seats in business class, they stowed their carry-on baggage in the overhead compartments. Atwell and James sat together to discuss planning and mission specifics.

Atwell pushed his back firmly against the seat and closed his eyes. Thirty-five minutes later, the Boeing 757 jumbo jet taxied to the runway in preparation for take-off. As the engines revved, the jet accelerated and shuddered down the runway. James gazed out the window, gripped his shaky hand, and tried to forget about the misfortunes of Beirut. The plane rocketed skyward and pierced a fibrous gray layer of clouds minutes later at twenty thousand feet. James considered his gifted team while Atwell dozed beside him. He admired Atwell's vision, experience, and mentorship. Physically, he appeared in good shape for a man in his late forties – lean and mean. His glasses made him look more like a college professor than an agent. However, his nickname was "Doc," a moniker he earned during Desert Storm, where he saved countless soldiers. He would follow the highly decorated veteran anytime and anywhere.

James glanced over his shoulder and to the other side of the aisle. O'Donnell played a video game while Wagner read a *Guns and Ammunition* magazine. Both agents possessed unsurpassed shooting skills and physical abilities, yet they appeared awkward next to one another. Wagner sported a wrestler's build, muscular and somewhat wiry. He stood slightly over six feet tall with a mustache and brown shoulder-length hair, but clean cut on the sides. Despite his ragged appearance, he served as a Marine Corps officer and retained a disciplined but rough demeanor. A diplomat by no means, he spoke his mind, bringing trouble to his doorstep. His technical proficiency meant he could recite any weapon's nomenclature as if he memorized the manual. He definitely wanted Wagner backing him up when kicking in a door or under a blaze of gunfire.

Conversely, O'Donnell's muscular and short build never slowed him down. His abundance of energy made him borderline ADHD. His technical savviness meant he could capture a critical moment on film. His years of martial arts training had toughened his hands, body and spirit; or was it the women he had wooed in his single days? His easy going, good-natured personality left broken hearts all over the world. With short blond hair and a Chevron mustache, O'Donnell portrayed the short man's version of the Marlboro man. It also masked an irresistible warmth and charm.

James felt a nudge on his shoulder; he turned to see Steele, who appeared relaxed considering the upcoming mission. Steele pointed to the cover of his book. "Have you read this new NYT best-selling bio-terror thriller?"

James shook his head. "Is it any good?"

"It's fantastic. By far his best work. I'll let you read it when I'm finished." Steele settled back in his seat and flipped to another page.

James leaned back in his seat. He counted their blessings for their business class fortunes. He could not imagine Steele's tall and husky frame being comfortable in economy class. A former Chicago detective, his street savviness and instincts reflected his experiences. His daily dealings with drug addicts, gangs, and guns never dulled his optimism and good nature. His street smarts, intuitiveness, and positive demeanor would be most welcome on this trip.

Glancing over his shoulder for a flight attendant, James spotted one next to Smith. "Hey Doug, will you allow the young lady to help us less fortunate? I could use another drink."

"I'll be right with you sir." She turned and resumed her conversation with Smith.

Smith's two-hundred and twenty pound frame could give Adonis a run for his money. Most agents envied him for the flocks of women he attracted. James valued his solid reputation as an agent which reverberated within DS' corridors. His confidence and equanimity spilled over to those around him. A definite team player, he would finish the mission, no matter what the cost.

The clatter of flight attendants serving dinner awoke Atwell. Ignoring the lighthearted banter the team typically engaged in to relax, he stared pensively at his plate.

"What's wrong George? You look troubled." James glanced at his colleague.

"Oh, just thinking about the West Bank. I've got a bad feeling about this mission; I just can't place it though."

James' mouth slackened. "This is unlike you. You're not afraid of anything. As a special forces medic, you've been in tough combat and witnessed many atrocities. You're also highly decorated with a Silver Star, two Bronze Stars, and four Purple Hearts for your heroics."

"Why do you always push it Matt? Stop living under your uncle's cloud. You had nothing to do with his mysterious death." Atwell sipped his orange juice.

"I know; I just can't let it go. He encouraged me to join the service. They say he messed up on the job, but I know better."

"As your friend and colleague, I'm telling you to let it go. You've nothing to prove. Many think you have a death wish. Now I know better, but still others think you take unnecessary risks in the name of country. Many even question your sanity."

"Like the Samurai, I have no fear of death. This lack of apprehension makes me a good agent." James pushed his shoulders back into the seat.

"More like an adrenaline junky." Atwell rubbed his eyes.

"I'd be worried if he expressed this sentiment." James pointed over his shoulder.

"I have that bad feeling as well." Steele leaned over the headrest. "It's the same bad feeling I had before I got shot in the Chicago projects area. I should've listened to my gut. It told me to avoid the area, but my partner raced into the building, so I followed."

"Well then, we better enjoy this five-star cuisine while we still have the chance. It may be our last sit-down meal for a while." James' demeanor became serious.

The team indulged in their dinners while chatting idly. They passed the time by reading, playing cards, listening to music, watching movies and occasionally dozing off. Each of them had a ritual in which they channeled their energies in preparation for their missions. They all knew once they landed that their time for routine play would diminish, and that would happen when they hit the ground in Israel.

# CHAPTER 5: THE BAD LANDS

The blazing sun pierced the oval window as nighttime turned into midday fourteen hours later. A sudden jolt and screeching wheels signaled their touchdown at Tel Aviv's Ben Gurion International Airport. James wiped the sleep from his eyes while peering out the window. Heat radiated skyward off the black tarmac. He popped two aspirin to counter his dull headache and the seven separate time zones he transited. Adrenaline flooded his veins. Rubbing his lower back, he turned to Atwell. "Welcome to the chosen land. Let the fun begin."

"This land has been disputed since the dawning of time. There's been so much death in the name of religion. Too bad they can't peacefully settle their differences. Only then will the fun begin." Atwell unfastened his seatbelt.

"Fair enough George," said James, "but at least the world's mayhem keeps us gainfully employed. Don't know how I'd make an honest living without all the flashpoints."

Atwell's head shook. "No chance of that ever happening in our lifetimes. There'll never be peace in this part of the world. WWIII is looming. Islamic extremists are hitting targets around the world while threatening another nine-eleven style attack on America. Political correctness obscures this reality to most, but you can't dispute the facts. They want to wipe out western ideology, dominate the earth, and enact Sharia law. Ironically, they use our democracy to spew their extremist ideology, recruit people, and threaten our very way of life."

James pondered his wisdom, admiring his candor in a world marred by political correctness. "You're right. Too bad our politicians don't act before it's too late."

The plane edged forward to the arrival gate as eager passengers stood to gather their belongings. James snapped off his seat belt, stood, and grabbed his black nylon bag from the overhead compartment. He handed Atwell his suitcase and then retrieved the diplomatic pouch from the overhead bin. He contemplated the secrets within the pouch and hoped none of them would appear on WikiLeaks.

"It's all yours George." He let out a loud breath. "You got it or should I get you a stroller?"

Atwell puckered his brow as he snatched the pouch and slung it over his shoulder. The team trailed the erratic movements of other passengers onto the jetway. Once inside the terminal, Atwell spotted Gene Tyler, the regional security officer (RSO). At five feet six inches, Tyler's waistline suffered from a lack of exercise and watching countless television reruns. In his early fifties, retirement loomed and he relished returning to America. A man known for his mastery of regulations, he thrived on administrative matters. He also enjoyed managing the daily security needs of embassy personnel and their families. His dislike of criminal investigations and protection lessened his operational understanding. Once the threat to the secretary emerged, he requested MSD support. Sixteen hours later, the MSD team arrived on his home turf.

Tyler introduced the team to his local investigator, who could easily navigate the labyrinth of Israeli government protocol. The team trailed the investigator, pressing through the buzzing crowd and bypassing two security checkpoints. They shuffled to the baggage claim area and fanned out around the carousel to look for surveillance.

"Hang loose. I'll have you through here in a jiffy." The investigator collected the team's passports and customs forms. He motioned for them to follow him. Approaching the customs inspector, his arms flapped prior to his hand extending. "Shalom, my friend. How's the family?" He released his grip.

The customs inspector motioned them to pass. "Mazel tov," said the Israeli official, winking. "Be safe out there."

James' stance stiffened. "Inshallah."

"Todah," Atwell answered before turning to James. "Stop messing with these people."

"I'm just returning the favor as they're always screwing with us." James bit the inside of his cheek.

Atwell shook his head. "Cool it. We need to stay under the radar."

O'Donnell vaulted forward pushing a cart full of equipment toward the parking lot. Smith marched alongside supporting the top cases with his right arm. The local investigator redistributed the passports to each team member as they exited the terminal. The other team members trailed O'Donnell and strolled to the vehicles with the remainder of the equipment. They hurled their cases into a van and two accompanying vehicles. Encircling their leader, sweat streamed from their faces and soaked their underarms.

Atwell pointed to the investigator. "Faisal will lead you to your quarters. Divide yourselves up equally in the cars and be observant. Once we arrive at the house, we'll offload the equipment and suitcases. James and I will go to the embassy to deliver the diplomatic pouch and meet with the CIA. Unpack, organize the equipment, and grab some shut-eye. There won't be much time for that later. Be ready for a post-specific briefing at zero-six forty-five."

James clapped his hands twice. "You heard the man. Let's get cracking."

"Oh, give James your visa photos so he can get embassy ID cards. They could save you if stopped on the streets." Atwell glanced at his watch.

"Let's go." James hopped into the van's front passenger seat. "Daylight's burning."

The team members piled into the cars which soon formed a caravan, rolling at moderate speed through streets teeming with the exotica of the Middle East. Women moved along with an odd dignity in their full-length black garbs. Children shrieked at one another in sing-song cadence. Speeding through the Old City, the team uniformly fixated on its narrow twisting cobblestone roads, ancient mosques, homes, open stalls, donkeys, and flocks of people.

After about thirty minutes of driving, Faisal interrupted their reveries. "We'll be taking the next left. You'll enjoy this area; it's one of the finest neighborhoods in Ramallah. Many foreigners and their families live here. You'll blend in much better here."

With one final turn, Faisal pointed to the right. "That's it. Not too shabby? You'll like the house's privacy and size."

Atwell radioed the other cars to hold their positions while Faisal backed the van into the driveway.

RSO Tyler stepped out from the carport's shadows. "Welcome to Ramallah. I'm sure this house will suit your needs."

"I know it will." James extended his hand.

"Let me give you a hand." Tyler grabbed a bag and led them inside. "The kitchen is fully stocked. All the beds have fresh linens. There are five bedrooms, so I had a cot delivered. Are there any questions?"

"It's nice," replied James, eying the locks on the door. "Thanks for arranging it."

Tyler handed two sets of keys to James, who tossed Steele a set while pocketing the other one.

"Come on." Tyler motioned to the door. "The communicator's waiting for us."

"We need to go George." James grabbed the diplomatic pouch.

"I'm on my way." Atwell set his suitcase on the living room couch.

James approached the awaiting van and pitched the diplomatic pouch into the back seat and jumped inside. The RSO tailed them back to the embassy. The deserted streets lessened the drive time back to Jerusalem.

Making an illegal left turn, Faisal drove onto a main roadway. The eerily quiet drive passed by quickly. Their exhausted state combined with the secrecy of their mission fueled their silence. Although Faisal was a trusted embassy employee, he lacked U.S. citizenship, requisite clearance, and the need to know.

The van pulled up to the embassy's front gate where a guard checked their diplomatic passports. The guard signaled a man inside a ballistic booth who remotely opened an outer gate to the sally port. The van drove into the bay and stopped short of an inner gate. Faisal turned off the ignition while the outer gate closed. A guard, utilizing an elliptical mirror and a flashlight, systematically inspected the vehicle for explosives. James studied the guard's three-hundred and sixty degree search of the undercarriage. His hesitation near the gas tank captured his attention.

"What did you find?" James asked, leaping from the car.

The local guard shrugged. "It's too small to be a bomb, but it doesn't belong on the van."

James grabbed the inspection mirror. "Let me take a look." He adjusted the mirror and illuminated the object by reflecting the flashlight's beam off the mirror and onto the car's underbelly. The rectangular, matchbook-sized box with a small blinking red light seized his interest. Kneeling down, he twisted and pulled the device to overcome its magnetic fix.

"Someone's interested in us." James' eyebrows arched as he tossed the device to Atwell.

Atwell inspected its craftsmanship. "It looks Syrian and similar to the tracking devices Hezbollah used in Lebanon on their adversaries. Let's get the CIA's assessment."

"I could go to a nearby hotel and plant it on a random car. Let them chase someone else for a while." James looked over his shoulder at the street.

Atwell shook his head and placed the device in the center console. "Let's leave it here so they think we aren't on to them."

The guard resumed his inspection, culminating with a perfunctory check under the hood. Faisal parked the van near the embassy's main entrance and leapt out to open the sliding door. Atwell exited last and reached back into the van to grab the diplomatic pouch. Seeing the strain on his face, James helped him lift it.

"I've got it," Atwell snapped, frowning. "I can carry it all the way."

Tyler led them through the main entrance. A Marine manning Post One, a bulletproof booth, punched the button and released a magnetically-locked, blast-resistant door.

"Good evening sir." The Marine Security Guard snapped a crisp salute.

"I see you're keeping us safe tonight Sergeant Williams." Tyler signed the logbook.

"It's quiet tonight. Just the way I like it." The focused Marine scanned the alarm panel.

Tyler winked. "Yeah, me too. Let's keep it that way."

The two agents followed the RSO through two corridors to a central elevator bank. They entered an awaiting elevator and ascended several floors. Upon exiting the elevator, they reached the Information Program Center. The isolated windowless area housed the essential and highly technical communications' systems that protected the nation's secrets. It served as the respiratory center for any post and allowed steady communication with the State Department, governmental agencies and other posts through transmitting and receiving all classified cable traffic.

Tyler pushed an intercom button.

"Yes," a raspy voice answered.

"It's the RSO. We need to handle that matter I spoke to you about earlier today."

"Just a second."

The metallic gate snapped opened. A portly man signaled for them to enter. They trailed him into a back room and then through another hardened door.

"How was your flight?" The man inquired while picking up a wire cutter off the counter. He clipped off the seal on the pouch and peeled off the orange cover, exposing a transmittal receipt. He then handed Atwell the small, wooden case.

"Great." Atwell watched the man notate the transaction. "Thanks for coming in tonight."

"No problem. I need the overtime. Sign here." He pointed to an "X" on the paperwork. Atwell scribbled his name like a doctor signing a prescription.

"Enjoy your stay here." The man led them to the gate and guided them toward the door.

"Let's go to my office and open the case." Tyler motioned them to the elevator.

After descending a couple floors, they exited, negotiated a hallway and arrived at a door marked "Regional Security Office." Tyler disengaged a spin-dial lock and punched a five-digit cipher combination, releasing the lock. Opening the door, he led the two back to his office.

Tyler walked to his desk and opened his bottom desk drawer. He handed Atwell two sets of pliers and a small crowbar. Atwell gave James one of pliers and together they cut a series of wires attached to each end of the case. They pried the lid open a second later.

James reached into the box and hoisted a sheaf of classified nuclear and biological manuals. "I'm sure this is riveting stuff?" He glanced at Tyler.

"Don't ask me to go into it." Tyler shook his head. "I'm only supposed to hold them for our political counselor."

"Let's get down to business." The portly man leaned back in his chair. "These items came for you earlier today." Dragging a heavy case from behind his desk, Tyler directed their attention to its contents. He picked up an MP-5K submachine gun. "You guys mean business with hardware like this. What type of scope is this?"

"That's an aimpoint." James pointed to the optic. "Just turn this knob on, look through the scope, line up the red dot on your target, and squeeze the trigger."

"Yeah, it's certainly handy when things get rough." Atwell stretched his neck. "The right equipment can give you an edge in a gunfight."

Looking at George, Tyler spoke. "You guys know your mission. I'm here to support you. The CIA will share their latest intelligence with you tomorrow."

James's face furrowed. "That's refreshing. Information is power."

Tyler's face relaxed. "The president would hate to lose one of his closest friends. Besides, who would he golf with in the summers?"

"Good point!" James shot a grin at Atwell.

"What time will we be briefed?" Atwell glanced at his watch.

"Zero eight-hundred. Is that okay?"

"That's fine." Atwell advanced his watch forward seven hours to the new time zone.

Has the place been swept?" James' eyes arched.

"Technicians will visit you tonight." The RSO winked. "Here are six welcome packets with area information."

"Can you make embassy ID cards for us?" James handed Tyler six visa photographs. "Official ID cards have saved us in the past. On one past occasion, Lebanese police discovered us conducting surveillance and drew down on us. None of us spoke Arabic, which compounded matters. We thought we were toast until I displayed my embassy ID. Without it, I may have been jailed or worse yet eaten a bullet."

"Okay James, that's enough stories. It's getting late. Let's head back to get some rest." Atwell tapped his foot.

"I'll have them processed first thing in the morning and bring them by your house." Tyler displayed the photographs. "Faisal will drive you back. Get some shuteye."

"Great." Atwell shook Tyler's hand. "See you tomorrow."

Arriving at their temporary quarters, the two entered the house and lumbered upstairs, discovering two vacant rooms.

"They must've flipped coins for the beds." Atwell cupped an elbow with his left hand while tapping his lips with the other.

James waved him off. "I'll bet you ten-to-one that Dutch took the cot. The bastard prefers them to beds. The Marine Corps convinced him that it helped his back. About the only way he'd choose a bed over a cot is if it came with a woman." James lightly backhanded Atwell to the stomach. "Sleep well George. Tomorrow's going to be busy."

It seemed as though James' head had just hit the pillow when the alarm's incessant beeps woke him at six in the morning. He rubbed a crusty film from his eyes and slid to the side of the bed; the groggy agent sat upright as his head throbbed. He staggered to the bathroom and swallowed two aspirin with a swig of bottled water. After washing down a handful of vitamins with another gulp, he then stumbled toward the shower.

James turned the hot and cold dials; a hard narrow stream of water sprayed from the showerhead. The water's brown color did not disturb him, as he realized it would clear. Following a rushed five-minute shower, he dressed and ambled downstairs. Playful banter filled the air as O'Donnell and Steele hovered over the stove.

"Good morning. What are you making besides a mess?" James asked, eying the flour on the floor and the counter.

"Pancakes are the only thing we could find to feed ten of us." Steele turned the stove's dial to medium.

"Ten? We're only six." James rubbed his chin as his eyebrows squished together.

"We counted Steele and Smith twice because they know how to devour the groceries." O'Donnell took a step back. "We thought the RSO and base chief might join us."

James raised his chin. "They're coming here. Who knows if they'll eat?"

"Anyhow, breakfast in two minutes." Steele resumed stirring the maple syrup.

The kitchen commotion, combined with the sweet aroma of hot maple syrup, had summoned Atwell, Smith, and Wagner to the dining room.

"Where's the meat?" Wagner grunted. "It's not breakfast without bacon or sausage, and the greasier the better."

"Damn, I knew I forgot something." O'Donnell snickered. "You just sit down Dutch and I'll call in a plane from the states."

Steele tossed three stacks of pancakes on the table. "Dig in guys. I've got more on the stove." The stacks vanished within seconds.

"Good thing I ate already." Steele retrieved the empty plates. "You guys are worse than piranhas in a feeding frenzy."

"Yeah, and we're as mean as them. So keep them coming," Wagner grumbled as bits of pancakes spilled from his mouth.

Steele shook his head. "Now I know why I was invited on this mission. It was to carry the bags and cook your meals."

"Don't forget our laundry." O'Donnell grabbed the last pancake.

Raucous laughter stirred the room.

"Listen up," barked Atwell. "Now that you guys have fed your mouths, we can get to work." Atwell glanced at his watch. "We have ten minutes until the RSO and base chief arrive. Dutch – since you liken yourself to a piranha – you can play in the water and scrub the dishes."

"I'll give him a hand." James stood with his plate.

Atwell's eyes gleamed. "Once we're briefed by the base chief, we'll divide into two teams. Smith and O'Donnell will accompany me. Wagner and Steele will go with James. Today we'll familiarize ourselves with the city and run route analysis. Identify and note available places to conduct fixed surveillance detection. FALCON is scheduled to arrive in two-and-a-half days, so time is limited. You know the drill, so I won't belabor the point. We'll meet back here at fifteen-hundred to compare notes. Wagner, did you encrypt the radios?"

"You bet. I did it last night. We'll probably need to talk in the clear because the encryption will reduce our range."

"Give me your call signs," James instructed.

Atwell..."DOC."

"Of course." James penned it in his small black notebook.

Steele..."SPLASH."

Wagner..."PEGASUS." James glanced around the room. "It should be devil dog."

O'Donnell..."Hmmm, let's see."

"Try weasel?" Wagner smirked. "You're not solving a complex mathematical problem. Spit it out. We don't have all day."

"That's funny." O'Donnell shook his head. "I'll use COBRA."

Smith…"CONAN."

"And I'll go by HITMAN." James pocketed his notebook. "Everyone got the call signs? I'll take it your silence means yes."

Suddenly they heard a knock; they all turned to look at the front door.

Smith leapt from his seat. Opening the door, a smiling face greeted him. "Good morning Gene."

"Good morning Doug. I hope you slept well."

"Not bad considering the time difference and a mattress made of concrete."

"By the way, this is Mike Olson. He'll brief you guys this morning."

Olson extended his hand. "Pleased to meet you."

"Likewise." Smith gripped his hand. "Come on in. The team is in the dining room finishing their breakfast."

Tyler eyed the bunch as they entered the dining room. "Good morning. I'd like to introduce you to Mike Olson who will brief you."

Olson stepped out from behind Tyler. "I'm the CIA's base chief for the Palestinian territories. "What I'm about to tell you is highly classified. It mustn't leave this room."

James remained expressionless, deducing the CIA taught its recruits this phrase during the initial stages of their tradecraft training. He had heard it enough.

The base chief panned the room. "Unfortunately, we haven't developed anything solid, but our officers are pursuing new leads. From what we pieced together, the terrorists will use a six or seven man attack element. The ambush will begin with the detonation of an explosive device. The attackers then will finish the assault with a barrage of gunfire. The Khorasan Group wants to make a heavy statement. We believe the attack will take place near the presidential palace, the site of the upcoming peace talks. However, we're still awaiting confirmation and candidly I don't know if we'll get any further specifics. We haven't penetrated this newly formed alliance. We'll pass you more information as we receive it. Are there any questions?"

After a few seconds of silence, Wagner raised his hand and asked, "So we don't know the location of the attack? At this point it's merely speculation."

The base chief tugged his ear. "That's correct."

"Great, that makes it easy. All we have to do is analyze the entire city, factor in FALCON's scheduled moves, and find the most probable place for the attack to occur based on chokepoints, escape routes, ability to blend in, and so on," grumbled Wagner. "That should be easy since we only have two days before the secretary arrives."

"The director informed me that you guys are the best in the business," said Tyler, interrupting Wagner's mini-rant. "He also told me about your recent successes in Pakistan, Gaza, and Lebanon. I recognize the time constraints, but I know your team will do everything within its means to protect the secretary and guarantee the success of his mission to the region."

Atwell cleared his throat. "We appreciate your confidence in our abilities. However, we had a little more intelligence to go on and they weren't without consequence. We lost Jeff Fraser in Beirut, so you can see our concern. Nevertheless, we'll do everything we can to accomplish this mission. We appreciate your insight and candidness." Atwell shook Olson's hand.

Tyler escorted the veteran spook to his armored Mercedes, but before he exited the door, James grabbed him. "We're going to start our surveillance operation. Do you have our badges?"

"Oh yeah, 1 almost forgot." Tyler reached into his jacket and handed them to James.

"Thanks. Incidentally, we'll call you on channel five on your embassy net if we have any difficulties. We'll see you later." James shut the door behind them as they shuffled out.

# CHAPTER 6: VULNERABILITY ASSESSMENT

James stopped at the kitchen's doorjamb to watch his team review the street maps of the West Bank. "Smells like another C-Y-A mission. I hate wasting our time."

"Me too." Wagner's eyebrows rose. "I had to pass on this incredible date with a voluptuous blonde that would rival Qaddafi's Ukrainian nurse."

"Yeah, and I'm missing that Caribbean cruise to vacation in this dusty, shit-hole." O'Donnell's head lowered as he closed his eyes.

"We need to focus on the mission." Atwell pointed at the maps strewn across the table. "Wagner has analyzed FALCON's routes. The primary and secondary routes are highlighted. Pay close attention to the circled areas. They represent chokepoints that provide the ability to blend in, certain avenues of egress, and a tactical advantage."

Atwell sipped his citrus-flavored green tea; its lemon-orange aroma permeated the room. "We should focus on three areas and one other target location. First, there's the presidential palace as the press published the secretary's meeting with the Palestinian president. It's a great place for an attack. If something happens to FALCON in that area, it could also embarrass the Palestinian government. Syria can flex its muscles over Hezbollah guerrillas in Lebanon; however, I'm sure the Khorasan Group desires to demonstrate their independence."

"Second, there's the Canadian representative's residence as it provides the terrorists with an element of predictability. The secretary will sleep and depart from there in the morning."

"Third, the routes from Ben Gurion Airport to the West Bank need to be analyzed. Thanks to the media, the secretary's arrival time has been released."

Atwell stroked his beard while scanning the group to ensure their attention. "Finally, FALCON will work periodically at the main hotel in Ramallah, where we'll set up his communications. This venue is less of a concern as the Palestinians will lock the area down."

"Let's work in three teams to cover the area. James and Wagner, you guys examine the presidential palace and the airport route. Steele and O'Donnell, you review the Canadian representative's residence and the hotel. Smith and I will do a primary on the airport route and conduct a secondary inspection of the presidential palace."

"You know the drill. Document your activities. We need to cover ourselves. Let's meet back here at three o'clock. Any questions?" Atwell eyed the group. "No, that's a first. Watch your backs out there."

"That's reassuring." James glanced at Wagner. "You're watching my back."

Wagner raised his head, arching his right eyebrow. "Let's get out of here. Our equipment is already in the car."

The two agents vaulted out the door with the other team members trailing them. Flashing the keys, Wagner sat in the driver's seat.

"By all means Dutch, take the helm. I still have nightmares about your little driving escapade from Quantico to Dunn Loring. There's something about warp speed that doesn't work on Virginia's congested roads." James holstered his pistol after chambering a round. "Let's film the airport route from the West Bank entrance from Israel."

"No problem." Wagner adjusted his rearview mirror, ignoring James' jibe.

James began to unfold a map when Wagner grabbed his hand. "Put it away. I once protected the Middle East Envoy on a ninety-day assignment. I have our routes memorized. Grab the video camera and hold it steady. I won't drive fast and take chances today."

"Easy day." James placed the map in the glove compartment.

After negotiating several turns, Wagner drove onto the main road to the Israeli checkpoint into the West Bank. Fifteen minutes later, he parked on the side of the road and pointed at a gate. "All VIPs or special guests usually enter/exit this checkpoint gate." Wagner leaned back and interlocked his fingers together behind his head.

James exited the vehicle with the video camera; he panned a hundred and eighty degrees and then focused on the gate.

"You're not making a motion picture," Wagner jeered. "Hurry up and get that damn camera hidden. The police get nervous around here."

James ducked back inside the car to review the secretary's schedule. "FALCON will land at fifteen-hundred and travel to the Canadian representative's residence to freshen up. Let's run the route to find the chokepoints and any other areas of concern."

"When dignitaries are moving, this gate has more police officers than a doughnut convention for cops." Wagner's eyes displayed a twinkle of mischief.

"Not too many places here to use as cover either. Let's go." James scanned the area and scribbled his observations.

Wagner drove onto the main roadway and accelerated to the speed limit. "Anywhere along this road is a good spot to plant explosives or park a car bomb. I recall a case study about a 1988 incident in Bolivia. Terrorists detonated a device near the secretary's limousine as it traveled from the airport to the capital. The bomb detonated between vehicles and caused only cosmetic damage to a couple of the cars."

"History's full of examples where people survived only by terrorist incompetence or blind luck. I doubt luck is something we can rely on with this group." James' belly fluttered.

Minutes later, the road veered ninety degrees and the neighborhood transformed into a commercial area. He sat the camera down and instructed Wagner to pull in front of a small roadside store. James leapt from the car, approached the merchant, displayed two fingers and pointed at an orange Fanta bottle. He paid with Jordanian dinars and received a handful of change.

"Did you notice the guy across the street?" Wagner asked as James returned to the car, handing him a soda through the driver window.

"I sure did Dutch. If he stared any harder, his eyes would explode. He must like you."

"That's all I need is a Palestinian pen pal." Wagner sneered.

"Hey Dutch, could you map out this area?"

"No problem." Wagner removed his notebook from his sport jacket and penned the road and various buildings.

"This place has all the hallmarks of a good attack site." James scratched his cheek.

"I'd make a hit here," Wagner said while diagraming the block.

"This isn't good." James' eyes swept the area again. "We stick out like Darth Vader at a Jedi convention. I hope the embassy has solid contacts in these stores. We'll need a place to conduct surveillance detection operations in this neighborhood." He jotted down the names of the stores.

"This place has it all." Wagner pointed to the intersection. "The motorcade has to slow down for the ninety-degree turn and a sudden rise in pedestrian traffic. The attack team could blend in here. They'd have cover for status and action."

"These side alleys and cross streets offer a good escape route either by foot or car. The secretary of state will be fairly predictable moving through this area. We have a bit of ground to cover Dutch, so we better get our asses in gear." James hopped back into the car.

The two agents drove and finished filming the route, but nothing offered the advantages of the first chokepoint. They spotted Steele and O'Donnell sketching the area around the Canadian representative's residence. Wagner beeped his horn, but the two agents snubbed their boisterous colleague.

Wagner rubbed the base of his skull. "I wonder if they heard us."

"Of course they did. They just ignored you flipping them off. Let's get a closer look at the palace." James snickered.

"I'm on it."

"How far is it from here, Dutch?"

Wagner's eyes narrowed. "It's about fifteen minutes in this light traffic."

"Hey Matt, can you pull my brown notebook out of my nylon bag? There's a map of the presidential palace and its immediate vicinity. I highlighted three chokepoints last night. They're circled in pink."

"Really Dutch, you like pink. You're probably a cat person and like to clean and cook."

"It was the only felt-tip pen I could find," Wagner grumbled as he adjusted his rearview mirror. "From my experience, this site is covered by a small security patrol during most events. The special envoy spent a lot of time here."

"Pull over." James vaulted from the vehicle to scan the area. "The attackers would have the advantage and could blend in here." He looked for a practical escape route. "Unless they're suicidal, this area is an unlikely attack site if they bolstered security here." He gave a quizzical stare, recognizing the statement's irony as al-Qaeda had recruited thousands of suicide bombers. James only hoped the wannabe martyrs were busy elsewhere.

"You're right Matt. Let's go to the next one. It's around the corner."

They jumped back into the car and sped away. With only an hour remaining until their deadline, they rushed to finish their reconnaissance before the fifteen-hundred briefing. The two agents reached the next location within minutes. Vehicular and pedestrian traffic swarmed the area. Grayish fumes permeated the air as honking horns chorused. James filmed the surrounding area while recording the active, chaotic pace of daily Palestinian life.

"Can you pull over Dutch? I need to record the businesses in this area."

"Oh shit! Here comes a few of Palestinian's finest." Wagner leapt from the car and displayed his embassy badge.

James listened to their conversation from the car. He lowered the video camera and wedged it underneath the seat. Listening through a partially rolled down window, he scrutinized Wagner's rusty Arabic. The soldiers laughed, pointing at the former Marine. Shaking their hands, Wagner handed them each a pack of cigarettes before returning to the car.

"What's going on?" James' eyebrows crumbled.

"No problem. I told them we work for the embassy and showed them my badge. I then told them a nasty joke that I learned in Beirut. Sometimes I amaze myself."

"Yeah Dutch, you're a genuine diplomat. You should write a book on how to bridge cultural differences and influence people."

"They additionally told me they plan to secure this area and the other location we just reviewed minutes ago. They're making our job easier without knowing it."

"Great, let's check the final area." James grabbed the video camera from beneath his seat.

Wagner drove to the last chokepoint on the other side of the palace. He rapidly parked with the inner wheels up on the curve.

"This location is another possibility," James said, writing in his notebook. "The channeling of the motorcade through this narrow street makes this a good chokepoint. The bus stops and street vendors provide them with excellent cover for status and action. Proper firepower and strategic positioning could give them the tactical advantage. There are several possible escape routes through adjacent alleys and side streets. Target identification could happen several different ways." James wiped his forehead with a handkerchief.

"This site is just as good as the first chokepoint we identified this morning." Wagner rested his shoulders back against the seat.

After mapping the area and noting the names of businesses, they entered the car and headed for home. Wagner's aggressive driving even got them there ten minutes before the meeting time. Arriving home, they found the team sitting at the kitchen table comparing their observations and analyzing their notes.

"How did it go?" Atwell motioned them to their chairs.

"Excellent. Dutch was an ass; I mean an asset on our excursion. He even practiced a little Arabic with the police. Dutch charmed them in his own way." James turned his palms up.

O'Donnell shook his head. "I'm sure that went over well. I guess we'll hear shortly from the embassy about a diplomatic incident."

"What joke did you tell them?" James' nose crumpled. "You didn't tell them how a one-armed man counts change. Did you?"

"Nope, maybe I'll share that one next time." He snorted.

"Grab a seat and fill us in." Atwell pulled a chair out next to him.

James sat and reviewed his notes. "There are three chokepoints on the route from the Israeli checkpoint into the West Bank. Two of them suck, but a third one is ideal. Let me elaborate."

After about fifteen minutes of explanation and a detailed look at the maps, Atwell interrupted. "We came to the same conclusion."

James pointed to the map. "We identified three problem areas around the palace. One of them is a great attack site, but it's heavily patrolled during official events. Another one has most of the necessary elements, except for a viable escape route. Unless we're dealing with a suicidal group, we won't have to worry about this one. Besides, it's also heavily patrolled during presidential events. That leaves us with one area of interest. This location is south of the palace. I'll let Wagner explain."

Wagner stepped forward and drew the team's interest to the vicinity of the palace; he pointed to a circled area on the map. The team focused on the crossroads. "This chokepoint is in a major commercial area and has all the required elements. It's a well-known travel route to the palace. If it was me, this site is where and how I'd conduct the attack." Within ten minutes of detailed explanation, the team's tightened faces reflected their thoughts.

"Excellent work." Atwell glanced at his watch. "Now we know where to concentrate our efforts. I'll draft our preliminary report and provide it to the RSO. He can enhance security in and around the chokepoints that we've identified as potential attack sites."

"Let's hope the embassy has great connections." James displayed a list of businesses.

Atwell surveyed his team. "It's agreed that we stick out, so we should rely on fixed surveillance. We can supplement our work from the vehicles. James and I will return to the embassy to report our findings while obtaining any new intelligence. We'll brief the ambassador and identify the businesses from which we can operate effectively. If they're not available, we can throw a few visas at them."

Laughter echoed the room.

Atwell sipped his tea before continuing. "You guys recheck all of the equipment to ensure that it's functioning properly. If you have time, I'd recommend playing a few *what if* scenarios. Maybe we can determine the terrorist's attack method or discover vulnerabilities in our identified areas of concern. We'll be back in a few hours. Try to behave."

Atwell and James jumped into their sedan and drove to the embassy. Upon arriving, they headed to the RSO's office to report their findings. Tyler watched the two entering his suite and motioned them to sit while he talked on the phone. James instead eyed five black and white photographs of the old city. Several desert sunset photographs that rivaled many of the ones he saw in National Geographic equally impressed him. Atwell sat across from Tyler and thumbed through several pages of notes.

"Sorry for the delay." Tyler slammed the phone down. "I had the management counselor reminding me how to serve the community." He shook his head. "They don't pay me enough to eat this constant barrage of crap. It's death by a thousand cuts. How did your operations go today?"

"We scored big." Atwell reseated his glasses. "We have several recommendations."

Tyler raised a hand. "The boss wants a briefing on your findings. Are you ready?"

Atwell raised his head. "No problem."

The RSO picked up the phone and dialed the four-digit extension to the front office. The ambassador's office manager answered and put him on hold.

"Hello Gene," the ambassador came on line. "Is there any news from the team?"

"Sir, the team leader and his deputy just arrived. Did you still want to meet with them?"

"You bet. Come on up. I'll tell my office manager to let you right in."

"We'll see you in a few minutes sir." Tyler hung up.

"Let's go. The ambassador's waiting to see you. He's a refreshing change from the other careerists that you've encountered. He appreciates and prioritizes security. Ever since our agents saved his life in Beirut in 1993, he's become a firm believer in DS."

"Too bad the whole community doesn't see us in the same light." James jutted his chin. "Some see our duties as in conflict with their diplomatic role. We're a necessary evil."

"More like an inconvenience." Atwell snorted. "Many still see us as gunslingers or knuckle-draggers."

Laughter filled the elevator.

When they arrived at the front office, the door's magnetic lock clicked allowing them access. "Gene, go right in," the office manager said while opening the suite's double doors.

Ambassador Williams stood five feet eight inches tall with a thin, almost fragile build. His receding graying hairline revealed a man in his late fifties. Known in the department for his remarkable dedication and fine-tuned negotiating skills, his deep blue eyes and unreadable face hid his thoughts and intentions. The dark circles beneath his eyes reflected the heavy cocktail circuit he frequented. He had reached the pinnacle of his career based on merit and not on his political connections. His baggy pants and oversized, wrinkled shirts had that freshly slept-in look. His voice projected like Goliath. When he spoke, people listened.

The ambassador stood from behind his desk and met them halfway. The diplomat extended his hand to both agents. "We're glad you're here. Have a seat." He motioned them to a sitting area that included a soft leather couch, a coffee table and four antique cherry wood chairs. "Can I get you anything to drink?"

"Not for me," Atwell said with a scratchy voice. The searing Palestinian heat had a way of dehydrating a person.

"Me neither." James looked up.

"Okay, tell me what you found." The ambassador clapped once, rubbing his hands briskly together.

"Well, sir. We've identified four areas of concern. They're the hotel, the Canadian representative's residence, the Israeli checkpoint route into Ramallah, and the presidential palace. By augmenting security around the Canadian residence and the hotel, we think the terrorists will avoid these areas. That's unless they're suicidal and we all know that al-Qaeda can be fanatical. Still, their results would be limited given the setback and other defenses in these places." Atwell stressed, peering directly into the ambassador's eyes.

The ambassador raised a hand. "What will you need to secure the hotel and the Canadian representative's residence?"

Atwell cupped his chin. "We need a full-time security presence in the chokepoints coupled by an additional roving patrol for the hotel and the Canadian residence."

"Can we swing it Gene?" The ambassador repositioned himself in his chair.

Tyler looked up expectantly. "Yes, but I'll have to authorize overtime for the troops."

"You have my full support." The ambassador sat back in his chair. "Make it happen."

"That still leaves us with two problem areas." Atwell's hands formed a steeple at his chin. "There are three main routes to the presidential palace. Each route has chokepoints, but only two are ideal attack sites. We've learned during functions, the Palestinians deploy full patrols, which should deter any attack in these potential chokepoints."

The ambassador nodded agreeably. "Gene, contact your Palestinian counterparts to ensure they deploy the requisite patrols in these areas."

Tyler eyed his boss. "I'll take care of it first thing in the morning."

Atwell peered up from his notes. "We'll recommend to the special-agent-in-charge of the secretary's detail to use one of these routes. We'll also recommend that a scout car be used in addition to our counterassault team vehicle."

"That's reasonable. What other concerns do you see?" The career diplomat sipped his black coffee.

"Our biggest concern is the airport route to the Canadian representative's residence into the West Bank. There are no real options for several miles. The press announced the secretary's arrival time, so he'll be predictable within an ideal attack site. Fortunately, our team has identified suitable surveillance detection points in the heart of the attack site. We need permission from one of the businesses to use their space to monitor the area."

"What businesses?" The ambassador looked over his glasses.

James pulled his notes out of his pocket and handed them to the diplomat who scanned the list. His eyes stopped on Abdul's fine jewelry store. "I know the owner of this store quite well. My wife shops there. Abdul can be trusted." He neglected to tell them that Abdul reported to the CIA. "If you want, I can phone him to make the necessary arrangements."

"That's great. Tell him we'll arrive around seven o'clock in the morning and he mustn't tell anyone." Atwell glanced at the ambassador. "Do you have any other questions for us sir?"

"Not at the moment. Thank you for coming in. Good luck." The ambassador shook their hands and escorted them from his office. His blistering schedule demanded his attention.

The three agents entered the elevator, reflecting upon the gravity of the situation. Atwell advised the RSO that they would be in touch as they parted ways. The two agents arrived home, exhausted from the day's activities, jet lag, and the region's energy-zapping heat.

Entering the house, they found O'Donnell rechecking their surveillance cameras, cleaning different lenses, and ensuring their operability. Wagner ensured the proper functioning of all the team's weapons, placing them in their soft cases. Steele analyzed the various maps and downloaded the material into the team's laptop computers. Smith tested the communication equipment and changed the antennas on their Motorola radios to boost their range.

"How did it go?" Smith looked up, turning the dial off on a Motorola handheld radio.

"Better than expected." Atwell shot a knowing grin.

James eyed the group. "The ambassador is very security conscious and extremely supportive of our mission. I just wish there were more like him. They'll implement all our recommendations. I'm going to eat and take a nap. We'll meet at nineteen-hundred."

The team assembled in the dining room at seven in the evening. Although it had only been two days on the job, their weary expressions permeated the air.

Atwell entered last. "I assume everyone ate."

The group remained silent and a bit lethargic.

Atwell sat upright. "Listen up. Tomorrow, we'll divide into two groups to begin our operation. James, you'll take Wagner and O'Donnell and operate out of Abdul's fine jewelry store. He's expecting you at the side entrance at seven in the morning. Set up your equipment and start your log. Feel free to go mobile if necessary. Notify me of any important developments. Remember, we only have a day and a half before FALCON arrives. Be alert."

Atwell sipped his sparkling water. "I'll take Smith and Steele to work the area around the presidential palace. There's a hotel in the heart of one of the attack sites. Steele has reserved a room and will check into it tonight to monitor the area. We have a perfect corner room that provides us an excellent vantage point. Are there any questions?"

"Yeah, I've got one." Wagner blurted out. "Who's buying the beers tonight?"

"I've got first round." James offered as the meeting adjourned.

James walked into the kitchen. He opened the refrigerator door, reached in, and retrieved two ice cold beers.

"Where did you get these beers Hitman?" Wagner tapped James' shoulder.

"I've learned a long time ago to conceal my sources. Cheers. I'm going to finish my book. Feel free to help yourself to more."

"Don't mind if I do." Wagner twisted off the cap and drank half the bottle in three gulps.

James read "*The Art of War*" for about an hour until his eyes crossed. He knew it would be a long and strenuous couple of days so he decided to sleep. He brushed his teeth and rested his Sig Sauer 228 pistol on the nightstand next to his bed. Turning out the lights, James sucked in a quick breath. His pistol's tritium night sights appeared as three small, glowing green eyes. He closed his eyes and dozed off within minutes.

# CHAPTER 7: EAGLE EYES

A knock at the door startled James awake. He rolled to his side and lunged for his pistol; his hands reach its soft rubber grip as his heartbeat skipped.

"Are you going to sleep all day?" Wagner peered through the cracked door.

James shook his head. "I'm up Dutch." He rolled out of bed, wiped the drool from his mouth, and stumbled to the bathroom.

"I guess you're working today," Wagner grunted, shutting the door.

James threw on his prepositioned underwear, shirt, pants, and socks from a wooden chair. He shuffled downstairs and skipped breakfast, guzzling a cup of lemon green tea instead. Having already loaded their gear into the car, Wagner and O'Donnell read the latest edition of "*Guns and Ammo*" from the comfort of their living room couch. James walked by them and opened the front door; his black nylon bag dangling from his shoulder. He pivoted to establish eye contact. "Let's go. Daylight's burning. I'm always waiting on you guys." James gave them an exaggerated eye roll.

They arrived at a seldom-used side entrance to the jewelry shop five minutes before seven. A man folded the morning newspaper in half and greeted them curbside.

"Good morning. I'm Abdul. Welcome to my humble shop."

Wagner stepped out of the car and opened the trunk, handing James and O'Donnell four black Pelican cases. Driving to the store's parking lot, Wagner backed into a space and eyed the block.

Abdul led the two agents inside his store and ascended two flights of stairs. He had reorganized the room, placing a phone and a small two-shelf refrigerator in it. "I hope this suite meets your needs." Abdul swung the door open.

James' eyes swept the twenty-by-fifteen foot wide attic; its Brazilian cherry hardwood floors covered with handmade Egyptian carpets. A pristine handcrafted Italian desk sat idly in one corner. An assortment of antique furniture, books and other belongings littered the room; a thin layer of dust masked some of the room's hidden riches. Priceless Persian antiquities and century old paintings lined the walls. Mice-sized cockroaches skirted for cover as Abdul flicked the light switch on. The skeletal remains of Lieurus Quinquestriatus or 'Death Stalker' littered the floor. Known as the deadliest scorpion to humans, it reminded James to tread lightly. The attic's musty stench fused the smells of mildew with a wet dog. Its two oversized windows graced the room with natural light and provided a panoramic view of the street intersection below.

"This room is excellent. Thank you." James gave a crisp nod.

"If you need anything else, just let me know." Abdul turned and departed.

James ran his hand across the desk. "Okay. Much appreciated."

"This seems nice enough." O'Donnell glanced at Wagner as he entered.

"We've all been in a lot worse. I can still smell that old rat-infested apartment in Mogadishu," Wagner shuddered with a down turned mouth.

"Forget the past. Let's get to work." James approached the window and adjusted the shade, sending more sunlight into the room. "We can see almost the entire attack site from this room. We sure lucked out. Sometimes it's better to be lucky than good."

"I don't know. I've always been just plain good." O'Donnell tilted his head back and snorted.

Wagner and O'Donnell unpacked and swiftly set-up the surveillance equipment. They moved the video camera closer to the window and readied it with a few minor tripod adjustments. O'Donnell fastened an HDMI cable to the nineteen-inch color monitor. He pushed the power button and the street life sprang to life on the display.

O'Donnell periodically scanned the street activity behind a digital camera supporting a powerful zoom lens. The lens allowed him to see the Arabic headlines on the newspaper across the street.

Sitting at the antique desk, James dated the logbook and entered zero seven-hundred hours – commence surveillance: Site – Abdul's Fine Jewelry Store; Agents – James, Wagner, and O'Donnell. James rubbed his burning, water-filled eyes. The approaching Palestinian summer, combined with the dry climate and cramped dusty quarters, exacerbated the discomfort he felt.

"Hey Dutch," James called out. "Go ahead and take a sequential photo spread of the area." O'Donnell quietly clicked off a number of photos.

James gently sat the Motorola lunch box radio on the corner of the desk and lifted the microphone: "Doc...Doc, this is Hitman."

Atwell answered immediately. "Doc, bye."

"Yeah Doc, radio check. We're operational."

"Hitman, I read you five-by-five. All's quiet here."

James pushed the transmit button. "There's nothing unusual to report here. We'll keep you posted. Hitman out."

"It sounds like they're having as much fun as us." James sat down the receiver and yawned.

"Yeah, and I gave up a Caribbean cruise for this crap," O'Donnell quavered. "It's as fun as watching paint dry."

"Nobody ever accused you of being smart. I can't believe you traded this suite for the white sands of the Caribbean." Wagner snorted.

The midday sun transformed the attic into a giant oven.

"I can't remember the last time I had so much fun." James reread the log's sparse notes.

"Wow, look at this." O'Donnell eyes gleamed as he rose up on his toes.

Wagner jumped from his seat and positioned his right eye over the camera's viewer. "Unbelievable. Could it be?"

James rushed behind them and peered over their shoulders. "What do you see? Let me look. What is it?"

"I see a problem." Wagner tapped O'Donnell on the shoulder. "She could take me out to dinner in a second."

O'Donnell handed James the camera and pointed in the direction of the unsuspecting woman; a five-foot six inch bombshell with long dark hair and a beautiful olive complexion sat at the bus stop. She sat, waiting for the next bus to the Old City. Her sudden fame lost upon her.

"That's outstanding work guys." James dropped his head and sighed. "Why me? I can't wait to report our findings to the ambassador. Let's grab lunch. Are you hungry Dutch?"

"You bet. I worked up an appetite sitting here."

"Sean, stay here and monitor the situation while Wagner and I find some grub." James grabbed his pistol off the desk, holstered it beneath his baggy shirt, and noted the time in the log.

The two agents hurriedly departed, returning thirty minutes later with enough food to feed a basketball team. Wagner walked to the window and picked up the binoculars. "I'll take it from here Sean. Go grab some chow."

O'Donnell bounced over to the desk. "What did you get? I'm starving."

James handed him a warm can of Pepsi. "Here are two chicken shawarmas and some fries. That ought to hold you for a while. This is probably as exciting as it's going to get today, so enjoy it."

O'Donnell grumbled, "I hope I don't get amebic dysentery, parasites, or some other form of funky bacterial infection. Liberian stomach bugs almost killed me last year. I've never been so sick. I just wanted to die. Thank God for ciprofloxacin."

"That's nothing," said James, quirking an eyebrow. "I once ate something in Peru that stayed in my intestinal system for four years until the latest generation of antibiotics cured me. I cringed every time I ate at an Iftar dinner in Iraq. No telling what was in the fish they caught from the Tigris River or, worse yet, the individual hands that speared into the communal food dish. And you couldn't pass or you'd risk insulting your hosts."

Time appeared frozen or so they all thought. Nobody complained as surveillance demanded patience. James likened their mission to watching a giant python digest a wild boar on National Geographic instead of the glamor reflected in a Hollywood spy blockbuster. At least the boar slid through the snake's digestive tract, whereas time stood still as sweat pooled on his forehead and collected in the small of his back.

The street activity picked-up tenfold around four o'clock in the afternoon as businesses reopened after their midday siesta. Wagner clicked off another routine photo spread, capturing some of the conditions common to third world countries. Garbage littered the streets; plastic bags floated haphazardly in the wind. Stray cats and dogs scurried about, withered to virtually nothing and frail from parasitic infections. Small children, in no better shape, played in the street and adjusted their baggy clothing. Americans undervalued their fortunes, taking their lives and freedoms for granted. Wagner reflected as he watched the daily street activity from a distance. The street vendors seldom sold merchandise. Men, woman, and children of all ages walked, talked, and shopped with purpose. Beggars attempted to exploit passerby; loiterers just stood around and watched time pass. Wagner understood the irony as they watched the clock.

The street activity abated at about six o'clock in the evening.

"How long are we staying?" Wagner grunted. "This overtime is blood money. The taxpayers aren't getting their money's worth out of us today."

"Let's work until seven o'clock and see how it looks." James raised his chin as he thrust his shoulders back. Street life appeared nonexistent at seven o'clock. James lifted the radio's transmitter. "Doc...Doc, this is Hitman."

"Go for Doc." Steele's voice boomed over the radio.

"Yeah, I'm calling it a day if there're no objections."

"It's your call Hitman."

"We'll see you at the ranch. Hitman out."

Wagner and O'Donnell anticipated the outcome of the radio transmission and threw all the equipment into their cases. The agents descended the stairs and met Abdul at the bottom.

"How did everything go today?" Abdul tilted his head to the side with his lips slightly parted.

James glanced up. "Not too bad. Thanks for letting us use the space. We'll see you at seven o'clock tomorrow morning. Goodbye."

The outside air reinvigorated them. The three agents gently placed the gear in their car's trunk and dashed off. They arrived home to find it empty.

"I guess Doc and the boys are working late tonight. Relax for an hour and we'll review today's highlights." James checked his cellular phone for a message while his right heel incessantly tapped the marble floor.

"I can't wait." Wagner's shoulders drooped as he collapsed onto the sofa. "It was so riveting watching it the first time."

James tapped his fingers on the table. "I'll spare you today's boring reruns Dutch. Just set up the equipment in the living room and I'll run through it."

"Thank God." Wagner flopped back on the couch, pressing his palms to his eyes.

"If you don't mind, I'll review today's still photos. I've set up a makeshift photo shop in my bedroom." O'Donnell displayed three SD cards.

"Sure, just leave me alone. I'll find solitude in this ice-cold beer." James sneered.

James grabbed a can of tuna, opened it, sprinkled salt on it, and devoured it from the container. He appreciated a safe and fast meal. He sat on the sofa and punched the play button as he sipped his beer and watched the video footage. Thirty minutes into it, he pushed the pause button and studied the screen. Pots and pans clanged in the kitchen.

"Hey Dutch, come here. Where did we see this bastard?"

Wagner scratched the side of his face. "I know. He's the guy we saw outside the roadside store yesterday morning. Remember, he stared at us."

"I knew he looked familiar. He certainly liked you Dutch."

James scribbled the time stamp for reference purposes. He reviewed the remaining material in forty-five minutes, frequently employing the remote's fast-forward button. Turning off the monitor, James sighed and closed his eyes.

"I've printed today's noteworthy pictures. Do you want to see them Matt?" O'Donnell barked from the balcony.

"Do you have anything interesting?" James leaned forward, his nose wrinkling.

O'Donnell motioned. "Follow me. I've printed sixty color photos."

James examined them one by one, slapping them down on the table. His eyes sparkled as he drew a photo closer to his face. "I see you captured the lady this morning. Look at those pair of tickets. You zoomed in nicely."

O'Donnell took a wide stance. "She could've been a terrorist used to distract us. I was just exploring all the camera's features."

"She sure distracted you." James continued sifting through the photos and halted on the individual that he spotted on two consecutive days. "Could you make three copies of this guy and enlarge the photo to obtain a good facial shot? My gut says he's bad."

"You've got it Matt."

"I'm going to grab some sleep. Get some rest Sean. I'll see you tomorrow." James stumbled to his bedroom. Restless in bed, his mind shuddered, replaying a thousand faces. His concentration waned as his suspicions intensified. He tossed and turned for about an hour before his anxiety subsided enough to sleep.

The sound of a high-pitched, annoying alarm woke him up at zero-six-fifteen. Feeling surprisingly rested, he showered, shaved and dressed in faded blue jeans and a white guayabera shirt he bought in El Salvador. Its loose design allowed air to circulate against the skin, reducing perspiration. It also concealed his pistol and spare magazine, making them readily accessible if left unbuttoned.

James met Atwell downstairs, pouring two bowls of whole grain cereal and handing one to him after filling it with milk.

"James, I want your team to conduct surveillance detection operations in the same location. I'll take my team and run the counterassault team in FALCON's motorcade. There are three other MSD agents on the secretary's plane, who will join me. Keep in touch and report anything unusual. Call me on channel five encrypted if you spot anything unusual."

James nodded once, placing another spoon of cereal in his mouth.

"After the move from the airport to the Canadian representative's residence is completed, cease your operation and go mobile. Set up around the Canadian's residence to observe the area. We'll improvise from there depending on the secretary's itinerary. The following day, my team will deploy in the area of the palace and conduct surveillance detection operations. You'll lead the counterassault team. Do you have anything to add?"

James glanced up from his depleted cereal bowl. "Yes. We've spotted the same person in our chokepoint on two consecutive days." He reached into his notebook and pulled out a photograph of the individual. "Keep an eye out for him. It's a gut feeling."

"I'll show the other guys." Atwell stared at the photograph. "Thanks for the tip."

"I'll see you around." James stood and walked to the front door. "Be safe out there and don't worry. We've got your backs."

James joined Wagner and O'Donnell at the car. "If you're finished undressing that woman with your eyes, then let's go. We have important work to do today." James scrutinized the woman. The three agents piled into the car and sped off to the jewelry store.

They arrived to find Abdul standing near the side door reading the morning newspaper. "Good morning, gentlemen," Abdul said in a raspy voice.

"Ah halan (good morning)," James replied, covering his heart with his hand and smiling.

Abdul opened the door and pointed. "You know the way. Call if you need anything. I'm at your disposal."

"Thanks. We appreciate your generosity. Is there anything we can get you?" James placed his fist on his hips.

"I've got everything I need." Abdul tilted his head, neglecting to tell James that the CIA bankrolled him.

James and O'Donnell navigated the narrow stairs, each carrying a full load of gear. Wagner strolled in behind them after parking a block from the store.

"It's showtime." James clapped his hands together. "Remember our mission. Let's look alive and get it right."

Wagner unzipped a long black nylon case and pulled out a Heckler & Koch G-3 sniper rifle. "Damn it's clean. You have to admire the German craftsmanship and ingenuity. I can reach out and touch somebody with this baby."

He hoisted the rifle, tightly seated its plastic stock into his shoulder and snuggled his cheek against it. Peering through the scope, he swept its crosshairs over the nearby rooftops and paused on a pigeon; its head centered between the scope's vertical and horizontal lines. "That's perfect." He gently laid the rifle on the ground.

James lifted the microphone on the Motorola radio. "Big Ben...Big Ben, this is Hitman. Radio check. How do you read?"

A Marine Security Guard staffing Post One came on line. "I read you Lima – Charlie. How do you read me?"

"Roger, I've got you five-by-five. Hitman out."

James placed the radio on the desk and sauntered to the window. He lifted his binoculars to his eyes and swept his gaze across the rooftops, storefronts, streets, and alleys; everything appeared normal. He walked to the antique wood desk and sat in the chair. Opening the logbook, he scribbled the date and time. Wagner and O'Donnell stood in front of two separate windows and snapped a series of photos of the area.

"Make yourself comfortable. We have about seven hours until FALCON arrives. It's going to be a long hot day." James felt a lightness in his chest as he drummed his upper thigh.

"Hopefully it will be a boring one." O'Donnell released the camera's shutter.

James brushed his fingers on the side of his nose. "Let's hope so."

O'Donnell grabbed a nearby antique wooden chair and placed it in front of the window. Wagner mimicked the move at the other window. Hours passed with little activity. They engaged their minds by photographing countless bystanders and lingering vehicles.

The stir of the radio captured their attention as they finished their lunch. "Hitman...Hitman, this is Doc. Come in."

James lifted the radio's microphone and responded, "Go ahead Doc."

"We're set up at the airport and awaiting FALCON's arrival. Switch to channel five encrypted and give me an update."

James dialed his radio to channel five. "Doc...Doc, this is Hitman."

A garbled voice answered.

"Doc...Doc, this is Hitman. You're broken up. Repeat your last transmission."

Once again, static consumed the airwaves.

James pulled the microphone to his mouth. "Doc...Doc, in the blind, you're unreadable. Switch to channel five in the clear." He turned the encryption switch off and heard Atwell inform him to remain on channel five.

"Roger Doc. All is calm." James sighed. "We'll keep you apprised of anything unusual. Hitman out."

O'Donnell's alertness heightened as he scanned the area. He froze and studied a group of men sitting idly at a bus stop across the street. Tension radiated from the three men's faces.

"Hey Hitman," O'Donnell barked. "Take a look at these guys. They're sitting at the bus stop watching their surroundings. They failed to get on the last bus and the one that departed twenty minutes ago."

James placed the camera's viewer to his eye, focused its zoom lens, and photographed the three suspects. "You're right and look at those bulky bags at their feet. They're large enough to contain rockets or rifles." He snapped a couple more photographs of the suspects.

Wagner repositioned the video camera and the individuals appeared on the television monitor. He held his arms out wide, pointing to the clear picture. "Look, the three stooges in living color."

The radio captured their attention as the agent-in-charge of the secretary's detail announced, "FALCON is wheels down."

"They're early. They must've had some brisk tailwinds. We have about twelve minutes to analyze this situation since there's no ceremonial greeting." James inserted his earpiece snuggly into his canal. "Wagner, keep the video rolling."

O'Donnell swept his binoculars left to right, observing the gradually increasing vehicle and pedestrian traffic.

"Hitman, did you copy that motorcade departure?" Atwell radioed.

"I did now." James scratched the back of his head.

"Hey Hitman." Wagner turned in his seat to look at him. "Are you going to notify them of our situation?"

"Not yet. I don't want them spooked unnecessarily."

"Hitman, this is Doc. We're about five minutes from your location."

"Copy that," James replied, turning to Wagner. "Keep your rifle handy."

"You've got it." Wagner lifted the rifle off the floor and rested it on the wall.

"I've got two guys at eleven o'clock on the roof." O'Donnell shifted in his chair as his scalp prickled.

James scanned the roof. "This looks bad." He keyed his microphone. "Doc...Doc, this is Hitman. We have a possible situation. Recommend you take the alternate route."

Radio static permeated the air. James growled, clearing his throat. "Doc...Doc, this is Hitman. In the blind, we recommend you take the alternate route."

An eerie silence remained as Murphy's Law surfaced.

"Hitman it's the same son-of-a-bitch that we saw the last two days. He's down near the turn with a buddy and it looks like he's talking into a radio." Wagner jutted his jaw and gritted his teeth.

James scratched his jaw. "Shit! It's going down. He must see the motorcade."

He turned the dial on his radio to embassy repeater channel one. "Post One, Post One, this is Agent James. "Please relay an emergency message on channel five to FALCON's detail. Tell them to use the secondary route. There's an ambush going down on the primary route."

"Roger." The Marine's voice cracked.

"We've got to do something." James' eyes narrowed as his muscles tensed. "Wagner, cover the bastards on the roof. If they even blink wrong, take them out. Continue to radio Doc. O'Donnell, follow me. Let's go hunting."

Adrenaline surged through James' veins as his heartbeat quickened. Recognizing the onset of an adrenal rush, he sucked in a sharp breath while visualizing a snowcapped mountain.

Calming his mind, James rocketed down the stairs with O'Donnell in tow. Reaching the side door's threshold, they drew their pistols, tucked them under their armpits, and trotted to flank the three suspects. Blue lights and sirens captured their attention as they crossed the street. The three suspects reached into their bags.

Wagner's voice pierced the radio. "RPG-7 on the roof, I'm taking them." A loud gunshot rang out followed by another.

Knowing Wagner culled the two on the roof, James' eyes fixated on the three at the bus stop. The Russian-made AK-47 assault rifles that emerged from their bags caused his stomach to churn. Sprinting toward the suspects, James raised his pistol and shouted, "Freeze!"

Bystanders darted into stores and behind cars as the terrorist nearest James snapped his head around; his hollow and lifeless eyes pierced through his as he raised his rifle. James squeezed his pistol's trigger twice. The terrorist's limp body dropped to the dusty sidewalk. He leaned to his right to gain a clearer shot at the other two.

A blast rocked the street, setting off a series of car alarms. James' skin tightened from the explosive's blast and heat wave. His feet floated skywards as his head and upper body slammed on the hard pavement. His ears rang as his eyes gazed probingly toward the explosion. A dust cloud and smoke engulfed the area. The Palestinian police lead vehicle overturned as a fireball erupted skyward; its carcass blocking the road. Shrapnel from the bomb sliced through its occupants. Four police officers and one DS agent's bloody and contorted bodies littered the street.

The DS lead car rolled to a stop, blocking the street; its engine compartment crumpled and dangling. The DS Suburban drove parallel to the limousine to shield it from the incoming gunfire. Two terrorists depressed the triggers on their assault rifles; sixty odd rounds peppered the

Suburban. The agents in the right front and rear slumped forward, blood gushing from multiple wounds.

Atwell's counterassault team Suburban streaked to the side of the limousine. Dust billowed skyward as the vehicle skidded to a stop. Atwell's team leapt out of the vehicle and darted for cover behind a van and a nearby curb. They sprawled out on the ground and fired their assault rifles at the two terrorists to the rear. Sustained gunfire echoed throughout the street, as civilians scurried for cover.

O'Donnell fired on the run and struck one of the terrorists in the shoulder. The other fired back; O'Donnell dove to the pavement, as six rounds whizzed over his head. The two terrorists dashed around the corner into a narrow side alley. O'Donnell sprung to his feet and pursued them. Dazed, James regained his footing and sprinted to catch his teammate.

The two terrorists fired from behind a car and a dumpster as the agents rounded a corner of a building. O'Donnell turned, pushed James back around the corner, and leapt for the building's corner. Three rounds pierced his back and neck; he collapsed breathless.

James peered around the corner and fired six shots at the terrorists. He grabbed his teammate's leg and pulled him back around the corner as the terrorists fled. He analyzed O'Donnell's back wounds; his wheezing and difficulty breathing indicated a collapsed lung. James rolled him to his side and pressed down on his wound. He picked up his radio. "Post One...Post One, Agent down. I repeat, agent down just off the corner of Ibrahim and Sabah streets. Send medical assistance."

James propped O'Donnell's head up on his lap and eyed his blood-drenched hands. "Hold on buddy. Help's coming." His voice cracked as he pounded his fist on the pavement.

O'Donnell's vitals plummeted. He struggled to remove a letter from his tactical vest, placing it in James' hand. "It's bad, real bad. I feel so cold and weak. Give this letter to my wife and tell her I'm sorry about missing our anniversary. Don't beat yourself up. It's my fault. I should've never removed the back ballistic plate." His voice shook as his eyes glossed over.

James shook his head. "You can give it to her, just as soon as we get you home. Now hold on."

Chills electrified James' neck; he glanced up to see a curious onlooker. "Please help me."

The man smirked, turned, and walked away.

# CHAPTER 8: THE WALK-IN

*American Embassy Rome*

Assistant Regional Security Officer (ARSO) Jack Kline rarely broke a sweat at work. He had spent the morning reading classified cable traffic, reviewing residential security surveys, signing police stipend vouchers, and rewriting portions of the Emergency Action Plan.

Known as a "hobby cop" by his agent colleagues, Kline had taken the job with Diplomatic Security after retiring from the army. He did so, not for the work or money, but for the chance of travel, prestige, and government security that came with the job. His easygoing nature, combined with his extroverted personality, allowed him to make friends, both young and old. His round, full face supported a well-groomed mustache and a full beard peppered with gray. Even at fifty-two, he had the mind-set of a college student with a genuine zest for life. However, his physical appearance reflected many years of bad eating habits. Kline preferred television reruns to recreational activities, resulting in a classical Buddha belly. Nicknamed the dumper, he often boasted, "A mission passed was a mission completed." Today, work blessed him as the only available agent in the office.

Kline's stomach rumbled as it approached his customary one o'clock lunch hour. He placed several secret folders in his Mosler two-drawer safe, closed it, and spun the combination lock. The desk phone suddenly rang, startling him from his deep reverie. He lifted up the receiver.

"Sir, this is the Marine Security Guard at Post One. We have a canary in the reception area."

"I'll be right there." Kline hung up and reached for his sport jacket. He grabbed a black ballpoint pen and a small green notebook off his desk.

Walking toward Post One, he bumped into his colleague in the inner courtyard, inviting her to join him. Special Agent Jeanna Wilson, an eight-year veteran, thrived on the job. Her education, integrity, and professionalism impressed many in both the private and public sectors. She had earned a reputation in the service as an even-tempered, levelheaded, no nonsense agent who could accomplish any task thrown at her with near perfect results. A natural and gifted speaker, she easily out-talked even the most seasoned of politicians. Her professional talents ran deep, but her Spanish, Italian, French and German language proficiency silenced many.

They strolled to the reception area in front of Post One and encountered a poised male.

Kline extended his hand. "Hi, I'm Jack. I work for the security office. This is Agent Wilson. Let's go somewhere more private." He motioned and escorted the stranger to a nearby ten by twelve-foot office within the chancery. He pulled out a wooden chair from a round circular table. "Please have a seat." The two agents sat down across from him. Only a small video camera with a flashing red light broke the room's sterile ambience.

Determined to get to the truth, Kline grilled the informant for thirty minutes. Wilson translated Kline's questions from English to French and then translated the informant's answers back into English. She also readied her pen, so she could take notes of the interview.

Upon finishing his interview, Kline summarized the information to ensure its accuracy. "Your true name is Sergi Abalakov, born on May 6, 1961 in Kiev. The documents you've provided us in the name Pierre Lafonte, born 18th of December 1959, are false. You're wanted by Interpol for drug and weapons trafficking. You want us to facilitate your arrest in exchange for leniency and relocation for your family. You're providing this information to us because you fear termination upon your merchandise's delivery. Is this correct?" Kline asked while Wilson simultaneously translated.

Abalakov looked over his shoulder at the camera and its flashing red dot.

"You're delivering five nuclear warheads from Iran to Vienna to Innsbruck to Milan, then to Rome and Naples." Kline flashed his five fingers. "All the warheads are broken down and stored in wooden crates. The cargo is bound for the Mexican drug cartels, where you'll receive $750,000 for their delivery. The shipment is protected by seven armed men and booby-trapped with high explosives. Only you and one other can disarm the bombs."

"Am I correct so far?" Kline asked, glancing at his partner while she translated.

Abalakov eyed the exit. "Yes. Tis correct."

"Unfortunately, you don't have a shred of evidence, and you fear for your family's lives," said Kline, tugging on his earlobe. "Your train departs in an hour to Milan, where you'll be greeted and taken to the truck. You'll drive to Rome tomorrow and the cargo will sail from Naples in four days. In Rome, a contact will call you with the meeting location and time to give you the paperwork."

Perspiration ran from Abalakov's brow as he squirmed in his chair. He spoke to Wilson who translated his request into English. "He wants to move further inside the building. He's afraid somebody might recognize him here. Is that okay?"

"Sure. As long as he's screened by the guard, then we can move deeper inside the Embassy." Kline's palm repeatedly stroked downward on his blue tie.

Abalakov wiped his clammy hands on his pants.

"Follow me." Kline walked through the magnetometer. He waited for Abalakov's screening. After a brief delay to inspect some coins and keys, the guard cleared Abalakov's admission. The Marine opened the hardline door based on the agent's wave. Kline led him to his supervisor's spacious office. His chief's busy schedule demanded half of his day at police headquarters, so his office provided sanctuary. Kline distrusted the informant and feared that his presence involved intelligence gathering. Directing him to a couch, he sat down opposite of him.

"Is this office better?" Kline leaned in as his eyebrows rose.

Abalakov sighed, nodding.

Kline glanced at Wilson. "Could you entertain him? I'd like to photocopy his French passport and confer with our boss." Kline walked out the door.

The Marine Security Guard rover arrived and stood in the hallway in case Abalakov acted up. The twenty-two-year-old Marine prayed for a reason to pounce on the informant as Rome lacked action. Many of the Marines – fresh from recent tours in Iraq and Afghanistan – hungered for a physical workout that differed from their typical weight and running routine.

Kline cryptically explained the source's information to the veteran security officer by telephone, relaying Abalakov's time-sensitive intelligence. He also described Abalakov's motivation and deemed his intelligence urgent, credible and vital to national security. The security chief overruled Kline and instructed him to turn Abalakov over to the Italians, given their jurisdiction. Kline hung up and immediately telephoned his contact in the Direzione Centrale Polizia di Prevenzione. The Italian police sought to arrest Abalakov as a con artist. The police instructed him to stall the man and wait for their arrival.

Kline returned to find his source fidgeting like a sugar-rushed child stuck in a car seat. The trafficker needed to leave the embassy within five minutes to catch his scheduled train. Kline pushed Abalakov for further information about timing, routing, and his Mexican contacts.

Abalakov rose from his seat, approached the door, and turned toward Wilson to request that she translate for him. After he rattled off a few phrases in French, Wilson relayed his message. "You think I'm a fool. I'm not playing games; no more stalling. The group will assume there's a problem if I'm late. Besides, I need time to grab my submachine gun and dump the car near the train station. I'm gone."

Abalakov vaulted for the exit, so Kline walked alongside him. "Just stay a few more minutes. I can accompany you to the station."

"No way." Abalakov scowled. "I can't. My colleague's waiting. Meet me in thirty-five minutes at the station." He darted from the embassy and disappeared around the corner in seconds.

Five minutes later, the Italian police stopped at the embassy's front gate and fumed at Abalakov's disappearance. The police futilely combed the posh neighborhood surrounding the embassy compound. They blamed Kline and Wilson for not holding Abalakov, even though they lacked the jurisdiction to do so. Abalakov freely marched into the embassy and could leave whenever he wanted, and this logic infuriated the Italians.

Kline defused the situation in minutes, advising the detectives that they could intercept Abalakov at the train station. He satisfied the police by providing them with copies of Lafonte's ID documents. Kline and Wilson jumped into their office vehicle and sped off to the train station.

The two American agents entered the staging area, observing the arrival and departure boards; two trains to Milan flashed on the board in pale orange letters. They sat on a bench and watched the police inspect each row, cabin, and compartment in both trains. Kline remained indifferent to their futile results. His eyes tracked the police as they canvassed the station's common areas in an effort to locate Abalakov. After ninety minutes of searching, the police abandoned their manhunt and returned to their precinct.

Kline analyzed the tactics and methods used by the Italians to locate Abalakov. He expected greater effectiveness from his Italian counterparts as he observed their bunching and saturation techniques. The portly agent identified twelve of the thirteen undercover officers during their surveillance and search of the station. He knew the savvy smuggler spotted them as well.

Kline believed in Abalakov's legitimacy and information. In filing his report, he would depict the officer's shoddy performance in their quest to arrest him. He recognized the botched operation jeopardized not only the validation of Abalakov's information but also U.S. national security. He knew that the CIA, FBI, and DHS would need to see his report.

# CHAPTER 9: REFLECTIONS

*American Embassy Jerusalem*

A thick pasty dirt covered James' flushed face. The tremor in his hands subsided as he washed the blood from them, fleetingly turning the sink red. James toweled his hands and buried his face in them as the door banged open.

Tyler stormed into the locker room with a stoic face. "O'Donnell's dead."

James already knew that. His blood-soaked shirt foretold his friend's fate.

The security chief leaned forward and handed James a cup of tea; its sweet orange-lemon effervescence permeated the room. "The secretary's safe and they've arranged another meeting with the Palestinian president. What the hell happened out there today?" Tyler asked, bearing a sheen of sweat on his cheeks, forehead, and chin. "I have to brief the ambassador. People want answers and they can't get them fast enough."

James sighed, massaging his temples with his fingertips. A persistent stabbing pain pierced his forehead. "We saved the secretary while losing a great agent. Sean saved me." James glanced up.

"Damn it James. Pull yourself together. Headquarters is breathing down my neck. They need to brief the deputy secretary who will then brief the president. They all want answers." Tyler raised his head, stretching his neck from side to side.

"How many times do I have to relive this nightmare? It's on film. Why don't you review it?" James rubbed his eyes.

"I did, but I need to hear it from you."

James threw his towel across the room; a vein on his temple bulged. "It was just after noon. My team was watching the area from Abdul's Jewelry Store. We spotted three suspicious individuals as we received word that the secretary was rolling. I weighed my options and decided to monitor them."

James slurped his tea before continuing. "I didn't want to jump to any conclusions or needlessly panic the detail. A few minutes later, we observed two Arabic males on the roof across the street. I attempted to alert the detail, but I encountered radio static. O'Donnell and I dashed towards the three persons at the bus stop while Wagner covered the two on the roof."

"Go on." Tyler licked his lips.

James dabbed a handkerchief to his forehead. "As we crossed the street, Wagner radioed that there was an RPG-7 on the roof. I heard two gunshots. The motorcade was approaching so I drew my pistol and shouted at the three at the bus stop to freeze. The closest one pointed his weapon at me so I shot twice, dropping him. I shifted to get a lock on the other two when an explosion swept me off my feet."

What happened next?" Tyler motioned.

"O'Donnell dashed by me and fired, wounding one of the terrorists in the shoulder. They returned fire at him so he hit the pavement. The terrorists shot the shift leader and the agent in the right rear of the follow car, and then darted down a nearby alley, so we pursued them."

James sat his tea down, picked up his plastic bottle and guzzled some water. "I then observed our counterassault team dismounting their vehicle and engaging the terrorists to the rear. Sean and I chased two terrorists down a side ally. As we rounded a corner, the terrorists unloaded on us. Sean pushed me back to cover and took three hits. I returned fire and dragged Sean around the corner. I applied pressure to his wounds and radioed for help. That's it."

"Now, if I understand you correctly, you saw a threat and attempted to communicate it. Unable to relay your situation, your team took immediate actions to counter the threat. Your actions saved the secretary, but you lost one of your agents. Between your team and the counterassault team, you killed five terrorists and wounded another. I count two on the roof, one at the bus stop, and two more near the ninety-degree turn. Two of the terrorists escaped, but one was wounded in the shoulder. Is that right?" The RSO patted James' shoulder.

"That's the way it went down." James' legs wobbled.

An unexpected ring broke the silence.

Tyler gripped the receiver; his head hunched. "Yes sir. We'll be right there." He hung up. "The ambassador wants a briefing. I'll go over the attack, but if he wants specifics, you give it to him. You got it?"

"I hear you." James stood, brushing some of the dirt off his pants.

The two agents strolled to the elevator and arrived at the front office moments later. Upon entering the suite, the ambassador greeted them and led them over to his conference table. He flicked his wrist at his office manager who shut the door.

Tyler summarized the attack and the enhanced security measures deployed in the aftermath of the assassination attempt.

"What's your assessment of the attack?" The ambassador turned toward James.

The agent leaned back in his chair. "If we hadn't intervened, the secretary would've been assassinated. The attack was thoroughly planned, coordinated, and had back-up provisions. The terrorists had excellent intelligence and conducted surveillance prior to the ambush."

The ambassador nodded. "What else?"

James' throat constricted and cracked. "They must've had excellent support and a well-organized network. Their use of assault rifles, rocket-propelled grenades, and high explosives indicate a solid understanding of tactics. If you asked me..." James stopped in mid-sentence, not wanting to overstep his bounds.

The ambassador waved him on. "Please, I need your opinion. There's no detail too small."

James' eyebrows arched. "Sir, I want to stress that this is only my opinion."

"Understood." The ambassador crossed his arms.

"Well sir, it's unlikely that the Khorasan Group could've conducted an assault in Ramallah without the Mukhabarat's knowledge. The intelligence service controls everything in the West Bank. It doesn't add up. Hell, a fly couldn't spit in the Palestinian territories without them knowing it."

The ambassador's eyes went wide. "That's interesting analysis, Agent James. It mirrors the CIA's assessment. If this is true, then we have a grave situation here. I appreciate your insight and excellent work. I'm truly sorry about the loss of Agent O'Donnell."

"Thank you Mr. Ambassador," said James, touching his Saint Christopher medal dangling from his neck.

The ambassador stood, signaling the end of the meeting. "Incidentally, the Palestinian president called me to express his condolences for the attack and loss of life. He pledged the Mukhabarat are doing everything possible to apprehend the perpetrators, stressing they're conducting a thorough investigation. He offered their complete cooperation."

The ambassador glanced at Tyler. "You need to meet with their investigators and take a good look at all of their evidence."

"Sir, I'll give them a call as soon as I return to my office."

The ambassador escorted them from his office, shaking the agent's hand at the door's threshold. "Great work out there today Agent James. I'm putting you in for the Secretary's Award for Valor. And Sean O'Donnell will receive the Jefferson Star for his heroic and selfless actions."

"Thank you sir, but the entire team deserves it."

"I'll see what I can do." The ambassador pointed to James' forehead. "Get that scrape examined by our nurse. Things get easily infected here."

"Yes sir, I'll have it looked at right away. Thanks."

Following Tyler's directions, James arrived at the Health Unit moments later. After the nurse cleaned and bandaged his forehead abrasions, he thanked her and ambled to the security office. Tyler telephoned the motorpool dispatcher to arrange transportation for James and then led him to the garage. He directed the driver to the team house and patted James on the back. "You take care. Get some rest. See you tomorrow. This isn't over."

Upon entering the house, James relished its solitude. He stumbled up the stairs, slugged down three aspirin, and staggered to his bed to rest.

A knock startled him awake. "Enter," James yelled out, groggy from his brief forage into a dream state.

Wagner opened the door halfway and peered in. "I can return if it's a bad time."

"No, please come in." James sat up. "What do you need Dutch?"

Wagner brandished an SD card. "You need to see this. When you bolted out the door, I pushed the record button on our video camera and captured the attack."

"Great work Dutch. Has anyone else seen it?"

"No, just me."

James tossed the covers aside and sprung to his feet. "Let's go look at it. Perhaps we'll catch a break." The two agents scuttled downstairs to the living room.

"I set up the footage on my laptop." Wagner eyed the screen and pushed the play button. Traffic congestion, incessant horns, and frantic people sprung to life on his seventeen-inch monitor.

"Dutch, can you fast forward it to the attack?"

"Sure, give me a sec." Fuzz filled the screen as Wagner advanced the video. He pushed the play button. "Okay, this is where I captured the three terrorists sitting at the bus stop."

"I know what you're thinking." Wagner grabbed James' forearm. "You couldn't have known they were terrorists just by looking at them. You needed confirmation and you got it. An unprovoked incident in the city could've easily sparked widespread violence here and around the world. Remember when a magazine outlet published a caricature of the prophet Muhammad. Large-scale and violent demonstrations sparked around the globe. Now imagine what would've happened if we jacked-up these people without cause."

James stared at the screen. Wagner's shots sounded like a cannon as he came into view, firing two shots and downing a terrorist. The explosion rocked the nearby buildings, shattered windows, overturned the police lead and blew James off his feet. It then captured O'Donnell and James' pursuit down a side ally, followed by the distant, faint, and rapid burst of a submachine gun. James' stomach churned as this salvo of shots took O'Donnell's life.

Wagner popped out the SD card and held it up. "Just think Matt, I could get a healthy piece of change if I sold this footage to the networks. Inquiring minds want to know."

"Don't get any bright ideas Dutch." James snatched the SD card from Wagner's hand, pausing, he said, "Make two copies. We'll each keep one. Don't be surprised if the original disappears."

"I'm on it." Wagner reached for the tiny card.

James walked to the dining room table, sat down, and broke out a pad of paper. His head pounded, but he knew that his office and leadership needed his report immediately; and they would want it sooner than later. He struggled, drawing a blank of the day's activities as each scene blended into one long event. Vivid images of O'Donnell's death flashed in his head; his heart fluttered once again. His stomach churned as he relived the rounds ripping through O'Donnell's torso.

Rubbing his eyes, he glanced down at the team's surveillance logbook. He reviewed the freshly scribed journal in several minutes. The diversion reenergized him as his words began to flow by following a chronological sequence of events. He finished his rough draft in a little over an hour and laid his pen on the table. He proofread the document one final time for flow, context, and grammar. His concentration faded as he heard Atwell, Smith and Steele's voices emanating from the front door.

Atwell trudged into the dining room. James peered over his laptop's computer screen and captured his eyes. The room became awkwardly silent.

"You alright buddy?" Atwell patted his friend's shoulder.

James shrugged. "I can't believe he's gone. He saved my life. It could've been me. He had a wife and kids. I'd trade places with him in a heartbeat."

Atwell's posture loosened. "It wasn't your time to die and you're still here. I remember when I lost my squad leader who took me under his wing. We were just over the border in Iraq, conducting a rescue mission. Bad intelligence led us into the middle of an ambush. We suffered several casualties as we fought for our lives."

Atwell's face lightened. "A salty army sergeant saved my life, but in doing so lost his. He died in my arms. I was the medic but I couldn't do anything except watch him die. I'll never forget his face and final words, but the hurt fades in time. Believe me."

James' mouth drooped.

"You did everything you could Matt, and sometimes that's the best you can do."

"Thanks George." James brooded.

Atwell's face tightened. "Oh, before I forget. Protective Intelligence Investigations (PII) and the Office of Special Investigation (OSI) have sent a joint team to analyze and investigate the attack. They want your assistance to bring the perpetrators to justice. They'll be here tomorrow afternoon, along with a dozen FBI agents."

"This is great. OSI is going to play armchair quarterback and second-guess my decisions. They're looking for a scapegoat." James lowered his head as his chest tightened.

"Don't worry." Atwell shifted back and forth. "They're required to investigate when there's a loss of life. Besides, I just came from the embassy and reviewed a cable the ambassador sent complimenting our team."

"You're probably right George, but that doesn't make me feel any better. I've seen OSI do their hatchet job before in Baghdad and Kabul." James pursed his lips.

"Get cleaned up. We're going out for drinks." Atwell rubbed his forehead.

They piled into two cars and drove to a nearby hotel; its lobby and bar buzzed with aid workers and westerners trying to close a business deal. After numerous European beers and repeated toasts to their fallen friends, they sat their empty bottles down.

"Let's head home. We need to prep for the arriving agents' many questions. This is the wrong time to nurse a hangover." Atwell stood and walked to the door with fast-paced strides.

A warm night air smacked James in the face as he exited the hotel's revolving door. The area teemed with pedestrian and vehicular activity. He paused in the covered vehicle staging area, glancing behind him with a wide-eyed look. His neck hairs straightened as his gut tingled.

Atwell nudged him. "You okay?"

James turned; his face pale. "I'm just tired George, real tired."

"I'm not surprised. Your body dumped a lot of adrenaline into your system. Let's head home and get some rest." Atwell squeezed James' shoulder.

James opened his bloodshot eyes; his head throbbed as he stared at his watch's blurry red digits. Rolling slowly out of bed, he stumbled to the bathroom and fumbled to open a bottle of aspirin; its cap fell to the tile floor as he extracted two pills from the nearly empty bottle. After showering, he shaved his five o'clock shadow and brushed his teeth. He hurriedly dressed and crept downstairs to avoid waking his team.

After flipping the lid to his laptop, he inserted the SD card and pushed the play button. He stopped the video intermittently and froze it on the three terrorists sitting at the bus stop. His muscles quivered as his face reddened. He glared at their facial features as his heartbeat quickened. Slamming his fist on the coffee table, he muttered, "I should've killed all of these bastards." He covered his face with both palms, sliding them down to form a steeple at his chin.

Viewing the video footage further, he discovered an anxious man lurking in the shadows. He froze the video again to examine the man; his cold eyes transfixed on the three terrorists at the bus stop. The brawny man appeared familiar to him. He zoomed in on the man's face and recognized him as the curious onlooker in the side alley. He speculated the CIA's facial recognition software and vast contacts could identify him. Extracting the SD card from the player, he decided to pay the veteran spook an impromptu visit.

The tenacious agent bolted out the door, hopped into his car, and drove to the embassy. Arriving just prior to business hours, he visited the cafeteria. Hickory-smoked bacon and the aroma of sweet maple syrup permeated the small cafeteria. James grabbed a bottle of orange juice from an open refrigerator and then walked to the cash register. He scanned the menu and ordered two fried eggs, bacon, and two slices of wheat toast. By the time he inhaled his breakfast and read the international newspaper, employees flooded the building.

James ambled through several corridors and back stairwells to arrive at the RSO's office. He pounded on the door with the heel of his palm.

Tyler opened the door. "Oh, come in Matt. Why didn't you ring the buzzer?"

James shrugged. "Hell if I know. I just felt like hitting something." He entered the suite and sat down in front of the RSO's desk. "Gene, I may have identified another bad guy."

"What do you mean?"

"I took another look at the video footage taken during the attack. I've identified eye contact between an unknown man and the three terrorists at the bus stop. I also saw him in the side alley where O'Donnell was slain."

"Are you sure it's the same person?" Tyler drummed his foot against the floor.

"I'm positive. I looked directly at him and sought his help. The bastard just turned and walked away. Yeah, it's him. Do you think the station can identify him?" James licked his lips with cautious optimism.

"I don't know, but it's worth a try." Tyler telephoned his CIA counterpart, who invited them up. Arriving at the entrance, they announced themselves through an intercom. A click sounded signaling the magnetic lock's release, so they opened the door and entered the suite. Proceeding to the office manager's desk, she escorted them to the chief's office.

"Go right in. He's expecting you." The frumpy office manager motioned.

"Thanks for seeing us on such short notice Mike." Tyler extended his hand and received a firm handshake. "You remember Agent James."

"You bet. It's good to see you Matt. I'm sorry about O'Donnell. He was a true patriot."

Nodding, James remained silent. Sensing the unease, Tyler said, "Matt has identified a new suspect and wants your assistance in identifying him."

James handed the CIA chief an eight-by-twelve color photograph of an Arabic male.

Olson eyed the photograph, shaking his head. "I don't recognize him; I know most of the al-Qaeda and ISIS characters operating in this part of the world. Our continued success against them has decentralized their network and regrettably brought many new faces into the game."

The CIA chief sat behind his desk, motioning for them to pull up a seat. Olson scratched his nose. "I'll run him by my sources and contacts. I'll have our experts run our facial recognition to see if we get a hit in our database. It might take several days given the size of the database. Is there anything else I can do for you?"

James straightened up in his chair. "Not now, but I won't hesitate to call if I do."

"We'll meet with the Palestinian explosive experts shortly. Do you want to accompany us Mike?" Tyler thrust his chest out as his thumbs hooked his belt.

Olson glanced down at his watch. "I can't today. Unfortunately, my schedule's full. Thanks for the offer." Olson looked up; he grinned knowingly as his sources had already provided him the explosive analysis.

"No problem. We'll let you know if we discover anything interesting." James rose. "I appreciate your assistance. Thanks."

"Don't thank me yet. Let's see what we uncover. Take care." The CIA officer motioned to the door.

"I know you're busy so I won't take any more of your time." James shuffled his feet as they walked to the door. He doubted the CIA's sincerity. Their agenda often diverged from others.

The two DS agents departed the suite and scuttled to the RSO's office. Tyler looked forward to his meeting with his Palestinian counterpart as he sensed their progress in the case.

He radioed his local investigator to prepare for departure in ten minutes. After going over a few notes, they departed the RSO's office and met Faisal in the parking lot. The local investigator swung his head around as Tyler opened the door and ducked his head into the car. "We have a ten-thirty appointment with Captain Makdad. Can you get us there in thirty minutes?"

"I'll see what I can do." Faisal waited for the doors to close and punched the accelerator. The veteran investigator bobbed and weaved in and out of heavy traffic to arrive on time.

James patted him on the shoulder. "I see the Bill Scott Raceway course paid off."

"The course was fantastic. I enjoyed the high-speed driving section." Faisal winked.

James leaned over the seat. "I thought so by the way you maneuvered through that tight S-curve and hit every apex flawlessly."

A sharply dressed man bearing captain's bars waited curbside in front of the Explosive Unit headquarters building.

"Ah halan, Captain." Tyler placed the palm of his hand on his heart as he exited the vehicle. He waved to James. "This is Special Agent Matt James."

James extended his hand. "It's nice to meet you captain. Thank you for meeting us. I know you have your hands full given the political pressures of this case."

"I'm glad to help." He smiled thinly. "Please, follow me." The captain marched through the front door and bypassed a security checkpoint; the Palestinian guards snapped their heels together and offered a crisp salute to the captain.

Passing an antique wooden case, the captain pointed out various inert explosive devices from past high-profile explosive cases. After a short pause and negotiating an additional security checkpoint, they arrived at the captain's office.

James' eyes panned the room as he paused to read the degrees neatly hung on the wall. This included a Bachelor's in Mechanical Engineering from MIT and a Master's in International Relations from Georgetown. A dated photograph of the captain shaking Yasser Arafat's hand sat on the corner of his desk.

The captain picked up two files marked confidential from his desk and handed each of them one. "Here's our preliminary report with accompanying photographs. I had it translated into English. As you can see, the attack utilized two well-placed improvised explosive devices. However, one – a shape charge – failed to detonate; otherwise, its fifty-five pounds of Semtex would've annihilated your fully armored Cadillac and instantly killed its occupants."

"It was fortunate for us it didn't detonate." James' eyes widened.

"Luck had nothing to do with it. Your elimination of the first terrorist saved the secretary, as he held the detonator. Your counterattack caught them off guard. They didn't even have time to alter their plan or detonate the device." The captain spoke boisterously.

"Captain, when will your final investigative report and analysis be finished?" James asked with a softened voice.

"It will take another three days. We're still awaiting our final forensics analysis. I'll bring a copy of the report to the RSO as soon as it's finished."

"I look forward to your visit," Tyler said. "Maybe we can have lunch. Thanks for meeting us on such short notice." The two agents shook the captain's hand prior to walking out of his office. They hurriedly strolled through the building and out to an awaiting car.

James froze in his footsteps shortly; his mind raced. "Faisal, can you drop me back at the residence? I've some unfinished business there that can't wait."

He arrived at the house to find it empty, so he embraced its tranquility to review his report. Perusing through the pages, his concentration intensified as his stomach churned. He vowed to capture or slay O'Donnell's killers. With investigative agents arriving in three hours, his mind relived the assassination attempt and death of his friend. He wanted to avoid any blame so he reread his notes a third time when the phone rang.

James lifted the receiver on the third ring as his thoughts wandered. "Hello."

Atwell spoke staidly. "Report back to the embassy immediately. I need..."

"Can't it wait?" James interrupted him in mid-sentence. "I'm prepping for tonight's debriefing."

"No, it can't wait," Atwell barked. "We have a mission that requires immediate action. Believe me Matt, you'll like this one. So move your ass and get down here. That's an order."

"Say no more." James reached for his gun off the table. "I'm on my way."

"Do me a favor Matt. Bring the leverage tools." Atwell cryptically referred to the team's special assault equipment; the case sat in the house's hidden vault.

James' face sparkled. "You've got it. I'll be there soon."

"It's time for some payback." Atwell's fist tightened as he hung up the phone.

# CHAPTER 10: INTELLIGENCE DRAIN

*Rome, Italy*

Abalakov paced back and forth in his musty hotel room. He studied the tattered and faded sheets covered by a stained salmon-colored comforter. Moans from the adjacent room echoed throughout his room, as did the rhythmic thumps of a headboard. Cockroaches skirted freely, feasting on a smorgasbord of crumbs. He glanced down at his watch, grabbed his mobile phone off the desk and hit the recall button at nine o'clock in the morning.

"Good morning, this is the American Embassy Rome switchboard. How may I direct your call?"

"RSO's office please," he said, crumpling his nose as he glanced down at a rat in the corner of the room munching some leftover Chinese food; its Cheshire smile and fat body reflected a long-term resident.

"Hold a minute. I'm transferring you now."

After a single ring, a familiar voice answered, "RSO's office, Jack Kline speaking."

"Hello Jack. Are you ready to deal or do you want to play more games? Halftime is over and the clock is ticking. Pay attention. I'm only going to state this once. These are my terms. Take it or leave it. It's your call, but let me remind you that the stakes are colossal. I'd hate to think what havoc the Mexican cartel could cause with nuclear weapons."

Kline clenched his teeth. "You made your point. What do you want?"

"Meet me in forty minutes across the street from the northwest corner of the Roman Coliseum. Don't screw it up Jack. Leave the cops out of it and come alone." The phone line hummed incessantly.

At the security chief's direction, Agent Jeanna Wilson telephoned the Italian authorities to inform them of the time and location of the meeting. The police reiterated their desire to arrest Abalakov, reminding her to avoid obstructing their investigation. This demand did not comfort Kline or Wilson. They had already witnessed the police's uninspiring work at the train station and feared a similar outcome.

The two assistant regional security officers arrived five minutes before the designated meeting time. Casually scanning the area, Kline observed an espresso bar across the street from the marvel of Roman architecture and engineering. He found the meeting choice ironic. In ancient times, the coliseum hosted reenactments of epic battles, gladiatorial contests, hunts, executions, and dramatic plays. The crusty agent attributed Abalakov's site selection as symbolic of the magnitude of the present situation.

The American agents strolled over to the bar, sat at a small glass table, and summoned a waiter. While waiting for his source, Kline ordered a cappuccino while his partner requested a small glass of orange juice. He anticipated the smuggler's tardiness as undercover officers swarmed the bar and the immediate area. Kline's eyes panned the vicinity; he effortlessly spotted them by the way they strutted around in their tailored Italian suits and sporty sunglasses.

The hairs on the back of Kline's neck abruptly stood and tingled as he felt an eerie presence. He glanced at the coffee bar across the street and then to the rooftop of an adjacent building. His sparkling eyes wandered from the ground level stores to a series of apartment windows and visible rooftops. He leaned back with his arm draped over the back of the chair. The bustling area presented hundreds of places to hide and observe; no doubt the reason the seasoned smuggler chose the location. Kline recognized there would be no meeting today, amassing his second strike. He doubted he would get a third.

The two agents sat idly for an additional hour. Kline took advantage of the lull in activity to order a ham and cheese Panini. They ate, talked, and watched the area for about thirty-five minutes. The supervising detective barged in and interrupted their brief respite from work.

"It's your fault that he didn't show up. You Americans can't follow the simplest of instructions." The Italian detective averted his gaze while rubbing his nose.

Kline's face reddened as he pressed his lips tightly together. He found the detective's rationale groundless.

The detective waved his figure in front of Kline's nose. "This is our turf. You're simply guests in this country. Stop meddling in our business."

"Your men's aggressiveness and lack of discreetness didn't help the situation. They were easier to spot than secret service agents guarding the president." Kline's voice wavered.

"You don't know what you're talking about. My men are professionals." The detective's hands now accentuated his words. "You can learn from us."

"Learn what not to do." Kline's diplomatic tongue vanished. "Your guys couldn't find their asses if their hands were in their back pockets. I liked the way they went from vendor to vendor showing his photograph. That work was real subtle." He pointed at the detective's chest.

The detective's face contorted as he stomped off; his hands flailing over his head.

"That was fun." Kline sipped his cappuccino while thrusting-out his chest.

Wilson peered down at the uneven cobblestone pavement. She understood the need for a robust partnership with the Italians. She also knew her boss would demand an explanation.

Kline eyed the bill and slapped ten euros down on the table. He lacked the time to wait for the inattentive waitress. The two American agents ambled several blocks back to the car. He opened the door to his Ford sedan as his eyes wandered frontward to a clacking noise; a sheet of notebook paper flapped under the driver side windshield wiper. Kline reached over and ripped it from the wiper blade. After his phone discussion earlier in the day with Abalakov, the English-written note seemed appropriate. He read it carefully:

*The shipment will leave tomorrow afternoon for Veracruz, Mexico. The Star Gazer is the name of the boat which will depart at about sixteen-hundred from Naples. The paperwork is legitimate and filed with the appropriate authorities. The cargo is only a small portion of a larger load. Keep the Italian police out of it if you want to deal. I don't trust them. I've bought too many of them in the past. Don't underestimate me. I'm smarter than you think. I know you understand the consequences if these things land in the wrong hands and on American soil.*
*Sergi*

Kline shook his head, grinning and admiring the smuggler's intelligence. "This guy's no fool and a cool customer. He conducted counter-surveillance at both the train station and at the bar. He concealed his English-speaking abilities during our interview, probably to assess our plans by our comments. I think he's legitimate Jeanna. What do you think?"

"You may be right. I don't buy he's a con artist, as there's no gain. It just doesn't make sense. It's not like he's trying to sell us red mercury or something else fictitious."

"The gain is in being arrested and thrown in the slammer. The guy wouldn't get a damn thing unless he hands over the goods. Let's return to the embassy to report our encounter to the RSO." Kline snickered, shaking his head.

# CHAPTER 11: PAY BACK

James darted in and out of traffic, dodging a steady stream of oncoming cars; their flashing high beams and blaring horns served as only a minor annoyance to him. Making it to the embassy in twenty minutes, he scampered up to the RSO's suite. The office manager redirected him to the CIA's conference room for an urgent meeting. James – bearing a cocky grin – tossed the equipment cases in the RSO's office and strutted out the door. He caught up with his teammates at the base chief's office. The team sat patiently at a conference table while waiting for the ambassador's arrival. His brown eyes circled the table; the team's tense faces and their unusual silence indicated something out of the ordinary.

"Have a seat and take a load off," said the veteran spook, "it may be awhile. The ambassador's dealing with Washingtonian politics."

James turned to Atwell. "What's going on?"

"The CIA has located the terrorist's safe house; the ambassador wants us to take it down, capture any suspects, and sweep up any intelligence or evidence." Atwell stroked his beard.

"You're serious?" James pulled at his ear. "This action is unprecedented. It's one thing to run after terrorists during an attack, but it's totally different to conduct a clandestine raid without host government permission. Look at the blowback from the Bin Laden raid in Pakistan. You have a law degree. All hell is going to break loose once our actions get out; the media's overzealous and self-righteous nature guarantees our mission will make the headlines, even if it compromises national security. Look at the 2010 European Terrorist Alert and the printer cartridge bombs in the UK and

Dubai. One day the information is classified top secret and the next day it's scattered all over the news."

"I understand your concerns Matt, but the ambassador is worried about possible Palestinian involvement in the assassination attempt. He's advising the deputy secretary about the evidence that may be found in the safe house. Besides, the Justice Department is chomping at the bit to prosecute these terrorists; they want us to take them alive if possible."

"I'm sure they'll invite us in, throw up their arms, and volunteer for the upgrade to Guantanamo." James threw up his hands.

Atwell rubbed his eyes. "We're only supposed to capture, search, and secure. The CIA's handling transport."

"Thank God. That's a relief." James wiped his forehead. "I'm sure that makes this rendition legal." He shook his head and slouched in his chair.

The suite doors flew open; the ambassador marched into the room supporting a long face. The team stood in unison to pay their respect to the senior diplomat.

"It's always a pleasure discussing business with those Washington bureaucrats. I reluctantly got approval for the mission, but it's my ass on the line if it backfires. So, you guys better get it right and handle it quietly and professionally." The diplomat motioned them to take their seats.

"You can count on us." Atwell took a seat. "We'll have to hit the safe house by surprise, otherwise it could go sideways and turn ugly fast..."

The senior diplomat interrupted. "I don't need to hear the specifics of your operation. Just get the job done. Watch yourselves. No doubt the Palestinians are watching your actions."

"We'll take every precaution possible." Atwell glanced at James.

"Then it's settled. Good luck." The ambassador rose from his seat. "I have to draft a cable. Mike will brief you on the source's information." He departed the room.

The base chief briefed for about twenty minutes, finishing with a short question-and-answer session. The intelligence officer described multiple unnamed credible sources and pinpointed the exact location of the safe house.

"My informants advise that two terrorists are being sheltered at this safe house. They're waiting for their new identity documents and transportation to Iran." Olson scanned the group. "I can't give you any further specifics.

Our sources and methods must be protected." Olson opened his briefcase, removed some papers, and spread them across the table. "Here's a map of the area and a floor plan of the apartment. Pay extra attention to the front window overlooking the street."

The seasoned case officer circled the area with his pen. "You'll need to quickly hit the house because if they're watching, they'll see you coming. They've already demonstrated their commitment and willingness to kill."

"This mission gets better all the time." Wagner slapped his hand down on the table. "We'll be sitting ducks out there; this is a suicide mission. I don't like it. Not one bit."

"You don't have to like it. Just get the job done. Are there any other questions?" The veteran spy eyed the group.

Atwell glanced at the map. "How's your source's reliability?"

"It's about as good as it gets." Olson's eyes twinkled as he leaned back in his chair. "His track record is impeccable. Oh, the RSO and one of his assistants are already at the site conducting surveillance. When you approach the site, call them on channel five encrypted and they'll give you an update. Two of my guys will drive you there in a van. They'll assist you in your search. Good luck." He stood and walked the team to the door.

"I wonder what these guys are really doing George," James whispered behind his hand, shaking his head. "They're definitely up to something."

"Who knows? It's anyone's guess." Atwell's stoic face signaled his operational concerns.

The team shuffled to the security office and donned their gear. The room's unnerving quietness reflected the situation's gravity. They could easily conduct the raid, but this mission fell outside their purview. Raids on foreign soil belonged to the clandestine agents that work in the shadowy underbelly of black operations. Unfortunately, the number of global hotspots had exhausted the CIA's resources.

Steele double-checked all his equipment. He dreaded an unrestrained piece of gear giving away their position.

"If you need a hand getting dressed, just ask. My eighty-year-old grandmother dresses faster than you." Wagner held his night vision goggles up to his eyes.

"I'm just taking my time to ensure that everything is secure." Steele shook his head as he buckled his low-ride holster around his thigh. He racked his pistol's slide to the rear and let it slam forward. He slid his weapon into his holster. "Now I'm ready."

Each team member sported soft-soled black boots, utility pants, and bulletproof vest with front and back ballistic plates. Special webbed gear held everything imaginable, including standard Sig Sauer P 228 9mm semi-automatic pistol, headset for communication equipment, flashlight, radio, and an assorted array of other tools for the job. An assortment of shotguns, submachine guns and assault rifles dangled from slings around their necks.

"Listen up," Atwell barked. "Wagner and James, you're the entry team. I'll follow. Steele, you're security and Smith will be rear security. The mission's simple. We're going to own the place and anyone in it, just as we've practiced and taught. We're short information, but we have a copy of the floor plan. Matt, take it away."

James rolled out the floor plan on the table. "The van's going to drop us as close to the front door as possible. We'll exit through the van's sliding door and move to the building's outer door. The van will hold in place shortly to provide us with partial concealment from the street. Steele, you should pay close attention to this upper window. If the terrorists are watching, then they'll see us coming. I don't anticipate a problem. We'll only be exposed for seconds."

James tapped the sketch three times. "Once inside, we'll proceed up the stairs to our target door which is located on the right. We'll do our standard scan and hit it accordingly. As we clear, the progression would be the common room and kitchen, followed by the bedroom and bathroom. Any questions?"

Wagner shook his head. "None here. This takedown is a piece of cake if we can surprise them."

"Anything to add George?" James glanced at him.

"Yeah, I've just one thing. Since it's already dark, we'll wait just a few minutes and use nightfall to aid our operation. Remember, these guys are highly skilled and dangerous. Let's do this assault by the numbers and cover each other's back. We're all going home after this mission."

Each member acknowledged with a customary nod and thumbs-up.

"Let's do a gear check." Wagner moved between teammates examining and tugging on their gear. "Everyone looks good George."

Atwell clapped. "Great, let's go to work. Remember, we want to capture them alive."

The team trotted down a seldom-used stairwell and scurried into an awaiting van.

"You guys ready?" The driver asked.

Atwell slammed the van door shut. "As ready as we'll ever be. Let's go."

The driver obeyed all traffic laws and drove the speed limit throughout the thirty-five minute trek. The clandestine operator avoided any undue attention.

"You guys are the best DS has to offer. Let's show everyone what we're made of and take this house down with precision. There's one more thing. Let's do this for Sean." Atwell's intense fiery eyes panned his team.

The team nodded their approval.

"Five minutes," the driver called out over his shoulder.

Atwell keyed his microphone. "Nighthawk...Nighthawk, this is Doc."

"Go Doc," Tyler replied over the radio.

"Can you give me a situation report?"

Tyler held his radio down in his lap, depressing the talk button. "There's no sign of any movement. There may be one person in the apartment. Take it down."

Atwell glanced out the window. "Copy that. We're four minutes out."

The team scanned the neighborhood as the van pulled to the curb in front of their target house; its deserted streets suited them. James relished the sign and good fortune.

Atwell slid the door open. Wagner and James leapt out, followed by Atwell, Steele, and Smith. The team advanced to the house with their submachine guns covering front, right, left, and rear sectors. Wagner and James darted toward the premise's outer door, taking a standing position on each side of it. The three other agents trailed and stacked up behind them. Smith kneeled and scanned the area behind the team. Wagner inserted a pick and torque wrench into the lock; his fingers maneuvered the pick and wrench until a series of pins disengaged with a click.

Atwell squeezed James' shoulder to pass the go sign. Wagner pushed the door open and sprung through its threshold with James following closely behind. They dashed up the stairs and stacked on both sides of the apartment door. Atwell signaled the others up the stairs. Wagner slid a pencil-thick fiber optic tube under the door; the team eyed the inside of the apartment on a small phone-size monitor. Wagner twisted the tube from right to left; the main living area of the apartment appeared empty.

Wagner quickly analyzed the door and its locking mechanisms; he raised his index finger and his thumb up, pointing to the top hinge and the lower one. Atwell stepped out to face the door and aimed his shotgun at the top hinge. He pulled the trigger. The impact of the frangible 12-gauge round instantly sliced through the top hinge. Atwell immediately racked another round into the chamber and fired into the lower hinge. He then shot the deadbolt lock, immediately lowering the shotgun and transiting to his pistol.

The team crashed through the door with James taking the lead, entering and moving to the left. Wagner followed closely behind him and moved to the right. Everyone else pursued and cleared the main room in a second.

James and Wagner darted to the bedroom door and awaited the go signal. Atwell stacked behind James and motioned for Smith and Steele to set up on the bathroom door.

Atwell nodded and the two teams simultaneously crashed through both doors. Wagner, James, and Atwell entered and cleared their areas of responsibilities. Wagner's gun sights captured the center of a suspect's head; he released his trigger to the rear, as the man remained motionless with a detonator in his hand.

Atwell crept toward the man and placed his fingertips on the side of the suspect's neck. "He's gone. It looks like he bled to death from his shoulder wound," Atwell stated and then barked, "Clear."

"Clear," Steele responded.

Atwell activated his microphone. "Nighthawk...Nighthawk, this is Doc. The site is clear. We have one dead tango. The room's wired. Give us a few minutes to disarm them and then send up our friends."

"Copy." A voice came over the radio. "They're standing by. We'll continue monitoring the outside."

"Roger. Atwell out."

Wagner crawled following the wire leading away from the detonator switch. "Shit!" He reached for his wire cutters. "Look at this device George. Good thing he wasn't alive to set this bomb off. The ten pounds of Semtex would've blown us to hell."

Atwell wiped the sweat from his forehead. "Can you disarm it?"

"Let's find out. Hmmm, I wonder if this wire will neutralize the power source." Wagner glanced at Atwell for a reaction.

Atwell cringed. "Do you know what you're doing?"

"I'm not sure. There's always a first and sometimes a last time for everything, but I've been lucky so far." Wagner raised his hands. "I still have ten fingers."

The other agents conducted a cursory search for other devices.

"Shit," James bellowed, "I've got another one."

Tension permeated the air.

James felt the room spin as his face turned pale; his mind flashed back to Beirut before he shook off the sensation. "Hey Dutch." He stared at the device as sweat pooled on his forehead. "Bomb disposal isn't my area of expertise. Do you mind taking it?"

"No problem. Give me a minute to finish this one."

While Wagner disarmed the devices, the team systematically searched the apartment and discovered notes, sketches, and maps. They also uncovered dozens of weapons and explosive components hidden in a couch and the bedroom's closet.

James held up a sketch. "George, you better have a look at this."

"Looks like a rough drawing of the embassy and its neighborhood." Atwell scanned the diagram. "No doubt plans for a car bomb given the elimination of the police and the placement of the car."

James glanced at the drawing and memorized it. "Yeah, it certainly appears so. We better get the hell out of here before Palestinian's finest join the party."

The team combed the place and discovered even more items. Steele popped open a gray, hard plastic Pelican case that the CIA officers brought up. They all worked swiftly together to load the notes, explosives, blasting caps, detonators, and various weapons. A laptop computer caught their interest; its hard drive could provide a trove of info.

James examined a pen gun and shook his head while smiling. "You could write a binding contract with this gadget." He unscrewed the top off it and removed a small caliber bullet, tossing them both in the case. He shut and latched the top to the case.

The squelch of the radio aroused the team. "Heads up! You've a hostile coming your way," Tyler radioed.

Steele hid behind a kitchen cabinet and aimed his pistol at the apartment's entrance. James crouched on the left side of the door and waited.

The suspect walked to the door and observed the splintered door and frame. His groceries crashed to the floor; eggs, oranges, and an assortment of vegetables spilled out of the bag and onto the wood floor. He drew his Makarov pistol from his waist belt. James sprang forward and trapped the suspect's arm to his side; his extended fingers speared into the man's nerve point on the side of the neck. The man's limp body fell to the ground. James glanced over at Steele and winked. Steele rubbed his forehead while looking down.

The CIA officers kneeled on the terrorist's neck, handcuffed and frisked him, and then duct taped his mouth. They covered his head with a black hood and cinched it up around his neck.

James patted the terrorist's head. "Enjoy your free visa and trip across the Atlantic to meet your new friends at Guantanamo."

"We need to go," Tyler shouted over the radioed. "Host country security forces are coming." Faint and ever-increasing sirens captured their attention.

The team grabbed the hard cases and scurried down the stairs. They threw the suspect and the evidence cases into the vehicle and leapt into the van. Atwell slammed the sliding door shut.

"Where's Matt?" Atwell surveyed his team.

Wagner shrugged. "He was right behind me and stumbled on a loose floorboard."

"He was removing something from underneath it when I passed him. I told him to leave it, but you know James. He must've uncovered something good." Steele winced.

Atwell tapped the driver's shoulder. "We've got to wait for him."

"Not a chance." The CIA man turned the key in the ignition switch. "We can't risk the police catching us."

Atwell drew his pistol and waved it at the driver. "Look asshole, we're not leaving him."

The driver threw the gear selector into drive and removed his foot from the brake. Before he could stomp on the accelerator, a Palestinian jeep screeched to a stop in front of them. The police charged their assault rifles and pointed them at the driver and front passenger.

"Freeze!" A police captain shouted. He motioned to his officers to check the area.

"This isn't good," whispered Steele.

Atwell raised a hand. "Quiet you guys."

Each team member pointed their pistols outwardly and turned their ears toward the commotion outside the van.

"If I'm going down, I'm taking all of these bastards with me," Wagner muttered.

"Safara Amerikeeya (American Embassy), Safara Amerikeeya!" Tyler panted from the dash over and held up his diplomatic credentials. "These U.S. diplomats are transporting a very sick American who needs urgent medical attention."

"He must be talking about Steele's mental condition," Wagner whispered.

"Show me," the captain insisted, strolling over to the van's rear doors.

Tyler shrugged. "Okay, but this person has a very contagious and deadly disease. Don't get too close to him. The doctors believe he's infected with a mutated and more deadly strain of the Coronavirus." Tyler donned a surgical mask.

"He'll catch lead poisoning," Wagner mumbled as he raised his pistol, grimacing.

"Ah, take him away." The police captain motioned with his hand. As the jeep backed up, the van darted off.

Atwell looked at his team. "I hope Matt is okay."

James' adrenalin surged as responding police blocked his egress down the stairs. He panned the apartment while stuffing countless documents into his vest's pockets. He grabbed a long overcoat lying on the sofa and scurried into the bathroom.

Arabic instructions emanated from the apartment's front door. James slung his MP-5 submachine gun behind his back and threw on the coat. He slid the window upward, ducked, and lunged out onto an eight-inch lip. His right foot slipped off the ledge as his hand grabbed the window's frame. The police officers' voices amplified as they stumbled upon the dead terrorist.

The resolute agent leapt and plummeted downward; the wind whipping through his hair. His left knee buckled from the impact. Rolling forward, he sprang to his feet and limped off to a nearby deserted side alley. He crouched behind a dumpster; its stench of rotten meat permeated the air. He gagged as countless police cars with their sirens wailing flooded the neighborhood.

James stumbled upon an empty four-door Toyota sedan and lifted the handle on the door; its locks were engaged. He moved down the street and approached a four-door 1995 Mercedes sedan. Opening the door, he climbed in and removed his Leatherman utility tool from his belt. He rammed the screwdriver into the ignition and attempted to turn it. He pushed it in further and jiggled it. He cranked it over and the engine roared as black smoke spewed out of the exhaust pipe. He sped off seconds later.

He detached his microphone and lifted the radio up from his waist. He pushed the talk button. "Doc...Doc, this is Hitman."

"Go ahead Hitman, this is Doc."

"Be advised that I'm alright and heading back to the embassy."

"What's your E-T-A Hitman?" Atwell looked at Wagner.

"I'm about twenty minutes out, but I need to dump this car. Could you meet me in the parking lot of the American Colony Hotel?"

"Hitman, this is Doc. No problem. We'll be waiting."

James read a map while driving. He passed several police cars, but they buzzed on by. Turning on the radio, he found the music distracting and switched it off. Not out of the woods, he drove the speed limit. Pulling into the lot, he spotted the white van and parked next to it.

Atwell popped out of the side door. "Glad to see you." He extended a firm handshake.

"Yeah, me too!" James wiped the sweat from his face.

"Nice duds Hitman. I hope you didn't pay too much for that coat." Steele shook his head.

"I got it on sale while running out the door."

Wagner smirked. "You're a little overdressed for spring?"

"I don't think so Dutch, but if you're nice to me, you can borrow it."

"Gee thanks. Let's get the hell out of here." Wagner jumped back into the van.

"That's a great idea." James hopped into the vehicle behind Wagner and they headed off, arriving at the embassy in ten minutes. They hurriedly offloaded the gear and the evidence through a dusty old emergency door. Once unloaded, the van departed with the suspect to some unknown destination. None of the team cared about the suspect. They just welcomed being back on U.S. soil, no matter its actual distance from America.

"I guess he'll fly first class to the U.S." Wagner turned away and busted out laughing.

"Without a doubt," James replied. "But it's a one-way ticket. The U.S. wants it known that we won't tolerate terrorism and we'll hunt them down whatever the cost. We're learning the Israel method of negotiation."

Wagner shook his head. "It took long enough. Remember how the Israelis tracked and killed the terrorists who assassinated their Olympic athletes in Munich in 1972."

"Terrorists only know revenge." James stretched his neck.

Atwell stroked his beard. "It's a shame as we'll never have peace in our lifetimes."

"That's a sad reality, but it's based on fact." James closed his weary eyes.

"Well at least we all have job security." Atwell felt a flutter in his belly.

# CHAPTER 12: THE AWAKENING

*U.S. Embassy Jerusalem*

Atwell pressed the video doorbell to the CIA's suite. James removed his agent credentials from his pocket and read their fine print.

Atwell displayed a wide grin. "What are you doing?"

"I'm just seeing if my badge changed, as the CIA gives us our orders." James frowned and pocketed his badge.

The office manager buzzed them in and pointed. "You guys know where to go. He's waiting to see you."

The ambassador trudged into the room supporting a long face. "I'm glad you made it back safely and without problems."

"Not quite," said Atwell, "we had a run in with the Palestinian police. Luckily, the RSO talked them into letting us go, so they never saw us or discovered our mission."

"What did you find?" The diplomat's eyes widened.

Atwell shook his head. "It's bad. We hit the place and captured a suspect. The other one bled out from his wound. They rigged the place to blow, but we deactivated both bombs and recovered a cache of weapons. We seized a laptop which needs to be analyzed. That could take weeks, depending on its encryption and how much useful information is stored on it."

James opened the case and scattered several items on the table. "Don't want to forget these documents." He reached into his vest pocket. "I found them under a floorboard." James felt a thumb drive in his pocket and retracted an empty hand.

Picking up several documents, the ambassador skimmed through them. "Oh my God, they were planning to hit my wife and other personnel." He glanced at the CIA chief. "You're on their list too."

The ambassador laid a diagram on the table and pointed at it. "This information is serious. Look at this drawing and note, showing a suicide car bomb attack on the embassy. They conducted surveillance over a three-month period to identify our vulnerabilities. We need to protect our personnel and this mission."

James vigorously scratched the base of his skull. "Sir, may I speak frankly?"

"By all means," replied the senior diplomat, eyeing the agent.

"We degraded this Khorasan cell and scored a victory, but they'll never stop."

The diplomat scanned the group. "I agree. What are my options?"

Atwell motioned. "First, we should increase the guard patrols and the Marine presence to deter them. Why go after the tiger when there are plenty of sheep? We also should harden all other U.S. facilities or they could hit one of them."

"That's easy. What else?" The ambassador looked around the table.

Atwell adjusted his glasses on his nose. "Next, we'll train your guards to conduct surveillance detection. These measures will only protect your facilities. We'll also have to provide security awareness training to your staff. They'll need to ensure their own safety."

Atwell cleared his throat. "You'll have to authorize flextime to limit your employees' predictability for their work arrivals and departures. They'll complain about some of the inconveniences; however, if they want to reduce their odds of becoming a target, they'll need to follow these procedures."

"I don't give a damn about inconveniences. They'll listen or I'll ship them home. How else can I help?" The ambassador leaned forward in his chair.

"For starters, you'll need to request the Department extend us here so we can conduct terrorist avoidance training. The training needs to be mandatory for all post personnel, including adult dependents."

"Consider it done. Washington will have a cable by C-O-B." The chief of mission glanced at Tyler. "Make it happen. Anything else?"

"That's it, but we'll let you know if we need anything else."

The senior diplomat exhaled while looking up. "Good. You did great work tonight. You must keep your mission a secret. The consequences of your operation may have drastic repercussions on U.S.-Palestinian relations and the entire Islamic world. Your op is highly classified and compartmentalized."

"Yes sir," the team unanimously chorused.

The diplomat shook each team member's hand and then walked off. "I must call the secretary. I'll also convey the appropriate message covering your actions."

"You heard the man. This information doesn't leave this room." Atwell raised his chin.

Smith's eyes narrowed. "What's going to happen to the terrorist we captured?"

"Don't worry about it. The CIA will handle that nasty business. You best forget the incident. It never happened." Atwell surveyed his team.

James started to repack the seized material. "Never mind those items." The veteran spy raised a hand. "Just leave them. We'll take care of it and apprise you of any intelligence."

Glancing at Atwell, James caught him nodding to do so. The team walked out of the room and returned to the RSO's office to remove their gear. They instead met agents from Protective Intelligence Investigations (PII), Office of Special Investigations (OSI), and the Explosives Unit.

James recognized them and shook hands with Mike Armstrong of PII and Ray Garcia from the Explosives Unit. He casually waved at Jerry Long, the sole OSI agent. Nicknamed the butcher by the agents, Long ardently investigated rumors of agent misconduct and reveled in doing so.

"What are you doing?" Long's voice reminded James of fingernails on a chalkboard.

The team looked at Atwell. "We were practicing room clearing techniques in preparation for our class with the Marines."

"You used real weapons?" Long shook his head.

Wagner rolled his eyes. "We know what we're doing and rechecked our weapons."

"That's enough kidding around. You have copies of our reports. The ambassador requested us to conduct training, so we need to prepare for class. We'll cooperate as much as time permits, but please be frugal with our time." Atwell glanced at Armstrong.

"I'm sure we can accommodate you." Armstrong patted Atwell on his shoulder.

"Let's head back to the ranch." Steele walked toward the door.

"Good idea. It's been a long day. We deserve a night off." James walked off, patting Garcia on the back. "Good to see you Ray. The explosive selection, detonation method, and planning indicate a high degree of professionalism."

Garcia's eyes enlarged. "I'll see you around. Let's grab a beer one of these nights."

"You've got it. Stop by the house. I'll have a few on ice for you."

"You're on, but you better make it a six-pack. I'm thirsty. It's something about the hot, dusty climate here. See you later."

# CHAPTER 13: FAREWELL

Time accelerated bringing the dawning of a new day. Although the sun recently crested the horizon, its rays baked the landscape and those within it. Sweat dribbled down the faces of the team, while pooling in their lower backs and armpits. The deadly events of the past days now resonated with them; the loss of their teammate and close friend drained their spirits.

The team inhaled their waffles and sausage before rushing out the door. They piled into one van and arrived at the airport's tarmac gate just prior to the arrival of a U.S. military C-141 transport plane.

A salty Israeli sergeant raised his hand at the gate's entrance. "Halt!" He stepped to the driver's window. "I need to see your identification."

Wagner handed him five diplomatic passports. The sergeant eyed the passports, glancing at each of the agents. He keyed the microphone to his radio and spoke in Hebrew. None of the team understood a word with the exception of Wagner.

"What did he say?" James peered at Wagner.

"He notified his command and asked permission for us to traverse the tarmac. The answer he received was basically – standby, we'll send an escort."

A marked Israeli police vehicle arrived minutes later; its flashing blue lights filled the air. A police lieutenant tapped on their window. "I need your passports." He compared their names to his list. "Okay, follow me."

The lieutenant led them across the tarmac as a large jumbo jet roared overhead. Wagner tailed the police lead, zigzagging around two parked commuter jets. They slowed as they neared a group of U.S. embassy vehicles parked neatly together in front of a large hanger. A fully armored black Cadillac parked separately; four Israeli bodyguards stood around the vehicle, one at each of the rear doors and front quarter panels.

Wagner parked alongside the other official vehicles, backing in so he could see the landing strip. The team eyed the runway as an American C-141 transport plane touched down on the hot Israeli pavement; its wheels screeched as the pilot hit the brakes.

Embassy personnel exited their vehicles and gathered at a central rally point. The ambassador, CIA chief and their senior staffs joined the somber crowd. James scanned the group and spotted Armstrong and Garcia; he pondered Long's absence and envisioned him rummaging through someone's trash.

The plane taxied for several minutes before coming to a complete stop in front of the crowd. James' heart sank as he watched a van pull up to the plane's cargo door. His brief contentment over the assemblage morphed into a sharp gut pain. He knew O'Donnell lay inside.

The MSD director exited from the passenger door. His taut face worsened by the thirteen-hour journey. The ambassador shook the director's hand at the base of the stairs. The seasoned diplomat turned partially to the right and presented the consul general and the CIA chief.

"We're sorry about Sean's death. He died in the line of duty. He truly served our country with honor, dignity, and courage." The ambassador gave him a solemn look.

The MSD director touched the ambassador's forearm. "Thank you for those kind words. I'll relay them to his wife at his funeral."

The ambassador dabbed his white handkerchief on his forehead. "Your team did a great job in thwarting the Khorasan Group's well-planned attack. I'm nominating them for the Department's Award for Valor. The secretary has already verbally approved, and he'll present the prestigious medals on the seventh floor."

The ambassador steered the director to the rear of the aircraft as the others paraded closely behind him. "I understand Sean had a small infant," said the ambassador consolingly.

"Yes," the MSD director replied, rubbing his bloodshot eyes. "I broke the news to her. She knew her husband's fate the minute I knocked at her door." His face abruptly turned pale as he relived her crying and collapsing to the floor. His stomach sank further as visions of her clutching her son resurfaced. Seeing the toddler pushing his mother aside and dashing out of the room crying repeatedly haunted him. He shook his head and blinked his eyes repeatedly to alleviate the image.

"You okay?" The ambassador asked as he patted the MSD director on the shoulder. "I can't imagine her pain. What a horrible thing to face." The four-star equivalent shook his head, grimacing.

"Sorry, I was just thinking," said the MSD director. "Breaking the news to her was one of the hardest things that I've ever done in my life." His one-thousand mile stare disappeared.

"I imagine." The ambassador's arm halted him as the embassy van pulled up to the plane's rear cargo door. The detachment commander, along with six of his Marines, sprang from the vehicle dressed in their blue ceremonial uniforms.

Gunnery Sergeant Bud Harris relished his first tour as a detachment commander. His voice projected like thunder and his face bore the experience that came with age. A daily diet of push-ups and sit-ups resulted in his muscular physique. He enjoyed running his Marines, in some cases twenty years younger, into the ground.

The detachment commander belted out his instructions. The Marines snapped to attention and awaited his next command. They marched in unison to the van's rear doors and stood three to a side facing one another.

"Side step left." The Marines snapped their heels and moved into position.

"Open doors." Two Marines reached up and opened the van's rear doors.

"Raise the casket." The ceremonial guard slid the casket almost all the way out and lifted it out in perfect harmony.

The ceremony mesmerized the crowd. An American flag draped the pine casket. Chills electrified James' body.

"Sean used to always say, if you must die, it's best to die defending our great nation. He was a true patriot." James nudged Atwell.

"He died in the line of duty, but it won't make it any easier for his wife." Atwell shook his head.

"It will be tough for her to raise their son alone. If she remains in the DC area, I'll stop by regularly to lend her a hand. I hear she might return to Florida, so she can be close to her parents."

Once the casket cleared the rear doors, Harris commanded them to face forward. The six Marines responded in uniformity, standing at attention while anticipating their next order. Harris spun one-hundred and eighty degrees. They stood transiently at attention. Even though a few seconds passed, it seemed like an eternity to James.

"March in place," the leader belted out. "Left...left; Left, right, left." He repeated this sequence. "Detachment forward."

They moved the casket to the plane's cargo ramp in standardized sequence. The detachment paused, turned ninety degrees, and marched up the gradual incline. The Marines rested the casket on the hard metal floor. Snapping a crisp salute, the ceremonial guard exited, maintaining their symmetrical formation. The Marines formed a straight line to the side of the ramp with their commander positioned slightly in front.

The ambassador approached Harris and gripped his hand. "Well done gunny." He withdrew a speech from his inside suit pocket.

Ambassador Williams briefly eulogized the fallen agent, speaking expressively of duty, loyalty and the country. He finished on a poignant and uplifting note.

"...And the greatest sacrifice you can make is in the line of duty and for your country. Sean O'Donnell made such a sacrifice. It's people such as Sean, who have died for our principles throughout our history so every American can enjoy the freedoms that make our nation such a great country. As a nation, we honor and remember this unselfish commitment." The ambassador placed his notes back inside his coat pocket and waved to the crowd, signaling the end to the brief ceremony.

The bodyguards encircled the ambassador and whisked him to his armored limousine. The driver confirmed the bodyguard's return to the follow car and punched the accelerator. The remainder of the embassy staff leapt into vans and departed on the tail of the ambassador's motorcade. Only the small DS contingent remained standing in the blazing heat.

The MSD director wiped the dust from his eyes. "Listen up. I don't have much time before this bird departs. The ambassador appreciates all your efforts. He asked the Department to extend you here. Naturally, it's been granted. There's a lot riding on your work and lives are at stake. Do what you've been trained to do. You have my backing."

His concentration waned from jet lag. "You guys watch each other's backs. Atwell, keep me apprised of what's going on. Hopefully, we'll see you guys back home real soon. I have to go. I've a family waiting to retrieve Sean at Andrews Air Force Base."

The rear ramp had already closed so the director trudged to the passenger door. The team waved goodbye as their boss reached the top of the stairs. He turned and boarded the plane. The door closed moments later. They returned to the van and leapt into it; the C-141's jet engines roared as it taxied out to the runway.

James pointed at the lumbering jet. "Sean's off to his final resting place. May God bless him and let him rest in peace." Silence permeated the air as they contemplated the permanence of his words. This realization blackened their hearts.

"Just remember guys, Sean's still alive as long as he lives in your hearts." James broke the awkward silence, as an Israeli lieutenant in a jeep motioned for them to leave. And, as instructed, the team departed the airport with Wagner at the helm.

# CHAPTER 14: FEEDBACK

*Damascus*

Seated around a table in a basement in old Damascus, the Khorasan Group leaders lambasted the setback. All their meticulous planning and exhaustive efforts led to a major embarrassment and a botched operation. The seven leaders stared pensively at one another. Their suspicions of each other surfaced as their tempers flared by the recent loss of their comrades.

Moussa Rahman's face flushed as his blood boiled. He sponsored three out of the seven attackers, including his favorite nephew. He had overseen the strategic placement of his personnel and helplessly watched the operation unravel from a nearby vantage point.

Rahman pointed his finger. "You're to blame for this embarrassment Nissan. You personally gathered the intelligence for this operation. All that meticulous planning and what did we get for it. We suffered a significant loss and a major embarrassment. This failure has hurt our cause. You better do some explaining or else..."

"Or else what?" Nissan raised his hand. "Don't blame me. Everything was going smoothly until the American commandos swooped in and hit us without warning. They were fast and effective. Like the leopard that lays camouflaged until the right moment. Then the beast leaps out and smothers its prey before it can react. They surprised us. We would've succeeded in our attack if it hadn't been for those American pigs."

"It's bad enough you failed in your mission, but to make excuses on top of it." Rahman shook his head in disgust. The six other members remained silent through his discord. They knew better than to interrupt him during his rant. Nobody wanted him as an enemy. He bore many scars from his incarceration by the Russians. A three-inch facial scar ran from just below his right eye down across his cheek; a wound he sustained while escaping from a Siberian gulag. Rahman broke the guard's back, leaving him paralyzed from the waist down.

"I'm not making excuses," Nissan fired back; his face reddened by the allegation. "I'm just relaying the facts, and while I'm being straight forward, we have a spy in the group. How else could've the Americans known about the attack? They countered our attack by being positioned at the right place and time."

Faisal Ahkmat fidgeted in his chair. "Are you accusing one of us as being a traitor? I resent the accusation. I've killed people for less."

"Alright, let's settle down. We're not the enemy. It's the Americans we want, but Nissan makes a valid point. How did the Americans know about our attack? It may not be one of us, but it may be someone close to us. We need to take added precautions before our major operation in America." Moustafa Yousef tapped his finger on the tabletop.

"You're absolutely correct. I just hope our plans for America are safe." Abdul Ramzi gasped.

An awkward silence filled the room.

"Did our men in the safe house know anything about our master plan?" Muhammad Ayud asked, glancing around the table.

"I doubt it." Nissan glanced at his watch. "The safe house only contained a few weapons, explosives, and some plans of our local operations. There shouldn't have been anything about our international operations."

"Great, you blow a perfectly planned operation, and I'm supposed to take your word for it. No thanks." Ahkmat's face reddened.

"What about their computer? Did they destroy it?" Ramzi asked, grimacing. "The hard drive could provide the crusaders some valuable clues as to our upcoming operation. The NSA can exploit everything."

Ahkmat's face tightened. "You've been watching too many movies; however, your point is valid. If their computer fell into their dirty hands, then our operations could be compromised. Let's just hope they practiced solid operational security, adhering to their Iranian Quds Force training."

Silent until now, Abdul Ramzi slammed his fist on the table. "The specialist sheikh will kill us if our critical mission was compromised. He's counting on us to crush the infidels with an unprecedented attack. An attack so devastating that it will reenergize the masses and reclaim the cause."

"Don't worry. We practice compartmentalization for a reason. The U.S. may discover there's a larger plot, and one directed at America, but that should be it. Nevertheless, our plan has been limited to only those that have a need to know. Even those transporting the weapon don't know whom it's ultimately destined for or where it will go. They only know it needs to be smuggled over the Mexican border. Likewise, the contents remain unknown to those receiving the package. All they know is that they're supposed to warehouse it until contacted," Khalil Moumad said. "Our plan will move forward and kill millions of infidels. You can count on it."

"We must succeed; we can all agree on that point." Rahman recognized the plan would kill hundreds of millions if executed properly.

"Yeah, 1 hope none of you blow this historic operation." Ahkmat smirked. "1 don't want to see poor execution disrupt our plans. My organization has never failed. The rest of you has-beens can give us a bad name."

Rahman fought his impulse to knife Ahkmat. "Let's not argue over the past. We came together to fight a common enemy. Only by working together can we overcome the Zionists and the American capitalist pigs. We still have much to do. I'll go to America to lead our upcoming plan, so we can ensure its success. Let's discuss our next move."

The group all agreed, so the meeting adjourned with a renewed sense of optimism.

# CHAPTER 15: PROACTIVE MEASURES

*U.S. Embassy Jerusalem*

The team's focus and enthusiasm faded following the morning's ceremonial activities. Trying to forget these images, James lifted a table and moved it to the side of the classroom. The thirty-by-forty-foot rectangular shaped room served their training needs. By rearranging the chairs and tables, the makeshift classroom could easily accommodate eighty employees and their family members.

The door flew open. "Coming through," Wagner shouted as he rolled in a large fifty-inch color monitor on a four-wheeled cart.

James glanced up from his notes. "Where did you grab that?"

"I borrowed it from the Public Affairs Office. They're well equipped. I've also got a SMART Board coming over here in ten minutes. The ambassador must've laid down the law. I've never seen such cooperation." Wagner glanced at the others.

James unfolded a metal chair. "Turnout is always better with the front office's backing."

"It sure is." Wagner attached the HDMI cable to the monitor.

"We'll have standing room only," Atwell announced, strolling into the room while waving an administrative notice. "The ambassador mandated the training for all American personnel. This directive will fill the classroom."

James' eyebrows rose. "I'm sure this notice is unwelcome news. Many people dislike security training and the disruption to their busy schedules. I'm sure the class will be dotted with work materials, papers and magazines."

Atwell twisted his head. "Oh well, what can you do? The ambassador ordered them to come."

"It's too bad he can't make them listen as well." James eyebrows rose. "Their lives may depend on it."

"It's up to us to grab their attention." Atwell cleared his throat, glancing down at his notes. "Listen up. Here's the schedule. Dutch, you'll teach the terrorism overview section. I'll follow with the surveillance detection class. Matt, you've got improvised explosive devices, and Steele will instruct the Marines in room clearing. Wagner and James will assist. Any questions?"

"Yeah, I've got one." Wagner snarled. "How come Smith gets to skate?"

"He's not sitting on the sidelines." Atwell scratched his head. "He's going to ride shotgun to evaluate the ambassador's protective detail. He'll provide protective security training if needed. He's also going to retrain the local guard force on screening procedures."

"Does anyone else have any bright questions?" Atwell glanced at James and winked.

An awkward silence permeated the room. The team knew the drill. None of them had anything to add as they preferred to avoid Atwell's feistiness. None of them wanted to be on the receiving end of his sharp wit. He could throw more piercing verbal jabs than a machine gun could spit out bullets.

It took thirty-five minutes to set up the classroom. Participants filtered in slowly causing the first class to start ten minutes late. The audience surpassed the classroom's capacity given the assassination attempt on the secretary. The audience asked a handful of questions, reflecting their concern for their own safety. A few even personally knew some of the victims cited as examples, making the lecture resonate with them.

The audience's enthusiasm slipped during the second class. A gifted teacher, Atwell captivated listeners around the world with his technical expertise, confidence and enthusiasm. James recognized that most people underestimated the importance of the surveillance detection course. He understood that early recognition of attack indicators could lead to countermeasures to avert a terrorist attack. This knowledge was critical for survival. Terrorists generally created an environment that gave them the edge, firepower, surprise and the tactical advantage.

Returning from their break, the class lumbered into the room. James surveyed their deadpan faces and knew that he had his work cut out. "Damn George, did you torture these poor saps with your class?" James shook his head.

Atwell shrugged and sat in the front row to observe and grade his colleague's performance.

"Okay. Let's get started. My name is Matt James. I've been a special agent with DS for nearly thirteen years. During that time and addition to my two overseas tours, I've served in investigations, dignitary protection, counterintelligence, and I've been with the Office of Mobile Security Deployments for about three years."

James scanned his audience from the front of the room to the back. "Today, I'm going to talk about improvised explosive devices or I-E-Ds for short. When I'm finished, you'll understand how devastating these devices can be and just how little imagination it takes to disguise them to be anything. In addition, you'll recognize the basic components of an IED and the many ways they can be activated. Finally, we'll talk about the appropriate response if you ever encounter one."

"You run like hell," a voice from the crowd shouted. Laughter filled the room.

"You're not far from the truth. What we like to tell people is to recognize, run, and notify the appropriate personnel. This includes the RSO's staff, Marine Security Guards, or local guard force. But we'll describe more details later on."

James pointed to a middle-aged man sitting in the front row. "Excuse me sir."

The man glanced up from his magazine. "You need something?"

"Could you please hand me that book sitting next to you? I want to demonstrate something to the class."

"Sure thing," the man replied, gripping the book. Upon lifting it, a high-pitched buzzer blasted the room. The man dropped the book and flew out of his seat. "Shit," he said, glancing down at the open book.

James snorted. "More like, no shit. Had that been an actual IED, then you wouldn't even have had time to soil your pants. The message that I want to make clear is that an IED can look like anything. The only limitation is the imagination of the bomber."

"Dutch, can you dim the lights?"

"You've got it." Wagner rose and adjusted three dimmer switches on the wall next to the door.

As the lights softened, James pushed the play button on a remote control to his laptop. The projection system shot an image of a man sitting behind a desk onto a garage-door sized screen. "Now pay close attention to the screen." James beamed a red dot from his laser pen, circling an item on the desk.

The screen displayed a secretary entering her supervisor's office to deliver a letter. She left moments later, closing a set of double doors as she exited. A yellow flash spiked the screen and scattered fragments throughout the room.

"It's a good thing the person behind the desk was just a test dummy; I don't mean just any other government bureaucrat." James directed his laser at the desk. "Look at the devastating effect that the letter bomb had on its immediate surroundings. A bomb doesn't have to be big to cause damage. Watch this next scene."

James unfroze the screen. A light blue sedan drove into a parking space in front of a building. Exiting the car, its driver entered the front door and disappeared from sight. Seconds later, a man walked toward the parked sedan and paused by its rear fender. He squatted and placed a small magnetic device in the wheel well, adjacent to the gas tank. He then wandered off. The driver returned moments later and started the car. As he backed out of the parking space, the car exploded and erupted into flames.

"You see how fast that bomber planted an IED. It doesn't take very long." James eyed the somber audience. "And you were probably wondering what the government did with all those surplus blue sedans."

The crowd erupted into laughter.

"Okay, one more video clip. You'll find this one very interesting. You saw what a pound of high explosives did to the last car. Watch what fifty pounds of high explosives does to this van."

Nearly two-hundred eyes stared at the screen. The van disintegrated into a thousand pieces as dark-gray smoke billowed skyward.

James scanned the audience. "Now imagine what two-thousand pounds of explosives could do to an area or building. Remember the bombing of our embassy in West Beirut in the early 1980s. That's what the experts estimated the truck to be carrying. That bomb alone killed eighty-six and wounded more than one-hundred people."

James closed the video and clicked an icon on his laptop. A PowerPoint presentation appeared on the screen. He wiped the sweat from his forehead. "I apologize for the slide's age, but it makes an excellent point. This slide represents the different type of attacks directed against Americans and our facilities from 1998 to now. The red line depicts the bomb as the preferred weapon of the terrorist."

"Why choose the bomb as your means of attack?" James asked, looking at the silent audience. He clicked the remote and advanced to the next slide. Multiple newspaper headlines littered the screen. "It gets media attention while promoting fear."

"Okay, why else?" James pressed the button on his remote control. A picture of the 1993 World Trade Center bombing in New York flashed on the screen. "Another reason is because there's no opportunity to establish a relationship or bond with the victim."

James stepped out from behind the lectern. "The bomb allows for physical separation from the crime." He gripped a red plastic training knife and thrust his hand forward at gut level. "If I stab a person, I must look at the victim. However, with a bomb, I don't have to see the death and destruction it causes. I merely plant it and I could be halfway across the city or country when it goes off."

James pointed to the next slide on screen, showing the aftermath of the 1998 bombing of the U.S. Embassy in Nairobi, Kenya. He slowed his talking down. "Until the rubble is cleared away, it serves as a constant reminder of terrorism."

The agent pressed the remote's forward button. "Anyone have any other reasons why the bomb might be used?"

A woman raised her hand. James pointed at her. "Yes, the young lady in back."

"Doesn't a bomb destroy most of the evidence?" She asked, looking down and away.

"You're correct. A detonating explosive device destroys or alters the physical evidence at the crime scene. This increases the difficulties associated with forensic investigation and identifying the bomber's signature," said James, raising his eyebrows.

"Anybody else?" He turned and looked at the screen which showed Pan Am 103's wreckage. "A blast doesn't completely destroy the evidence. Look at how much evidence the investigators recovered from sifting the ground over many square miles. They eventually connected two Libyans to this terrorist plot."

James' face sank. "One of my uncle's friends was on that plane. They worked together in DC. Anyway, look at how this act changed airport procedures. There were huge financial costs to upgrade security screening, and we know al-Qaeda wants to hurt America economically."

Advancing through a series of slides, James demonstrated the simplicity and cheapness of making a bomb. He paused on a slide that showed a female concealing a bomb around her stomach. "This case took place in Germany and was copied more recently in Iraq. The terrorist circumvented security by pretending she was pregnant. Instead of using the bathroom, she went to the garage and planted the bomb on the target's car. So, I must stress the only limitation on bomb construction, initiation, concealment or placement is the bomber's imagination."

Proceeding to the next slide, he pointed to the screen. "RECOGNIZE, RUN AND NOTIFY. This is all you need to remember. Look for items which are out of the ordinary."

"What's unusual about this slide?" James directed his laser pointer at the screen.

A man in the front row raised his hand. "There's an unattended briefcase."

"That's right," James responded, surprised by the man's enthusiasm. "And how about this next slide, do you see anything out of place?"

A woman in the middle row raised her hand. "The package next to the wall isn't right."

James nodded. "You're correct. Never touch an IED or what you suspect is an IED. Recognize its potential danger and clear the area. Notify the proper authorities, but don't use your hand-held radios. Remember the slide of the remote control device. Your radio signal could potentially activate the device."

James sipped from his bottled water. "Keep a minimum safe distance of one-hundred yards. Remember, if you can see the bomb, then it can see you. Take cover."

"So, what does a bomb look like?" After a slight pause, James answered. "It can look like anything." He repeated. "What does a bomb look like?"

The class chorused, "Anything!"

James pointed at the audience. "You're correct. Remember that point. A bomb is only limited by the bomber's imagination."

"IEDs generally consist of four components. First, there's the container. It holds the explosives in place. It could be the paper wrapper around dynamite or a coke can that contains homemade explosives. The container could also provide fragmentation, as in a pipe containing black powder. In some cases, a container may be absent, such as in cast TNT."

James cleared his throat. "Second, the main charge is considered the explosive or incendiary filler. Third, the detonator causes the main charge to explode. This could be a blasting cap, flashbulb, or percussion primer. Finally, the fuse fires the detonator. It could be a simple burning time fuse or it could involve a complex system of electronic booby traps. The fuse can be electric or non-electric."

"Are there any questions?" His eyes swept the room. "I know I've covered a great deal of information in a short time. It's important you understand the components and basic functioning of an IED. This will allow you to know what to look for when conducting a search."

"No questions? IEDs can be initiated electrically or non-electrically. Electrically initiated IEDs are those that use electric blasting caps or flashbulbs; they require a power source such as a battery, wall plug or charged capacitor. Non-electrically initiated IEDs are those that use a burning fuse or percussion primers. Military booby traps are a good example of percussion primers."

James stepped forward and handed a young Foreign Service Officer an old VCR tape. "Please examine the tape and tell the class what is unusual about it." The officer flipped the tape over. A buzzer pierced the room. The man jumped skyward.

"So, how does an IED activate? I'll tell you how. IEDs can be categorized into four different types."

He punched a button on the remote control; the screen displayed a bomb with a stopwatch. "The first category is known as time delay."

He continued flipping through his slides to reinforce his teaching points, finishing his presentation thirty minutes later by asking if there were any other questions. A majority of the people in the class responded by shaking their heads negatively. The rest of the audience remained silent, anticipating a break.

"Okay, grab all your things," James instructed, stepping towards the door. "Now let's see what you learned in today's class. Divide yourselves into groups of twos and come with me." The class trailed James to an adjoining room.

"Do I have any volunteers?" James eyed the group.

A man and woman raised their hands. James pivoted to face the group. "The object of this exercise is to conduct a room search to identify suspect devices. You must remember to conduct a thorough room search, just like I demonstrated in class. You need to be both systematic and cautious in your search."

"You two begin." James motioned to them.

The two-person team crept into the room. Moments later, a buzz echoed throughout the room.

"Damn it," the man bellowed, loud enough for the class to hear.

"Don't worry about it. Keep on searching," James instructed. They continued the search and identified three mock IEDs before tripping another one.

James patted them on their backs as they exited the room. "Not too bad. You must remember, the bomber has the advantage. He can set up his device to look like anything and activate it by one or more means."

James allowed Atwell and Wagner several minutes to reset the training devices before he called out, "Next two." An hour later, the class finished.

Atwell slapped James on the shoulder. "Nice job. Let's head home and grab a bite to eat. Steele should be finished by now. We'll pick him up on the way."

Wagner cocked his head to the side. "Matt, you obviously know a great deal about explosives. Why didn't you disarm the one you found in the safe house the other night?"

"I don't feel like going into it now," James grumped.

Wagner tapped James' shoulder. "Why not? You owe me an explanation."

"Piss-off Dutch. I don't owe you anything." James glanced down and stomped off.

Wagner turned to Atwell. "What's eating him?"

Atwell stroked his beard. "Remember his uncle and Jeff Fraser?"

"Of course I do." Wagner looked up. "Both died on protective missions."

Atwell sighed. "When Fraser died in Beirut, he was deactivating a device attached to one of our vehicles. Fraser chose to disarm it instead of calling the explosive ordinance disposal unit. The bomb appeared routine, but it exploded as he cut the main wire. He somehow missed a collapsing circuit. It was a messy site. James did everything possible to save him, but his injuries were too severe. He lost both his arms and a portion of his head, including his right eye. He survived almost a day before succumbing to death." Atwell shook his head. "I think Matt blames himself for Fraser's death and his uncle died in a similar situation."

"It wasn't his fault." Wagner clenched his jaw.

"Try telling him Dutch. James led the mission. It was his responsibility to bring everyone home safely." Atwell patted Wagner on the back as they headed for their vehicle.

The drive home seemed longer than the usual thirty minutes. The awkwardness caused by the incident left everyone a bit tense. They arrived at the house and ate while discussing a scheduled emergency response drill. The team wanted to test the Marine's ability to handle a bomb threat and a hostile intruder.

They relaxed while waiting for their 7:30 pm departure time. They had one final lesson to teach before returning to America, one that would test the Marine's preparedness for the realities ahead.

# CHAPTER 16: DESTINATION AMERICA

*U.S. Embassy Rome*

Frustrated by the CIA and FBI's lack of responsiveness to his request about Abalakov's background, Kline contemplated his options. He learned the Italians had prioritized the threat, running traces and combing the streets of Rome and Milan. Still reeling from Abalakov's disappearance and continued elusiveness, the Italians blamed the American agents for his disappearance. Determined to overcome the setback, the Italian police launched a countrywide all-points bulletin to arrest the arms trafficker. Abalakov became their number one priority for the near future.

Kline understood the ease of conducting name traces and anticipated a quick turnaround. He canvassed his embassy sources and discovered that the CIA had requested local and world traces on Abalakov. Even so, the agency admitted nothing openly, so Kline called an impromptu meeting with his CIA interlocutor. He believed in the reasonableness and honesty of his counterpart, especially since he funneled the walk-in's information through him.

The officer's punctuality delighted him. He directed him to a chair, but the officer insisted on standing.

"We ran name traces through our database and failed to get any hits." The CIA man glanced away.

Kline shook his head. "There has to be more. The guy's a known arms and drug trafficker."

"Who told you that?"

"Abalakov told me that he's a trafficker. He stressed that INTERPOL had records of his activities." Kline glanced at the company man.

"If INTERPOL had a warrant for him, I would've received a hit. Are you sure that you heard him accurately?" The spy peered into the agent's eyes.

"I heard him correctly. There was no misunderstanding. So what else can you tell me about your findings?" Kline rubbed his temple.

"We'll conduct further checks, but I doubt we'll uncover anything more. We'll be in touch if we hear anything else." The officer looked at his watch. "I'm late for another meeting." He turned and walked out the door.

Kline would not hold his breath as he suspected a hidden agenda. An office manager unwittingly alerted him to the CIA's exhaustive manhunt. The station teemed with activity as their assets canvassed the countryside.

He decided to test the embassy's other 800-pound gorilla and scheduled a meeting with the FBI Attaché. Cynical about the outcome and the FBI's willingness to share information, Kline opted to pay them a visit. He marched past Post One and waved at the able-bodied Marine on duty within a ballistic booth. The Marine returned the gesture and resumed his duties of safeguarding the embassy, its personnel and classified holdings. The Marine controlled all access into the building, dozens of monitors, and hundreds of sensors and alarms. Serving as the nine-one-one react force, these Marines would doggedly pursue an intruder to neutralize them. Once a breach occurred, Post One would pinpoint the location and instantly dispatch well-armed Marines to intercept them.

Kline entered the elevator and pushed the button for the first floor, arriving there, seconds later. A large seal of the FBI hung on the wall next to the door. He scrutinized their motto – Fidelity, Bravery, and Integrity – and wondered its origin. The determined agent pressed a button centered on the faceplate of a cipher lock; a buzzer sounded. A split-second later the office manager released the magnetic lock by pushing a button affixed under her desk.

He pulled open the door and met a bubbly woman. "Can I help you Jack?"

His eyebrow arched. "That depends. Did you conduct the checks on the walk-in the other day?"

"I sure did. The guy was wanted by INTERPOL for arms and drug trafficking. Ken was supposed to pass it to you."

"No problem. I'm sure he'll pass it soon. Thanks."

He hurriedly exited the office; his face remained expressionless as he pondered the FBI withholding information from him in the post nine-eleven era. Most other local, state and federal agencies resented them for this practice. Kline now understood this practice firsthand. He begrudged any agency that placed publicity and statistics over cooperation. He recognized the politics in play, and it sickened him. The nation relied on its government to protect them from all of the emerging threats. The populace also desired a cost-effective security apparatus that tackled record deficits in the trillions. As a taxpayer, he expected more from his government.

Kline shared his interview reports with the FBI on two occasions. His naiveté frustrated him as he realized the FBI would take everything and provide nothing in return. He recognized their sidestepping of the matter. Both the CIA and FBI vied for that headline-breaking case. His stomach churned.

He understood the FBI's uncooperative nature given their notoriety for such behavior. However, the CIA's duplicity troubled him, as he knew they queried the same computer indices as the FBI. He deplored their dishonesty about the weapon's charges, unless they uncovered something so big it demanded total secrecy.

. . . . .

Meanwhile, about one-hundred and thirty miles south of Rome, Abalakov considered his upcoming overseas journey and his fate. He brushed aside thoughts of a pine casket, thinking at least it would be finally over. Constantly looking over his shoulder frayed his nerves. Life on the run while waiting for an assassin's bullet troubled him. He regretted not saying goodbye to his wife and child.

Abalakov's fifty-thousand dollar bribe ensured that the ship passed inspection by Italian Customs. He doubted the captain even knew the cargo's contents. This skipper's ignorance increased his survival odds while lessening any risk to his prized merchandise.

With the inspection completed, the vessel prepared to embark on yet another voyage. The ship had obviously made its rounds; rust lined the ship from fore to aft. The ship showed its forty-plus year's age as it lacked general and customary maintenance in all areas. The powerful diesel motor sputtered upon the captain's order to the engine room. It took the portly engineer several tries before the engine started and spewed a cloud of thick smoke.

The seasoned smuggler eyed the eight-man crew; their frantic activities in prepping the ship for departure eclipsed their drab appearance. Two men retracted the gangplank while others scurried to untie the ship's mooring lines. Others shuffled boxes of food supplies into the galley. Their unfriendliness hit like a wintry blizzard and matched his two Middle Eastern escorts. His stomach churned, as he presaged his own death. His uneasiness briefly overshadowed by awestruck visions of one last score and sipping margaritas on a Panamanian beach. The ship's ear-piercing horn echoed throughout the harbor and interrupted his reverie. Abalakov's voyage to America through Mexico began as the ship motored away from the pier. He leaned back in his seat and rested his eyes.

# CHAPTER 17: ONE LAST SALUTE

*Arlington National Cemetery*

A light crisp breeze whisked over the 624-acre field strewn with over four-hundred thousand white tombstones and situated across the Potomac River from Washington, D.C. The springtime sun radiated through the Old Post Chapel's stained-glass windows; beams of light blessed those in attendance with warmth and color. The chapel teemed with law enforcement personnel from every agency. James understood the community's common bond; its jurisdictional boundaries set aside during times of tragedy. Hordes of people lined the pews and the back of the chapel. A hundred separate conversations droned into one and reverberated throughout the place of worship.

James relished the normalcy of America. His departure from the West Bank delighted him; he disliked the dust, cuisine, hot humid weather, and now its memories. O'Donnell's death overshadowed their mission's success; the loss of his friend blistered his heart. He recognized his death would haunt him for an eternity. O'Donnell's wife, son, parents and other relatives sat somberly in the front row. Their pained stares accented by darkened skin bunched around their eyes; tears streamed down their faces. O'Donnell's mother clutched a bible to her chest. James' eyes moistened at the sight. Nausea radiated throughout his intestinal tract as the back of his throat ached. O'Donnell's death transformed his invincibility. The two had shared several near-death experiences, which exacerbated his pain and loss of his close friend. Hardened terrorists almost killed them both in Karachi and Beirut, but they always managed to survive and triumph. Their luck ran out this time as death finally captured the heroic agent.

O'Donnell's altruistic nature spared James' life. His stomach constricted at the thought. He desired to trade places with his friend. O'Donnell had a beautiful wife and child, a loving family, and a job he thoroughly enjoyed. James' life paled in comparison and revolved solely around his work. He pondered the impact to O'Donnell's son and whether he would live a normal, healthy, and productive life.

The crowd stood as the president and the secretary of state strolled into the church. A procession of special agents surrounded the two and ushered them to their seats at the front. After some introductory remarks and a prayer, the chaplain yielded the podium to the secretary. The diplomat ambled to the lectern and removed his notes from the inside pocket of his suit jacket.

Secretary Jackson cleared his voice. "We're gathered here to honor a great patriot. One who put country above all and paid the highest price in defending freedom. Katherine, John and Patricia, son Jacob, and the rest of Sean's family, I'm truly sorry for your loss. Mr. President, we value your attendance today in paying your respects to a fallen hero."

James watched the secretary as he spoke elegantly for another ten minutes. The secretary underscored duty, honor, bravery, and self-sacrifice for the country. He spoke about the qualities of patriotism and accomplishment. However, in the end, he focused on O'Donnell's rare qualities that made him such a remarkable human being. He concluded by emphasizing that he wouldn't be in attendance if it weren't for Sean's personal self-sacrifice. His heartfelt speech honored the fallen agent and touched every member in the audience. James surveyed the crowd. He searched for a dry eye, but found none.

Atwell spoke briefly next as James declined to give a eulogy; his emotional state vacillating. Atwell reiterated many of the same things that the secretary addressed, only his speech hit closer to home. His personal touch reflected countless heroic instances in Sean's life. An eerie silence filled the chapel upon his closing words.

The Catholic priest walked to the podium and blessed Sean and his family. He called on the audience to view Sean one last time before journeying to his final resting site. The orderly audience lined up and one by one passed the raised casket. James shuffled in turn and eyed his friend who appeared poised and peaceful. He preferred to remember his playful side and quickly turned away. He vowed to avenge his death by apprehending or killing his assailants.

The audience lumbered out of the chapel, emotionally drained and somber. Most of them walked to their cars and then drove home or back to work. The official delegation and family walked toward the gravesite. The "Old Guard," members of the U.S. Third Infantry, gracefully positioned the pearl-colored casket on the symbolic ammunition carriage; its six well-groomed and beautiful horses affixed to it would deliver the downed agent and Distinguished Service Cross recipient to his grave site. Eight members of the Old Guard, four per side, flanked the ammunition carriage. A rider-less horse, symbolic of the warrior who would never ride again, participated in the ritual. The small group followed behind the carriage as the Old Guard marched in perfect rhythm to the site.

James' blurred vision and fogginess accentuated the events moving in slow motion. A three-volley salute woke him from his self-induced trance. By this time, the priest said a few last words. James glanced over at O'Donnell's wife and child. Tension and fatigue gripped her face. The permanence of the event evaded her two-and-a-half year old son.

The president approached Katherine, extending his hands forward. "On behalf of a grateful nation, please accept this flag in honor of your loved ones honorable and faithful service."

"Thank you, Mr. President." She clutched the flag and held it firmly to her chest as tears gushed down her face.

This triggered a chain reaction with her son and other family members. James spun ninety degrees to the right and observed all of the other white headstones in the cemetery. Freedom came at such a steep price. Following the playing of Taps, James turned and walked away, vowing to avenge his friend.

# CHAPTER 18: UNSOLVED BUSINESS

*CIA Headquarters – Langley, Virginia*

With a glance behind her to make sure no one else noticed her less than graceful maneuver, Katharine Davis backed out of the crawl space between her desk and the filing cabinet, carefully protecting the sheaf of photographs she had unearthed. Freshly graduated from the CIA's intensive career trainee program, Kate had been thrilled to begin her first assignment with the Agency's celebrated Counter-Terrorism Center (CTC) two years ago. Her enthusiasm slipped a notch or two when it became apparent that she was to be treated more like a glorified file clerk than an active desk officer. With an undergraduate degree in international relations and a master's degree in Middle Eastern Affairs, her under-utilization signified yet another instance of wasted resources from the CIA's old-boy bias.

Instead, she smartly used this time to develop her knowledge base by reading every file she could find. At some point, they would have to assign her to lead a case, and she had a feeling she would only get one chance to demonstrate her knowledge and analytical abilities. She comforted herself with the knowledge that she probably had reviewed more obscure photos, teltap reports, and raw intelligence than anyone else in the center.

Kate brushed herself off, mentally kicking herself for the bout of self-indulgent daydreaming. Her eyes widened at the huge file she had accumulated. Bob Mortimer, Chief of CTC, had asked her to collect all available photos of known or suspected Khorasan terrorists that operated in the Middle East. Thanks to her forays into the back file rooms, she had more material than he had probably anticipated. Checking her watch, she noticed that she had wasted more time than she realized in retrieving the old photo files. She had less than five minutes to get the paperwork to her boss before meeting the DS special agent and escorting him up to the center for his meeting with the CTC chief. Although she had little hope of being included in the meeting, she looked forward to viewing the video footage he couriered back from the West Bank.

Upon her arrival at the main entrance, she found the special agent sitting in a waiting area; his punctuality surprised her. Most government types tended to mask their awe of the CIA with a calculated arrogance. She had heard DS was different, maybe so. After signing him in and collecting his visitor badge, she punched her code into the turnstile and escorted him through the security gauntlet. Noting the way he handled the procedures, she gave him a fleeting grin.

The elevator whisked them to the designated floor where they exited and strolled to the CTC. Meandering through the corridors, the MSD agent received numerous inquisitive looks from the many employees in the section. He eyed their activities with interest. The place buzzed with activity. He pondered their work as they arrived at the office of the chief of the CTC.

Bob Mortimer sat behind his desk reading the morning's cable traffic when his secretary informed him that his appointment had arrived. "Send him right in Jane." Mortimer stood and shuffled halfway around his desk to greet the DS agent with an unyielding handshake. He politely dismissed Kate, thanking her for retrieving his guest. James pivoted to thank her, but she had vanished.

James turned and extended his hand to another individual in the room. The man shook his hand, but neglected to introduce himself. He thought it a bit rude and unusual; however, he blew it off as a simple oversight. Maybe he preferred to remain nameless. It did not matter. He hunted for information regarding O'Donnell's killers and those responsible for the attack on the secretary of state.

They each sat at a solid cherry conference table situated to the left of the desk. James surveyed the plush room. A bachelor, masters and a doctorate degree hung on the wall behind his desk. Signed photographs, even one from the U.S. President, bordered his degrees. A number of awards and certificates for achievement covered an adjoining wall. Assorted photos of his wife and two sons sat prominently on his desk. He pegged him as a dedicated bureaucrat and looked forward to matching wits with the scholar.

"We've been expecting you Agent James. Our chief in Jerusalem alerted us that you need assistance in identifying a possible Khorasan terrorist." Mortimer reseated his glasses on his nose. "What do you have?"

James opened a brown envelope and removed three sequential photographs taken during the assassination attempt on the secretary. He placed them on the table and directed the CTC chief's attention to the center one. "Look at this enlargement. You can clearly see his face."

Mortimer lifted the photo. "You sure can."

James remained expressionless. "This is the same bastard I saw in the alley following the assassination attempt. You read my report. He was only ten feet from me. I pleaded for help, but he just turned and walked away. I'll never forget that scar-faced son-of-a-bitch."

"In this photo it appears he made direct eye contact with the terrorists at the bus stop." Mortimer observed. "If this is the same guy you saw in the alley, then it would be one hell of a coincidence if he's not connected with this attack. At the very least, he's a witness who should be interviewed."

"So, I guess you can see my concern." The agent rubbed his neck. "You heard about the safe house we hit in the West Bank. There's a lot more at stake. The Khorasan Group is determined to destabilize America all over the world, whatever the cost. Anything you can do to shed light on this guy would be appreciated." James leaned forward, sitting on the edge of his chair; his stomach fluttered as his eyes glowed.

"I'll see what we can do. No promises, but we'll send out a request to all stations in the region to identify him. If any of them has information, you can bet we'll hear back in no time. Just give me a week to get back to you." Mortimer turned to his right. "Pete, can you get a message out to our stations at once?" The chief handed him the photographs.

"Consider it done." He grabbed the photographs and extended his hand to James. "It was a pleasure meeting you."

"Likewise." James returned a firm handshake before the man left the room.

"You should find this interesting." James handed his host a copy of a thumb drive that showed the assassination attempt on the secretary and extended his hand in appreciation. "Thank you for your time Bob. I'll call you in a week if I don't hear from you. Hopefully, you'll have the answers we need to crack this thing wide open." James quirked an eyebrow.

"Don't get your hopes up." Mortimer returned the handshake. "My secretary will have an officer escort you out. Goodbye."

"Thanks again." James strolled out of the office and bumped into Kate. He questioned the result.

"I hope you got everything you needed." She smiled and motioned to the door.

James shrugged. "I'm not sure. I gave them some photos and other information. I imagine it will eventually make its way to you for analysis."

"It usually does. My staff will review it and then run all traces, crosschecking our electronic and hard copy files. It's a lengthy process given the size of our terrorism database." The analyst appeared calm and focused.

"The thoroughness of your work's very comforting. My service is happy just to pass the information off to another agency and let them handle it. Not me though. I lost a close colleague and great friend in the assassination attempt. I'll find his killer at any cost."

"I'm sorry for your loss. I understand Agent O'Donnell had a wife and a small son." Kate's face sank.

"Do you remember the briefing you provided us prior to our departure to the West Bank?" James blew out a long breath.

"Of course I do." Kate brushed the hair from her eyes.

The two strolled back to the main entrance, meandering their way through myriad corridors. The lunch bell lessened the operational tempo while clearing the halls.

The DS agent looked over his shoulder. "There's a lot going on behind the scenes on this case. The CIA and FBI are acting as if it's a competition versus working together. The stakes are great. If our government fails, the results will be catastrophic."

"Go on. What can I do to prove that we're all on the same side?" Kate's shiny eyes captured his.

James removed a thumb drive from his pocket. "I'm going to take a chance; I want you to have this important piece of evidence. I attempted to download the documents to my computer, but I can't access its files. I need you to break the encryption. Please call if you find anything?" He handed her the thumb drive, releasing his steely grip.

"Where did you get it Matt?"

"It was under the floorboard in the safe house we raided in the West Bank."

Kate displayed the drive. "This thumb drive could be a critical piece of the puzzle. I'll analyze it immediately and call you if I find anything."

She handed the agent her business card after writing her home phone number on the back of it. "You can call me anytime. In fact, why wait for the analysis to be completed. I could use a nice dinner out." She winked at the agent as she ushered him through the front turnstile.

"Do you like Peruvian food? I know a quaint place not too far from here in Arlington." He turned toward her.

"Awesome. It's a date." She beamed.

James walked to the visitor's parking lot. His reservations surfaced. He hoped his gut was right. He needed an inside ally.

# CHAPTER 19: SHADOWS

*DS Training Center – Dunn Loring, Virginia*

Life taught James many lessons that heightened his guarded nature. He knew that his daily routine could be a source of tension. Having driven routinely on Route 66 to and from work, he personally observed a daily accident. People often paid more attention to their mobile phones and accompanying texts than the roads.

The agent recognized that crime alone in the greater DC-Metropolitan area should have kept people on their toes. He volunteered his time at a local police department and hunted the brazen criminals that lurked the backstreets and side allies. He truly despised criminals and the manner in which they preyed on society. Protecting the public interested him from an early age. He chose the feds over local law enforcement given the clientele. He recognized his limitations and knew that he needed to stay away from the dregs of society. His cynical nature required no further poisoning by a justice system that appeared to cater more to the criminals than to their victims.

He specifically detested drug traffickers, dangerous motorcycle gangs, pedophiles, and terrorists. All of these groups preyed on society and disregarded a civilization's acceptable norms. He deplored their immoral behavior and the way they preyed on some of society's most vulnerable persons. Although these groups all sickened him, he truly hated terrorists because they preyed on innocent men, women, and children and then justified their deaths in the name of religion or some other obscure cause. This misguided rationale troubled him. He thought of them as nothing more than cowards. A terrorist murdered his close friend, which required justice or retribution. His resolve made it a certainty.

James awoke from his self-induced trance as his workday ended. Reading the cable traffic at the office often had an unintended hypnotic effect. He gathered up the classified material and neatly placed it in the second drawer of his safe. He spun the dial repeatedly – first to the left and then to the right – to ensure that the lock fully engaged.

On his way out, he stopped by the DS registrar's office to say goodbye to Jennifer O'Brien. She stood five-feet seven inches tall with long, well-sculpted dancer's legs that talked as she walked. Her soft, silky blond shoulder-length hair had a gentle radiance that mirrored her outgoing and dynamic personality. Her sensuous blue eyes and beaming smile could entice even the happiest of married men. An independent woman, she did not mix words. Jen valued a hard work ethic and did more than the job demanded, provided she respected the person. If not, then it was best to avoid her. Her tremendous bark equaled her bite and the scars left from either could run deep.

James found her irresistible in many ways and contemplated dating her over the years. He sensed the mutual attraction, but neither wanted to jeopardize their true friendship. After a five-minute chat, he walked down a flight of stairs to the garage and hopped into his car. Turning the key in the ignition, warmth radiated through his chest as its finely tuned engine hummed. He frequently questioned his chosen career path. As an honor graduate, the U.S. Air Force attempted to recruit him to fly jets. James realized the pilot's utility in wartime, but feared becoming stale and unchallenged during peacetime. Instead, he chose to become a federal agent for the diversity the job offered. The prospect of frequent travel, not to mention an occasional bout with danger, closed the deal for him.

Punching the accelerator, James' shoulders sank deeper into his seat as his tensions left his body. He maneuvered his car from his office onto Gallows Road and blended in with the afternoon rush hour. He checked his rearview mirror in preparation for a lane change. The astute agent observed a silver Ford Taurus pulling in behind him about two car lengths back. Disregarding his observation, he habitually followed his normal route by turning left on Idylwood Road. He continued straight and then turned right onto Leesburg Pike before entering the eastbound ramp to Route 66. Merging onto the freeway, he settled in at sixty-two miles per hour and engaged the cruise control. Preparing to pass a car, he checked both side view mirrors and swiftly changed lanes.

The DS agent eyed his rearview mirror after passing and spotted the same Ford Taurus. Only this time he observed its Virginia license plate and its two Middle Eastern-looking occupants. His senses heightened as his gut wrenched. He found the prospect of being tailed in suburban Virginia intriguing. His eyes darted between his rearview and side view mirrors while scrutinizing everyone and everything in his path. He drove for another four miles while eying the Taurus five cars back in the far right lane.

His patience waned, so he punched a button on his GPS to examine a map of the area. He spotted a nearby residential neighborhood with multiple routes into and out of it. Exiting Route 66, he drove into a mixed commercial and residential area in Arlington. After skirting Ballston Common Mall, he conducted a basic surveillance detection route. He knew that DS' Protective Intelligence Investigations would demand proof of his encounter. James had used the same technique on foot overseas to confirm terrorist surveillance while deployed to Amman.

Welcoming the diversion, James' eyes sparkled. He opted for a left turn and then three consecutive right turns within a residential neighborhood. Upon turning left, he watched the silver Taurus follow him. He knew it would be highly coincidental for the car to make multiple turns with him. After turning right, the Ford Taurus broke off and continued straight, never to be seen again. Anxious to get home, he punched a button on his GPS and followed it back to Route 66. His abrupt detour confirmed his suspicions. He would ponder the people and their purpose the remainder of the evening.

Throughout the week, James' vigilance heightened while driving to and from work. Alternating his routes and times, he practiced the due diligence he often preached in classes overseas. His failure to discover additional surveillance troubled him, as did his newfound paranoia. He reflected back to the possible surveillance incident and second-guessed his powers of observation.

. . . . .

Entering the cramped quarters, the scar faced man's eyes swept the alcove studio apartment. A cloud of light grayish tobacco smoke wafted skyward creating a light haze throughout the room. Two dark-haired men hunched over a glass table looked up expectantly. An assortment of timers, electrical wires, mercury switches, and cellular phones scattered between them. One man sat his soldering iron down while another tended to explosive residue cooling in the kitchen. Their lower jawlines, necks and chins appeared lighter than the remainder of their faces. Empty Chinese takeout containers and pizza boxes littered the kitchen counter.

"You guys clean up well and almost look like Americans. You'll draw less suspicion without your long beards," the scar faced man said while crossing his arms and thrusting out his chest. "I see you purchased all the electronics we'll need to build our devices."

"We're almost ready to carry out your orders. Another man turned around from his binoculars. "We've monitored the target for three weeks now. He runs every morning, showers and then goes to work. He shops at the same grocery store – usually on Saturdays – and eats largely fish, poultry, fruits and vegetables. He recycles his trash and shreds most of his documents. He's a real choirboy."

"More like a crusading pig. Did you find the right spot to carry out our work?" The fresh traveler asked with a focused gaze. "Have you been detected?"

"We found a great place to greet him. He usually goes there on Friday nights after work. He meets some friends and a woman who seems to be close to him. He parks in a multi-layered garage and then walks to the bar. The infidel has no clue that we've been monitoring him around the clock. We've used multiple cars to tail him both day and night."

"Excellent. I look forward to catching up with him, and then we'll execute our landmark mission." The man picked up the group's surveillance photos and studied them. He sat them back down on the table and withdrew a wooden handle from his pocket and depressed a button; a four-inch steel chisel shaped blade sprang out. The man slammed the blade's tip into the face portrayed on the photo, thrashing it side to side. "I look forward to gutting this American pig. I'll make him regret the day he crossed me." His face and neck reddened as he walked to the window and picked up the binoculars. He peered through them, scanning a condominium and single-family dwelling across the street.

# CHAPTER 20: A NEW YORK MINUTE

*One Week Later*

James glanced at the wall mounted clock as the minute hand edged toward the top of the hour; the blistering pace of work and the regular demands of his profession hastened time. His job required both mental prowess and physical endurance. Given the extreme climes they frequented, combined with the sixty pounds of gear they regularly donned, they faced challenges that could tax even an Olympic triathlete. Frequently challenging his body's physical limits on a mission, he pushed himself to the edge in his workouts. He feared blowing an assignment from his body's inability to handle the stress of an operation. His missions often had national security implications.

Finishing a five-mile run, James sat on the mat with his legs extended in front of him. He grabbed his toes and held them when another agent, Dave Johnson, challenged him to spar. With protective equipment covering their bodies, the two agents threw an assortment of kicks and punches. A third-degree black belt in Tae Kwon Do, Johnson's overconfidence surfaced.

James recognized the style's high, jumping, and spinning kick techniques. He landed a barrage of punches to Johnson's body and head while his low kicks kept him guessing. The MSD agent glided in and out of his opponent's kicking range, either blocking or slipping anything thrown at him.

Instructors, agents, and students stood elbow-to-elbow and encircled the two fighters. James' powerful hits echoed throughout the adjoining weight room. Johnson's face reddened as his skilled opponent dodged or blocked everything thrown at him. James admired the agent's determination, energy, and talent, despite its misplaced focus. Blocking a punch thrown at his torso, James stepped in and gently threw his challenger to the ground.

"Hey Matt, if you're done showing off, you're needed in the director's office." Atwell treaded through the crowd, grinning.

"What's going on George? I'm right in the middle of showcasing the merits of Jeet Kune Do." James gave a half-shrug.

"You need to catch the next flight to New York. The boss has an urgent mission for you to lead."

James winked. "It's always something urgent."

Johnson kicked the back of James' knee, causing it to buckle.

"Be with you in a minute George." He disliked cheap shots and decided to teach his opponent a lesson. As Johnson kicked, he trapped his leg and forcibly immobilized his knee. He flipped him to his stomach and twisted his knee.

"I give, I give," pleaded Johnson, slapping the mat repeatedly."

Atwell tossed James a towel. A light sweat pooled on his forehead.

"So what's up George?" He dabbed the white towel on his forehead.

"A special session of the United Nations General Assembly is being convened. You'll lead a counterassault team for the Russian foreign minister. The Russian president is unable to attend. It's rumored that he's attending secret peace meetings with the Ukrainian government." Atwell looked at James with concern.

"I'd like to see those talks result in a breakthrough. We haven't seen a major war in Europe since WWII." James rubbed his eyelid as they walked into his director's office. "Why are we providing the Russian's with a counterassault team? We've never done that before."

Atwell's brow rose. "The Chechens want revenge for his purported war crimes and ethnic cleansing when he was a military commander."

The MSD director reiterated Atwell's information, concluding his two-minute meeting by outlining some logistics regarding James' latest assignment. "Miss O'Brien has booked you on the 6:00 pm shuttle out of Reagan National Airport. The rest of your team will meet you at the hotel. They have all your gear and equipment. They drove up earlier today with one of our fighting follow cars. Just go home, pack, and get yourself to the airport on time. Give me a call when you get in."

"No problem boss." James walked out the door.

James strolled down the stairs to the garage, opened his car's trunk and grabbed a black suitcase. He left the other one replete with slacks, sport jacket, and undergarments for another day. He maintained two suitcases in his trunk, one for teaching and another one for tactical missions. This trip called for the black suitcase. Atwell drove him to National Airport. Upon settling into his aisle seat, he considered the UN's special session and the disruptions it causes to the already chaotic pace of New York. Motorcades blasted down city streets at all hours of the day; their blue lights flashing and sirens blaring. People watched in awe as these motorcades maneuvered through heavy traffic to transport their dignitaries to meetings.

The DS agent thumbed through the Russian foreign minister's dossier as the plane lifted off. He remained unfazed by the Chechen's accusations of war crimes. His eyes widened as he studied several photos showing men, woman, and children slain and their village destroyed. The dedicated agent questioned taking a bullet for the man and then shrugged it off as his job.

The Russian president canceled his trip to America as economic sanctions strangled and crippled its currency. He instead entrusted his foreign minister with leading his delegation as he remained familiar with his governing priorities. The minister provided a stabilizing effect on the president who often relied on his sage advice and counsel. This division of duties allowed the Russian president to concentrate on his secret war in the Ukraine.

A naturally gifted and skilled diplomat, Vladimir Smirnoff influenced mainstream Russian circles and all the countries surrounding it. His close friendship and counsel with the president kept him calm and focused during the toughest of times. Not surprisingly, there had been quite a few of them over the past couple of years. Daily crises seemed to be the norm, not the exception.

Smirnoff's three years in office accelerated his aging process by a dozen years. No doubt his love for Russian vodka and fine Cuban cigars aided in this metamorphosis. His large round face supported a full mustache and gray beard; he appeared more like a salty farmer than Russia's top diplomat. A perceptive politician, he tenaciously brokered countless deals.

James scanned the city's skyline as his plane descended into La Guardia Airport; its sheer size and splendor amazed him. His Seattle roots paled in comparison, and he preferred the Emerald City's small-town feel. He looked down at the dozens of skyscrapers that literally pierced the clouds. These architectural wonders impressed him; they displayed the ingenuity of American builders whose spirit, creativity and vision turned drawings into reality. The city's around the clock lights, pace and action both intrigued and astounded him.

As the plane came to a halt at the gate and the fasten-your-seat-belt sign flashed off, he grabbed his carry-on luggage from the overhead compartment and dashed off to the baggage claim area. Thirty minutes later, the spry agent hailed a taxi. "Take me to the Global Plaza Hotel."

"No problem, hop in back," said the driver. His accent hinted to his Pakistani roots.

James watched the sprawling city's bustling activity as they made the thirty-minute journey in moderate traffic. Arriving at the hotel, he checked in and ordered room service. His meal arrived thirty minutes later; he enjoyed eating a green salad and a crab cake sandwich with fries. After watching some news, he read a few chapters of a New York Times best-selling bio-terrorism thriller. His eyes tired after two chapters, so he set the book aside and drifted off to sleep.

James ambled downstairs to the command post and met his team at eight in the morning. He received their itinerary, a detail briefing, and specific operational orders. He surveyed his team; five others wore dark blue jumpsuits etched with the DS emblem on the front and large gold "POLICE" markings on the back. With black webbed gear covering their torsos, all their weapons and equipment remained exposed and readily accessible. More than a dozen other agents and New York Police Department (NYPD) plainclothes intelligence officers entered their cars.

An NYPD squad car led a procession of sedans, Suburbans, and a Cadillac to Kennedy International Airport to retrieve the Russian dignitary. Given his diplomatic status and the threat directed against him, the nine-car motorcade drove out on the tarmac. They staged in succession with the limousine positioned at the base of the stairs of an Ilyushin Il-96 four-engine long-haul wide body jet. James glanced at the foreign minister as he descended the staircase. He was flanked by his wife and wedged fore and aft by two Federal Security Service (FSB) agents.

James eyed the female agent leading the group as she marched down the stairs; her intense eyes scanned the area. Her gaze captured his eyes before leading the foreign minister into the black armored Cadillac. He recognized that the KGB still lived within its successor agency. He pondered her purpose on this mission. The incisive agent knew the FSB often masked its clandestine activities within legitimate undertakings. The thirty-something, posh, and highly professional female agent leapt into the limousine's backseat, after seating the foreign minister.

The motorcade drove off the tarmac and exited the airport through the VIP gate. Seventy-plus demonstrators lunged through the barriers and engulfed the limousine; protestors hit the cars with signs while standing in the vehicle's path. Raucous chants filled the air, compounding radio communication. James ordered three of his tactical agents to dismount and clear a path through the crowd. His DS colleagues vaulted from the follow car to trot alongside the limousine's fenders.

Approaching the limousine's right rear fender, James grabbed an unruly male attempting to open the limousine's door. He pushed him back into the crowd, assuming his place as the protector of the door. James turned and winked at the female FSB agent safely tucked within the limousine. She smiled thinly, admiring his determination and aggressiveness. After the motorcade broke through the demonstrators, the driver gradually accelerated; the agents sprinted back to their respective vehicles. Garbage and spit pelted them for their efforts.

The motorcade continued on its fifty-minute journey, first stopping at the FOX news studio for a quick interview. It then traveled to the Russian consulate for secure consultations before arriving at the Global Plaza Hotel; the foreign minister needed downtime to freshen up and prepare for the day's events. The agents' shift rivaled anything they had experienced in the past. Their long and sweaty faces signaled the challenges they faced. Two bomb threats and a hostile demonstration highlighted the day's activities.

James wiped the sweat from his forehead with his sleeve. Lifting the strap of his submachine gun over his head, he laid it on the Suburban's front seat. "We should be finished for the night. You guys standby. I'll go up to the command post to see what's planned for tomorrow."

"Tell the agent-in-charge we'll have that cold beer he promised tonight. I could use it after handling that suspect bomb." Wagner removed his ballistic helmet.

"Don't worry Dutch. I'll tell him." James snapped his head around. "Getting you a beer is the least he could do for you, along with buying you a steak and lobster dinner."

James lumbered up a small flight of stairs and stumbled as he reached the top. His fatigued body struggled to carry the sixty pounds of gear and weaponry. He longed for his youth, realizing his aging body's limitations. He briefly imagined the doldrums of a desk job and then discarded it as he still enjoyed protective operations. The elevator doors sprang open interrupting his reverie. He sidestepped so a protective detail and their dignitary could exit unimpeded.

The counterassault team leader and five disparate agents piled into the elevator. He scanned their faces, not recognizing any of them. After making four stops, he arrived on the thirty-first floor. Exiting the elevator, he veered right and, after a few steps, marched into room thirty-one-zero-five and the DS Command Post; it intersected the hall housing the elevators and a row of suites. He recognized the room's strategic position; anyone transiting from either the stairwell or elevator had to pass the suite to access the dignitary's quarters. Police officers, augmented by stairwell cameras and alarms, made accessing the area a daunting task for the unauthorized.

Entering the room with a broad grin, James took a deep breath.

"Hey James," a member of the detail called out. "Do you have another outfit for me? I need to change my car's oil."

James cocked his head to the side. "Only when you graduate from hump duty and that could be another ten years in your case."

"Nice job on that demonstration." Another one snickered. "Better they spit on you than me in my five-hundred dollar Italian suit."

"You've got to be kidding me. I thought that was a JC Penny polyester special." James gave him a playful nudge.

The agent's face sank as he stood; he brushed the tips of his fingers against the front of the suit. "What do you mean?"

"I'm sorry. The suit looks fine. It's you that looks like a dumb ass and no suit could remedy that."

Thunderous laughter erupted as the agent-in-charge (AIC) strolled in.

"Okay, quiet down you guys," AIC Stan Kulowski bellowed out. "The foreign minister's going to hear you. We're finished for the evening. Our first move to the UN is at eight o'clock tomorrow morning. The foreign minister wants to get some exercise and walk."

Kulowski was not a stereotypical man of Polish ancestry as his name implied. He had a Sicilian's fiery temper and the physique of a six-foot four, underweight Sumo wrestler. Deep blue eyes accented his round face topped with gray thinning hair. These soft facial features combined with a politician's smile masked his true personality. A malcontent by nature, he frequently voiced his displeasure with the wrath that shook windows like a sonic boom. His favorite pastime was chewing ass, regardless of your grade or the audience. He frequently exercised his sarcastic wit, throwing more acerbic darts in an hour than thrown at a British dart tournament. A devote Catholic, he attended mass weekly, probably to repent for his surplus of sins.

"Are you kidding?" James shook his head.

"Nope, I tried to dissuade him, but it was like talking to a wall. Anyhow, we're faced with a walking move in the morning. James, could your team cover the vulnerable ground away from the diamond, including the high ground?"

The MSD leader grunted. "That's impossible. There's too much area to cover. I'll talk to the head of protection to see if he can temporarily allocate three other teams for this move. I'll also talk with NYPD Emergency Services Unit. Maybe they can deploy some additional teams to assist."

"I doubt it. NYPD is strapped," Kulowski said, shoving his hands in his pockets.

James' posture slumped. "This walking move is crazy. There's no way we can cover all the vulnerable areas. The guy must have a death wish. If he makes a habit of walking and the terrorists get wind of this trend, then he'll be talking to his maker in a New York minute."

"Well, just do the best you can," Kulowski groaned.

"No problem." James leaned back in his seat and scanned the facial expressions of the group.

Kulowski droned the schedule. "Internal move at the UN to meet with the Pakistani Foreign Minister; meeting with Turkmenistan Foreign Minister; UN General Assembly; lunch at the suite of the Indian Foreign Minister at the Waldorf Astoria; meeting with the U.S. Secretary of State at the UN. Then he'll return to the hotel for some private and staff time; 6:00 pm – reception for delegates hosted by the UN Secretary General; 8:00 pm – dinner at Antonio's; and finally, a night tour of the city. The locations and route will be determined. Looks like you guys will get some overtime. Are there any questions?"

Rookie Agent Mark Hayes' hand shot up. He volunteered for the midnight shift, knowing he could explore New York City during the daytime. A Midwesterner, Hayes' idea of a big city was Kansas City prior to his first trip to the Big Apple.

Kulowski pointed his finger. "Well son, speak up."

"What time will we be relieved in the morning?"

Kulowski popped his earpiece out and rubbed his eyes. "C-P-ers (short for command post or residence watch), be here at 7:00 am. Are there any other questions? No. Okay, you're dismissed. Matt, can you remain behind a minute?"

"What's on your mind, Stan?" James asked, knowing what was coming.

"Who in the hell do you think you are disobeying my direct order during the demonstration today?" Kulowski's voice rattled the ceiling, as the agents scurried out the door, not wanting to bear his wrath.

James contemplated the question. He resented the ball busting. "If you're referring to the way I deployed my team today, then it was the correct response. I left two men in the car to cover the team and the nearby rooftops. Besides, my team worked in conjunction with your guys on the fenders and had everything under control. If you have a problem with the way I handled the situation, go talk to my boss." His jaw clenched as he folded his arms.

"Take it easy Matt. I was only kidding. Your team did an excellent job out there and you know me. I'd much rather have someone willing to speak up than be an ass-kisser." Kulowski softened his voice, seeing he hit a nerve.

The MSD agent waved him off. "I'm sorry Stan. I'm just tired and a little pissed-off. I can't believe that scumbag spit on me at the demonstration. I felt like breaking his face with my expandable baton."

"I don't blame you." Kulowski tipped his head to the side, patting him on the back. "I need your opinion."

The MSD agent's head cocked heedfully to one side. "Shoot, what is it?"

"Matt, as you're aware, this protective operation is the highest threat detail DS is running here. I'd appreciate any input."

"I don't know what more I can tell you." James' chin dipped as he rubbed his eyes. "So far, our surveillance detection teams have come up with zip. Our motorcade includes a marked NYPD police lead, NYPD intelligence car, DS lead, fully armored limousine, DS follow, DS counterassault team car, Emergency Services Unit (ESU) vehicle and an NYPD police tail car."

Kulowski held his hands loosely behind his back. "It's a solid motorcade with enough firepower to start a small war."

"Indeed, I definitely don't see an attack on the motorcade. Who would mess with us? If our guys didn't get the terrorists, then the ESU team would have them for lunch."

"True." Kulowski pulled in a deep breath.

James glanced down at his watch. "There's good support at each site, and the sites we can't control are unpredictable. I think their best shot would be to assassinate him with a car bomb or here at the hotel."

"Get real Matt." Kulowski's jaw dropped. "This hotel's swarming with cops. It would be hard to get in the front door, let alone find a doughnut. Do you have any other thoughts?"

"None right now, but I'll sleep on it. I'm sure I'll have the answer by the morning." James supported a playful grin.

"I bet you will." Kulowski winked.

"I'm out of here." James patted Kulowski on the shoulder. "Get some rest. It's going to be a long week. Don't forget you owe Wagner that beer tonight."

Rounding the door into the hallway, James collided with the female FSB agent as they stood toe-to-toe. "Excuse me." He gazed at the woman, practically standing eye-to-eye with the five-foot seven inch blonde bombshell.

"Your team did nice work protecting the limousine from that angry mob as we departed the airport. I liked the way you tossed aside the protestor who tried to open the limousine's door. Allow me to introduce myself. I'm Svetlana Ivanoff Andropov of the Federal Security Service."

His head tipped back. "It's a pleasure to meet you Miss Andropov. Your English is perfect. Where did you learn it?"

"I've studied English since I was four years old. I have master's degrees in both English and International Relations." The FSB agent beamed.

"That's impressive Miss Andropov."

"You haven't seen anything yet, Special Agent Matt James. Please call me Svetlana."

His eyebrow arched. "How do you know my name? I never mention it."

The Russian beauty's stance widened. "I know a great deal about you and your service. Your recent work in Ramallah was remarkable. I'd like to stay and talk, but the minister needs to speak with me about his schedule. I'll catch you later." She winked and strutted down the hallway.

Turning to watch the foreign agent saunter down the hall, he hoped she would turn back toward him. She pivoted briefly and smiled as she knocked on the minister's door. Warmth radiated throughout his body as Andropov disappeared inside the suite.

James hesitated at the suite door. His thoughts jumbled. She dispelled his notion of the evil empire. His mind refocused on his protective responsibilities and a number of prospective scenarios. His concentration waned as his stomach churned. He snapped his head around. "You guys be extra careful. The midnight shift can drain your mind and body."

"When you're as good as us, there's nothing to worry about." Mark Hayes grinned.

James took a wide stance, pondering his own cockiness. He shuffled to the elevator and pressed the down arrow; its heavy use caused it to arrive five minutes later. He knew agents routinely held the elevators for their arriving and departing dignitaries. In their eagerness to do their job, they sometimes acted too early.

He walked into the elevator; its lone foreign-looking waiter glanced up from his dishes. The waiter inconspicuously scanned James from head to toe. He sensed the waiter's scrutiny as more than curiosity, but his tactical gear often garnered attention. The elevator stopped at the lobby whereby James hurriedly exited without looking back. He walked to the Suburban.

"It's quitting time. Before you guys bust loose, break down the equipment and park the vehicle in the designated area." James stretched from side to side. "Our first move to the UN is at zero-eight hundred. Be here and set up by no later than zero-seven hundred and have the vehicle swept by the bomb dogs no later than zero-six forty-five."

"Aren't you coming out with us tonight?" Wagner threw up his hands.

"Not tonight Dutch. I have to go to the command center to speak with the director of protection. We need some additional support for tomorrow's stroll to the UN. Deal me in for tomorrow night. On your way to the garage, could whoever's driving drop me off at the Marriott?"

Wagner glanced at Mattson. "Mr. Gadget can drive you."

"No problem. I'll have you there in no time."

Mattson dropped James at the hotel for his meeting with the director of protection. James knew the director had been handpicked for his position based on his superior management style and skills. He never pulled rank, even though he could. His oversight of the overall protective operation meant he could reallocate manpower as needed.

His meeting disappointed him as costs and resource limitations meant no augmentation to his detail. Stunned by the news, James walked to the Global Plaza Hotel. His preoccupation with the meeting's outcome left him oblivious to a group of vivacious college girls waiting in line to get into a yuppie bar, ogling him with more than idle curiosity.

The agent arrived back at his hotel room to find it much neater than when he left it. Tossing his gear on a nearby chair, he sat down on his bed to ponder the day's activities. He habitually clicked the television remote and channeled surfed until he arrived at a local news channel. The news blended together as his focus diminished. After a few minutes, he turned off the television and decided to sleep. Upon finishing his nightly ritual – washing up, brushing his teeth and doing a light stretch – James hopped onto the bed and slid under the goose-feathered down comforter. Reaching over to turn out the lights, he observed his battery-operated traveling alarm clock. It had traveled the world, waking him in places like Lebanon, Liberia, Israel, Iraq, Pakistan, Peru, and Libya. He set the alarm for 6:00 a.m. and then duplicated the procedure with the hotel alarm clock. Neither one would wake him up the following day.

# CHAPTER 21: ABRUPT AWAKENING

Special Agent Mark Hayes stood the suite post at 5:00 am, a time known as the dead zone. His erect and ready posture – hands in front of his body – prepared him for anything. He periodically scanned up and down the hallway. Intermittent faint buzzing from the overhead lights occasionally eclipsed the eerie silence. He paced a small strip of carpet to ease his dull backache. The fatigued agent glanced down at his watch. It now read 5:27 am. He inhaled deeply to ward off his sleepiness. Time felt frozen to the rookie agent. The clanking of the service elevator doors captured his attention. Unsure, he scuttled to the neighboring service area as cable news blared out of the command post. He opened the door and noticed a waiter stooped over a serving cart.

"What are you doing?" Hayes asked, gripping the handle of his holstered Sig Sauer 9mm pistol.

An older Middle Eastern looking waiter snapped his head around. "I'm collecting the dishes to return them to the kitchen. It will be breakfast time soon and room service will be very busy. The kitchen needs all the dishes we can find. I'm sorry to have disturbed you. Can I get you anything while I'm here?"

Hayes' nose crumpled as he eyed the man's facial scar. "No thanks," he said, stepping back into the hallway. The waiter departed seconds later with a trove of dishes. The rookie relaxed and imagined myriad contingencies ranging from terrorist attacks to unscreened packages arriving at the suite. His confidence spiked as he ran through all possible scenarios and his actions to them.

"Hey Mark," the other DS agent whispered. "I'll relieve you in a few; I just need to hit the head first."

He glanced at his watch again. It read 5:58 am. The agent walked to the suite post to relieve Hayes.

"Did you hear that noise Mark? It sounds like our man's up and about."

"He's right on schedule; room service will arrive in about fifteen minutes." Hayes peered down at the schedule and returned it to his inner jacket pocket.

"I've got it. Go to the C-P and grab a cup of coffee."

"Are you kidding? I need to sleep as soon as our shift's over, so we can explore Manhattan later." Hayes slapped his hands against his cheeks.

Strolling toward the command post, he paused at the door as an explosion sent shock waves throughout the floor and building. Wall fragments sliced through Hayes' body, almost severing him in half. A partial wall collapsed on the other agent.

The fire bell echoed through the room, hallways, and building. James rocketed out of bed. His alarm clock read 5:59 am. He contemplated the upheaval, as he slipped into his jumpsuit and put on his gear. Realizing the clamor originated from above, he feared the worst as he wiped the sleep from his eyes. He sprinted to the nearby stairwell and rapidly climbed five flights of stairs in under thirty seconds. Arriving on the thirty-first floor, the MSD leader, panting, touched the stairwell's emergency door. The ear-piercing ringing of the fire alarm fleetingly disrupted his thought. Wagner and Andropov joined him seconds later and jarred him into action.

James cracked the door; his eyes enlarged as they scanned the hallway. Large beams and supporting structure dangled freely from the roof and sides. His eyebrows drew together as his throat constricted. He paused at the doorjamb as his mind envisioned large chunks of concrete burying him alive. Fire raged throughout the floor as the overhead sprinklers doused the area. James gasped from the smoke-filled hallway, which surged into the stairwell and obscured his vision. He knew they had to go in, despite the risks.

The three agents crawled toward the command post. Passing the suite, they directed their flashlights into the room; their intense beams diminished by the thick smoky haze that filled the room. They scanned the room, but found no signs of life. James panned the area with his thermal imager. "All clear," he barked as he met up with the others outside the door.

Wagner led the group toward the dignitary's suite and stumbled over a body partially covered by rubble. The smoke intensified with each passing step, as did the eerie blackness. James shined his light downward to find Hayes motionless on the ground. After removing a piece of debris, he reached down and felt for a pulse on his neck. "He's gone. Let's move on." James looked down and away.

Lifting his radio, he depressed the button to activate his microphone. "DS Command Center, this is Agent James."

An unfamiliar voice came over the radio. "This is the DS Command Center, Agent James send your traffic."

"I'm on the thirty-first floor of the Global Plaza Hotel. I have a major blast that has caused considerable structural damage near the Russian foreign minister's suite. I have one confirmed DS casualty and an uncontrolled fire. Request immediate medical and fire personnel. I'm continuing my search with Agent Wagner and FSB Agent Andropov. James out."

James crawled forward, disregarding the garbled reply; his concentration intensified as his hands felt the hallway floor and walls. After a few more feet, he heard a faint, agonizing groan. Shining his light forward, he discovered an agent pinned down by a sizable chunk of the suite's wall. He crawled to the fallen agent in an effort to assist Wagner who had bolted ahead. James knew they could not last much longer given the dangers posed by the fire. The fire's heat and toxic smoke presented burn and respiratory hazards as it raged uncontrollably. Andropov skirted forward, making her way to the minister's suite.

"Hold on pal, I'll get you out of here," Wagner muttered as he wiped black silt from his face.

The MSD team leader struggled to lift a substantial beam and portion of the wall off the downed agent. A surge of adrenaline supercharged his muscles, enabling him to toss the sizable debris to the side. He analyzed the agent's injuries, noting a fractured right leg, some broken ribs, a concussion and internal bleeding. His rapid shallow breathing, cold clammy skin, and weak pulse reflected his fading state as shock took hold.

"God, I hate to do this. If we don't move him, he's dead for sure." James glanced at Wagner.

Wagner clenched his jaw. "Let's do it."

They worked harmoniously together to lift the agent from the floor. The man's two-hundred and thirty-pound frame and the billowing thick smoke exacerbated the task. Weighing the odds, Wagner threw the man over his shoulders in a fireman's carry. His adrenaline surge simplified the undertaking. Wagner trotted to the stairwell and heard a scream emanating from the foreign minister's suite. Wailing sirens approached the hotel.

Wagner nudged opened the stairwell door with his hip as panicked persons bumped into him. "Hey, you there. I'm a federal agent. Calm down and give me a hand with this wounded agent," Wagner shouted.

Regaining his composure, the man turned to his wife and motioned her to continue down the stairs without him. She reluctantly complied. The elderly man assisted Wagner in carrying the agent down a floor.

"Stay with him," Wagner ordered. "He's in shock. I've got to go back. Firefighters will be here soon."

"You can't go up there. That inferno will kill you. Let the firemen handle it," the man pleaded.

Wagner's eyes intensified. Shrieks emanated from the dignitary's suite. He knew James' tenacity sealed his fate; he would not abandon him.

"I have to go. Remember, stay with him." Wagner trotted up the stairs and swiftly crawled to the dignitary's suite. The expanding fire cracked loudly; his ears rang. He arrived at the suite to find James hunched over the FSB agent who was picking the lock.

"Where's the key? It must be with one of the other agents," James said, scrubbing a hand over his face. He dashed back to the C-P and grabbed three towels from the bathroom. Turning the bathtub's faucet on, he soaked the towels and darted out of the room.

He handed the towels to Wagner and Andropov who covered their heads and mouths. He did the same.

"Take it down Dutch," James shouted over the crackling flames. "We're out of time."

"Wait, I almost have it," said Andropov while her fingers worked the pick and torque wrench. "I just need another minute."

"We don't have another minute. Move aside." James grabbed her shoulders and guided her away from the door's frame.

Wagner drew his pistol from his holster and racked the slide to the rear; Andropov shielded her eyes. He aimed the sights to the door's lock and rapidly fired three times. James gripped the doorknob, but it remained locked. Wagner realigned his sights to the lock and fired off three more rounds in a second. James kicked the door; it flew open as the doorframe splintered.

Standing face-to-face with a blazing inferno, James stared into the flames as dark toxic smoke filled the room. The three agents disregarded their bleak survival odds. They repositioned the sopping wet towels over their faces and scampered through the roaring flames.

James and Andropov scurried through the main living area dodging the fire while looking behind sofas and chairs. Their continuous shouts went unanswered. Fire crackled and roared, creating a deafening howl. James wheezed as his heart thumped against his chest. He felt his life fading but with single-mindedness, he forged ahead. He arrived at the bedroom and eyed the intense blaze that engulfed the room.

"Matt, over here," Wagner yelled.

James crept low to the ground, zigzagging through the inferno. His skin reddened and tingled from the blaze's blistering heat. Rounding the bed with minor burns to his arms and legs, he found Wagner with the lone survivor. Her husband's fate evaded her; ball bearings from the explosive device peppered him.

James briefly rested his two fingers on the side of her neck and lifted them; her weak pulse meant they had little time. He scanned the blaze and looked for a path out of the fiery nightmare. Wagner dragged the woman by placing his arms under hers and clasping them around her chest. He followed James out and tugged her around a gauntlet of smoke and flames. They found a nearby door that provided them an egress to the hallway. The two exited and met three firefighters, who led them to safety. Only Wagner collapsed and lost consciousness.

James turned to look for the FSB agent, but she had vanished. He dashed back into the dignitary's suite and found her lying unconscious, clutching a metallic briefcase. He pondered its contents for her to have risked her life. He hoisted her over his shoulders and grabbed the briefcase. Finessing his way out of the suite, the determined agent carried her down a flight of stairs. He set her on an approaching gurney and instructed the paramedics to take the Russian to the hospital. They agreed and then ushered the silt-covered agent to another gurney, provided him oxygen, and whisked him away.

. . . . .

Wagner opened his eyes and repeatedly blinked them, staring up at the sterile white ceiling. An IV dripped medicines and electrolytes into his arm, while a thin clear tube fed his nose oxygen; respiratory and heart sensors led to a monitoring machine. "Thank God you're alive. Hell of a job you and Matt pulled off this morning. You're at the hospital being treated for smoke inhalation. Try to maintain your energy. The doctor advised us that you need to rest." Atwell leaned in and peered into Wagner's eyes.

"Man, I feel like a sledge hammer hit me in the chest," Wagner groaned, coughing uncontrollably.

Atwell's hand flew to his chest. "You're fortunate that's all you feel. The doctor stressed you're lucky to be alive."

"Well George, you know me. I'm one stubborn bastard."

"I won't argue with you there." Atwell pressed the palms of his hands to his eyes.

"Did the people we saved make it?"

"The DS agent's doing fine. He wanted to personally thank you. He'll be down to see you later."

"What about the foreign minister's wife?"

"It's too early to tell; she's in critical condition. The doctor stated she's lucky to have survived through the morning, but he underscored that was a good sign. They'll know more tomorrow." Atwell gulped his 7-UP. "Can I get you anything?"

"I'm so thirsty. Could you ask the nurse if I could have something to drink?" Wagner examined the IV line that rested slightly above his wrist.

"Theoretically, the IV drip was supposed to replenish any missing fluids from his system. We probably just need to adjust the flow rate." Atwell increased the IV's drip rate.

"That's better, but I'd prefer a shot of Jack Daniels and an ice-cold beer."

Atwell disappeared into the hall and returned with the nurse. She carried a plastic tray with both apple juice and plain water. "Young man, I recommend you start with the water." She sat the tray down next to the bed. "I'll be back in twenty minutes to check on you. The doctor will examine you then." She departed without saying another word.

"That's just my luck George. All of the pretty young nurses in this hospital and I get Nurse Ratched."

"Well, you get what you deserve." Atwell's booming laugh filled the room.

"Now, if that were true, I'd have five model-like Thai nurses here attending to all my needs. Where's Matt?" Wagner pulled on Atwell's sleeve as his nose wrinkled.

"Matt was released earlier today. He suffered a mild case of smoke inhalation. I'm sure he's resting at the hotel. Try to get some rest Dutch. Matt and I will come by later."

Wagner tossed from side to side. His mind raced as he thought about the circumstances behind the Russian foreign minister's death. He studied terrorist tactics, recognizing their repeated utilization until effectively countered. "What can you tell me about the attack method?"

"Are you sure it can't wait Dutch?"

"I have to know, George. Otherwise, it will eat at me."

Atwell shook his head. "We can't have that. The blast utilized high explosives and shape charge technology. The bomb was set in the service area and activated by noise at a certain decibel. The explosive experts believe that the bomb was pointed at the bathroom area. So when the foreign minister flushed the toilet or something else, it activated the bomb. These findings are preliminary, but they demonstrate the terrorists had the hotel's floor plan and the requisite access."

"Do you have any leads or suspects?" Wagner's eyes furrowed briefly.

"Not really. Some witnesses have reported an unknown person wearing a waiter's uniform leaving at about the time of the blast. The only identifying features they mentioned were his Middle Eastern appearance and a three-inch scar under his cheek."

"Get some rest. I'll see you later." Atwell walked out the door.

# CHAPTER 22: BEHIND CLOSED DOORS

*One Week Later – Washington, DC*
Walking down the sidewalk, the long-legged blonde woman adjusted her white Italian hat. Although its large brim shielded her face from the sun's intense rays, it did little to stop the sweat from pouring down her face. Sweat pooled at the small of her back, causing her long summer dress to stick to it. She hadn't anticipated the uncharacteristically hot and humid day for the time of the year; the type of day where tempers easily magnified. She approached the house and hoped its shelter could provide her relief. She rang the doorbell.

"Who is it?" A masculine voice emanated from behind the door.

"It's me, Svetlana. Can I come in?"

"Okay, hold on a minute." Igor Chirtoff disengaged a heavy deadbolt lock and unhooked the chain from the frame to the door. Opening the door, he motioned for her to enter his early nineteenth century Victorian home. He ushered her to a tiny circular glass table adjacent to the kitchen. "Can I get you some tea?"

She sat and glanced at the Kusmi tea tin can on the table. "I see you have a little taste of home."

He smiled as he poured water into a glass teacup. Steam drifted skyward. He set a plate of rugalach next to his guest. "Internet shopping is wonderful. I can get anything." He touched her hand as he sat beside her. How is my favorite and most accomplished student? I've been watching your career closely."

"Uncle Igor, how did you survive all those years in the KGB running counterterrorist operations?" She looked up.

His lanky body and gray balding head leaned toward her. "I've spent my entire life serving mother Russia. I've seen the fall of our mighty empire and the rise of capitalism. The Americans will not survive much longer. It's hard to believe some American politicians openly tout socialism over capitalism." Populist messages of socialism disguised as communism have ended tragically for numerous countries; too many have fallen for its false promises and ideological appeal." He shook his head. "There are certainly plenty of fools among us."

He understood all too well the shortcomings of both communism and capitalism. He knew that democratic principles created vulnerabilities in border security and civilian control. He believed that freedom of movement favored the insurgents. It made it easier for them to penetrate Russian defenses to strike deep within his beloved country. He recognized he needed to change the current political trajectory before it was too late.

"The Americans aren't the evil I was taught in school. They're like us in many ways." She glanced into his eyes.

Chirtoff raised a hand. "Don't be seduced by their lifestyle. Why have you called this meeting?" His eyebrows rose.

She looked up. "It's getting too dangerous. The Chechen terrorist we've been hunting for years just assassinated our foreign minister. Who knows what he's planning next in America, but it may involve a nuke. If the prime minister finds out about our operation, then we're finished. I'm sure he's happy about America's distraction, so he can concentrate on his Ukrainian activities."

Chirtoff waved her off. "Forget the prime minister. If the SVR finds out, then we'll have bigger problems. Don't worry Svetlana; I worked with Russia's external security service on joint operations for over twenty-five years. I know their methods. Besides, I still have allies on the inside that support our plan. They've been funneling vital intelligence to us all along. Our deep undercover source gives us the inside edge and tactical advantage. They've been trying to get a source to infiltrate a group like this for many years. We've done it in just a few months. They need us." Chirtoff's eyes gleamed.

He sipped his tea, peering over the rim of his cup. "There's more at stake than you know. Our country's in grave danger. The breakup of the former Soviet Union has caused some of our bordering countries to pursue democracy. If they're successful in joining NATO, we'll have the Americans and their technology on our doorstep. This is dangerous with their development of their missile defense system. I can't believe that President Reagan's Star Wars dream is turning into reality. His vision will haunt us to the end."

"Reagan was a visionary and a great communicator," she said with glossy enlarged eyes.

"I miss the Cold War era." He shook his head. "At least we knew our place and our chief enemies during that time. With the breakup of the republic, we have to monitor a number of countries neighboring us. This uses resources that we could deploy elsewhere in keeping the Americans and now the Chinese in check. Fortunately, the prime minister's intelligence background understands this point. This could be used to our advantage." He touched her arm.

She appreciated her longtime mentor's wisdom. She disliked operating in a vacuum and without the implicit consent of the prime minister, the FSB, and the SVR. She knew defiance could get her shot or sent to a Siberian gulag, and she did not relish either prospect.

"Look at our border security with the North Caucasus." He thumped his finger on the table. "Islamic rebels use the North Caucasus as a staging ground to attack us. I'm sure you remember the 2002 Moscow theater hostage crisis that led to over one-hundred civilian deaths; and the 2004 Beslan school hostage crisis led to close to four-hundred deaths. The FSB tracked down and killed the responsible leader in a brilliantly executed assassination. But in any insurgency or terrorist group, a new leader inevitably rises and assumes control of the group. Moussa Rahman of Al-Qaeda in the Caucasus is one such leader. He is even more dangerous than his predecessor, as he thinks big and uses asymmetrical warfare. He's also linked to key Taliban leaders in Pakistan and Afghanistan."

Andropov shook her head. "I don't get it. Why's Rahman going after America instead of us? And why join the Khorasan Group? They make a formidable force, but it diverts his actions from us. He'll consolidate his position by striking America and see if the next president is more amenable to negotiations."

"In other words, he's buying time. He understands politics and the will of the people. This makes him more dangerous than past Chechen leaders. He must be stopped. This is where you come in. You're to neutralize him in America. Don't screw it up this time." Chirtoff's eyes narrowed. "The president will leverage this achievement with the United States in the ongoing Strategic Arms Reduction Treaty negotiations.

"Won't the FSB target him for the killing of our foreign minister?" She looked away.

He shrugged. "Only if they can prove he was involved, and that might be difficult. He's like a ghost and always a step ahead of us."

"Well then, what's next and how do we find him?" Andropov grumped.

Chirtoff rocked on his heels. "I see the doubt in your eyes. We're in too deep to call it off now."

"I agree, but we're losing control. Did you know that he was going to assassinate our foreign minister in New York?"

"I didn't." He leaned back and tucked in his upper lip. "The minister was known as a hardliner when it came to Chechen independence. Perhaps Rahman saw him as a possible threat to his plans. Who knows how he thinks." He shrugged, dropping eye contact.

"How come our source didn't alert us?" Her face reddened. "His death happened on my watch."

"He did." Chirtoff sighed. "He just didn't know any specifics. There's a lack of trust between the different factions. They may be working together, but that doesn't mean they're talking freely. Some of these groups still have their own agenda, and they don't always want to share the credit. Nobody knew this group had the contacts to mount a successful attack inside America. Our analysts always speculated an assassination attempt against one of our ministers would occur closer to home."

"This proves my point. It's out of control and could blow up in our faces." Andropov's chest tightened as she twisted her watch.

"You may be right Svetlana, but it's a chance that we'll have to take. There's no backing out now. There's only one objective left. We must neutralize him. He'll be most vulnerable in America where he doesn't have his full complement of armed security."

"Can't we just wait until the FSB assassinates him in retaliation for killing our minister? He has crossed a red line." She wet her lips.

He grunted, "We can't wait that long. The FSB's very efficient and patient. Rahman needs to be eliminated as soon as possible if we're to succeed in our plans."

"Okay, what do we know about his plans in America?" The female protégé muttered, clasping her hands together while staring off to a distance.

"Our source informed us that Khorasan will assassinate a Pakistani delegation on their upcoming visit to the United States. He further advised that Khorasan wants to hit the Pakistani delegation for their move toward reconciliation and their pro-peace stance currently in the works between Afghanistan and the Taliban. Pakistan is the key to obtaining a peace settlement. We're seeking their delegation's schedule, so we can anticipate the Khorasan Group's attack location. Rahman will be leading this group, so if you find the group, you'll find him."

She shook her head. "What? Security will be impenetrable, making it impossible to get close to him. The Americans maintain excellent security in their homeland. And after the recent assassination on our minister, I imagine they'll leave nothing to chance."

"Perhaps that's where the nuclear weapon comes into play. You don't have to get too close to kill your target. Khorasan could kill two birds with one stone. A nuclear attack on American soil would have tremendous impact, both psychological and tangible in casualty figures." His gaze wandered the room.

"Don't worry Svetlana. The intelligence is accurate. According to our source, Khorasan will attack the Pakistani delegation at a diplomatic reception in Washington, DC. Two al-Qaeda sympathizers penetrated the catering service. They're planning to bomb the event."

"Can we trust the source's information, Igor?"

The seasoned spy shrugged. "About as much as we can trust any of these bastards." He felt a slight heaviness in his stomach. "The Pakistani foreign minister is expected to make the opening speech to discuss the Afghani-Taliban peace process. It will be his last remarks if the terrorists succeed. This is where you come in. I want you to thwart this attack while you find Rahman."

"And how am I to do that?"

Chirtoff handed her an invitation to the Pakistani reception. "Here's a file on the two al-Qaeda sympathizers and floor plans to the reception site at a prominent DC hotel. Study the information closely and covertly thwart the attack by locating the bomb and calling the bomb squad to handle it. We don't want to blow your cover, but there will be Russian diplomats of prominent families in attendance."

"This mission sounds easy enough, provided I can find the device. I'm sure security won't give me access to the entire venue."

He cleared his throat. "This isn't your primary tasking. If you can't accomplish the mission, then abort it so you can go after Rahman. I'll ensure that all the Russian diplomats get recalled to the mission or call in a bomb threat to the site."

"That recall should save our people." She had become accustomed to saving lives, not taking them. Her foreknowledge of this plot meant she needed to handle it.

"From there, you'll need to find Rahman and neutralize him." His eyes glowed. "If things go as planned, no one will ever know about our involvement. There will be no awards or medals. Only the satisfaction of knowing we defended our country and that our children will sleep safer at night. We can be proud of this accomplishment. Rahman's death must look like an accident. This toxin should help you. It's the latest derivative of thallium." He handed Andropov a metallic box about the size of a pack of cards. It contained the deadly poison and its antiserum.

"Okay Igor. That's not bad for starters. What about the leaders of the Khorasan Group? They're still in Syria and considered a liability, to include our source. Are you going to liquidate them?" She inquired looking up and fidgeting in her chair.

"It has to be done. I'll have our source deliver a present, which will eliminate them." Chirtoff's eyes darkened.

"What about our source?"

"After he finishes taking care of the terrorists, then he'll go back to farming."

"Can we trust him?" She fingered her gold necklace.

"Absolutely, look at the risk he's taken to infiltrate this group. Besides, our financiers have agreed to pay him handsomely for his work and silence. He knows the consequences of betrayal."

"I'm sure that you've made it perfectly clear to him," she snarled.

"How about we toast our successful operation?" He went over to the bar and poured a scotch.

"No thanks, I'll have a toast upon our completion of this mission."

"By all means Svetlana, have it your way. We still need to meet with our local informant face-to-face," said Chirtoff, nodding repeatedly.

"I know. I'm making the drop at 2:30 pm. Do you want to add anything specific?"

"No, just arrange the meeting at our secondary safe house for tomorrow afternoon. I have to run some errands in the morning. The SVR has requested an emergency meeting." Shaking his head, he added, "I don't know what it's all about."

"My God Igor, I hope they're not on to us." She bounced her curled knuckle against her mouth.

"Don't jump to any conclusions Svetlana. They probably just want an update on our informant's activities. Unfortunately, I don't have much to tell them, but I'll satisfy their curiosity with select information. More importantly, I'll see what information they have. My meetings with them are challenging. I thought it was difficult dealing with the KGB even when I worked for them. Now, it's worse than playing a chess game with a high-speed supercomputer. I'm always trying to anticipate their true intentions or their next move. So far, I've been successful. I only attribute my success with them to the fact that I spent my whole career as one of them. It's a different mindset. It has to be."

She moaned, "Oh, enough stories. Do you want me to assemble the entire group for tomorrow's briefing?"

"No. I only need to see Vladimir and Yuri. What we're discussing tomorrow only requires a limited amount of people. It's very specific. The fewer people that know about it, the better it is for us. You understand secrecy?"

Nodding her head in agreement Andropov said, "I understand completely. Look Igor, I have to go. I need to study these files and figure out Rahman's location."

"Good luck. Don't forget to bring the technician with you. He needs to sweep the conference room prior to our briefing."

"You must've read my mind Igor. I'll notify him tonight that his services are needed. Bye."

She slammed the door as she departed the safe house. She hoped that her mentor did not think she did it intentionally. The man was unpredictable and dangerous. He would do anything and give everything for country. She twisted her hair, hoping that he did not expect her to swallow a cyanide pill. She knew that he would.

# CHAPTER 23: BETRAYAL

*Atlantic Ocean*

Dawn brought a new day and renewed optimism. Orange, pink and yellow hues spanned the entire eastern horizon as the sun climbed skyward. Yet, this tequila sunrise escaped Abalakov. Twelve-foot swells pounded the hull; the vessel rocked as seawater poured over the railing and flooded the deck. Feeling queasy from the eight day long journey, his insides churned as he concentrated on keeping his breakfast down. A combination of diesel fumes, salty air, and frayed nerves exacerbated his condition. The trafficker recognized the importance of the next four hours, as they approached Veracruz, Mexico. His anxiety had spiked ever since their departure from Naples. His fate depended on the integrity of an infamous drug lord. He considered a few inventive methods to boost his survival odds. He yearned to live and his looming retirement from smuggling meant greater safety, comfort, and stability.

The seasoned smuggler knew the element of surprise could surmount overwhelming odds. He crept aft and located a wooden emergency storage container; it held life jackets, rescue tubes, medical kits, and other miscellaneous materials. He reached into the container and felt under six life vests. Smiling internally, he gripped a flare gun; it felt awkward compared to his Glock pistol. He reached around his waist and tucked it into the small of his back underneath his jacket.

Locating five two-gallon containers of kerosene in a common storage room, he redistributed them throughout the ship. He knew ship fires presented a significant threat to the vessel and his high value cargo. His adversaries would no doubt recognize the danger as well. He appreciated the fires dual purpose and its ability to mask his escape. He also valued his life more than the money, even if it secured his retirement.

A faint high-pitched buzz from the west captured his attention. He set his last canister down and glanced across the water to see a distant boat rapidly approaching. His mind raced as he pondered surrendering to the Mexican authorities in exchange for the hidden cargo. Their willingness to negotiate served as an opportunity; he speculated that U.S. authorities had been tracking the vessel since its departure from Naples.

Abalakov peered through his binoculars at the streaking boat. The vessel's limited markings reflected its private origin. He correctly assumed that security concerns necessitated a change in the meeting time. He dashed toward the emergency boat and eyed the twelve-foot long dinghy; he hoped its thirty-five horsepower motor provided sufficient power. The boat dangled by pulleys that permitted a person to disengage and lower it into the water. This option suited his needs; however, the dinghy's limited horsepower left him unable to outrun the other vessels. Disabling both boats simultaneously required perfect timing and execution.

He eyed its thirteen-person crew as the boat throttled back and pulled alongside the Star Gazer; their Arabic speaking troubled him as he anticipated Mexican cartel members per his earlier negotiations. This betrayal disturbed him given the threat that nuclear-armed terrorists posed to America and the world.

Abalakov mentally kicked himself for his naiveté; he failed to recognize the false narrative of the cartel's acquisition of nukes for deterrence purposes. Chills ran down his neck upon observing the group's leader; he bore a ravenous wolf's menacing eyes and the spirit of the devil. He feared the terrorists would not honor their agreement to keep their acquisition a secret.

After tying their boat off, the group's leader boarded the cargo vessel first, wielding an AK-47 assault rifle. His hardened features portrayed a cold and fierce man. The savvy smuggler rightly concluded the scar beneath his eye meant he engaged in routine battles.

The leader raised his weapon. "Spread out and sweep the ship. Leave no area untouched. Move it!" Ten men appeared and searched the ship in pairs from fore to aft and from top to bottom. The leader, accompanied by two bodyguards, ambled to the command and navigational center. He embraced the ship's captain. "Captain, it's great to finally meet you. Is everything in order? I have the money."

"Everything's as you requested. The items are in the cargo hold. We'll offload them onto your ship shortly." The captain motioned the leader to a table. "Show me the money?" He bounced on his toes as his tongue moistened his lips.

The leader snapped his fingers. One of his bodyguards set a suitcase down on the table. "You'll find it all there. I'm sure you will enjoy your retirement in the Bahamas."

"And what will become of my crew?" The captain rubbed his forearm while looking around.

The man's arms hung limply at his sides. "You leave that to me. We can't have any witnesses."

Abalakov despised the treacherous bastard for his underhandedness. By finding alternate buyers, the captain willingly violated an unwritten honor code among criminals. Abalakov had to work quickly before time ran out. He walked toward the storage room and its adjacent cargo area. He traversed the rear ladder well; his undetected descent surprised him, given the cargo's value and the stakes of the transaction.

Turning the door handle to the storage room, he sensed someone's presence. Pivoting, a terrorist pressed the barrel of an assault rifle into his back.

"What are you doing down here?"

Abalakov froze. "I...um...um...I was told to come down here to deactivate the booby-traps that protect the warheads. If you'd rather I return topside, then I'd be delighted to do so. Bombs can be tricky, and you never know when one will get a little finicky." He stepped backwards and bit his lip.

The man stared through him. "Alright, go about your business. Just remember, I'm watching you. If you do anything foolish, I'll shoot you. Got it?"

"Yeah, I hear you, but I don't recommend you hanging over my shoulder and making me nervous. I'd hate to slip and accidentally set off ten pounds of high explosives. It would be a bad day and your boss would be furious."

"There's nowhere for you to go. You're surrounded by ocean. Besides your job isn't finished until we've smuggled the warheads across the Mexican-American border at Nogales. I understand the tunnel systems will allow us to slip into America undetected."

"Drug traffickers control a number of elaborate tunnels to smuggle their merchandise. These tunnels will guarantee your group easily arrives in the United States unnoticed." Abalakov gave an easy nod.

"You better be right for your sake. Your life depends upon it." The man turned and left the room.

The smuggler closed his eyes and inhaled deeply. His brief brush with danger aroused another idea. For the first time, he felt optimistic about his survival odds. After deactivating the booby-traps, he removed the blasting cap from the Semtex high explosive. His sweaty hands trembled as he sliced the explosive into five parts. Assorted weapons, ammunition, and other fusing components filled the shelves in the cargo area. He frenziedly fabricated four smaller bombs and one larger device.

He placed five pounds of the Semtex together with a timer, battery, and blasting cap. He set the countdown timer for ten minutes and crept to the ladder well. Feet scurrying on the wood deck above captured his attention; it appeared he lost the element of surprise. Ear-piercing shrieks echoed through the hull as automatic gunfire erupted. Following a short pause, he heard a succession of large splashes into the ocean. He knew the sharks would not go hungry.

Hiding behind a door, he stood frozen; his heart pounded as he slowed his breathing. A group of four men vaulted down the stairs frantically searching for him. He slipped by them, knowing that nine others lurked nearby. He emerged topside seconds later and darted aft. Tiptoeing around the side, he tossed one of his explosive devices onto the terrorist's speedboat. A second later, a blast wave rocked the Star Gazer; fiberglass fragments shot skyward as the boat's cabin erupted into flames.

Abalakov poured one of the pre-placed kerosene containers over the boat's deck. He flicked a match onto the floor; flames exploded skyward and singed his eyebrows. He hoped the blaze would protect his flank while buying him time to lower the dinghy. Carefully navigating his way to the boat's stern, he removed another explosive device from his backpack; he set the timer for ten seconds. After initiating the fuse, he dashed around the corner and cocked his arm back to toss the bomb. A terrorist spotted him and fired a burst of rounds at him. Abalakov felt his right side go numb as two bullets sliced through his shoulder and bicep. He dropped the bomb to the wooden deck; the terrorist fixated on it. Abalakov pulled himself back around the corner. His legs wobbled as he stood and staggered toward the dinghy. Blood soaked through his shirt.

The blast rocked the boat and swept him off his feet. The explosion and resulting fire only caused cosmetic damage to the ship's stern. He prayed the next blast would sink the ship to the bottom of the ocean.

Abalakov sprang to his feet, dashed to the rail, swung the dinghy out, and disengaged the pulley system. The boat effortlessly slid downward and splashed into the water; a light salty mist filled the air. He stepped over the side rail and descended a small ladder in seconds, landing in the dingy. Clearing the ropes, he lowered the outboard motor into the water. Terrorists scrambled in the background to extinguish the fire.

After pulling out the choke throttle, he tugged on the starter cord; the engine sputtered so he pulled it again and it roared to life. The engine's revving alerted the terrorists to him. A barrage of rounds flew by his head and body. He twisted the throttle wide open; the engine propelled him away from the danger. The fleeing smuggler zigzagged back and forth, as rounds splashed in the water all around him. He stared off to the horizon as he headed for the shores of Mexico.

Abalakov trekked one-hundred meters from the ship. He glanced over his shoulder to see the ship ablaze; his confidence in escaping spiked. Removing his phone from his pocket, he scrolled to a draft email that he had prepared earlier; the note advised ARSO Kline that the merchandize had arrived in Veracruz, Mexico. After providing Nogales as the smuggling point, he depressed the send button and pocketed the device.

The terrorists opened the lid to a wooden trunk and rifled through it. They grabbed a Russian-made FSU SA-16, or "Gimlet," man-portable missile system amongst the weapons' stash. The Gimlet devastated targets with its cooled infrared homing guidance system and a two kg HE-fragmentation warhead. The two men looked around the area. The missile's backblast could cause additional boat damage while endangering those directly behind it.

The leader approached them. "Give me the launcher. I want the honor." He gave them a curt nod as his muscles tightened. With a maximum engagement range of five kilometers, Rahman knew he had plenty of time.

The two men watched with great anticipation as their leader flipped a switch to the missile delivery system; the battery required five seconds to charge before he could fire the missile. Unfazed, he could be a patient man when required. He sighted in the weapon and beamed as he depressed the trigger; the missile blazed the three-hundred meters to the target in seconds, leaving a grayish exhaust trail en route.

The missile slammed into the dinghy's stern and engine, blowing Abalakov from it. His flaccid and lifeless body plunged into the water and bobbed in the waves. The two terrorists high fived one another as a black smoke cloud billowed skyward. Rahman stumbled back a step as one of his cohorts displayed a disarmed bomb. The efficiency and effectiveness of these high-tech weapons amazed him. He would show America a new level of terrorism. He ordered his fellow warriors to call for their backup boat. He would transfer the weapons about fifteen minutes later.

# CHAPTER 24: NEED TO KNOW

*Greater DC Area*

Andropov strolled down a few isolated side streets in Crystal City, stopping to view a boutique's display case. The leggy blonde eyed a pair of Jimmy Choo's classic black suede pointy toe pump shoes; her eyes dulled from their four-figure price tag. The window's reflection imaged a man in a light blue windbreaker and jeans across the street. Her heartbeat raced and stomach churned. She grimaced at her predicament. This cautious temperament suited her occupation. She disliked jumping to conclusions, so she waltzed down three more backstreets.

Increasing her strides, she darted around the first corner. Her peripheral vision gaged the man's movements as he trailed her. She clutched her purse, contemplating the man's motives. Walking another city block, she turned right and slowed her pace; she glanced over her shoulder, worried about the stranger's intent and her need to evade him. After rounding the third corner, she ducked into an ally and pressed her back against a brick wall. She stared out at the street.

"Freeze! Give me your purse," a man shouted, brandishing a revolver.

"Don't shoot. Take what you want." She eyed the man.

"I definitely will." The man looked directly into her eyes.

The female agent snapped her purse up and hit him in the nose, gripping his wrist and twisting. The gun fell to the ground as she slammed her elbow into his face. He staggered back on his heels as she drew her pistol.

"Turn around and get on your knees." She pressed her lips together forming a slight scowl.

The man kneeled and faced the brick wall. "You don't know what you're doing," the man replied in perfect Russian.

She slammed her pistol's handle down on the crown of his head. His body fell limp to the ground; blood trickled from the top of his head. She rolled him over, rifled through his sport jacket, and removed a credential and opened it; her chest tightened as she read, "the Foreign Military Intelligence Main Directorate of the General Staff of the Armed Forces of the Russian Federation." She rubbed the back of her neck, pondering the GRU's sudden interest in her.

Clutching him under his armpits, she dragged him behind a green dumpster and winced. A rotten meat stench emanated from it. She glanced out on a clear street, scanned behind her, hailed a cab, and hopped into it.

"Take me to Constitution Avenue NE and 12th Street NE near Lincoln Park," she said, rubbing her forearm and looking back over her shoulder. Eighteen minutes later, the cab pulled curbside. She exited the vehicle, paying the cabby with a crisp twenty-dollar bill. She beamed, displaying a bit of renewed confidence. "Keep the change."

The driver waved his right hand. "Thanks. Have a nice day."

"You too." She waved and walked away.

The blonde-haired woman stood eying her surroundings until the cab drove out of sight. The cautious agent retraced her path by walking back four blocks and turning right. After two blocks and a friendly three-minute conversation with her neighbor, she arrived at her temporary home.

She dashed up the stairs, entered the master bedroom, and changed into white slacks and a light blue shirt. Placing her hair up, she covered most of it with a plain white hat. Her efforts to mask her natural beauty proved difficult, even in dull clothes.

Andropov mentally prepared for work, grabbing a small leather briefcase off an easy chair. She strolled down the stairs to the front door. Exiting, she activated the alarm system and engaged the deadbolt lock on the door. The front yard and street appeared normal. She then walked east for about fifteen minutes and arrived at a nearby coffee house. Her eyes swept the place; fourteen customers were scattered throughout its divided space.

Stepping up to the counter, she ordered a double latte from a second-year college student. The Russian agent paid and strutted to an isolated section of the shop. Sitting down with her back against the wall and near a gas fireplace, she eyed the customers within earshot.

Even with her senses vibrating, the shop seemed ordinary. She lifted her briefcase from the floor and placed it on the chair beside her. Taking a small sip of her latte, she pulled out a white laptop from its leather case and placed it on the wood circular table; she opened its lid and depressed the power button. She slurped her latte while waiting for her computer to start up. Her sparkling blue eyes scanned left to right. She entered her twelve-digit password, which allowed her to access the computer's countless applications.

She logged on to the shop's Wi-Fi service and connected through its ISP. After confirming a speedy connection, she triggered an application that provided an additional layer of encryption. She typed a brief message to her five colleagues:

*It was great to see you all recently and I'd like to see everyone very soon. With appreciation, Svetlana.*

*PS: The meeting is scheduled for 1500 tomorrow at location two. The technician should arrive one hour before.*

She highlighted the PS message and then minimized the font to one. The cautious operative then changed the font color to white to conceal the entire phrase. Pressing the return key, she sent her cryptic message.

The relaxed agent sipped her latte for another ten minutes. She departed the coffee shop, hailed a cab, and drove to the Russian Embassy. She entered the building and passed through several security controls, displaying her FSB credentials. Arriving at the intelligence service's office, she met FSB Station Chief Stanslov Levchenko, who provided her new orders.

The top spy pulled a half-empty bottle of Russian vodka from his lower desk drawer. "Moscow has provided me your new instructions. It seems that you're to undertake a fresh covert operation here in America," he said while hurriedly filling two scotch glasses to their brim.

"Can I see the orders for myself?" She lifted a single eyebrow.

Levchenko slapped a folder down on the table. She observed its "Top Secret" stamp on the outside of the folder. "Read it for yourself. You're to capture and protect Moussa Rahman who is in America to conduct some sort of attack. You'll smuggle him out of America and transport him to Moscow for interrogation. It would be quite embarrassing if he carried out an attack on American soil. After all, the KGB provided him advanced military and tradecraft training in the early 1990s."

Her eyes narrowed as her face reddened. "This terrorist's responsible for the death of many Russians. He should be tortured and killed, not protected. He just assassinated our foreign minister."

"Orders are orders. It's not our right to question Moscow's wisdom or instructions. As I understand it, this order comes from our prime minister." His face tightened. "I'll forget your little outburst and leave your insolence out of my report."

"I apologize." Her head sank. "His attacks are personal. My cousin was killed in the Moscow theater bombing." Tension eased from her face. "He planned the operation and sent his 'black widow' suicide bombers to do the job."

"Don't worry. I understand." He squeezed her hand. "Rahman and our P-M's past are intertwined. Rumor has it that Moscow's sweating his capture by the Americans as he maintains knowledge that could incriminate Russia. It's real big."

"What did Rahman do that could be so classified?" Her demeanor froze.

"I don't know, and I don't think we should be discussing it any further." He glanced over his shoulder with widening eyes. "Don't get on the prime minister's shit list. Look what happen to Alexander Litvinenko in London in 2006. Poisoning is a painful way to go."

"I won't bring it up again. Nostrovia." Andropov held up her glass of vodka and knew otherwise. She would ask Chirtoff about the Litvinenko case next time she saw him.

Levchenko drank his vodka in one large gulp. She slugged it down like water.

"How about another round?" The station chief asked as he poured himself a full glass of their national drink.

"No thanks." She waived him off. "I must prep for my mission."

"It won't be too hard." The FSB chief gave an easy nod. "You have a team on standby to assist you. Our intelligence indicates that he'll be coming over the border at Nogales in two days. You'll greet him there. A private jet is waiting for you at Reagan National Airport. You leave tomorrow afternoon. So, finish your work, go home, and pack. Keep me apprised of any pertinent developments. You have my contact numbers. Call me anytime and good luck." The senior Russian spy departed, leaving her to fend for herself.

She perused Rahman's file and appreciated his tenacity and proficiency. He had waged war in many parts of the world and developed a huge network. His merciless nature frightened many. She pondered the prime minister's desire to keep him alive given all the atrocities he committed. She knew secrecy often came at a steep price. After reading the terrorist's dossier, she walked the two-inch thick file to another officer in the section. The young officer relished the opportunity to converse with the Russian woman. Excusing herself from the conversation, she departed the embassy and took a cab home.

Andropov awoke the following day invigorated. She finally got a full night's rest, something that remained elusive since her operation in Grozny. She milled around the house for most of the morning without any real sense of purpose. After lunch, she read a number of online articles regarding Litvinenko's life and his assassination. She recalled the case, but the FSB seldom talked about it, given its sensitivity with the prime minister. The circumstances surrounding Litvinenko's death fascinated her.

After reading a few in-depth stories, she remembered his poisoning involved radioactive polonium-210. This information caught her attention, as she recalled learning about assassination at a secret FSB training facility outside Grozny. She understood polonium-210's limitations in assassinations because of the difficulties in containing it; nevertheless, the FSB studied the tactic. She wondered if the KGB killed Litvinenko to keep their secrets. She did not know what to believe anymore; her government often stretched the truth, hid lies between two truths, and admitted nothing. Her preoccupation with Litvinenko jeopardized her arriving to Chirtoff's meeting on time, so she rushed out the door.

Approaching her car, she scanned the neighborhood. Other than the birds' chirping and a mother strolling her daughter down the street, the area remained quiet. She leapt into her car, backed it out to the road, and checked traffic from both directions. Backing her Mercedes sedan into the inside lane, she then drove forward. Her preplanned route traversed the Maryland countryside and then returned towards the city. This extended her drive time from thirty to ninety minutes. Nearing her destination, she sped through two different neighborhoods, whereby surveillance specialists checked for a tail. Five minutes later, she arrived at the safe house; the upper middle-class two-story dwelling with brick facade appeared identical to all the houses on the street. She hoped the others had practiced similar tradecraft.

She arrived ten minutes early and found Chirtoff observing the technician work his trade. The small wiry man ran a metal wand-like device over the wall and checked several different bandwidths. His grid search covered every inch of the room's wall.

"No anomalies here." He adjusted his radiofrequency detector. "Let me double check it one more time since we have time."

The "Bug Man," as they called him, was one of the youngest and brightest in the field. He had a blossoming career with the FSB when a terrorist bomb meant to kill his protectee crippled him. The Riyad-us-Saliheen Brigades had somehow received information on the location of the safe house and penetrated security, planting a remote-controlled explosive device. When he scanned the walls for listening devices, his scanners activated the bomb, practically killing him. He worked tirelessly to rehabilitate himself and restore his ability to walk, albeit with a slight limp. Immigrating to America a few years later, he joined his father at his electronic repair shop. This provided him the cover needed to carry out covert operations. Chirtoff realized his talent, played to his sense of loyalty, and recruited him to work in America.

With the room cleared and the others now present, Chirtoff stood. "Let's get started. The SVR are watching me. This is why we need to take extra precautions like this secondary safe house. What I'm about to reveal is extremely sensitive and the reason I've summoned you here. I need to tell you about my recent meeting with the SVR and discuss its ramifications." He scanned the group.

The Russian sleepers eyed their leader.

Chirtoff cleared his throat. "The SVR were primarily interested in our knowledge of nuclear proliferation and biological weapons. It was obvious from their questioning that they were after certain details and confirmation. It appeared they knew about al-Qaeda's acquisition of either biological or nuclear weapons, including their imminent use. They further implied that these weapons would be used in Russia and in other countries. The U.S. was specifically mentioned."

He scanned the group to assess their commitment. "From what I've gathered, they had strong evidence, but they failed to disclose their sources or methods. I sensed they thought our source had better access. I believe they have an independent source funneling them information on the intentions of the Khorasan Group. This means our source is in danger. It also indicates that the terrorist group is planning something larger than we ever imagined. We need to uncover their plans or we could lose control over this operation. This is a luxury we cannot afford." Chirtoff tilted his head back.

"If I understand you, we've possibly lost control of the terrorist coalition. Worse than that, we're unaware of a biological or nuclear attack they're planning. We should turn this whole mess over to the SVR while there's a chance to salvage our operation. The SVR can shut them down before they gain too much momentum. They are better resourced to handle this situation." Andropov looked at her colleagues.

"Are you kidding?" Chirtoff slapped his hand down on the table. "We can't give up now. We've devoted too much energy to this project." His nostrils flared as his gaze intensified.

The others remained composed, faces stern as they digested and analyzed the information they had just received.

The bug man's face turned bright red. "What about our source? If he's been discovered, they're just waiting for the opportunity to kill him. We must extract him now."

Chirtoff raised his voice. "Alright, let's settle down and think this decision through. First, we should alert our source to the danger and let him decide his fate. If he wants to continue, then we should have him find out whatever he can about their plans. Meanwhile, we'll conduct our own independent checks. I'm confident we can get this operation back on track."

Appealing to their sense of duty, the cell leader steered them to his way. "Let's see how it all unfolds. If it looks negative, then we'll give it to our SVR brothers. However, if it appears manageable, then we'll continue the operation. Our countrymen will be proud. We're achieving what our government failed to deliver and that's the security of our homeland."

He scanned the group's faces to assess their continued enthusiasm to his covert operation as the meeting adjourned. Smiling, he sensed their unyielding stance. He would continue the operation, one way or the other.

His goal of bogging down American with multiple wars would advance. America's distraction would make it possible for Russia to play hardball with its rebellious neighbors.

"Igor, do you have a minute?" She asked, motioning.

"What is it?"

"The FSB has tasked me to go after Rahman and take him back to Moscow, so he can be debriefed. They advised that I'll find him in the southwest, and I have to leave late this afternoon. They have a team waiting for me on the ground. What should I do when I catch up with him?" She inquired, smiling wryly.

Her mentor stared out the window. "I don't understand why they want him alive. He must have some important information that they're after. Make sure you capture and interrogate him first. We must discover what he knows, and then make sure he has an accident, one that our skilled FSB colleagues cannot detect."

"No problem. I have to go. I've a plane to catch. Bye."

# CHAPTER 25: COLD STEEL

*Arlington, Virginia – June*

It began like any other day for James. An ear-piercing alarm permeated the room at six o'clock in the morning. He rolled to his stomach and flung his hand to the on/off button on top of his alarm clock. Hitting the button, he felt instant relief as the room returned to its normal state of tranquility. He contemplated shutting his eyes, but knew if he succumbed to that desire, he would miss his daily morning stretch and run.

The dedicated agent yawned, rolled out of bed, and stumbled to the bathroom. He squinted in the mirror to examine his bloodshot eyes. His pale complexion indicated a rough day ahead of him. Splashing cold water on his face, he tried to invigorate himself, but it failed to counter his unsteadiness. Cupping his hands together under the faucet, he bent down and gulped about a cup of water. He felt only marginally better for his efforts.

The dedicated agent walked over to his dresser and pulled out his morning exercise attire. This included white shorts, a shirt with the DS emblem embroidered on the chest area, and tube socks. He dressed and tied his laces to his running shoes, a gift from the U.S. Ambassador to Lebanon. When he gratefully accepted the shoes, he failed to realize their heavy price tag. This involved daily grueling forty-five minute runs with an ambassador who ran marathons for pleasure. Situated in East Beirut, the embassy compound's steep terrain challenged even the most proficient of distant runners. Nevertheless, he kept pace with the seasoned diplomat. He found distance running reduced stress, but the prolonged jarring harmed his knees and back.

He trotted out of the bedroom and stubbed his toe on a slightly raised floorboard. He liked his two-bedroom, one and a half bath condo situated in an old established part of Arlington. Its fifty-year-old frame needed repair and remodeling, but he liked its convenient location to restaurants and headquarters. He also bought it as an investment thinking he could restore it, as he enjoyed woodworking and carpentry. However, home improvement came second to the job; temporary duty missions requiring travel occupied eighty-five percent of his time. When he landed home for several weeks, he undertook the necessities, such as bills, paperwork, and home maintenance.

The dedicated agent disliked running on either an empty or a full stomach. Devouring a green banana, he grabbed his daily supplements organized on the kitchen counter next to the sink. He opened, withdrew, and closed each bottle until a multivitamin and seven others rested in his hand. He tossed them into his mouth and washed them down with a single gulp of orange juice. Drinking his remaining juice in two swigs, he began his stretching regimen to avoid pulling a muscle. He recognized that his age increased his recovery time.

Recalling his basic agent training days, he could run twenty miles and be completely recovered the following day. These glory days had long passed. A mere five-mile run would generally mean a mega dose of ibuprofen before going to bed; otherwise the unbearable pain and swelling would make for a restless and sleepless night.

The resolute agent recognized the continued need to push his body, recalling a poster in a Seattle gym. It showed a burly convict bench-pressing over three-hundred and fifty pounds and captioned, "Get in shape because they are." This poster left a lasting impression on him. He dreaded a terrorist or criminal overpowering him or having his partner or an innocent bystander harmed.

He understood his physical limitations compared to the bigger, faster, and stronger persons that roamed the earth. This trepidation alone might have contributed to his martial arts prowess. More likely than not, his instructor's direct links to the legendary Bruce Lee amplified his skills. He truly missed the esprit de corps, challenge, drills and sparring. No training device could ever replace his teacher's one-on-one instruction. The job had cost him many things over the years; yet his sudden transfer from Seattle to Albania made his Jeet Kune Do training a distant memory.

Twisting from side to side, he visualized his running form and morning route. He rushed out the front door and heard his phone's Bluetooth application engage his smart lock. Trotting to the street, he quickened his pace. After two miles, sweat trickled from his forehead as the early morning sun bombarded him with ultraviolet rays. He passed a steady stream of houses and an elementary school. Running down a path through nearby woods, he skirted a small creek, reemerging on hard pavement minutes later. About five miles into his run, he sprinted for home and finished in under thirty-five minutes. He gasped for oxygen as his heart pounded; his knees throbbed as his legs wobbled. He glanced forward; his elation interrupted as a dark haired man with olive skin bearing a designer running outfit approached him.

He eyed the stranger as butterflies multiplied in his gut. The runner's unorthodox posture skewed his jogging form. Converging on the man, he noticed his right hand hidden behind his back; the man glared at him. His senses heightened. Nearing the foreigner, he darted across the street and sprinted toward his condominium. The runner maintained his course, casually turning to observe the agent's actions. James failed to see the cold steel blade concealed behind the stranger's palm and wrist. His remerging paranoia surprised the steely agent.

The week passed quickly as he kept busy with his daily office routine. He wrote a trip report, revised two lesson plans, and completed the Pressure Point Control Tactics instructor's course. On those rare occasions when agents remained in Virginia, they honed their shooting, counter-terrorist driving, and physical skills. They also refreshed their abilities in tactical communications, defensive tactics, evacuations, and over fifty mission essential skills.

The opportunity to train with America's premier military and law enforcement units initially attracted him to the office. James valued MSD's forward-leaning mentality and specialization. Many in the service thought of them as cowboys, some of whom wanted to join their ranks. The cost of joining the office meant frequent deployment to hostile areas, such as Iraq, Afghanistan, and Pakistan.

Early Friday evening finally descended upon the office.

"Let's head over to TGIF's," one of the agents yelled out.

"That sounds great to me." James centered his report on his desk. "I could use a cold beer after this week."

Larson, who had recently finished his six months in-service training, asked the bar's location. The prospect of his first mission thrilled him. The recent doubling of MSD's budget from post-Yemeni initiatives granted him his wish sooner than anticipated. With more than twenty flashpoints boiling around the world, he would be on the road the following week.

Atwell's brow arched at Larson's statement. "You need to follow us. We'll introduce you to the Jackson State penitentiary." He waved the young agent over.

"What the hell's that?" Larson grumbled, smiling thinly.

"You don't even want to know. I can hardly wait until you find out." Atwell's booming laugh carried across the reception area.

The rookie remained oblivious to the drink's two-part potency as the outer glass mixed vodka and grapefruit juice; the inner one held a shot glass of tequila. Most new recruits endured the ritualistic hazing. However, only one of MSD's battle-tested agents, who had defied death, could administer it. They reasoned that if a newbie could endure the potent drink, then the agent could handle any crisis.

James hoped it gave them bad "Ju-Ju," a term he learned in Liberia. Bad "Ju-Ju," as the locals called it, made them invincible to their opponents or so they thought. Only the Liberians utilized different ingredients than the American version. They consumed the hearts and blood of their victims. They actually believed in the superstitious ritual as countless warriors died by their own guns as they tested their battle preparedness on themselves.

Disregarding the abhorrent thought, James once told a group of agitated Liberian soldiers he had already devoured an enemy's heart for breakfast after they threatened to cut his out and eat it. Receiving concerned looks for his statement, his retort shocked and silenced the Liberian soldiers.

Approaching 5:00 pm, the agents decided to party at Fridays, situated a mile from the DS Training Center. Piling into their cars, James led the procession with Larson following behind him to ensure his arrival there. James maneuvered his Dodge Stealth onto Gallows Road and approached Leesburg Pike; he glanced at his rearview mirror to ensure Larson's presence. He feared losing him in rush hour traffic as he waited for the light to turn green.

James floored his gas pedal as the light changed and glanced into his rearview mirror; a procession of ten cars crossed the intersection with a blue sedan following and running a red light. A Ford Mustang whose driver punched the accelerator with the efficiency of a drag racer nearly clipped it. The driver's recklessness perplexed him. He shrugged it off, given the area's high rating for the worst drivers in the nation.

After proceeding through another intersection, he turned into a covered parking garage with the other agents in toe. He contemplated his millionaire status if the bar paid him a small commission for the patronage he assembled. Most MSD agents liked to work hard, exercise vigorously, and blow off more steam than an eighteen-century locomotive.

Upon entering Fridays, the bartender waved. "It's good to see you Matt. Where are you back from this time and where's my DS hat you promised me months ago?"

"I've got the hat Bobby. It's out in the trunk of my car. I'll make you a deal. You pour me a beer and I'll be right back with the hat."

"That's a deal. Your first round is on the house," said the bartender, winking.

James glanced at Larson and removed a stool from the bar. "Sit down, my friend. I have your first round." He yelled across the bar, "Bobby, could you send my boy a Jackson State?"

Shaking his head, the bartender gave him a thumb's up and a broad grin.

"George will administer the exam in my absence." James beamed.

Atwell raised his eyebrows. "With pleasure."

Wagner savored the occasion and pulled up a seat next to Larson. With his good friend Jack Daniels in hand, he emulated "Crockett" from Miami Vice, wearing a white sports jacket with a black collarless shirt and dark sunglasses.

Minutes later, James arrived back at his car and opened the trunk. The blue baseball style cap bore a gold special agent patch at the front. Bobby had been hounding him for one for over three months. Today he would finally get the hat for his expansive collection.

Reaching up to slam the trunk shut, his peripheral vision caught a flash behind him. He pivoted and instinctively raised his right hand, effectively blocking the attacker's right hand wielding a knife. The stainless-steel blade easily sliced through James' forearm; blood dripped to the pavement. The accomplished agent effortlessly blocked the attacker's reverse slashing motion with both hands; his left hand caught the attacker at the wrist while his right merged simultaneously with it and folded the wrist straight back toward the attacker. The man shrieked as James snapped his wrist back. The knife fell to the pavement, echoing throughout the garage. The tenacious agent kicked the attacker's groin and then smashed an uppercut to his chin. The assailant dropped hard to the ground; a semi-automatic 9mm pistol popped out of his waist belt.

The proficient agent admired his victory, but just briefly as another man raced towards him. Only this time, the man brandished a pistol and called for his partner in Arabic. He ducked as a round whizzed over his shoulder missing him by inches.

James overheard several faint but distinct Arabic orders, indicating a third man's involvement. His concealed position prevented him from seeing the man, who bore a three-inch scar underneath his eye. O'Donnell's assassin lurked just thirty feet away. Had he realized it, he would have extracted his revenge or at least died trying.

Taking cover behind the left rear tire of a Toyota Camry, James reached for the downed assailant's gun. Stretching his arm, he grabbed the pistol off the pavement, as hurried footsteps closed in. He racked the slide back to the rear, chambering a round.

Hearing a round being loaded, the stranger crept forward as his weapon followed his wide eyes. The attacker's demeanor, crisp movements, tactics, and coolness indicated an assassin to him. James dropped to a prone position, shielding most of his body with the car's rear tire.

The assassin discovered his accomplice sprawled out on the ground. "You'll pay for this you American pig." He fired off five consecutive rounds, all hitting the rear quarter of the car. The passenger and driver side windows exploded; glass shards scattered into the air and sprinkled the agent's legs.

Studying his adversary's footsteps, James waited for his opportunity. He sighted his gun on the lower shin of his unsuspecting enemy and fired twice in under a second. Two rounds sliced through the attacker's legs, allowing gravity to intervene. Powerless, the assassin slammed to the ground, groaning. The DS agent sprang to his feet and moved to cover the fallen man. Rounding the trunk of the car, he aimed his weapon at the attacker.

"Don't even think about it!" He shouted.

The man casually rolled over and raised his pistol. "Allah Akbar."

James fired twice at his heart. The man plopped lifeless to the ground. He found the Islamic extremists' suicidal mindset perplexing. He knew this type of resolve would be difficult to defeat. Unbeknownst to him, Rahman ducked behind a van and slipped away.

Carefully placing his fingers on the side of the assailant's neck, James confirmed his fate. "Fucking fanatics," he bemoaned. He then scurried to cover the first attacker as he awoke from his induced sleep. James recognized the steadily increasing sounds of police sirens converging on his location; he removed his credentials from the inside of his sport jacket in preparation to meet his police brethren.

The first police officer on the scene screeched to a stop about twenty feet short of him. The cop positioned his vehicle to shield himself from possible danger. Using his car as a shield, the officer raised his pistol and instructed James to drop his weapon.

"I'm a Federal Agent." He raised his credentials skyward exposing his gold badge. "I've one dead and one slightly wounded. Call for an ambulance and back up." He could hear his reinforcements rapidly approaching.

The second squad car maneuvered to the side and behind the composed agent, avoiding a crossfire situation. The officer exited his patrol car and aimed his pistol at the agent. "Drop your weapon. Make no sudden moves."

"I'm a Federal Agent," James replied, remaining frozen. "Here are my credentials. I work as a special agent for the U.S. Department of State."

"I don't care if you're the President of the United States. I'm ordering you to drop your weapon," the officer barked; his posture erect with a relaxed face.

Glancing at the fallen suspect, James ensured his passivity. "Okay. I'm going to gently set my weapon down."

The agent sensed a veteran officer by his command presence and confident demeanor. He deliberately transferred the weapon to his left hand, careful not to point it at either officer. He knew the dangers of any furtive movement. The officers had the advantage and the rookie's jitteriness saturated the garage.

"I'm going to lower my weapon now and set it on the trunk of this car," James stated clearly.

"Do it very slowly," the senior officer ordered in a calm voice.

Unaware of the officer's rank, he probably could have guessed it by his composure. He gently set the pistol on the trunk of the car. James dreaded dropping it as instructed, fearing it could discharge from the impact.

"I'm going to take two steps back, turn and face you." The agent interrupted the officer's commands and back stepped unhurriedly, turning to face the officer.

The sergeant realized his suspect's identity. The DS agent clearly understood arrest protocol. The sergeant approached him, holstering his weapon. His partner remained pointing his pistol at the agent.

The fallen attacker sprang to his feet and seized James, holding a knife to the agent's throat. "Stay back or I'll kill him," the attacker shouted, shuffling backward to create distance between them.

"Don't do anything stupid," the sergeant ordered, raising a hand.

James pondered the recipient of the veteran's caution as it applied to both his partner and the terrorist. The attacker gripped his throat and wielded a knife just in front of his Adam's apple. Poised, his heartbeat stabilized as he watched his captor's arm movements.

Motioning toward the officers with his knife, the man shouted, "I don't want to tell you again. Get back assholes."

Seizing the opening, James shot his right hand up and seized the attacker's right hand at the wrist; a fight ensued. He struggled to keep the knife's blade away from his throat while fighting the left forearm of the man trying to crush it. Releasing his grip on the man's left forearm, the agent slammed his left elbow into the attacker's ribcage. He struck three more times, fracturing several of his ribs. The man's grip on the knife loosened. His left hand converged with his right and forcibly bent the terrorist's wrist against its tendons; he sidestepped and jerked him down to the ground.

The officers vaulted forward to assist him in controlling the attacker. The rookie handcuffed the suspect and double locked the cuffs to prevent them from injuring the assailant.

"Thanks." James wiped the sweat from his forehead with the tips of his fingers. He handed the sergeant his credentials. "I'm Special Agent Matt James of the Diplomatic Security Service."

The veteran officer gave the DS agent a handkerchief. "It's nice to meet you. Do you mind telling me what happened here?" He asked wiping his forehead.

"Sure." Brushing the dirt off his clothes, he stood, took the handkerchief, and pressed down on his forearm's cut. The cloth turned red as blood saturated its fibers.

The patrol officer escorted the wounded suspect to his squad car, but before he could get there, an ambulance arrived. After frisking the suspect, the rookie instructed the medical crew to examine him carefully.

"Go on." The sergeant motioned the agent to continue as he scribbled in his journal.

"Well, I arrived here at about five o'clock with some friends from work. I'm guessing the attackers followed us. I saw a blue sedan at the intersection of Gallows and Leesburg Pike busting ass to catch us. If you guys discover that these terrorists were driving a blue sedan, it will be more than coincidental," he said, sucking in a deep breath.

"Terrorists, what do you mean?" The sergeant's eyebrows rose as his pupils enlarged.

James looked up. "These bastards are obviously from the Middle East. In fact, the dead one had a very distinct accent. At least he did before I sent him to Allah. I had the drop on him. He just looked up at me with a cold stare and chanted 'Allah Akbar' as he raised his pistol at me. I granted him his wish. I blasted him twice sending him to his maker."

"Look at these passports." The sergeant handed them to the agent.

James studied them, noting the nine-digit passport number beginning with zero-seven. "These were issued in Seattle, Washington this year. Place of Birth is New York. The pictures matched the suspects. Appears to be genuine and not a counterfeit. No photo-sub. They've never been used." He looked up.

"How do you know all that?" The sergeant's eyes widened at the agent's encyclopedic knowledge.

The DS man straightened up. "We do primarily two things domestically as new agents – dignitary protection and passport fraud investigations. I spent over two years in Seattle investigating mainly passport fraud. You'd be amazed at the types of cases you can uncover once you dig into them. Countless illegal aliens attempt to obtain these documents. It's the best document for proof of citizenship and identity. In the majority of these cases, the only crime perpetrated by the illegal is document fraud. They just want to work in America to secure a better living for themselves and their families."

"Sounds boring to me," the sergeant grunted.

"Sometimes they are, but if you keep digging, you'll sometimes find impostor, deceased identity, and counterfeit cases. People want to become someone else for many reasons – fugitives, drug traffickers and, in some cases, terrorists. We've worked numerous cases with the Marshals Service to apprehend fugitives who applied for a U.S. passport. It was our lead that enabled us to track down some of the top ten most wanted criminals. The same holds true for some of the narcotic traffickers. These bastards want multiple passports to conceal their travels and identities. We've even seen people using deceased identities to collect multi-million dollar insurance scams."

"Unbelievable. Who would've thought?" The sergeant's eyes twinkled.

"Not too many people do." The agent cleared his throat. "Congress readily identified passport fraud as a major problem and enacted tougher laws and penalties. This action was largely based on the World Trade Center bombing and the blind Sheik. Did you know that a conviction could bring up to ten years imprisonment and as much as a two-hundred and fifty thousand dollar fine? If we link them to drug trafficking, it goes up to fifteen years, and if connected to terrorism, a person could receive twenty years with a similar fine."

James slapped the passports into the palm of his hand. "And all this for only a document crime which is easy to prove. On every passport, there's a picture and a signature. A passport case involving a deceased identity is generally easy to prove. All you need is a copy of the death certificate or the parent's statement. It's also simple for counterfeit cases to have a State's Bureau of Vital Statistics send you a letter of record of no birth. I've had a number of these cases. Impostor cases can take a little more time, but in the end, there's generally no problem proving these as well. Consequently, we see a very high plea bargain rate for these types of offenses. It's great for the U.S. attorney's statistics."

James rubbed his eye. "A lot of the different agencies complain about the U.S. Attorney's Office not taking their cases. We've never had that problem."

"Well, if you're right and this guy's not who he claims to be, he'll vanish if bail's set." The veteran cop let out a heavy sigh.

"You catch on fast sergeant." The agent glanced away. "It's up to us not to let that happen."

"No, it's up to you. I'm just a patrol officer, but let me give you a word of advice from my experience here. You've better put together a case fast. He'll be held until Monday. After that, there's no guarantee. All we have is an assault and no real harm. He'll say that he was robbing you and provide a sob story. He has no record but is down on his luck lately. He'll show remorse. With prison over-crowding and a liberal judge, he could be out on bail Monday waving goodbye. This outcome has happened too many times. These guys were eventually captured and returned for prosecution. But if this guy's a terrorist with a solid network, he'll have a different identity and be out of the country before you can put together your case."

"Not bad for just a patrol officer," James replied, appreciating the officer's insight.

"I wasn't always a patrol officer. I was a detective for twelve years in New York. I got tired of all the drugs, gangs, guns, child abuse, and homicides. I even had some exposure to terrorism as part of a local, state, and federal task force."

"That sounds interesting to me. Why'd you give it up?"

The officer glanced down. "It killed my family life, working long hours and being so cynical. When I had a chance to transfer, I took it, but things have followed me. When I first moved here, only minor crimes existed. Within the last five years, I've seen a large increase in violent crime. Well, another six years and I'll let somebody else handle the criminals."

"I understand," the agent said with a wry face.

The officer extended his hand. "I've got to run. Here's my card. The number at the bottom is my home phone. Call me if I can be of further assistance. Take care of that arm. You may need a few stitches."

James gripped the officer's hand. "I'll be in touch."

"I'm sure you will." The officer turned, walked to his patrol car, and radioed dispatch.

The EMT bandaged James' arm. He walked to his car to pick up the DSS hat and brushed it off. Entering his car, he picked up his cellular phone and dialed the number to the DS Command Center.

After three rings, a familiar voice answered. "This is the DS Command Center."

"Earl," James said boisterously.

"Who is this?"

"This is Matt James. I need your help, buddy. I was attacked off duty and I ended up shooting one of my assailants." He glanced at his bandage, grimacing. He knew that the paperwork would take days to finish, and worse than that, he would have to answer a number of questions posed by the Office of Special Investigations.

"I hope it wasn't your duty weapon." Earl snickered into the receiver.

"Fortunately not." James sighed. "I borrowed his partner's after he attempted to slit my throat. He's in custody and hence the problem. In their possession, the police found U.S. passports. We've a hell of a passport fraud case, and there's more. I was the intended victim of a terrorist assassination."

"That's a bold statement." Earl's voiced cracked. "Do you have any evidence to back that claim?"

James wiped his forehead with his hand. "Given the case's sensitivity, I can't go into details right now. Could you notify the director and the Office of Special Investigations? And could you patch me through to Dan Jackson at the Washington Field Office?"

"Sure, wait one."

The line went silent before the command center agent came back on line. "Ok, go ahead with your call."

"Hello Dan," it's Matt James. I need your expertise on a passport case involving possible Middle Eastern terrorists." He appealed to Jackson's curiosity.

"What do you have for me?" Jackson asked grabbing a pen.

James motioned to the sergeant who ambled over and furnished his notes. "I have two U.S. passports issued to Arabic speaking males. The first one's bearing the number 078854473 and issued to an Isaac Harold Johnson with a D-O-B of 04/23/65 and a P-O-B listed as Brooklyn, NY."

"Hold on a second. I need to get all the information correctly. Okay, what about the second one?" Jackson tapped his pen on the table, ready to scribble down the info.

James glanced down at the officer's notes. "The second passport number is 078854569 with the name Michael David Washington, born 03/09/68 in Queens, NY. His passport was issued on 12 April 2020."

"What about Johnson's passport? When was it issued?" Jackson's eyes narrowed.

"Let's see." The MSD agent scanned the notes. "Here it is. The passport office issued it on 9 April 2020. Could you contact the Seattle Passport Agency's fraud coordinator and get her to dig up the passport applications? And have them sent directly to you. I'll meet you at your office in about forty minutes. I'll explain everything in detail. Believe me Dan; you won't be disappointed with this case. I think we could get the guy twenty years."

The criminal investigator checked his watch. "That's great. I'll be here. Maybe I'll have copies of the applications by the time you arrive."

"Thanks Dan. I owe you one." He hung up and turned to the sergeant. "I'm going to need everything you have on this one. No matter how small the detail – driver's license, social security number, car rental papers, hotel receipt, address book. You name it. You know the routine."

"You bet. It's going to take a little time. I'll give you what we've got to this point and update you as more information's uncovered."

"Fair enough. What's your name?"

"Leroy Smith. My friends call me Roy."

He patted him on the back. "Thanks for all your help Roy."

"No problem. That's why I'm here."

After twenty minutes of information gathering, James leapt into his car to drive to the front of Friday's. Exiting the vehicle, he left the car idle and strolled into the bar. Tossing the hat at Bobby, he twisted his head. "I went through hell to get you this."

"I bet. You look like you got the shit beat out of you." The bartender mixed Smirnoff Vodka with crème and Kahlua; he pivoted and handed the White Russian cocktail to a blue-collar blonde celebrating her 25th birthday.

Atwell turned in his stool and scanned James from head to toe. "What the hell happened to you?"

"I got jumped. Didn't you hear all the commotion?" James squinted to relieve some of the dust from his eyes.

"Yeah, you get used to it in our work. Besides, we administered Larson's exam."

"Did he pass?" James grumped.

"He winced, but managed to chug it down. I gave him a B-plus." Atwell gave a knowing grin.

"Well done, Larson." James patted him on the back, glancing to his left to see Wagner engaging an attractive bartender. He turned his ear toward him as Wagner explained to her how they shared the same dream. Her puzzled look morphed to a beaming smile. He tilted his head. "Where does he come up with that crap? He's certainly original. I give him that."

"I need your help." James turned to Atwell. "That commotion you heard involved me. Two terrorists attempted to assassinate me. I killed one of them and the other one is in police custody. They both possessed fraudulently obtained U.S. passports. Dan Jackson is waiting for me at the Washington Field Office. I'll explain the rest en route. Can you help?"

"You sounded like Dragnet's Joe Friday reading an official police report." Atwell slammed his half-full glass of beer on the bar.

James shrugged. "That's how I talk when it comes down to business."

"Let's do it." Atwell rose from his stool. "The beers can wait."

James bent over the bar and whispered into the ear of a female bartender with a rock-hard body. Being regulars did have its advantages. She gave him a kiss on the cheek. "You can count on me." She waved.

"Larson, you see that young lady behind the bar?" James pointed.

"You mean the clean one," the rookie replied, smiling.

"She's going to take care of you. So, if you need anything to drink, see her. And if you have too much to drink, she'll drive you home." James' eyes widened.

"I guess I'll overindulge." Larson arched his eyebrows.

"You watch yourself. That young lady can handle herself. You would be a mere snack for her." James grinned as he turned to face Atwell.

"George, you ready? We're out of here."

# CHAPTER 26: ANALYSIS OF MISTAKES

*Damascus, Syria*

Igor Chirtoff glanced out the window as an American F-22 raptor's sonic boom rattled his safe house's windows; his mind wandered to the upcoming Israeli election. He pondered the impact to his relatives, who immigrated there for a better way of life. With Likud taking over power in a close election, the Middle East peace process grew more complicated. A hardline policy towards reconciliation would prolong al-Qaeda's ability to summon new recruits to the Palestinian cause. He considered the upcoming elections in Russia, the Republic of Georgia, and Pakistan. Political outcomes often depended upon the shifting situational winds. He valued and applied this sentiment to all of life.

Pacing back and forth, he glanced at his watch and peered through the window's blinds. His stomach churned by his source's tardiness. The man walked a mine-laden path; a wrong step or miscalculation meant a certain death. Hearing a knock at the front door, his concerns elevated as his source customarily used the back door. Chirtoff crept toward the door and reached for his gun tucked in the small of his back. He firmly gripped a .22 caliber pistol in his right hand and cocked its hammer. Cracking the door, he braced his foot against the door's base. His guest's face allayed his trepidation.

"Nissan, you're late. What happened? Come inside at once." Chirtoff bolted the door behind him.

"I may have been followed." Nissan hunched over and took a deep breath.

The seasoned spy grabbed his radio off the kitchen table and called his counter-surveillance teams. They all responded negatively to his call. "You must've imagined it. Who do you think was tailing you and how did you detect them?" He appreciated good instincts in his profession and pondered his informant's skills.

Nissan glanced up and looked into his superior's eyes. "I don't know. I just felt a presence as I traveled my route."

Chirtoff had experienced similar feelings over his career. He doubted that terrorists could slip past his surveillance teams and suspected the SVR's involvement. His operation appeared compromised.

Chirtoff motioned his guest to the kitchen table. "Have a seat. Can I get you anything?"

Nissan leaned his head back against the top of the chair. "A glass of cold water would be nice."

He patted him on the arm. "You're an easy man to please. Tell me, Nissan, what do you know about the Khorasan Group's plans?" The spy handed him a glass of water. "Since we don't have a lot of time, I'll be direct. Are you aware of any plans by the terrorists to use either a biological or nuclear weapon?"

Nissan shook his head. "No one has mentioned it. Distrust permeates the group. They talk in riddles and codes. As I mentioned before, Rahman traveled to the states to oversee a large operation. I heard a couple of the others talking about a shipment of weapons inbound to Mexico. They didn't mention the cargo, but they implied it was a game changer."

"What do you think they meant by this?" His face tightened.

"Something big is going on. They're mounting a major operation in America and possibly at some high-profile sporting event." Nissan chugged the rest of his water. "It's more than an assassination of the Pakistani delegation or America's top diplomat."

"How do you know this?" His brows narrowed.

Nissan rubbed his eyes. "I overheard them talking about mass casualties. It could mean only one thing. They're planning an attack at a large event and I'm guessing they'll utilize a car or truck bomb. That's the only way they could inflict such heavy casualties."

Chirtoff agreed, knowing otherwise. The SVR had mentioned other methods to inflict massive casualties during their last meeting – biological or nuclear weapons. Only they lacked the specifics of when and where. He had acquired another key piece to the puzzle. A catastrophe far surpassing nine-eleven would occur in America and soon.

Terrorism was about to take a dramatic turn for the worse. The Russian spy had played the game too long. A new era and rules offered the terrorists a distinct advantage. He contemplated providing the SVR the information and then decided against it. He would return to the United States immediately and use his own internal network to stop the terrorist's revised plans.

"Are you alright Igor?" Nissan tapped him on the shoulder.

"Sure. I was just contemplating a few options. There's nothing to worry about though. I need to ask you something. Please think about it before answering." He studied his informant's eyes. "Have you been compromised? Do you want out?"

"I don't know." Nissan shrugged. "They're suspicious of me. Maybe I should get out now."

"That's nonsense. You only have to hold on a little longer and then you'll deliver a small present to them. It will take care of them permanently. You'll do your country proud." He patted him on his shoulder.

"Perhaps you're right." Nissan scratched his head. "The stakes are high. I shouldn't be selfish when it comes to the security of our great country."

Chirtoff patted him on the back. "That's the spirit. Now go back and wait for further instructions." He escorted his source to the back door. "Good luck."

The longtime operative reflected as Nissan walked away, locking the door behind him. He regretted his instructions. He liked Nissan, but the stakes involved individual sacrifice. He doubted they would meet again.

• • • • •

Meanwhile, halfway around the world, six men in the CIA's Counter-Terrorism Center in Virginia evaluated INTERPOL's urgent information. Bob Mortimer glanced at the cover page and read the executive summary. The report reflected the Mexican Coast Guard's investigation into the wreckage of the Star Gazer; it detailed its discovery about twelve miles east of Veracruz, having originated in Naples, Italy. The Mexican authority's inability to identify the remains propelled them to send dental records and fingerprints to INTERPOL. It had taken a while, but INTERPOL identified five of the six bodies.

Mortimer's eyes widened as he read the list of names. One name captured his attention – Sergi Abalakov, DOB: 6 May 1961, AKA: Pierre Lafonte. He immediately connected the name to previous reports filed by his station chief in Rome. Abalakov's death off the coast of Mexico elevated his concerns that a nuclear weapon had been successfully smuggled into the U.S. "Oh my God, this news is bad." He handed the list to his senior case officer.

Pete Johnson scanned the list, shaking his head. "This development is a nightmare. If our citizens discover that nuclear warheads reached our soil, there will be hell to pay. Millions of Americans will be in danger."

"It's up to us to ensure that this doesn't happen." Mortimer glanced to the Director of Central Intelligence (DCI) for his insight and direction. George Mathison had been DCI for three years and enjoyed making the tough decisions. A former U.S. Attorney, he relentlessly pursued truth with the aggressiveness of a pit bull protecting his master. This unique quality brought him to the attention of the president who sought a transformative CIA director. It took a special leader to reorganize the CIA to achieve greater efficiencies. Mathison welcomed the career change. He had zealously undertaken the president's mandate. His popularity in the elite spy agency plummeted as a result.

Mathison's shoulders dropped. "We need to pass this information to the FBI and DHS. Gentlemen, we've missed the boat on this one. Even though the warheads haven't reached America yet, this is a sad day for the agency. We knew this day would come but didn't anticipate it so soon. Our experts predicted a decade to prepare for it. I need to brief the president. You're dismissed." The director rubbed his eyes.

Johnson followed Mortimer out the door; his body rigid with a down turned mouth. "The fucking cut-throat is going to gut this agency and at a time when it's needed the most."

"Settle down, Pete." Mortimer smirked. "My plan will restore power to the CIA. Let's head back to my office and I'll brief you on the operation."

Arriving at his office, Mortimer sent his newest case officer to retrieve Abalakov's file, code named "Red Lightning." Katharine Davis returned moments later, stopping at the door to read the cover page. Her ears perked up.

"You take things too seriously Pete. My operation will embarrass the president and the DCI." Mortimer pushed up his sleeves.

She knocked at the door and witnessed their shit-eating grins disintegrate.

"Come in." Mortimer closed the file and crossed his arms.

She opened the door and walked directly over to Mortimer, handing him the requested file. "Can I get you anything else?"

"No thanks. Just the door on your way out." He glanced over to Johnson who grinned at the treatment of the female case officer. They resumed their discussion of the ultra-secret operation once the door shut. They would limit dissemination of the plan's operation to just themselves.

Davis' face reddened. She smelled something big, but failed to decipher it. She would concentrate her efforts on the contents of the thumb drive that Special Agent James had provided. The determined case officer realized the gravity of the situation given the latest INTERPOL report. She hoped the thumb drive's contents would reveal clues to thwart the Khorasan Group's plot.

# CHAPTER 27: DIGGING DEEP

*Washington Field Office – Dunn Loring, Virginia*

Weaving through rush hour traffic, James and Atwell screeched to a stop at the Washington Field Office. People flooded the expressways, as they anticipated their weekends, blissfully unaware of the catastrophic threat to the nation. Celebratory weekends seldom occurred for the two dedicated agents. Duty now called for them to investigate a new fraud case under severe time constraints. They had to solve the case by Monday or risk setting a cold-blooded terrorist free.

After parking in front of a building, the two agents vaulted through the building's double glass doors. They marched through a series of corridors and up a central stairwell. Walking to the back entrance to the Washington Field Office, they rang the intercom. Minutes passed as the agents stood patiently; their eyes scanned the sterile cream-colored walls. The door snapped open.

Special Agent Dan Jackson, a veteran of criminal investigations, motioned them inside the office. He converted a decade ago from the Foreign Service (FS) system into the Civil Service. Although this transfer essentially finished his promotion prospects, it also meant he would no longer have to move. FS personnel could spend no more than six consecutive years domestically before being mandatorily reassigned overseas. Overseas tours ranged from one to three years, the tour length dependent upon the assignment, hardship, and danger. Jackson realized a longtime ago that overseas life and the RSO job did not interest him. DS realized the advantages of having continuity in their criminal program. He volunteered his service with no regrets.

"Matt, I understand being around you is considered hazardous duty." Jackson grinned as he led them back to his office area.

"Yeah, keep your distance. There's a bullseye on my back. And like all targets, people sometimes miss and hit what's next to them." He looked down.

"I'll take your thoughts under advisement. How are you doing George?"

"I'm still alive. Not bad for a guy that's been frequently deployed with Matt." He patted James between the shoulder blades and ended up shaking him lightly by the neck.

"Take it easy George. I think that terrorist bastard loosened a few vertebrae when he tried to snap my neck." James massaged his neck.

"So tell me Matt. What happened and why do you think this incident was a terrorist attack? If we're going to get the enhanced sentencing for the assault, then we need to prove his motivation."

James' face crumpled. He described the sensitive West Bank mission, the attack on the secretary, and then linked it to his near death in the parking garage. After about ten minutes, the criminal investigator waved him off.

"If Matt says so, then that's all I need." Atwell glanced at Jackson.

"We first need to prove passport fraud by Monday. Otherwise, the bastard will get out on bail and disappear. We can't let this situation happen." James clenched his jaw.

"Proving this will be difficult. I'm sure all of my contacts have left for the day. Let me show you what we've got so far." Jackson led them to a nearby conference room. Myriad documents, photographs and papers littered a wooden rectangular table.

"Looks like you've been busy Dan." Atwell stroked his beard.

"I do my best." Jackson lifted up copies of the documents. "These passport applications came in on the fax machine not more than five minutes ago. The fraud coordinator even sent us copies of her case notes. Apparently, she was concerned about the applicant's proof of citizenship and identity. In both cases, the applicants presented fresh documentation. Her notes indicate that a duplicate social security card was issued just before the driver's license. It was the same for the other person. She ran driver's license checks in New York and Washington State. Small discrepancies existed in height and weight, but they were not considered great enough to deny the passports. She requested a copy of the Washington driver's license and it matched the passport applicant in each case. The NY Department of Licensing's copies of driver's license photographs are hit or miss. She even checked death records in both Washington and New York, both negative. She was pretty thorough." Jackson looked up.

Picking up the applications, James grumbled, "Dan, you know that New York's records are a mess. Oftentimes, if a person dies in another state than where they were born, the death sometimes doesn't get reported back to the birth state."

Atwell stretched his shoulder. "It would take too long to check death records in all states. And, even then, the death may not be recorded."

"I've got a solution that may streamline the process. Dan, do you have any contacts with either the IRS or the Social Security Administration?" James' voice cracked.

"I sure do." Jackson rambled back to his desk and retrieved his Rolodex. He dialed his contact's mobile phone, but got voicemail instead. He then tried his home phone unsuccessfully as well. He hurriedly returned to the conference room. "He wasn't there. He must be out for cocktails."

James glanced at Atwell. "You have any thoughts?" The Asian American agent's head lowered. The weekend brought many challenges in locating key personnel, even the most dedicated of government servants.

Atwell removed his glasses, pulling out a white handkerchief to clean its lenses. "Unfortunately, I don't have any contacts that would help in this matter. I haven't been assigned to a field office lately." He looked at his watch. It read 7:47 pm. "Matt, you were in the Seattle Resident Office a few years back. Well, it's now 7:47 pm here, but in Seattle it's only 4:47 pm. You could call your old contacts there and they should still be at work."

"You're a genius George. My contact list is in the office. I'll call the Seattle Resident Office and get the number to my contact. When I went overseas, I gave him all of my best contacts. This guy's incredible. He's handed me many leads on cold cases." James bounced on his toes.

James punched in the number to DS' Seattle Resident Office. After three rings, an agent answered. "Seattle Resident Office, Special Agent Thorne speaking."

"Thomas, this is Matt James. How are you doing?"

"Awesome, I think I've found paradise here in the evergreen state."

"I need a small favor Tom."

"Sure, name it. I owe you one. After all, you helped me get this plush assignment."

"I need the telephone number for Randy Wyatt."

"Hold on a second." Thorne ran through his Rolodex and stopped on W. "Ah, here it is." Thorne gave him the area code followed by the seven-digit telephone number. "I just spoke to him an hour ago. You had better call him fast if you want to catch him. What's going on?"

"I'll tell you later. I've got to get on this right now. Thanks. Goodbye."

James dialed the number and after four rings, his old friend answered. "This is Randy Wyatt."

"Randy, it's Matt James. How are you doing? It has been far too long."

"I was just about to call it a day, if that matters. How can I help you?"

"I need a big favor and it's urgent."

"Isn't it always?" Wyatt replied, chuckling. "Hold on a minute, I've got to get to my terminal. Ok, go ahead Matt. Tell me what you've got."

"I have two possible Middle Eastern terrorists bearing recently issued U.S. passports. The Seattle Passport Agency issued both of them in April. The names and other pertinent information listed on the passports applications are as follows: The first person, Isaac Harold Johnson with a D-O-B of 4-23-65 and a P-O-B of Brooklyn, New York listed his social security number (SSN) on the application as 012-57-0987. However, on his application for a Washington State Driver's License he listed his S-S-N as 012-57-8709. Could you run these numbers to see what you've got?"

He heard the crackling of the keys as Wyatt entered the information. "Let's see. 012-57-0987 comes back to another person – a female. Let me check the other one." A brief pause occurred as Wyatt inputted the other number into the computer. "Ok, that number comes back to an Isaac Harold Johnson, born 04-23-65 in Brooklyn, New York."

"So, what can you tell me about Mr. Johnson?" James rubbed his forehead.

"Hold on a minute. I have to go to another screen." Wyatt came on line again and the sound of his fingers banging on the keyboard rattled like machinegun fire. "This sure looks strange. The guy lived a meteoric existence up until virtually twenty years ago; I have nothing reported on the person until this year. It's possible that he just spent time in the slammer. The other possibility is that the real Johnson is deceased. Let me see where he last worked. In 2000, he worked in Philadelphia for a local restaurant chain. In 2001, he remained in the Philadelphia area, but changed jobs. He appeared to be involved in the construction field. The same holds true for most of 2002 and then I have nothing on him until this year. He just literally disappeared. If I were you, I would check death records in New York, Pennsylvania, New Jersey, Maryland, and Delaware. At least that's where I would begin."

"I wish we had the luxury of time, but time's a luxury we just don't have." James sighed. "Randy, do you think you can locate the father or mother?"

Wyatt snarled. "It may be difficult, but I'll give it a try. I hope their names aren't too common, but with a name like Johnson, it will be unlikely. Can you read me their names off the birth certificate and provide their dates and place of birth (DPOB)."

"Yeah, here we go. Peter Issac Johnson, born March 21, 1944 in Trenton, New Jersey."

"Okay, hold on a minute while I run it." Wyatt anticipated the results. "Nope, there was no Johnson born on that date, and I get about thirty possible matches. That's the problem with birth certificates. They only give the age of the parents at the time of birth. You can subtract the difference to obtain a birth year, but that's all you have. Given the number of people born every year, you need an uncommon name to narrow it down. Peter Issac Johnson isn't unusual enough. Tell me the mother's name."

James' voice cracked, but when he read the mother's birth information, his face illuminated. "How's this for a name? Rebecca Meredith Wheatly, born August 8, 1945."

Wyatt inputted the name and punched return. "I'm sorry there's no Wheatly born with that date of birth. However, there are only three possibilities. Let me punch them up individually." After a brief delay, Wyatt had the information. One of the three was deceased. Another lived in Dallas, Texas, and the last one lives in New York. "Your best chance is this woman who lives in New York. She's currently receiving entitlement benefits at a Bronx address – 917 Kilmer Street, Apartment #18. How's that for service?"

"Outstanding. You're always amazing." James beamed.

"Okay, if you don't mind, I'm going to start my weekend. Let me know Matt how it all turns out."

"Sure thing. I owe you big for this one." He tapped a loose fist on his heart.

"You still owe me for the Reggie Tyler case." Wyatt let out a deep, gratifying sigh. "You know I don't do it expecting anything. Just remember, you didn't get this information from me. Bye."

"You've got it. Thanks. Have a great weekend. Out." James placed his phone back into his pocket. The guy certainly worked magic with his keyboard. He probably could hack into the NSA.

"Hey Matt, so where does your contact work?" Atwell quirked an eyebrow.

James' eyes arched. "Some things are better left unsaid."

"I bet your contact works for another governmental agency." Atwell gave a curt nod.

"You guys know there are certain sources that you don't give up. Let's just say my contact either hacks the computer for a living or works for another government agency. Maybe he does both. End of story – alright." James winked.

Atwell gave a single nod.

He relayed Wyatt's information to the others. They called directory assistance and encountered an operator who would not assist, despite it being a federal investigation. A check of the cross directory also proved negative. Their narrowing options led Jackson to place a call to DS' New York Field Office (NYFO); he requested that they send one of their agents to the address to knock on the door.

Unfortunately, NYFO's flood of dignitaries left the office deserted; agents donned their gear and weapons to protect royals, the secretary of state, and countless foreign ministers. Jackson telephoned the DS Command Center to be patched through to NYFO's duty agent. After listening to Jackson, NYFO's agents drove to the address, but came up empty. They even questioned her neighbors, but none of them knew much about her. She obviously kept to herself. Despite their diligent efforts, a dangerous terrorist would most likely walk on Monday.

# CHAPTER 28: HIDDEN PROMISES

*Arlington, Virginia*

James arrived at the Costa Azul restaurant fifteen minutes early. He found predicting DC-area traffic comparable to playing Russian roulette and wanted to make a good impression. After surveying the dining area, he bellied up to a small bar supporting a beautiful Mahogany canopy. He ordered a Pisco Sour while he waited for his date to arrive. It had been sometime since he indulged in the Peruvian national drink; it contained pisco brandy, lemon juice, egg whites, sweet syrup, and bitters. He found it surprising that Katharine had called him, suggesting they meet for dinner. His expectations remained neutral. He needed a little social courage given her vigor and inquisitiveness. She certainly knew her desires and aggressively pursued them.

The bartender approached him a few minutes later and placed the freshly blended drink down on the counter. "You'll no doubt enjoy this Peruvian delight. It's the house specialty."

"I certainly hope so." James leaned forward. "I served a tour in Lima, Peru and I often enjoyed it with a plate of Cebeché. Let's see if you know the secret Incan recipe." He sipped the frothy, dirty-white, cold and refreshing drink from an oversized martini glass.

"So, how did I do?"

"It's fantastic and just how I remembered it. It's been more than five years since I've had one of these babies."

"Que magnifico!" The bartender beamed, pointing over the agent's shoulder. "If that's your date waltzing in, then you're one lucky hombre."

He turned in his seat. Davis strolled into the establishment and cursorily scanned the room from left to right.

"Katharine, I'm over here." He toasted his new interest. Atwell may have got the digits first, but he landed in the driver's seat.

The immaculately dressed woman approached the agent with glossy eyes. "I see you started without me. You must have had a tough day. What are you drinking?"

"It's the Peruvian national drink." He took a sip. "Would you like to try one? They certainly are good for you. The Inca believe they increase your fertility."

She grabbed his martini class. "Don't mind if I do." She took a small sip, followed by a larger one. "That's pretty refreshing. I think I'll have one as well." She smiled at the bartender.

"Jose, you heard the lady. Can you whip her up one and bring it to our table? And could you make that two? I'm sure I'll be ready for another one by then."

"Absolutely amigo, you go grab your seats. I'll have it to you in just a few minutes."

James rose from his seat. "So, how was your day? I assume you're coming directly from work. You look absolutely ravishing."

The CIA lady glowed. "It was a decent day. I got a lot of work done and even finished an analytical product for my boss." She liked the fact that he showed interest in her day and his compliment; it indicated a degree of consideration she sought. She disliked self-absorbed, pretty boys. Instead, an educated manly man with a degree of sensitivity appealed to her tastes. So far, he fit the bill.

The two approached a young vivacious Hispanic hostess who ushered them to a middle table within the eatery. The restaurant's quiet ambience would soon overflow given its four-star rating. Its close and tidily arranged tables resembled a cafeteria-style line. A white tablecloth covered each rectangular table.

"We need something more private and quiet. Can we sit in the corner next to the window?" She winked at the hostess who nodded approvingly.

James walked around the table, pulled out a chair, and guided his date into it. Returning to his chair, he sat down and placed his white cloth napkin in his lap.

"I thought chivalry was dead. It's nice to see a modern man with old fashion manners." She beamed.

"My parents taught me well." He peered into her eyes. "I'm just delighted to encounter a modern lady who still appreciates chivalry in a man. I'm glad you called, but a bit surprised."

"I had to." She gave a half-hearted shrug. "I finally got tired of waiting for you to call. Besides, I've information you need to hear and I couldn't do it officially or at the office."

His head hung as he hoped for more. The dedicated agent desired a meaningful relationship with a woman who could understand his job and its pressures. Her beauty, intelligence, wittiness, and outgoing personality certainly helped. "Let's order and then we can discuss your information."

"Great idea, but I'm unfamiliar with Peruvian cuisine. Do you have any recommendations?" She gazed into his eyes.

"I'm full of recommendations. Do you like chicken or beef?"

"I prefer chicken. I limit my red meat intake and save it for a nice juicy New York cut steak." She eyed the menu.

"May I suggest we start with Cebeché, a Peruvian delicacy where the fish is marinated in lemon juice? I would then recommend Aji de Gallina for you and I'm going to sample the Lomo Saltado." He tilted his head back.

"That sounds interesting. Please order and tell me how you know about Peruvian food."

The well-traveled agent signaled the waitress and ordered the three dishes. Contemplating the suitability of her dish, he wanted her to taste authentic Peruvian food. He hoped the traditional chicken stew in a spicy, nutty cheese sauce would appeal to her tastes. He knew piquant foods were an acquired taste and speculated she would drink more Pisco Sours; this could relax the dinner conversation.

"Okay, now that our meals have been ordered and our drinks are here, let's get down to business." He caressed her hand, leaning in.

"What, no foreplay? What kind of date is this?" She leaned in. "I see you're a business before pleasure type of guy."

"You could say that. I just want us to get to know one another better over dinner without job talk." He licked his lips.

Davis beamed. He continued to reinforce her positive impression of him. She liked his demeanor and words. Her immediate attraction to him surprised her, as it encompassed physical, emotional, philosophical, and spiritual realms. "That makes sense Matt. I'll have to talk cryptically since we aren't in a secure area. The information I'm about to tell you has been buried by my agency and is highly classified."

"Just cut off the headers and send it from your private server to my phone. We could just claim we did it for convenience." He winked. "No seriously, I understand. I'm all ears. Besides, the salsa music should mask everything you tell me."

"The information you requested on the key player comes back to Moussa Rahman. He's a top rebel leader for Al-Qaeda in the Caucasus. Rumor has it that he and his merry band are planning a tour and something big in America. He killed an informant who was found floating in the water off the coast of Veracruz. I'm sure you already know this information; your agent in Rome interviewed the walk-in who alleged that five Iranian broken arrows were coming to America." She sipped her drink.

"What about the thumb drive I gave you? Did you break the code and learn anything good?" His eyebrows arched.

She leaned in and put her hand on his knee. "We pulled up a few items of interest. There's a connection to both Nogales and New Mexico. The encrypted drive used code words on top of it. We needed to transcribe the Arabic information. Hence, we cannot be sure about the accuracy of the translation or information. It's a calculated guess in many regards, but it represents our best analysis about what's going to happen. It appears that the arrows will travel overland from Mexico through Nogales via tunnel. From there, they're destined for some place near either Santa Fe or Roswell, New Mexico. After that, we're clueless as to their final destination. I wish I had something more for you."

James' phone rang. "Good evening. This is Matt James speaking."

"Mr. James, please hold for Mr. O'Reilly?" An all-business secretary transferred the call.

"Hello Matt. This is National Security Advisor Pat O'Reilly calling."

His eyes went wide as he glanced at his date. "What can I do for you sir?"

"You're needed at the White House tomorrow for your insight regarding Ramallah, the raid, and the group's intentions. I've already cleared it with your service. Can you be here at ten o'clock in the morning? I'll make sure you have the requisite pass for you to get in. I'm going to turn you back over to my secretary to provide you specific instructions. I look forward to seeing you tomorrow. Bye."

The phone went silent before his secretary returned to explain the parking and admittance procedures. Upon finishing his conversation, he hung up and looked up at his date. "Well, that conversation certainly was interesting," he said, pondering the invite.

Davis looked curiously at him. "Who was that?"

He lifted a single eyebrow. "You wouldn't believe me if I told you. I'm not sure what it's about. I've been invited to brief the national security advisor about the West Bank and the terrorist's next moves. It's at the White House tomorrow and has been cleared by my service."

"Then this is great timing for our get together. Let me give you the remainder of my team's discoveries," she muttered. "The group appears to be planning a mass casualty event with one or more of the broken arrows."

"You think?" James winced. His shoulders sunk as he pinched the bridge of his nose and squeezed his eyes closed.

She lowered her head. "I didn't deserve that. I'm trying to help you and at great risk to my career."

"I'm sorry. I didn't mean for it to sound that way." He glanced down fleetingly.

Her face shined. "Apology accepted as long as you buy me another drink and tell me ten things about yourself."

He covered his face with his hand. "You drive a tough bargain; I hate to talk about myself, but that's a fair deal. So what do you want to know?"

Her eyes glimmered, recognizing him as the strong silent type. She had so many questions. She knew men tended to hide their feelings. "So Matt, what do you want out of life?"

He gritted his teeth and looked away. "I want what all red-blooded Americans want, like a tax cut, world peace, and a strong military." He dodged the answer she wanted to hear.

She pinched her lips together and shook her head.

"I also want a family, a wife who is my best friend, a nice home, and a dog."

"You like kids." She leaned in.

"I don't have any; I thought about having a boy and a girl, separated by two years. The boy should come first so he can protect his sister's virtue later on in life." James winced, dreading the prospect of eight more questions.

Fortunately, dinner arrived and changed the dynamics of the conversation, which focused on his Peruvian experience. Time accelerated as they both enjoyed each other's company. By the time they finished dinner, she had elicited a hundred questions from the reserved agent without him knowing it. He found her both intriguing and fascinating. His clear disappointment in calling it an early evening surfaced. He needed to be well-rested for tomorrow's White House meeting.

After paying the bill, James accompanied Davis to her car and opened the door. She turned back toward him, so he gave her a light kiss on the cheek. He checked to make sure her body was clear of the door as she sat down and closed it. The sporty fiery-red Toyota Corolla appeared a good fit for a classy and stylish woman.

She rolled down the window. "I forgot to tell you something. Can you come closer?"

He stuck his head through the window as she started the car. "Yeah, what is it?"

"I just wanted to thank you for the wonderful time I had tonight." She leaned forward and planted a lingering soft moist kiss on his lips. "I hope we can get together soon. Good luck with your meeting tomorrow. Goodnight."

James watched the car back out and maneuver from the parking lot onto Wilson Boulevard. She disappeared from sight seconds later. He certainly hoped to see her soon, but first he needed to handle some urgent business.

# CHAPTER 29: A CONFLICT OF INTEREST

*The Oval Office*

The meeting began like many before. The president sat behind his desk reviewing the latest intelligence briefs from his national security advisor. Current threat reports on Afghanistan, Iraq, Pakistan, Iran, North Korea, Syria, and Libya dominated his agenda. All of these flashpoints presented unique dilemmas for any administration. Alexander Johnson, a conservative democrat, blew into office on the wave of change, which he portrayed and promised. Elected as the second youngest president in U.S. history, he represented a new era of thinking. He was conservative on the typically republican issues of crime, welfare reform, national defense and immigration. The Oklahoman combined this with a passionate mindset towards the environment, health care, education and other social programs. A fiscal conservative, he remained a hardcore blue dog democrat, which created several problems within his own party.

The president towered over most people at six feet five; his medium build suffered slightly around the waist from a sedentary lifestyle and a love for fast food. An intellectual, he had served in government all his adult life. Known to closely weigh his options, he relied on the input of a few trusted people within his administration. His recently appointed national security advisor (NSA) remained his top and true confidante.

Patrick O'Rielly was as Irish as his name implied. Born and raised in South Boston, the fifty-two-year-old politician had a tremendous career. Some attributed his success to the luck of the Irish. However, in reality, he excelled through hard work, discipline, and diligence, although a little luck may have helped. He brought impressive credentials to the office as a successful businessman, mayor, and U.S. ambassador.

A savvy politician, O'Rielly could see well into the future with almost mystical, yet accurate results. He had predicted the abrupt turnover in power in Egypt and ISIS' comeback in the Middle East. Although he had held his current position for four months, his insight had served the president well. O'Rielly had suggested a meeting to discuss the possible use of nuclear, chemical and biological weapons by terrorists. The timing and the Iranian president's recent proclamation about joining the nuclear club made it essential.

Experts from the CIA, NSA, and DIA predicted that weapons of mass destruction terrorism remained a decade away. However, O'Rielly knew otherwise from his service as the U.S. ambassador to the Vatican. He received intelligence from myriad sources in Syria, Pakistan, North Korea, and elsewhere. His contacts had repeatedly advised on ISIS' efforts to acquire nuclear, chemical and biological weapons. Prior to departing Italy, O'Rielly learned that Iran had acquired biological weapons and Shkval-type torpedoes from the Russian black-market in preparation for a conflict with the West.

The intelligence material flooded the Oval Office, emanating from numerous sources and agencies. It included a unique combo of RUMINT, HUMINT, EMINT, and SIGINT. O'Reilly had to digest it all and brief the president on only those items with foreign policy significance. They had just concluded their daily briefing when a knock came at the door.

The president looked up from the briefs on his desk. "Come in."

The vice president, the secretaries of state, defense, homeland security and energy, as well as the chief of staff and the directors of the DNI, CIA, NSA, and the FBI strolled into the room. They each greeted the president and his chief security advisor. The Oval Office's normal grueling pace could overwhelm a president without proper assistance.

The president motioned for them to their seats and scanned his outline for the topics of discussion. He then glanced up and surveyed his closest advisors.

"Gentlemen, my schedule is packed so we need to get down to business." He turned sharply to his left and motioned to O'Reilly.

"Pat thinks we have a serious situation on our hands. During his tour as ambassador to the Holy See, he came across a great deal of raw intelligence; it reflects that some of our greatest enemies have obtained sizable quantities of biological and chemical weapons. Furthermore, they're attempting to obtain nuclear weapons by any means possible. Now, I don't have to remind you what a threat this means to our national security. I need to hear your thoughts and solicit your advice. Nonetheless, I'll first have Pat address the problem as he sees it. Pat..."

O'Reilly rose in his seat. "Thank you Mr. President. I've heard through my reliable sources that Syria, North Korea, and Iran have acquired weapons of mass destruction. And by this, I mean specifically chemical and biological weapons. My sources have repeatedly told me they've recently acquired nukes from the former Soviet Union and North Korea. I find this disturbing, given ISIS' stated goal of killing the West. Our intelligence now suggests that Iran has developed nuclear weapons or is on the cusp of a breakthrough. Our sanctions have barely slowed them down. It's also problematic that they have the delivery systems to reach Israel. One of the most troubling is their acquisition of the Shkval high-speed torpedo capable of exceeding two-hundred knots. This is four times the speed of any U.S. torpedo, making it difficult to avoid. It can also carry a nuclear warhead."

The vice president interrupted. "Pat, we all find this of great concern, but we knew it to be inevitable. What makes you think that they'd be willing to use these weapons against us or our closest allies? These countries must know we'd strike back hard and that this action would be a prelude to war."

O'Reilly nodded casually. "Yes, but with peace looming in Afghanistan, they're finding themselves with their backs against the wall. If we forge peace there, then these extremist countries will lose another inroad into this region. Besides, they won't attack us directly. They'll use certain terrorist groups to accomplish this goal. It will give them plausible deniability, yet allow them to carry out their agenda."

"Isn't this too soon? Most reports that I've seen suggest that nuclear terrorism is at least eight to ten years away," said the secretary of defense. "I suppose it's possible. What makes you think that it will happen now and on U.S. soil?"

O'Reilly glanced down at his watch. He knew that the meeting would exceed the allotted time. "The timing is right given the current political climate. They have the will and the ability to conduct this type of attack now. I see no reason for them to wait. There was the recent discovery of a body and boat remains off the coast of Veracruz, Mexico. Fingerprints and dental records identified the remains as a well-known weapon's trafficker. In this incident, he was part of a small group attempting to smuggle nukes into America through Mexico. We all know how porous our borders are adjoining Mexico. This belief is supported by other intelligence."

The president caught the CIA director shaking his head in disagreement. "You've something you wish to add George. Please, speak up."

"Mr. President, the CIA has no knowledge that a nuclear attack will happen now and on American soil. We're aware of all of the intelligence on the subject and we're continually checking our sources. The intelligence indicates that Iran, North Korea, and Syria are in possession of biological and chemical weapons. We've known this for many years. The CIA has thousands of reports of black marketing of nuclear weapons by the former Soviet Republics. However, we've no credible evidence that any of these extremist countries currently have nukes, other than North Korea. And the Stuxnet worm caused havoc to Iran's nuclear program, setting them back several years. Pat's intelligence is likely with the break-up of the Soviet Union. It resulted in the formation of highly organized criminal networks comprised of former KGB and GRU officers. Yet, at this time, the evidence doesn't suggest they've this capability. You can rest assured that we're closely monitoring the situation."

"That's comforting. What about the 'walk-in' source in Rome? He informed that a shipment of five nuclear warheads was being transported to America through Mexico. He's later found floating face-up just off the coast of Veracruz. Don't you find this intelligence the least bit peculiar?" O'Reilly shrugged waiting for an answer.

The CIA director raised his chin high. "The agency can neither confirm nor deny this intelligence. We're checking through our sources and other methods to corroborate this intelligence. To date, there has been simply no corroboration or physical evidence."

The president glanced over to the FBI director. "Henry, does the FBI have anything on a possible WMD attack by terrorist groups on American soil?"

The FBI director rose slightly in his seat. "Sir, my agents throughout the world are working closely with their counterparts to uncover any information on the trafficking of nuclear, biological and chemical weapons. At this time, the FBI has no evidence to prove or disprove this possibility. I think everyone here in this room understands the importance of this type of work. There are literally thousands of leads out there and the FBI's looking into every one of them. Nevertheless, we presently have nothing on a possible WMD terrorist attack on our soil. We're looking into several aspirational reports regarding possible terrorist attacks at upcoming major events and our transportation sectors. However, we've been unable to corroborate any of these reports, but the FBI will continue to investigate. We are also looking into the individual found off the coast of Veracruz. The FBI's working with the Mexican authorities and other agencies around the world to corroborate this informant's information. My agents have interviewed his wife and daughter, but they disavowed any knowledge of his smuggling activities. This case has top priority, given the ramifications. That's all I have sir."

The secretary of state decided to weigh in. "For the record Mr. President, it was DS agents who first interviewed the dead informant's wife and daughter. The wife stated her husband was involved in something big, but she was unsure of what. She relayed her husband's deep concern for his life. And from his fate, I guess his fears were well founded. It was also a DS agent in Rome, who handled the 'walk-in' there. He felt that the informant was telling the truth by his demeanor and body language. The walk-in would only benefit if the proper organization received these five nuclear warheads. DS doubted the Italian's claim that he was a con artist. The agent's report also indicated that both the FBI and the CIA were hustling to follow-up."

"Is this true?" The president looked at his number one crime fighter and his top intelligence expert.

The FBI director deferred to his CIA colleague. The top spy director spoke persuasively. "Mr. President, given the ramifications of a nuclear warhead landing on U.S. soil, the natural response of our stations is to do everything possible to confirm or refute the intelligence. And that's precisely what all stations are instructed to do given its importance to national security."

The FBI director turned in his chair. "My agents are instructed similarly."

"Alright." The president scrubbed a hand over his face at the lack of certainty in the room. "What types of contingency plans do we have for this type of thing? As you're all aware, we have a number of rapidly approaching major events. Besides, we have a responsibility to protect our citizens from harm. When I was elected, I promised to protect the American people from foreign and domestic terrorism."

The secretary of energy interjected, "Mr. President, the Department of Energy (DOE) is working with the FBI and FEMA to prepare for a nuclear contingency. We've already run joint exercises in Houston with these groups and elite military entities to combat a nuclear warhead or disaster. The results were very promising. With the FBI and CIA providing intelligence, teams of DOE, DHS, FBI and military experts systematically searched the city with state-of-the-art technology until they isolated and contained a mock nuclear device. Once it was uncovered, military experts deactivated the mock nuclear device. I'm sure everyone present read the reports on operation 'RAINY DAY.' It couldn't have gone off much better."

"It was indeed an impressive operation." The president scanned the group. "Can we discover a chemical or biological weapon with the same shining results?" The president rubbed his forehead. His advisors' tense faces reflected the answer. "I didn't think so. I want to meet back here in a week. By then I want answers on how to handle a biological or chemical weapon. And be sure to invite the director of FEMA to this meeting. Please pass all relevant information to our allies to ascertain if they've any information regarding a nuclear attack." He glanced over to his chief of staff who made a note. "This meeting is adjourned."

O'Reilly motioned to the secretary of state to remain behind as the group filtered out of the room. A minute later the Oval Office sat empty except for the president, the secretary of state, and the national security advisor.

Harold Robinson appeared slightly perplexed by the request. He was one of the most active secretaries of state in the nation's history. He traveled frequently to broker deals in all parts of the world. While this work would have exhausted most people, Robinson thrived on such a busy and chaotic schedule. Although he was sixty-five, he appeared more like a well-conditioned athlete in his early forties. This youthful appearance probably could be attributed to his daily regimen of swimming and a Mediterranean diet. "Alex, what's going on?" He turned to the president.

The president shifted in his chair. "Sorry for the unscheduled appointment Hal; Pat thinks I ought to hear something directly from one of your men. So, I thought you should be naturally included on this somewhat clandestine meeting. Pat believes that the CIA and the FBI have their own agendas."

"That doesn't surprise me. It's hard to know exactly what they're up to these days." Robinson sneered. "Who are you bringing in from my Department?"

The president glanced over to O'Reilly who stood while pouring a cup of coffee. "Pat has invited DS Special Agent Matt James. He is intimately familiar with much of the information – your assassination attempt, the raid on the safe house, and a great deal more. Pat thought it best if we spoke candidly to him."

"He's one of our best; a fine young man." The secretary nodded once.

The president walked over to his NSA. "Okay Pat, tell the Secret Service agent to escort him in. I've a very busy schedule today."

O'Reilly walked over to the Oval Office's main door where an agent stood outside. He opened the door and instructed the agent to have the DS agent escorted to the office. A half-minute later James entered the Oval Office in awe of the splendor of the room.

The president stepped forward, extending his hand. "Agent James, welcome. We're glad you could make it here today. Would you like coffee or something else?"

"No thank you, Mr. President. This is indeed an honor and a privilege to be here today. I only hope I can be of assistance." James turned to greet the secretary and the NSA.

The president walked back around his desk and sat. "Gentlemen, please be seated so we can get started."

O'Reilly patted James on the back and directed him to his chair. The agent scanned the room while pondering his invitation. His sudden appearance before the president on the issue of terrorism and WMD sent chills down his spine. He valued Davis' information more than ever; he did not have much more to go on other than her information and his instincts. He hoped it would suffice.

O'Reilly took the lead. "Agent James, we're all aware of the role you played in thwarting a terrorist attack on the secretary and the raid on the terrorist safe house in the West Bank. What we'd like to hear is your thoughts regarding a possible WMD attack on U.S. soil. Do you feel that the Khorasan Group has the means to conduct this type of attack on America? Give us your candid thoughts."

James sat back in his chair and took a deep breath. "Mr. President, I'm not an analyst. I'd estimate there's better than an eighty percent chance that a major attack will take place in the U.S. this year. The most likely scenario would involve a large and highly televised sporting event. This newly formed terrorist coalition has the network and the will to operate around the world. They successfully assassinated the Russian foreign minister in New York and almost murdered me in Virginia last week. They were using false U.S. documentation. We've built a case on them, but it was too late. Not surprisingly, the terrorist failed to show for his hearing. We later identified the terrorist as an associate of Moussa Rahman, head of the Riyad-us-Saliheen Brigades. This group is more commonly known as Al-Qaeda in the Caucasus. DS is continuing its investigation and is working with the FBI. Nevertheless, if Rahman's in America, then something big is going down and soon. It's just a hunch, but I believe it to be true."

"What about the plans your team discovered in the safe house? Did they mention any use of WMD by this terrorist coalition?" The secretary probed.

"Unfortunately, I couldn't review the notes as I was in a hurry."

"I imagine so." The president's voice softened. He recalled the report where James leapt out a second-story window to evade capture by Palestinian forces.

"When the team returned to the embassy, we reported to the CIA chief. We handed over all the evidence, including notes, a laptop, weapons, explosives, maps, and other drawings." James cleared his throat. "I tried to examine the notes, but they took them and I never heard anything more about them. Mr. President, the CIA would have to answer that question. The ambassador instructed me not to discuss the mission with anyone. So, I didn't bother probing for further answers."

"You did the right thing." The secretary assured, patting him lightly on the shoulder.

"Is there anything more to add Agent James?" The president rubbed his eyes.

The agent took a deep breath. "I glanced down at one document following our raid on the safe house. It was written in code, but it indicated that something would happen at a major event in America. I couldn't get anything more from the notes before I handed them over to the CIA."

The president's voice softened. "What about anything else you might of heard or suspect from your knowledge of this case?"

"A CIA contact recently advised of the death of a weapon's trafficker off the coast of Veracruz, Mexico. A DS colleague who handled this informant received a corroborating email from him prior to his death. According to the email, the merchandise would be smuggled overland from Mexico through Nogales." James scanned the three politicians.

"Segments of the intelligence community have also heard that the merchandise they're referring to is a nuclear warhead." The NSA shook his head.

James caressed his chin. "Per a thumb drive I later supplied to the CIA, Moussa's group was going to conduct a kidnapping or some form of takeover, but the agency couldn't elaborate further. Our own DS investigation discovered that some of Rahman's associates are connected to Santa Fe and Roswell. There are addresses linked to a post office and a temporary storage facility in Santa Fe."

"This information is helpful." The president turned to his closest advisors. "Do you think this terrorist coalition is orchestrating a multi-pronged attack against the U.S. and our close allies? The Khorasan Group has repeatedly stated their intent on attacking our closest European partners and Israel."

The secretary nodded. "It would make sense given our close alliance with the Brits and their stance alongside us in Afghanistan. The Brits have raised their profile on the world stage. This would make them more of a target with their democratic roots."

"Agent James, do you have any last words?" The president rubbed his chin.

"I'm sorry Mr. President. I don't have any other pertinent information on this issue. In closing, I want to stress it's going to take the complete cooperation of all U.S. law enforcement and intelligence agencies to deter a WMD attack. Candidly, there's still too much competition between the different law enforcement agencies, the FBI in particular."

The president rose from his chair, extending his hand. "Thank you for coming in. We appreciate your insight."

The DS agent returned his firm handshake. "It was a pleasure for me to be here today. I only wish I could've been more helpful." He shook hands with the secretary of state and the NSA before turning towards the exit.

O'Reilly escorted the agent to the door. "I appreciate your insight. Now if you hear anything else, please contact me anytime, day or night." He handed James his business card and opened the door. I need you to run down the leads in New Mexico. I'll clear it with the secretary.

"I'm handling tactical support for the Pakistani reception tomorrow. If I leave now, it will cause some questions." James looked up.

"Okay, wait until after the reception and then catch the next flight out. Tell no one else and advise me of what you find. If necessary, I'll dispatch backup upon your request. Good luck."

A Secret Service agent escorted him out a back door.

# CHAPTER 30: DIPLOMATIC DILIGENCE

*Pakistani Reception – Washington, DC*

Driving past the front entrance of the Five Corners hotel in Washington, DC, James admired the building's aesthetics. Its unique reddish-brown blend of brick architecture, combined with circular arches and glass, portrayed a futuristic look. Internal and external courtyards complemented its design, which blended ornamental trees and flowers in full bloom. Its extravagance, combined with its accessibility to the seat of government, businesses, restaurants and monuments, solidified its five-star rating. Nevertheless, he would never pay for such luxury. He frugally saved his money for his retirement property on a fishing lake.

With the sun descending behind the taller buildings to the west, the hotel's activity would soon increase tenfold. They parked their counterassault vehicle on a side street across from the prestigious landmark hotel. The MSD leader and his team scanned the area looking for unusual people, cars, or suspicious activity. Lifting his binoculars, James panned the front of the building while focusing on the main entrance. Given his team's uniforms and tactical gear, politics dictated their placement outside and he preferred it this way. He disliked diplomatic functions because of the elitism, arrogance, wealth, and pretentiousness that came with the throng. His uncomplicated nature and simpler tastes did not mix well with the crowd. He had no time for the privileged.

An influx of people began to arrive twenty minutes early to the lavish reception in the Jefferson Ballroom. James had seen the room earlier in the day when bomb dogs swept the expansive room for explosives. A rich display of mauve, blue-green, and rose colors stylishly decorated the magnificent ballroom. Its crystal chandeliers radiated soft light throughout the room, accenting the warm honey-toned moldings and luxurious ornamental drapes. With the capacity to hold over four-hundred people, the reception would be the highlight of the DC circuit. Dignitaries, politicians, entertainers, businesspersons, and other affluent people from across the globe blanketed the invitee's list. His photographic memory and site familiarity meant his response to the ballroom in twenty seconds should trouble arise.

James watched the guests with great interest as they filtered through the front door. Protected dignitaries arrived almost every minute. He knew there would be more guns inside than in a SEAL platoon deploying to a war zone.

The counterassault team leader glanced at his watch. "Gentlemen – and I use the term loosely – we're much safer out here than inside the hotel. I'd hate to be caught in the crossfire if a single shot rang out."

Wagner chuckled from behind the driver's seat. "No shit, talk about the gunfight at the OK corral. There would be more lead flying through the air than people in the room. It's better that Atwell's inside doing the babysitting than us."

"Finally, there's a job worthy of his immense talents and skills," James cracked.

The Suburban erupted in laughter, but an abrupt radio transmission stifled their jocularity. The DS-protected Pakistani foreign minister would arrive at the hotel in five minutes. The reception would go full blown and live in the next fifteen minutes.

"Let's look alive. It's game time." James bit his lip.

"This mission is a cakewalk. The site has been locked down for over four hours with security, police, and feds." Wagner lowered the air conditioning.

James shrugged. "I wish it was that simple, but intelligence indicates terrorists will hit the event. We'll need to stop them cold in their tracks."

Wagner tapped James' shoulder and pointed. "I didn't know the Russian ambassador had protection these days. Look at the lead agent. The guy's a monster, but the girl's hot."

James lifted the binoculars to his eyes. "She sure is. Don't you recognize her Dutch? That's Svetlana Andropov."

Wagner rubbed his chin. "Who is it? It's hard to believe I don't recall her."

"It was kind of early and dark when you met her in that smoke-filled hallway. She was with us in New York, protecting the Russian foreign minister." James cocked his head.

"I don't feel too bad now. We faced hell that morning," Wagner scoffed.

They sat idly for thirty minutes, watching the parade of the worthy enter the hotel in small groups. People trickled into the reception as the event reached its apex. Glancing at his watch, James recognized that they still had another three hours left until the event culminated. He sent the well agent to a local sandwich shop for some dinner.

Meanwhile, George Atwell combed the reception for anything that might pose a threat to the Pakistani foreign minister. The director of protection handpicked him as the hotel's site lead given his diplomatic prowess. Walking systematically throughout the floor, he scrutinized everyone except his DS colleagues. Dressed in a solid black tuxedo, he resembled a host, apart from the pistol beneath his jacket and the white one-eighth inch coiled tubing leading to his left ear.

He ambled toward the food table when a call came over the radio. Atwell placed his left index finger on his earpiece and seated it firmly into his ear.

"Atwell...Atwell, this is Larson."

Atwell activated his miniaturized microphone clipped to the front of his shirt collar. The three-quarter inch long microphone ran beneath the shirt collar and clipped to its backside. "Atwell by."

"Could you come to the kitchen? I've something that requires your attention. Larson out."

"Wait one. I'm on my way." Atwell strutted back to the kitchen; his lengthened stride and tense posture indicated its urgency. Myriad five-star aromas bombarded his olfactory senses as he opened the kitchen door. His sinuses instantly cleared from the fiery vapors. He glided through a gauntlet of cooks and received more than a few idle stares. His intrusion into their domain ruffled them and their frantic pace. Advancing around the corner, he discovered Larson interrogating one of the cooks.

"You have no idea where this suitcase came from or who owns it." Larson's eyes narrowed as he pointed his index finger at the man.

The pudgy cook shook his head and shrugged.

"I wonder if he speaks English." Larson turned to Atwell as if he knew.

"What do you have?" Atwell scanned the cook.

"You've got me. I've interviewed everyone in this room and received the same response. Nobody knows a damn thing. It's as if this suitcase magically appeared."

Atwell stroked his chin. "Let's figure this out."

"Should we evacuate the building?" Larson's voice cracked.

"Larson, if you thought it was a bomb, why did you radio me and risk it going off." Atwell shook his head. He tapped his fingers against his trousers as the young agent's face flushed.

"I'm sorry George. I guess with all the excitement, it slipped my mind that my radio's signal could've detonated the device."

"No harm done. You've learned a valuable lesson and not the hard way. Now open the damn thing up. First, let me get around the corner and duck behind that industrial size oven." Atwell displayed a wide grin.

Hesitating, the rookie glanced up. "You're only kidding, right?"

"This is what we'll do Larson. I'll telephone James and have him dispatch a bomb dog our way. The canine will give it a whiff and we'll see if there's anything to worry about. Stay with the case. I'll be right back."

Atwell found a nearby phone in a back hallway, just off the kitchen. The hallway led to a multitude of banquet and reception rooms; all abandoned in the name of security. He punched in the telephone number to the counterassault vehicle.

After two rings, a familiar voice answered, "MSD, Matt James speaking."

"I see they found you a job worthy of your secretarial skills." Atwell snorted.

"You're a regular comedian George, but don't switch professions. All kidding aside, I'm answering the phones because Wagner's stuffing down a steak and cheese. It's awfully quiet out here, except for the hordes of weirdoes descending upon Georgetown. You'd think it's Halloween. We're like a lightning rod for their curiosity. They all want to know what's going on tonight."

"No shit."

"Yup, there must be a full moon, given all the lurking lunatics. We should've staffed the car with Dr. Phil. He would've had a field day analyzing these people. What's up?"

"Could you dispatch an EOD team to my location? I've a suspicious suitcase and I need a bomb dog to check it out."

James grunted, "Unfortunately not. Our teams have leapfrogged ahead to check out other scheduled sites. The U.S. president is scheduled to arrive at the Kennedy Center; our teams are busy assisting the president's protective detail. Sorry George, the Secret Service would have it no other way. And as you know, the president always has priority."

"This situation is just great." Atwell shook his head. "We're left out in the cold to fend for ourselves."

"Not exactly. How about Wagner and I come to your location and bring the portable x-ray machine? We can look into the case without disturbing it. If there's a concern, we can get a team here on a priority basis."

"Sure, how fast can you get here?" Atwell peered down the hall to a side exit.

He glanced at Wagner. "Well, with Dutch driving, we ought to be there in about ten seconds. We're only across the street. We'll bring the water cannon just in case we need to deactivate it."

"Thanks Matt. We'll see you shortly. Bye." Atwell hung up, confident that the problem would soon be resolved.

"Dutch, let's roll. George needs our assistance in the hotel's kitchen. Tell me we have the portable bomb equipment in the rear of the Suburban?"

Wagner gave a thumbs-up. "I packed it myself."

James pointed at the other four agents. "You guys hold down the fort. We'll be back after we check out a suspicious suitcase."

The two agents bolted out the door leaving behind some slightly perplexed faces. James lacked the time to brief them on the situation before leaving. They trotted to the hotel's rear doors; Atwell met and greeted them both with a handshake.

"Where to?" James motioned to Wagner to bring the x-ray machine packed away in a hard plastic Pelican case. Atwell led them down a side corridor where they entered the kitchen area. Larson stood precariously nearby entertaining a sharply dressed and sophisticated looking woman.

James beamed. "Good evening Svetlana. You look absolutely stunning. What brings you here tonight?"

"After the assassination of our foreign minister, I was assigned to protect our ambassador. I saw your agents scurry this way, so I decided to check out things for myself. I see you have a suspicious suitcase. Is it time for me to leave?" She glanced at Atwell.

Atwell normally would have cleared the kitchen while conducting this operation. He abandoned procedure this time as some of DC's finest chefs delicately prepared countless and costly exquisite dishes. Interrupting their cooking ritual would degrade the cuisine's quality and sidetrack the monumental event. He could not risk hitting the panic button unless looming danger mandated it. He had worked too hard to risk his stellar reputation by acting too abruptly. Nevertheless, he cleared the general area around the suitcase.

"Aren't you going to introduce me to the lady?" Atwell turned to the Russian agent.

"George, this is Svetlana Andropov. Svetlana, I'd like you to meet my close personal friend and colleague, George Atwell."

"The pleasure is mine Mr. Atwell." Her eyes sparkled.

"Miss Andropov, the pleasure is mine." Atwell shook her hand and then kissed the back of it.

"A true American gentlemen." She beamed.

"They don't call us Diplomatic Security for nothing." James gave a cocky smile.

"Svetlana, are you related to the past KGB chief and the former General Secretary of the Communist Party." Atwell released her hand.

"He was my grandfather and the reason I joined the FSB. It's not easy living under his shadow."

"Can you all quiet down so I can work here?" Wagner shook his head. He prepared the film for the x-ray machine and positioned it squarely behind the suitcase. He needed to reposition the machine around the suitcase to get a thorough look at its contents. After several minutes of precise work and processing, Wagner placed the developed x-ray film on a nearby countertop. He spread out the x-rays to match the order in which he took them.

"Have a look at this." Wagner admired the device's craftsmanship. James, Atwell, and Andropov peered over his shoulders to catch a glimpse at the device. Larson remained at a distance and patiently waited for the verdict. Their collective focus lingered on the device, while two food preparers scrutinized their bomb procedures and techniques.

"Dutch, we have an I-E-D on our hands. Look at all the wiring." James pointed to the second photograph. "The guy that built this device must be a professional. There are multiple fusing systems, to include a clock as a possible safety mechanism. There's also a mercury switch attached to the lid to detonate it if opened or tilted. In addition, look at the pressure release button. It's a good thing that Larson didn't have a closer look at this baby." He turned to the rookie. "Good work bringing this suitcase to our attention."

"Something isn't quite right here." Wagner refocused the group's attention to one of the x-rays. "Now we know this discoloration represents the explosive. Look at this side-view photo. The explosive is very thin. More like what you would find in a letter bomb. Considering this, the overall quantity appears to be quite small. Sure, it would kill or permanently maim whoever handled it, but it wouldn't hurt too many people in this room. Other than giving them earaches, this device was meant only to be an attention getter."

"I agree." James snapped his fingers, motioning for Larson to clear the kitchen.

"Do we want to evacuate the banquet area as well?" Larson looked at Atwell for guidance.

"What do you guys think?" Atwell turned to Wagner and James.

"If this thing blows, there's only going to be minimal damage to this corner of the kitchen." James pointed to the adjoining hall. "With the hallway and additional space separating the banquet room from here, the people at the reception will be completely safe. I'd doubt they'd even hear the blast with the idle chatter and music. Besides, maybe the person that..."

"You mean terrorist," Wagner blurted.

"Yeah, maybe the terrorist who planted this damn thing is waiting outside with his friends. All ready to spray and pray." James eyed the exit.

"That's a good point. Larson, only clear the kitchen while we disarm the device." Atwell's face relaxed. "Okay, how can I help you on this?"

"George, there's no need for you to be in this room if something goes wrong. You should go entertain the guests and take Svetlana with you." Wagner snorted. "Let the men handle this."

"Wagner's right George. We can handle this. It will only take a few minutes to disarm it. We'll keep you posted." James looked up from examining the suitcase.

Atwell nodded affirmatively, but decided to wait until the very end. Wagner trotted to the Suburban to retrieve the water cannon while James studied the x-rays one last time; the device's simplicity troubled him. He knew precisely where to focus the water cannon to interrupt the power source.

"Something's not right. This deactivation is too easy." James' stomach churned.

"In Russia, the Chechen rebels frequently use two devices. The first one draws in the responders, such as the police, firefighters, and medical personnel. The second one's larger and meant to kill them." She checked her cell phone for a message. "I bet there's a larger device placed somewhere else in the ballroom." She neglected to divulge Russian intelligence reflecting two terrorist sympathizers working the function.

"I don't see how that's possible. We conducted bomb sweeps of the entire area and then posted it with our agents." Atwell puffed out his chest, placing his hands on his hips.

Andropov folded her arms. "Did you check the rooms above the ballroom?"

Atwell caressed his cheek. "We ran the dogs through there, added cameras and alarms, and then posted the only entrance."

"Damn it's hot in here. What's wrong with the air conditioning?" James glanced up to the air duct situated in the ceiling. His guts contorted. "George, it's time to get dirty. I need to go up into the vent. Larson can assist Wagner with disarming this device. I recommend you and Svetlana return to the ballroom to monitor the situation and prepare for an evacuation. I think she's right. There's another device here."

Larson's face sunk. "I'm not an explosive's guy. How about I go into the ballroom and assist Atwell? My first child's due in three weeks. I'd like to be around to meet her."

"I specialized in explosives at our academy. I don't mind staying here to assist Special Agent Wagner," said Andropov, winking.

"Alright, it's settled. Matt will check out the vent. Dutch and Svetlana will disarm the device, and Larson and I will prepare for an evacuation." Atwell exited with Larson in toe.

Wagner popped in through the door with a hard plastic, three-foot by two-foot, gray case. It had special markings affixed to the top and sides – "Handle with Care," and "Fragile, Security Material Inside." He laid the case on the floor and unlocked its latches. Raising the lid, he admired the high-tech device capable of shooting a high-speed water pellet. Its remote operation reduced the chances of injury or death to its users.

Wagner assembled the three-piece unit. He did not miss the old days, which instead used a shotgun and a long string. He always appreciated advancing technology, whether it was in the security, medical, or the space industry. After a minute, the water cannon stood fully assembled and ready to prove its worth. He could literally put any weapon, device, or water cannon together blindfolded.

He got up from kneeling, joining Andropov at the counter. "It looks like I got the best deal as I'm here with you."

Her eyes glimmered. "Let's disarm this thing."

The two agents conferred briefly and decided precisely where to set up the cannon to ensure its success. They moved to the suitcase. Andropov displayed the photograph while Wagner placed the cannon.

"Just a hair to the left Dutch." She guided his hand and the tip of the cannon to the precise location.

James climbed up a small ladder and opened the vent. "Don't have too much fun while I'm gone." He disappeared abruptly into the bowels of the ventilation system.

Wagner adjusted the water cannon; they then compared the estimated point of impact on the suitcase to the x-rays one last time.

"That should do it." He looked at the Russian who nodded her approval.

They walked around a corner, concealing themselves behind both the wall and large convection oven.

"You want the honors?" He already knew the answer, handing her the remote control. "Hold on a second." He pulled out two earplugs from his pocket and inserted them into his ears. He signaled the FSB agent with a nod and the thumbs-up.

Grinning, she flipped the switch. The cannon fired its high velocity water pellet; it sliced through the suitcase and the battery, rendering it useless. The lack of a blast served as evidence of their success. They paused to be sure and then moved forward to inspect their work.

Kneeling beside the suitcase, they scrutinized the water pellet impact. It blasted clean through both sides and left a quarter-sized hole at their targeted area. They snapped one more x-ray as a precautionary measure. Wagner repositioned the x-ray machine, slightly embarrassed that he left it before firing the water pellet. He clicked off a final x-ray. They analyzed it together seconds later and appreciated the results.

The two moved cautiously and worked harmoniously together while breaking down the remaining components. They first secured the pressure release switch with a small metallic sheet and some electrician's tape. Drilling a hole in the suitcase, Wagner scrutinized the wires and grabbed a small wire cutter. His hand remained steady as he inserted the cutters through the opening; he clipped both leads to the mercury switch.

"That should do it. Let's hope we didn't miss anything." He wiped the sweat from his hands.

The suitcase used its factory combination of 0-0-0. Andropov simultaneously pushed on both releasing mechanisms. The case clicked open. Wagner shined his Surefire flashlight inside to check for additional booby traps.

"Okay Svetlana, it's clear to open."

She set the case on its side and flipped open the lid. There in plain view laid the various bomb's components. They eyed the bomb's fusing systems, which included an alarm clock, a mercury switch, and a pressure switch. The alarm clock functioned as a safety fuse; it would only activate when the hour hand touched the screw drilled through the rear of the faceplate. The mercury switch served as an anti-disturbance device. It would detonate the device if someone attempted to open or move it. Finally, there was the pressure release switch. If someone lifted the suitcase, the switch would spring open, closing the circuit and detonating the device.

They both knew that the bomb could have only harmed someone handling it and that bothered the FSB agent. "What's the true purpose of this device," she asked rhetorically, glancing at the American agent.

Wagner ignored the question as he studied the evidence. He recognized ATF forensic experts could produce a fingerprint or some crucial DNA evidence. After taking numerous photographs from different angles, he broke down the components, bagging and labeling each piece separately.

Bagging the explosive, Wagner shook his head. "This explosive is odd. Look how the thickness varies with much it rolled out like pizza dough. This is strange."

"I'm glad you agree. Let me call Atwell. Doc...Doc, this is Pegasus."

"Doc by."

"Yeah Doc, we're clear here. Come on back."

"Good copy. I'll be there momentarily."

"Larson copies direct."

"Larson, could you get the cooks back into the kitchen?" Atwell directed the young agent.

"Copy that, Larson out."

The chefs resumed their cooking postures, but hastened their pace. Their lost ten minutes put them slightly behind schedule. They appeared to be frantically making up time through their meteoric, but frenzied pace. The head chef noticed two men lollygagging and motioned for them to resume their duties. They stepped to their stations and started chopping voluminous amounts of vegetables. Unfazed, they had acquired all of the information they needed. They would be receiving four-thousand dollars when they passed the information later in the day.

Atwell rushed through the kitchen door. "What did you guys come across?"

Wagner took the seven sealed evidence bags from his case and laid them on the counter. "Here are the bomb's components. It was an easy job. Everything went smoothly. The small quantity of explosive is puzzling. It just doesn't make sense."

"If I didn't know any better, I believe someone's testing us," Atwell voiced. "I've seen this behavior happen several times in Lebanon, where the terrorists tested our response procedures. We know this, because during the subsequent attack, they revised their plans to compensate for our presumed response."

Wagner's face tightened. "What the hell does it mean?"

Atwell shrugged. "Beats the heck out of me. I believe something bigger is coming. The only question I have is where and when."

Wagner stared down at the items; he took several minutes to organize and pack up the equipment. Given the evidence's crime scene value, packing it required a cautious approach. With the cases packed, Wagner walked out the door.

"Where's Matt?" Atwell snapped his head around.

"He must still be in the vent. He's probably napping." Wagner shrugged.

"Dutch, where's the Russian agent?"

"I don't know. She just disappeared."

Mumbling under his breath, James backtracked from a dead end of one of the duct's tentacles; he had one last path to check. Crawling backwards to the main junction, he heard someone approaching from behind. Looking over his shoulder, he took a double take at the approaching sight. Andropov wore only her black undergarments.

"You could've just waited for me at the end of the evening?" James winked. "I would've gladly shown you my bedroom and you'd be much more comfortable."

"That will happen only in your dreams." Her ears reddened. "I didn't want to rip my dress and it's hotter than hell up here."

His skin flushed. "True. I just have this one remaining track to check and then it's all clear." Crawling down the final duct, he peered briefly through a vent to gain his bearing over the ballroom. Immaculately dressed people laughed and talked business in small groups. Their pomposity filled the air as did the shine from their gold and diamond jewelry. His track propelled him toward the podium where the Pakistani foreign minister was scheduled to speak. His hand directed his flashlight down the duct; its beam illuminated a rectangular case. He knew it looked bad, but he crawled forward anyway. Approaching the case, he heard rhythmic ticking resembling a clock. He speculated the bomb's detonation would coincide with the foreign minister's speech in less than five minutes.

He peered over his shoulder at the Russian agent. "This case contains enough explosives to kill the Pakistani foreign minister and many in the room below. You have to backtrack and evacuate the building. Tell Atwell where I'm at and then get out of here."

"What about you? There's no room to work in here and insufficient time to deactivate the device." She looked at the case.

"Please, you have to go now. I'll take care of this. Trust me." He gave her a darting gaze.

Andropov retreated from the duct, dropped down into a storage room, and threw back on her dress. She sprinted to the ballroom holding a shoe in each hand. She glanced left and saw Atwell. Running to him, she alerted him about James' discovery. "George, we need to evacuate. Matt found a larger device in the vent." She bent over and put her shoes on.

"Let's move." Atwell pulled the fire alarm, assessing the need to get people out of the building. Protective details whisked away their dignitaries through side doors and other circuitous routes. The remainder of the crowd moved in an orderly fashion up a flight of stairs and then out through the lobby.

The blaring alarm interrupted James' concentration. He doubted they could evacuate the hotel given its full occupancy and the thousand plus people in it. The inability to evacuate the entire building made his decision easy to do the unthinkable. He waited another minute for the ballroom's evacuation and then dragged the case to the kitchen's intake vent.

Upon exiting the vent, he glanced down at his watch. Two minutes remained before the scheduled speech. Time seemed frozen as he watched the second hand tick down another minute. With time running out, he lifted the case from the vent and dashed out the back door. He held the case level to the ground and jogged down to the Chesapeake and Ohio Canal. Scanning the canal for its deepest and widest section, he tossed the case into the water. It sank a second later and detonated, sending a fireball skyward; its blast wave violently rattled the area and swept him off his feet.

Getting up off his back, he brushed a portion of mud off his shirt. Returning to the hotel, he radioed Atwell. "Doc...Doc, this is Hitman."

Atwell responded a second later. "Are you okay? Meet me at the front of the hotel."

James limped to the front of the hotel and met Atwell and Wagner. Police and fire personnel had cordoned off the area.

"What the hell were you thinking Matt with that bold, but very foolish stunt? You could've been killed." Atwell shook his head.

"There was no way to evacuate the entire building in time. I assumed the device that Wagner disarmed was merely a test; its multiple fusing systems were meant to assess our response procedures while distracting us." James took a deep breath.

"We concluded the same. But, how did you know the device in the vent wouldn't detonate if you moved it?" Atwell pushed his glasses up.

"I didn't, but it was a logical assumption." James interlocked his hands behind his head.

Andropov joined the small contingent of DS agents, stealing the spotlight. "Nice work guys. I see you took care of the second device. Now what?"

James touched her arm. "You look lovely in that dress, but I liked the other outfit better."

Wagner and Atwell glanced at one another, puzzled by James' comment. Neither Andropov nor James would clarify the remark, instead smiling at one another.

"As much as I'd like to stay and play with you boys, I've real work to do. I must take our ambassador to a dinner function." Andropov neglected to advise them she had an early flight in the morning. Her mission in America was about to take a new course. She would go hunting for a notorious Chechen who desired to kill millions of innocent citizens. The FSB agent knew that only she could stop him. She sauntered away, glancing back over her shoulder.

"Now that's a sight for weary eyes. Look at her strut. She's so hot." Atwell's eyes remained focused on her.

James closed his eyes to savor the image. "I won't argue with you there. Her body combines the muscular tone of an Olympic gymnast with the leanness of a super model. She's absolutely stunning."

"Easy Matt. She's Russian, not to mention the granddaughter of the former head of the KGB. You don't even want to go there." Atwell patted him on the shoulder. "They'll try to recruit you if they see a vulnerability."

James gave a half-shrug, recognizing their intelligence tactics. He relished the thought of being the victim of her honey trap. Andropov would get nothing from him other than a good time. He could resist her interrogation techniques and possibly even recruit her.

Atwell snapped his fingers in front of his face. "Are you okay Matt? You should have your head checked. The blast might've jarred it."

"No, I'm fine and just a little tired. I must've sweated ten pounds off in the vent's ducts." He wiped his forehead.

Wagner snorted. "Yeah, you smell like a wet dog."

Atwell escorted the two MSD agents back to the Suburban. "That was great work today. I'll see you later. I've got the first two rounds."

"We'll be there." Wagner's posture slumped. "Take care George."

"You too. Bye."

They hopped into the counterassault vehicle and sped away. James anticipated more calls in the near future, given a rise in terrorism. Their skills would be tested again shortly. This event marked only the beginning; the true test was yet to come.

# CHAPTER 31: INTERNAL DECEPTION

*Mexican-American Border*

The eerie darkness, dampness, and sewer stench churned his stomach; a unique sensory combination that revived distant yet vivid memories in the North Caucasus he tried to forget. His subconscious often repressed his battles and near-death experiences with a pursuing Russian army. Relying on guerrilla tactics, Rahman and his warriors often retreated to a labyrinth of tunnels and connecting caves. These irregular tactics increased as the war reached the town of Grozny. His anti-tank teams resurfaced and fought fiercely from basements, ground floors, and the second and third floor apartments. The destructive force of the heavily armored Russian T-72 and T-80 tanks presented a dangerous and formidable challenge. Their advanced weapon systems could instantly turn buildings into rubble while extinguishing countless lives within them.

Nevertheless, he knew that for every challenge, an opportunity waited. The Chechen leader organized his twenty men into roughly three and four man fighting cells. They simultaneously attacked the tanks with rocket-propelled grenades from multiple directions. The tenacious rebel leader destroyed more than twenty tanks in the first couple of months of the war. His teams fought against overwhelming forces with superior firepower and held their own using their ingenuity and determination. Rahman knew it would take this sort of resolve and resourcefulness to allow him to succeed once again. Only this time, he would fight a greater superpower and he would have to attack on foreign soil.

Rahman suddenly awoke from his flashback and shook his head. His eyes wandered in the tunnel's dim light, causing him to feel its sides to ensure his position; its damp surface chilled his fingertips. The meticulously chiseled passage cut through rock and compacted dirt; wooden support columns placed every five feet reinforced the structure. It would take years to excavate the lengthy passageway without mechanical tunneling equipment. He admired the cartels' patience, not for the riches they amassed, but for their ingenious smuggling operations. Fortitude and inventiveness are something they both shared. Drugs killed a person from inside out while his diabolical plan killed them from outside in. The fact that drugs killed more people than terrorism did little to persuade him against his plan's merits. He would change the phenomenon in one instant.

Stepping deeper into the tunnel, he now stood twenty feet beneath the road above. The cool breeze would have normally been a welcoming reprieve. However, it also brought a heady, one-year-old mold mixed with sewage back to life. Carefully stepping over a rail, Rahman dragged his feet along the tunnel's surface to ensure his footing. He sloshed sporadically through small puddles, remnants of a hearty rain that occurred the previous week. Hundreds of bats scurried about, awoken by the puddle trudging of ten men while skirting their unwelcome visitors.

The two Mexican guides kept a slow even pace. They received payment by the load and not by the hour; neither smuggler relished a lengthy prison sentence if caught. Five coffin-sized crates along with their eight new foreign acquaintances accompanied them into America. Not unlike the drug loads they often carried on their carts, the two Mexicans pondered the crates' contents. Their curiosity waned as they approached their exit point.

The irony amused Rahman as he slipped back into the country he recently had fled. His strict schedule precluded delays and his rendezvous with destiny rapidly approached. He had only one shot to execute his ambitious plan. His inside source cost him greatly but delivered time sensitive and critical intelligence. He persuaded the leaders of the Khorasan Group to accept his handpicked team for the landmark operation. The Chechen leader never failed in a mission.

"Why are we stopping?" Rahman tapped his guide's shoulder.

"I think someone's coming. Get down and be quiet. U.S. agents or Mexican police sometimes discover these tunnels and clear them." The guide raised his American-made M-16 assault rifle while his finger caressed its trigger.

Rahman hunched down, canting his ear toward the tunnel's exit. The wind whistled through the hollow. He drew his Russian-made pistol, determined to defend his cargo. He aimed forward; his finger rested on the trigger, ready to shoot first, and forego any questions. His heart remained steady, as time slowed.

After a minute, the guide rose from his crouched position. "Okay, it's clear. Let's move out."

"Who's waiting for us?" Rahman asked, as his head cocked to the side. He disliked surprises.

"We'll surface in a warehouse; three other men will load the merchandize onto an eighteen-wheeler. If you want, they can drive you to your destination." The Mexican leaned into the man with the facial scar.

Rahman shook his head. "That's not necessary. We have maps and GPS."

The ten-person group trudged toward the end of the tunnel; increasing light filtered in through the cave's exit. Rahman let out a huge breath. He had his fill of caves from the war, barely surviving a tunnel collapse orchestrated by Russian technicians. Besides, his emergence in America meant his plan's looming climax, something he had sought for years. He recognized that revenge required patience, proper timing, and precision.

Rahman climbed a small aluminum ladder through the floor's trap door; a Mexican guide extended his hand.

"Welcome to America amigo. It's the land of freedom and opportunity. Here you can do anything you want. So, what's your dream?"

"I'm here to even an old score. Soon it will be the dawning of a new world order and balance of power," Rahman said with a gleam in his eye.

The guide's prolonged laugh halted as he helped the other men out of the tunnel. He needed to return to Mexico in two hours to collect another payload. He preferred to smuggle during the daytime because its pedestrian and vehicular traffic masked his illicit underground activities. He corralled the foreigners out of the quaint office as they cleared the trap door.

"Now watch closely." The Mexican pushed a button concealed on a lamp. An entire wall pivoted open, exposing an office suite. Two of the guide's associates wheeled in a small crane to the five-by-five opening in the floor. They lowered two cables with sturdy steel hooks affixed to their ends.

The guide ushered the group into an adjacent room. "Please have a seat. I have some food and drinks coming for you while you wait. We'll have the trucks loaded in thirty minutes." He snapped his fingers as an adolescent Hispanic female entered the room carrying a plate of sandwiches. She dashed out and returned a minute later with an assortment of sodas, water, and fruit juice.

Rahman glanced at the young woman. "Thank you. We appreciate your hospitality after our long journey."

"You're welcome. Please let me know if you need anything else." She leaned away from the men.

Rahman left the group carrying his glass of orange juice and a half of a chicken salad sandwich. He joined the guide as he marshaled his workers to ensure the rapid transfer of the cargo. The guide's command presence impressed him. His workers raised and offloaded the crates onto the warehouse floor. A forklift driver then rammed his forks into the pallet and moved them into the truck.

"Do you know how much longer it will be until you're finished? I'd like to get on my way?" Rahman's eyes swept the area. He wanted to account for everyone at the facility.

"We're moving as fast as we can, so you should be ready in ten minutes." The guide looked up from his watch.

"Excellent, do you mind if I take a look around?" Rahman's eyes widened.

The guide shook his head. "Suit yourself. There's very little here, as this warehouse is nothing more than a front for our smuggling activities. We act as a small storage facility to explain the trucks coming and going."

"Doesn't that draw the police's attention? I bet they're suspicious around the border."

"The ratio of agents to smugglers is skewed in our favor. The border is so wide open and expansive; most available law enforcement resources are concentrated on the desert areas where human traffickers work. It's hard to believe that America doesn't secure its borders with better fences and more patrols; the drug violence overflows into its territory. I just read that Ciudad Juarez is one of the murder capitals of the world. So where's the greater threat to America?" The guide gave a slow, disbelieving shake of the head.

Rahman raised his chin. "It's all driven by politics, the Hispanic vote, and getting reelected. America has invested so much in enhancing their airport security. Yet, they leave both the Canadian and Mexican borders vulnerable. The American taxpayers should hold their politicians' accountable. Porous borders jeopardize their national security."

"It's fortunate for us. If America clamped down, it would be difficult to make a living. I provide a product that people are dying to have." The guide puffed-out his chest.

"Yes, you're a regular humanitarian. I suppose you don't traffic innocent people as well." Rahman tilted his head away exposing his downturned mouth.

"I don't traffic people as it's too risky. Once they're caught, they could give up my operation to the police. I've invested too much time and money to have it shutdown. Besides, drugs don't talk. So all you need is to surround yourself with a few reliable people and become rich. It's capitalism at its finest." The guide thrusted his shoulders back while his eyes glimmered.

Rahman considered the guide's deviation in his case. He enjoyed his political point of view. He glanced at his watch and realized his looming operational deadline. Walking to the truck's cargo doors, he examined the five intact crates strapped to its floor. He appreciated the extra warheads, but he only needed one to execute his plan. He would show the world true shock and awe, and he would use ingenuity instead of massive firepower.

"It looks good. You run a professional operation." Rahman scanned the room.

"Thanks, where's the money?" The guide rubbed his hands together.

"I understand." Rahman snapped his fingers and motioned his top lieutenant to approach. "I trust an electronic transfer of funds is suitable. I feared criminals traveling with all that cash." He crossed his arms.

"It all spends the same and it will save me time in the end." The smuggler closed his eyes and sighed.

Rahman's lieutenant placed his laptop computer on the bed of the truck, flipping up its lid. After inputting some data, he turned to Rahman and nodded. The Mexican slipped the financier a note with a routing number and bank information. Rahman's man hit a few key strokes and then had the Mexican review it. The man appreciated the million dollar figure.

"Everything looks great. Hit the send button and then we'll verify the transfer. Once that occurs, I'll give you the keys to the truck and we can go our separate ways," the guide said.

"Not so fast." Rahman signaled to his men who rounded up all the guide's workers at gunpoint.

"What kind of bullshit is this?" The Mexican gave a quick, disgusted snort. "We had a deal. I've done my part. I got you and your cargo safely into America as promised."

"You should've maintained your policy about dealing with drugs only. I can't have any witnesses." Rahman crossed his arms while taking a wide stance.

"We won't tell anyone. There's honor in my profession and you may need our network in the future." The man raised his hands skyward.

"I'm sorry. I can't take any chances. Besides, this trip is a one way mission." Rahman snapped his fingers.

His men pushed the four Mexicans to the floor. "You need to kneel." One of his men bounded their hands with plastic flex-cuffs, while the others stood behind the kneeling smugglers. Withdrawing their silenced pistols, they simultaneously racked the slides back and let them slam forward. Rahman flicked his wrist. Four muffled shots sliced through their heads; the smugglers slumped forward and then fell to the ground.

The guide's face contorted. "What about me?"

The Chechen leader's eyes appeared flat. "You've done your part. Now finish the job. Open the trap door and dispose of the bodies in the tunnel. Dump them on the Mexican side of the border, so it looks like just another gang killing."

The guide dragged his limp colleagues one by one and dumped them into the tunnel's entrance; each body thumped as it hit the compacted dirt floor. His preoccupation with his orders caused him to miss the financier canceling the electronic transfer on the laptop.

"Okay, close the hatch." Rahman typed a text message. The man bent over to grab the door; Rahman drew his pistol and shot him in the back, causing him to fall forward into the tunnel. "What a dumb ass." He shook his head.

A feminine gasp stirred the air. Rahman turned to his right; the Hispanic girl vaulted from under a desk and fled toward the back door. He leveled his pistol and fired three shots. The rounds sliced through her upper torso as she skirted through the door into a side ally.

"Do you want us to finish the job?" Rahman's men looked at him.

"We don't have time. Let's get out of here in case someone calls the police." Rahman walked over to the hatch and pushed the door forward as it slammed to the floor. Walking over to the lamp, he depressed a button and watched the room revert to an office area.

"Let's go. Our important work is ahead of us. You six jump in the truck to protect the merchandize." He signaled to his lieutenant to jump into the driver's seat and start the truck's powerful diesel engine. Rahman strolled over to the wall and depressed a button to the garage bay door. It opened as its rollers and automatic opener did their work. The driver waited for the metallic door to open fully. He then put the gear selector into first and drove from the warehouse. Upon clearing the door, Rahman pushed the button again and the door descended to the asphalt pavement. He stepped out and walked over to the truck's passenger door to climb up into the compartment.

"You ready?" Rahman sighed. "That went like expected." He considered his duplicity. He relished killing his Russian enemies, but disliked killing those that meant him no harm. Yet, his sudden remorse over killing the smugglers troubled him. His conscience after all these years finally resurfaced. He brushed the thought aside. He knew Allah would understand it as part of the greater good. At least he hoped so.

"Are you alright?"

Rahman glanced at his top associate and friend. "This is a great day."

"Absolutely, let's get to our next destination."

The Chechen mastermind closed his eyes as the truck rolled out of the parking lot. The driver had already programmed the GPS system for its next location. It would take a few hours and then they would prep for the next phase of their mission. If all went well, they would be national heroes in just days.

# CHAPTER 32: BREAK TO THE HUNT

*Nogales, Arizona*

Piercing through the stratus clouds, a sleek Gulfstream G150 twin engine jet descended upon Nogales International Airport. Its four passengers understood that the prime minister ordered this risky rendition. The Chechen threatened the prime minister's standing and Russia's national security as long as he remained at large. Their FSB bosses reminded them about the costs of failure. Russian leaders ruled and motivated by coercion since the days of Lenin. The four Russian operatives all knew the Kremlin's involvement reflected their mission's importance. None of them wanted to bear the prime minister's wrath for a botched operation, nor spend a long vacation in a Siberian gulag.

Seated at a small rectangular table, the agents finished their box lunches while discussing their mission's specifics. They concentrated on the latest human and signals intelligence. Andropov welcomed her new team leader role, except for her conflicting mission. She wrestled with her incompatible directives from FSB headquarters and Chirtoff. Having three other team members – or witnesses – to report on the operation compounded her underlying orders; she pondered just killing the Chechen and claiming self-defense. The female agent walked a tightrope that required her brains and ingenuity to succeed. She needed to delicately balance the risks and the consequences of her team's actions. The success of her mission relied on teamwork; Yuri's assignment to the mission guaranteed their success.

Opening two black Pelican hard plastic cases, the team examined their choices of non-lethal weapons. They reviewed their options of electro-shock and chemical weapons.

Yuri picked up a taser gun and pointed it at his comrade. "They shot me with this in training, which caused temporary paralysis as fifty-thousand volts surged through my body. I tried to fight it, but because it made my muscles contract, I couldn't fight back. This weapon is what I'll use. I look forward to electrifying the Chechen scum."

Andropov shook her head. "Don't you have to be within twenty feet of your target to use it? Rahman won't let you get close to him. He'll be shooting at you while you're trying to get him to throw his hands up."

"We all have our orders. I can sneak up close enough to him to get a clean shot. I'm very skilled at the art of camouflage and stealth as a former Spetsnaz sniper. Russia spent a great deal of time and money on me to develop these important survival skills."

"I certainly hope so. Our orders don't mention anything about taking Rahman's associates alive. Let's see what else is useful in these cases." She rummaged through the case. "I hope we have something more reliable from a distance."

Andropov picked up a pepper spray canister and set it aside. Its oleoresin capsicum-based component could bring down the biggest and fiercest of men. However, it also had a limited effect on a small portion of the populace. She studied the three-methylfentanyl gas grenade pondering its use, recalling the 2002 Moscow theater hostage report; many innocents died, some reportedly by the gas itself. She set aside a sleep grenade, tranquilizer gun, and a pistol with plenty of rubber bullets. She questioned the opportunity to use any of them. Rahman would never surrender. Unless they could take him by surprise, she anticipated a gunfight and savored the prospect.

"Remember, we won't take any extra chances to accomplish our mission. If any of you are in imminent danger, then shoot to kill. We're all going back to our families after this mission." Andropov eyed her comrades.

The FSB team grabbed their weapons, gear and suitcases as the plane touched down at Nogales International Airport. They anticipated a short visit. They would take the captured Chechen rebel back to Moscow for interrogation when they completed their mission. This prospect motivated the team. They all welcomed returning home with the exception of Andropov who liked western culture and living. She planned to request a transfer to their Russian Embassy in Washington, DC, provided her mission succeeded.

Upon exiting the plane, the four FSB agents met the Southwest's sweltering heat as a gust of searing wind made its introduction. They walked down the steps and marched to a bald stout man standing next to two cars. The man handed her a folder with two pages of signal's intelligence. Andropov glanced at the report before conducting her briefing.

"Yuri and I will ride in the sedan. You two follow us in the SUV. Our intelligence indicates that Rahman crossed in this grid." She pointed to a map sprawled out on the hood of the sedan. "Don't be discouraged by a six block area. We can cover the ground in hours once we get there. Let's go." She motioned them to the cars.

The two vehicles departed the tarmac, making their way out a side gate used for private charter passengers. Yuri inputted their destination and activated the car's GPS system. With light traffic, he anticipated making the twelve-mile journey to their target in twenty-five minutes. They both remained silent and hoped for Rahman's detention without incident. Rolling down I-82 at sixty miles per hour, Yuri flipped a switch to the car's police scanner. They listened closely to an ongoing nearby sweep at the Mexican-American border. They looked at one another and contemplated Rahman's fate.

The leisurely drive entailed a straight shot to their destination with only several turns at the trip's end. Pulling down a side street, the traffic decreased as it transformed into a mixed residential and industrial area. They sensed the Chechen's presence as an eerie silence overtook them. Fortunately, the search for some human traffickers occupied the police in an adjoining neighborhood. This permitted her team the opportunity to inconspicuously search for the Chechen rebel.

"Let's pull over next to that restaurant and walk on foot." She pointed.

"What are we looking for? This search will be like finding a needle in a haystack." Yuri's eyebrows furrowed and then released.

"He'll need a truck to move his merchandise. Let's ask the shopkeepers if they've seen a truck leaving the area. Perhaps we could get lucky and lead us back to its origination point." She exhaled while her eyes looked up.

"That's brilliant Svetlana. Let's hope they feel like talking. Perhaps a little bit of cash could stir their memories."

Andropov directed her other team members to conduct a grid search of the adjacent block. The SUV sped off, disappearing around the corner seconds later. She walked into a small family-owned grocery store to buy a bottle of orange juice. Handing a five-dollar bill to the cashier, she inquired about the traffic. The man provided little other than her proper change. She anticipated a long day unless luck intervened. Moving to the next location, Andropov discovered a family-run bakery and sauntered into it; aromas melding fresh bagels with an assortment of sweet fudge and chocolate cakes bombarded her olfactory senses.

The head baker approached the blonde woman. "What can I get such a beautiful lady?"

"I'd like a bagel with cream cheese and a dozen of your assorted doughnuts." She beamed.

"Our bagels are the best in the region. I brought my secret recipe with me when I moved from New York about fifteen years ago."

"I thought I detected an east coast accent. How do you like the weather and pace? It must be quite different." She handed him a twenty-dollar bill.

"My family loves it. We sold our house in New York for a healthy profit. I bought a brand new house here and financed this bakery."

"It sounds like you're doing well. I see it's a very quiet area for business. I don't even see many truckers in the area." The Russian's eyes sparkled.

The veteran baker pointed southwest. "Although it has been quiet today, many trucks come from that direction, oftentimes bringing their business my way. Come to think of it, I've only seen one depart this morning."

"I need to get some things shipped. Can you tell me exactly where the truck came from? I'll see if they can ship some personal effects." She licked her lip with cautious hope.

The man rubbed his chin. "I believe it came from that small warehouse across the street. I wasn't paying too close attention.

"I must be on my way. Thanks for the delicious bagel. I'll see you later." She strolled out the door.

She met Yuri outside their car and handed him the box of doughnuts. "Save some for the other guys."

"I'll save them one or two. We cops like our doughnuts. It's the breakfast of champions. You forgot my coffee?" He gave a dismissive glance.

"Get it yourself." You have two legs and money." She bit her lip.

After waiting a minute for Yuri to get his black coffee, they drove the block to the warehouse. The two crept to the front door; a dog's sporadic barking from the back interrupted the warehouse's unnerving quietness. Yuri twisted the doorknob, but the handle remained frozen. Peering through the window, they observed a sparsely furnished, vacated facility. They scuttled to the side ally and discovered a door ajar. Yuri stepped in front of Andropov, drew his pistol and nudged the door open. His eyes followed a trail of red droplets past a double oven, sink, and refrigerator to another internal door.

Andropov drew her pistol and shadowed Yuri to the door. She tapped his shoulder. "Go."

Yuri scanned right to left as he moved through the door; the large thirty-foot high structure supported two garage bay doors. Its emptiness in the middle of a workday puzzled them. They trotted across the room and then checked two other adjoining office spaces. The two agents looked at one another upon clearing the last room.

She shrugged. "There's nothing here. We should try another location in this neighborhood."

"What's this place? It looks like it's hardly used." Yuri panned the area.

Retracing their steps, Andropov glanced down at a half-full plate of chicken sandwiches and empty glasses. She lifted a sandwich to her nose. "Someone's been here recently. These sandwiches aren't more than an hour old. The lettuce is still crisp." She returned the sandwich to its tray.

"Yeah, they're gone now. We don't even know if it was Rahman or the owners of this dump." His eyebrows squeezed together.

"You're right Yuri. Let's get out of here."

The two agents barreled through the kitchen and out the back door. A faint moan from a side ally captured their attention. They combed the area and encountered a young Hispanic woman sitting upright against a dumpster; blood trickled from her shoulder.

Andropov kneeled beside her. "How bad are you hurt? We need to get you to a hospital."

"Please don't call an ambulance or the police. I'm here in your country illegally. They'll send me back to Mexico and I don't want to go back there. There's too much violence, corruption, and poverty."

Yuri glanced at Andropov. "We don't have time for this. We must carry out our mission."

"I just can't turn my back. Yuri, please run to the car and get our medical kit. I'll take care of this wound the best I can with my medical training."

Yuri trotted off and returned to their side minutes later with a black nylon medical bag.

"What's your name?" Andropov cut away a portion of the woman's shirt to expose her upper shoulder.

"My name is Patricia, Patricia Calderon."

The female agent examined the front and back of the shoulder. "Well Patricia, it was a clean shot that went through you. The bleeding is subsiding. I'll need to stitch it up and give you a shot to counter a possible infection."

After about ten minutes, Andropov finished her bandaging. She glanced at the young woman and then brooded. Walking to her car, she removed a shirt from her suitcase and handed it to the shaken woman.

"Thank you. You're very kind." The Mexican teared up.

"What happened to you?" She helped the youth get her wounded arm into the shirt.

The woman sighed, pointing. "I work in the warehouse across the street."

"You mean the one we just left." Andropov's eyes widened.

"Yes. Eight Middle Eastern men arrived this morning from Mexico, along with five crates. The leader killed everyone there and then shot me. They left in a truck a little over an hour ago. I thought I heard them say to Santa Fe."

"I take it you mean Santa Fe, New Mexico." Andropov touched her forearm.

"That's the only Santa Fe I know of in this area. They were driving a large truck that was loaded with their crates." The girl winced as she pulled the shirt over her head.

"You've been extremely helpful. Now you need to go home and get some rest. Have a doctor look at your wound as soon as possible to avoid infection. Now go." She helped the girl to her feet.

"There's one last thing. If you want to see the tunnel, you'll need to activate a concealed switch hidden on the lamp next to the office." The girl turned and trudged away.

"Yuri, assemble the others. I want to search the warehouse again for clues. And bring the Geiger counter from the car." She pointed to the trunk. "We need to see if there are any trace remnants of the nuclear weapons."

Watching Yuri disappear around the corner, she walked back into the warehouse and entered through the kitchen door. She arrived at the office to survey the room. There was only one lamp as most of the light came from the florescent lightbulbs above. Bypassing the lamp's switch, Andropov slid her hand up the lamppost and felt a small circular protrusion. She depressed the button and shuffled backward as the wall opened up. A desk moved to expose a five-by-five foot trap door in the floor. Yuri and his two other FSB associates entered the warehouse; their eyes widened by the abrupt transformation.

"Now that's what I call an open air design." Yuri gasped.

"It's amazing how far these traffickers will go to smuggle their drugs. If they used that much energy in a legitimate business, they could rival the rich." Andropov bemoaned. "Yuri, check the door."

Yuri walked over to the trap door and lifted its handle. Raising the door, he saw a stack of fresh bodies piled at its base. "I see Rahman's been here."

Andropov and her two other teammates walked over to peer down into the tunnel. She found it odd to be chasing the infamous Chechen rebel in America. He left a trail of death wherever he went.

"It won't be too hard to track him. You just need to follow the bodies. Yuri, scan the area with the Geiger counter. Let's see if there are sufficient trace levels to verify he has the nuclear weapons with him." Her eyes glowed.

Yuri lifted the small-enclosed case from the ground with his left hand. He held the detector with his right hand. Turning on its power, the device instantly chirped at the low levels of ionizing radiation. He glanced down at the Giger counter's needle; it jumped and vacillated at a heightened level, reflecting the recent transiting of nuclear material.

Andropov shook her head. "That's all the proof we need. Let's intercept Rahman in Santa Fe before it's too late."

The four strolled away from the area. They recognized the high stakes and hoped they could capture the illustrious rebel before he executed his plan. Otherwise, the Chechen would leave an even greater trail of casualties.

# CHAPTER 33: PASSPORT TRAIL

*Santa Fe, New Mexico*

Walking down a row of cars, James glanced over his shoulder as he shook out his hands; an empty feeling in the pit of his stomach radiated into his chest. He contemplated his sanity in pursuing the world's most dangerous terrorist without backup. Rahman's possession of the most destructive weapon on the planet exacerbated the situation. His rudimentary knowledge of nuclear weapons troubled him. Russian-made thermonuclear warheads contained an explosive power greater than three-hundred thousand tons of TNT. He understood the fundamentals of the process; plutonium compression with a chemical explosive triggers a fission explosion that is boosted by the fusion of DT-gas. X-rays then compress the second component, causing a larger fission/fusion. This precise science resulted in a mushroom cloud that would annihilate a population and the surrounding structures. The consequences of an explosion in a densely populated area would be horrendous.

James had to act quickly. Everyone and everything within five miles of the hypocenter would be destroyed from the blast and its thermal effects. With roughly one-hundred thousand people, Santa Fe's population paled in comparison to Washington, DC or Los Angeles. He speculated the Chechen chose the city for its remoteness and its low level of protection. He pondered the terrorist's plans for the four other nukes. Perhaps Rahman intended to threaten the president or to terrorize the populace. He detested the message as he contemplated the sudden importance of a simple passport case. His fingers spread out into a fan over his breastbone as his skin tingled.

The MSD agent hopped into a dark blue sedan and drove out of the airport terminal. He reviewed the addresses that he had preprogrammed into the vehicle's GPS. His index finger tapped the selection bar to a post office box located near the center of town. After a twenty-five minute leisurely drive, he parked in the lot of Jose's Mexican Kitchen. His eyes twinkled at the restaurant's visibility of his target. After eating lunch, he paid his bill and then removed two passport photos from an eight-by-twelve brown envelope. Bypassing his car, the dogged agent ambled across the lot and opened the front door of Mail Express. Its emptiness delighted him.

Walking through the front door, a smiling face greeted him. "Can I help you?"

"I hope so. I'm Special Agent Matt James with the Diplomatic Security Service." He raised his credentials and then displayed his gold badge with a flip of his wrist.

The owner's eyes widened as he read the credentials. His eyes studied the photo and then matched it with the agent standing in front of him. "That's you, but what's the Diplomatic Security Service?"

"DSS is the law enforcement and security arm of the U.S. Department of State." He hooked his thumbs into his belt loops.

The man gave a crisp nod. "What can I do for you?"

The agent reached into his front jacket and pulled out two photographs. "Do you recognize either of these men?" He placed the first picture down on the counter next to the cash register.

The man picked up the photograph. "I don't know him, and I recognize all of my clients. This is a small city."

James scratched his elbow and placed the next photo on the counter. "What about this man?"

The man raised the photo, reseating his glasses on his nose. "Yes, I've seen this guy. He was here about a week ago. His English was poor. He asked about a storage facility near here and retrieved a small package."

"What can you tell me about him and his activities?"

The man shrugged. "Not much. He has only been here a couple times, checks his mail, and departs immediately."

"I need you to focus. It's a matter of national security. Is there anything else you can remember about him that could help me find him?" The DS agent jittered his foot against the floor while checking his watch.

The man cocked his head to the left. "You know, he's always driven here by another foreigner who waits for him with the car running. I thought they were going to rob me at first."

"That's good. Can you tell me anything more about the vehicle?"

"What did these guys do?" The shop owner's nose wrinkled as he caressed his chin.

"I'm not at liberty to say, but they're a threat to our country. They're considered armed and dangerous. Here's my business card. If you see them again, call me as soon as it's safe to do so."

"No problem." The man clapped once. "What about their car? Don't you want to know what they were driving?"

"Absolutely." The DS agent's eyes glowed.

"It's a green four-door sedan, either 2010 or 2011."

"That's excellent and very useful."

"And I can do one better than that. He's pulling in now. Are you going to arrest them?" The man's eyes squinted before blinking repeatedly.

"I can't yet. I need more information. I'm going to walk out the door, but I'll be watching from the restaurant. You won't be in any danger. Just act normal and stall them. Any questions?"

Striding out the door, James' eyes darted away from the sedan's occupants as he ignored the owner's query. He strolled across the sparsely filled parking lot to arrive at his car a minute later. Lifting the trunk, he removed a small black nylon backpack. He closed the trunk and walked to the driver's car door, which shielded him from his target. Opening the door, he placed his bag on the ground, unzipped the top, and removed a miniature drone; it resembled a hummingbird on steroids with blue and white color tones.

He launched his drone into the sky and started his vehicle as his suspects exited the parking lot. Sitting behind the steering wheel, he pushed one of his laptop's hot keys to activate the drone's camera. He maneuvered the hummingbird skyward to about one-hundred feet and tailed the two terrorists east on Cordova Street. He followed them for another quarter of a mile before they turned right onto Luisa Street. Their use of backstreets suited him given the drone's distance and speed limitations. After heading south on Luisa for three blocks, the terrorists turned right onto Columbia

Street. Approaching an underpass, he piloted the drone upward to two-hundred feet, narrowly missing the concrete highway structure.

Losing the car, the resolute agent drifted the bird over the expressway and focused on the other side. Seconds later, the green sedan emerged, so he resumed tailing them. After two blocks, the terrorists came to a T intersection and turned left. James rolled his finger back on the mouse; the drone descended to eighty feet and trailed the vehicle for another block. It turned right into a storage facility. Hovering, the drone relayed the video back to the agent; it showed the two driving to the back of the facility and parking. They exited their vehicle and walked to a nearby unit and disappeared through its door. James twitched his finger on the mouse; the hummingbird swooped in. The video displayed a closed door. He glanced down at the drone's computer interface; its low battery indicator light blinked continuously. Recalling the drone, it landed next to his car only minutes later. He grabbed the miniature bird and placed it back into its protective hard case within the backpack.

The determined agent jumped into his car and retraced the terrorist's route in five minutes. He arrived across the street from the storage facility and parked behind a building. This vantage point allowed him to discreetly observe the mixed industrial and residential neighborhood. Replacing the hummingbird's battery with a fresh one, he readied it for flight.

Launching the bird, his sharp fiery eyes scrutinized his laptop monitor; he steered the bird around a corner, across a field of uncut grass, and over the storage facility. Hovering the drone above the area, he counted four cars, one being the green sedan. He zoomed the drone's camera down and discovered a series of skylights that peppered the roof. Descending to five feet above the roofline, he let the aerial acrobatics of the bird do the rest. One by one, he floated the bird over each skylight, pausing briefly to view the room below. The agent's eyebrows rose as a sudden gust of wind barely jarred the drone; its seven inch wingspan and height remained steady in the sky.

After checking eight different rooms, James hovered the bird above the ninth one. Two persons sat in a pair of recliners and watched a movie on a laptop computer. His hand tapped a key six times to zoom in on a workbench area supporting many tools. He slid the contrast bar to the right to enhance the image; blasting caps, C-4 explosives, remote controls, and soldering equipment appeared on his screen. Assault rifles, pistols, grenade launchers, machine pistols, and silenced weapons littered the corner. Maps and photographs lined the container's wall. He descended the drone until its feet brushed the skylight. A dirt film and an acute angle to the photos obscured his view. He now possessed sufficient evidence to alert the national security advisor and request reinforcements.

James picked up his phone; a truck's revving diverted his attention. Grabbing his binoculars, he examined the driver and front passenger. Spinning the focus dial, a man bearing a nasty scar along his cheekbone appeared in his viewer. His cold-blooded stare caused a vein in the agent's temple to bulge.

The truck pulled around back and stopped next to the green sedan. His binoculars swung to the truck's back door. Six Middle Eastern-looking men wielding assault rifles sprang from its compartment. The men scurried to several cars and stood behind their engine blocks, facing out to the perimeter. A forklift rounded the building's corner and approached the truck's rear cargo doors while raising its forks. The men removed one palletized item off the truck and into the storage room. The forklift operator set the pallet down in the center of the room. He then reversed out and drove back to the truck to offload a second crate. The driver placed it in the adjacent storage room.

James observed another vehicle pull into the back and park next to the green sedan. Two Arab males exited the vehicle and shuffled over to the Chechen leader. Rahman hugged them and then handed them a small envelope. He called out instructions before the two boarded the truck. The engine roared a second later as the eighteen-wheeler moved around the facility and exited out the front. James lost sight of it a minute later.

Panning the parking lot, the tenacious agent counted ten armed men in possession of two nuclear weapons. He picked up his phone and dialed the private number of the National Security Advisor; the phone immediately bounced to voicemail. He hung up without leaving a message given the sensitivity of the information.

Instead, James typed a message: *"Merchandize and main character plus eleven arrived in Santa Fe. Three pieces of merchandize continued on its journey in a truck; its destination unknown. Two items remain in Santa Fe. Send reinforcements at once."*

The DS agent reread the message and depressed the send button. He knew the NSA could read between the lines. He only hoped it would be in time.

James clenched his jaw and sat idly, realizing the dangers of intervention given their numbers and weaponry. He looked down at the small drone. Changing its batteries, he glanced up as two more vehicles arrived at the facility and parked in front. He focused his binoculars on the unknown Caucasians in an SUV and then transitioned them to a sedan. His eyes widened. Tracing the Chechen leader's location, Andropov had no idea of his tactical advantage. He needed to warn her.

His index finger flipped a switch on the hummingbird; its wings flapped sixty times a second as it lifted off and streaked toward the Russian FSB agent. Andropov led three others toward the rear of the facility with their silenced submachine guns drawn. Anticipating a bloodbath, he joggled the drone up and over the roof to watch the operation. He touched his St. Christopher medal and hoped for the Russian's success against all odds. Peering through his binoculars, her team split into two; one approached from the north and the other from the south.

Andropov approached the building's back corner cautiously and remained concealed behind its brick wall. She peeked around it to see Rahman's men while waiting for her other team to reach their position. She clicked her radio once and her second team acknowledged with two clicks. The four Russian agents broke cover and moved toward the Chechen rebels. Muffled shots stirred the air as the Russians downed three terrorists in seconds. The remainder sprinted behind several cars and a forklift; they returned fire, spraying the general area. Rounds tore through metal doors and ricocheted off the concrete. With the element of surprise gone and the Chechen terrorists barricaded and concealed, she halted her assault. The female leader contemplated her dwindling options to thwart a nuclear attack. She feared that Washington might interpret an attack on American soil as a Russian first strike; Rahman's training and past connections to her government made it a distinct possibility.

James gritted his teeth as the female FSB agent darted forward. His stomach churned as one of her colleagues dropped lifeless to the ground. He gripped his car door's handle and then released it. The terrorists scrambled into a tight line formation to counter the assault; another one snuck around back and climbed to the rooftop. His drone shadowed the man on the roof as he crept into position. The man centered his rifle's scope on Andropov's head while resting his finger on its trigger. James dove his drone at the man; its beak struck his neck and knocked him off balance. The man staggered off the roof and plunged to the pavement with a dull thud; blood oozed from his head. Andropov glanced at the fallen man as her grimace morphed to a thin smile. Three against six odds still favored the Chechen, but at least she had a fighting chance.

The drone rested lifeless on the warehouse's roof. James needed to act forcibly to assist his Russian counterpart. He pressed his pistol's slide a quarter inch to the rear; the light silvery yellow hollow point round laid properly seated within its chamber. Holstering his pistol, he then turned the key in the ignition and slammed the gear selector into drive. He floored the accelerator, sped to the storage facility, and raced around the corner to the rear. Screeching around the final corner, rounds peppered his car as its windshield exploded. James steered toward the closest Chechen as rounds whizzed by his head. He opened the passenger door and leapt out as the car slammed into one of Rahman's warriors. Tumbling side to side, he crawled behind a wheel well of a nearby vehicle. He muttered, "That was fun. I'm glad I purchased the vehicle insurance."

James' eyes scanned the area. Bodies littered the ground, including Andropov's men and seven terrorists. Andropov, Rahman, and two other terrorists remained at large. Kneeling behind the car, he aimed his pistol at the opened storage door. His eyes spotted the nuclear weapon in the background, but nothing more. Rahman abruptly stepped out from the doorjamb, clutching the female agent by the back of her hair; the barrel of his pistol snuggly planted in her temple.

"Don't move or I'll kill her and detonate the nuke," Rahman barked.

James glanced left and right; his gun's sights aligned squarely on Rahman's head. "Perhaps I'll pull the trigger and see what happens." His eyes pierced the Chechen's eyes.

"You wouldn't dare. You can't risk me detonating the nuke and killing thousands of people. Now I'm only going to tell you this once more. Drop your weapon and come out. I won't kill you, at least not yet." Rahman smirked.

James lowered his weapon, squatted, and sat it on the pavement before standing again. "Now what?"

"I'm going to interrogate you. After I find out what you know about my operation, I'll leave you to gather your thoughts." Rahman offered a bemused smile.

The agent's peripheral vision captured Andropov's partner reaching for his taser weapon to unleash its voltage on the Chechen. Rahman clutched Andropov's throat, aimed at Yuri, and pulled the trigger. The round struck the shoulder of the once invincible Spetsnaz sniper. His finger wilted.

"You bastard." Her shoulders sagged. "You'll pay for that."

"My dear, you have so much anger. Actually, you'll pay for your ill-timed assault." Rahman pushed the female agent to his two associates. "Tie her up nice and tight. I don't want her to escape." Rahman flicked his wrist.

"Do you think you can get away with your plan?" James raised his hands skyward.

Rahman's eyes narrowed. "What exactly do you think I'm doing here?"

"You and your al-Qaeda cronies are here to terrorize America, releasing nuclear weapons on millions of innocent people." James stepped toward the Chechen.

"That's indeed the Khorasan Group's plan, but I'm Chechen and I fight for my country. Now shut up and walk toward the storage container. Let me show you the great equalizer. America's creation has proliferated. It will now be used against the mighty country that fashioned it. Ironic, isn't it?" Rahman rocked back on his heels.

"There's nothing ironic about mass murder." The DS agent walked toward the storage area.

"Tie him up." The Chechen stroked his chin. They grabbed James by his arms and escorted him to a metal chair opposite of Andropov. A nuclear weapon rested between them.

James eyed the FSB agent as he was tied to the chair. "Fancy meeting you here Svetlana. I looked forward to seeing you again. Can't say I like the conditions."

"That's sweet." Rahman snickered. "As much as I'd like to stick around and watch you two meld together, I've a plane to catch. I must personally take care of business."

Rahman strolled over to the warhead, inserted a key, and set the timer for sixty minutes. "That should give me plenty of time to escape the blast zone. Try not to have too much fun." He sneered as he tugged on the ropes binding the two agents.

"Come along men. We need to close the door and activate the motion-sensor bombs. This action will prevent anyone from entering until it's too late."

The American and Russian looked at one another. They listened to Rahman and his associates scurry about in the adjacent room, gathering myriad items. Screeching tires drew their attention outside. Listening to the sound of its sliding door, James speculated a van. The American agent crumpled his nose regarding Rahman's casualness as the nuke ticked down to Armageddon. He suspected something bigger in play. With time running out, he rubbed the ropes up and down on the chair's smooth aluminum frame.

"I'm sorry about your team Svetlana."

Andropov glanced down. "Yuri was a great agent and a dear friend. We wouldn't be in this predicament had we killed Rahman in Chechnya."

"You can't blame yourself. It's all Rahman's fault. Now let's just think of how we can break free and deactivate this nuke." He exhaled.

James heard the forks of the lift clinging as it drove into the neighboring storage unit. "They're moving the other nuke. We need to stop them before more people die."

They both paused to listen as the metallic door slammed to the ground. The two agents heard three car doors shut and then the sound of the engine faded. Andropov remained silent; her concentration intensified. Moments later, she broke the rope binding her hands and reached down to untie her feet.

"How'd you do that?" He jerked his head back.

"I used my ring which has a sharp corner on it. Now let's get you untied so we can deactivate this weapon." She examined the knots binding his wrists.

After a minute, she freed the ropes from her American counterpart. They remained stuck with the bomb as the booby traps precluded exiting. The two agents pondered their options as they watched the nuke's timer edge down to nineteen minutes.

# CHAPTER 34: UNIFIED EFFORT

*Santa Fe, New Mexico*

James' eyes panned the room before staring at the nuclear device. Sweat pooled on his forehead as he fought off a bout of sudden dizziness.

"Svetlana, as you can see we only have about eighteen minutes to disarm this device. Rahman claimed he could command-activate the warhead. We must assume the warhead is booby-trapped."

"That's correct." She fiddled with her watch. "Don't trust anything the Chechen bastard said. His word means nothing."

"Good point! What do you suggest?" His eyes met hers.

"Can we circumvent the motion-activated booby-traps to allow a military team to disarm the bomb?"

"I wish we could." The DS agent sighed. "The roof's skylight is the only way to penetrate the facility; it's time consuming and it looks like Rahman's booby-trapped it. Besides, there's no way a team could get here in time."

"We're on our own Matt. We have to disarm it. Lucky for you, I'm an experienced bomb technician."

"Great, knock yourself out." He glanced at her and rubbed his hands. A mushroom cloud and its destruction supplanted his thoughts. He brushed it aside.

"Matt, are you ready?" She grabbed his hand. "You're familiar with the concept of a firing train."

"Sure." James gave a slight head shake, not quite sure of her angle.

"Think of the nuclear device on different terms. The container is the outer skin of the warhead. The main charge is the nuclear material, plutonium 239, uranium 238 or 235. The booster will be some form of high explosive. The detonator is electric in nature, and the fuse is undetermined. We know it will function by time delay and may be command activated. It may also employ victim activated traps, such as pressure release or trembler switches." The female agent looked up from the device.

"Now I feel better." His eyes widened. "What else?"

"Let's simplify the process. There's a three-step firing train. The initiator or its equivalent sets off a high explosive, in this case, well, it's not important. Anyhow, we must interrupt the fusing system – the clock and whatever else. Let's analyze the control panel. The digital read-out indicates it will activate upon a zero countdown. We need to access the panel to kill the power source. I'd assume the fusing system is wired as a complete parallel circuit." She winked, giving him a casual nod.

"I get the point." He glanced at the clock; it read fourteen minutes and seven seconds.

Their pace quickened. The unlikely partners first analyzed the underside of the control panel. They saw nothing to indicate the device employed a pressure release switch. The Russian agent broke out a metallic pen containing sulfuric acid from her shirt pocket; she applied it to the upper right corner of the panel box. It fizzled upon contact, creating a small opening. He reached into his pocket and pulled out a mini-Maglite flashlight. He affixed a six-inch long fiber optic tube to it and directed its light into the box. Using his telescoping dental mirror, he observed the inside of the box.

The multi-colored wires tangled around the electrical components complicated the device's deactivation. James followed the wires from the digital clock, looking for any deviation or addition to the fusing system. The DS agent hoped for no breaks in the circuit. He glanced at the clock showing twelve minutes and twenty seconds.

Approaching the main power source, he recognized a familiar switch. "Svetlana, we have a problem." His chin sank.

Her eyebrows crumpled. "What is it?"

The American scratched his forehead with his right index finger. "There's a collapsing circuit mechanism." Sweat dripped from his forehead as images of his colleague's death in Beirut surfaced. His vision blurred.

"Go on." Her right eye arched. She sensed the American knew more about bombs than he admitted. His ability to distinguish different types of electronic switches impressed her.

"I see a secondary power source. The main power source maintains the switch or relay in the open position. The other meanders off. I can't follow it, but I imagine it runs to the detonator. By cutting power anywhere on the parallel circuit, this collapsing mechanism will reroute power to detonate the device. Is that correct?" He masked his trembling hand behind the device while blinking and squeezing his eyes shut.

"By breaking the circuit which maintains the firing relay open, it permits the open relay to close. This allows power to flow from the secondary power source to the detonator. The only way to disarm this device is to kill both fusing systems at exactly the same time." Her hand wiped across her face.

"This is a tricky and nearly an impossible procedure." His face cringed as his hazy vision subsided.

Tension permeated the room. He glanced at the Russian with a solemn look. "If we can't disarm it, can you pass through the motion sensor to explode the booby traps? The ensuing explosion may interrupt the fusing system and ensure that the nuclear device doesn't detonate."

"I seriously doubt that would work, but I can do it no problem."

He pressed his hand to his temple. "This isn't good."

"Don't give up on me now Matt. I know we can deactivate this device if we work together. Besides, these devices won't break apart the nuclear weapon given their distance and outwardly explosive tract."

"Then, we better get started disarming this damn thing." He wiped his forehead with his sleeve and took a calming breath.

His suggestion to have Andropov detonate the booby trap triggered a possible solution. If he could fabricate a shape charge, he could aim the blast to destroy the entire fusing system.

"Svetlana, I've an idea. Can we improvise a shaped charge to take out the control panel and the two fusing systems?"

"That's brilliant Matt. You're definitely on to something. A shaped charge directed at both fusing systems should render the device safe. If we do it precisely, our chances of survival are excellent. It's unlikely the blast will penetrate the warhead and disperse the uranium; thereby minimizing the chances of contamination to the general area."

"That's comforting," the agent muttered. He scanned the room's booby-traps and chose a device with overlapping coverage of the rear door. It appeared to be an improvised claymore mine utilizing a motion sensor as its fusing system.

With the clock showing just less than six minutes, he hastened his pace. He crept toward the device from the rear, careful not to cast his head beyond it. Eying it, he analyzed the basic passive infrared device. He examined the back plate and battery compartment. He needed to avoid jarring it, so he calculated the location of the battery and connecting wire. Borrowing the Russian's pen, he twisted off its top and squirted its acid directly at his target area. The acid fizzled and released a small plume of whitish smoke; it effortlessly melted through its plastic covering and left a small pea-size hole. He shined his mini-Maglite with fiber optic tubing into the hole. The acid destroyed the battery's top and its connecting wire.

He lifted the device and carried it to a nearby table. He placed it next to his Leatherman utility tool, flashlight, and a roll of electrical tape. The determined agent then separated the high explosive from the IR sensor and the blasting cap. Unfortunately, the sulfuric acid damaged the nine-volt battery. He glanced at his flashlight, knowing its AA batteries could work as the power source. Now, he needed to improvise a fusing system. His eyes darted around the room while his hands rummaged through his pockets. His hand brushed against a pen.

"Svetlana, I need your assistance. You're the explosive's expert. We only have three minutes and twenty seconds."

"What is it?" She stared at him.

"How much explosive should I utilize? And what angle should I cut the cone to ensure the jet's effectiveness is maximized?" His fingers trembled.

Her face crumpled as she calculated the amount of explosive needed. "You should employ a linear shaped-charge. From the half pound block of explosive, cut a small rectangular block, approximately one-half inch by one-inch by five inches."

James sliced the explosive to size. "I'm done."

"Next, cut a 'V' angle lengthwise through the block with an angle of about fifty degrees." She caressed his shoulder.

He lifted the explosive to eye level, made two incisions, and peeled the cut portion away. "Got it. What standoff distance should I use?"

She stretched her arms skyward. "That's easy. You need one point five times the cone's diameter or roughly three inches. Before you attach the explosive, line the cone of the shape charge with steel, copper, or glass. These coned liners control the cutting ability of the charge by adding to the jet fine particles of cone liner. This raises the temperature of the jet while providing abrasive materials to assist in cutting the material."

James simpered. "Great. This place isn't exactly an Ace Hardware store." He examined the area before focusing on the hinges of a nearby camera case. Grabbing his Leatherman tool, he gripped the hinges and ripped them from the case. He glanced at the clock; only two minutes and forty-six seconds left.

"The hell with it." Separating the hinge flaps, he turned them inward so the straight edges formed the crux of the 'V'. The innovative agent hurriedly slapped them into position and embedded them into the explosive, disregarding the overhang. He removed his Smith & Wesson handcuffs and cut the chain with his Leatherman, forming two separate pieces. Using the tape, he attached them to each end of the device to create the requisite standoff distance. He estimated the location of the two fusing systems. He then affixed the shaped charge to the control panel by wrapping it with electrical tape. Only one minute and thirty-two seconds remained.

"We're running out of time Svetlana. Get ready to activate the booby trap."

She looked down.

James thrust the blasting cap into the explosive at a downward twenty-degree angle. He rapidly attached one end of the wire to the battery, taping it in place. He considered touching the other end of the wire to the battery's positive end, but opted against it. He instead grabbed his pen and separated it into two pieces by twisting both ends in opposite directions. The resourceful agent removed the ring, spring and pen filler.

He carefully attached one of the wires from the blasting cap to the ring taken from the pen. He then embedded it into the top portion of the shaped charge. Pulling the small spring off the front of the ink cartridge, he placed it halfway on the rear of the cartridge. It took several seconds to attach an eight-inch long piece of wire into place to form the ad hoc trembler switch; one wire attached to the back of the ink cartridge/spring and the other end connected to the battery.

His hand quivered while estimating the arming distance to his switch. He noted the location and stacked a dime on top of a quarter. His hand remained steady as he avoided touching the ink cartridge or spring to the ring. He carefully threaded the front end of the ink cartridge through the ring. The focused agent then affixed the spring and rear of the cartridge to the dime and quarter. The upward angle provided by the dime-quarter platform appeared to compensate for the load of the ink cartridge. Not sure whether he calculated correctly, he inhaled before releasing the front end of the ink cartridge. His heartbeat skipped as he steadied his hand. Gently releasing the front end of the cartridge, his heart fluttered as the tip dipped toward the ring. He moaned slightly when it rebounded and froze perfectly centered in the ring. The slightest bump of the control panel or switch would detonate the shaped charge.

James glanced at the clock. His improvised explosive disrupter needed to be detonated within nineteen seconds. Throwing the table on its side, the two agents shielded themselves from the pending blast.

"Svetlana, if I fail to detonate this device when I bump it, then you pass through the infrared sensor." Through his peripheral vision, he could see her nod. He nudged the table into the nuclear warhead, but his jolt failed to detonate the device. He considered bumping it again, but realized he would only have one more chance; the nuke's digital clock now read five seconds. He waived Andropov off as he stood, grabbed his flashlight, and tossed it at the triggering system. He ducked behind the table. The flashlight hit and pushed the ink cartridge against the ring; the electrons flowed to the detonator of his disrupter.

The blast echoed throughout the small storage unit. Shrapnel from the Smith & Wesson handcuffs ripped into his right calf muscle. He knew he should have used something soft to create the necessary standoff distance. This mistake didn't bother him. He rolled to his left and glanced at Andropov. Her smile indicated her condition. Explosive residue filled the air. They detected nothing unusual, but James remained unaware of uranium's smell or impact to the body. He prayed for a precise deactivation. A single error with the disrupter would have meant a slow agonizing death from radiation exposure.

Without another word, the two agents disarmed the other two perimeter explosive devices. Upon deactivating the bombs, they stepped out into the fresh air, grateful for their work. The Russian agent walked to her car and returned a minute later with a Geiger counter. She walked toward the nuclear warhead while eying her high-tech gauge.

His stomach churned as the Geiger counter came to life, making a rhythmic clicking sound. He glanced over his shoulder and could see Andropov hovering over the warhead.

"It's all clear. The radiation levels are within acceptable parameters." She turned to him, smiling.

He looked directly into her eyes; his hand now steady. "So, there's no radiation exposure?"

She shook her head. "No. You did an excellent job disarming the device. I couldn't have done it any better."

James used the phone in his car to call the national security advisor. After two rings, O'Reilly answered.

"I got your message. A Department of Energy team will be at your location in twenty minutes." O'Reilly's hands clutched together.

The DS agent sighed. "That's great news. We disarmed the device, but Rahman got away with another one. I'm going after him. I'll apprise you when we have something more concrete. Get your men to the Frontier Storage facility in Santa Fe. It won't be too hard to find the device. You'll see the blood trails. Bye."

# CHAPTER 35: EXTREME MEASURES

James scampered over to Andropov who had entered the adjoining room in search of the Chechen's future intentions. The room's sterile ambience impressed the dogged Russian agent. Her concentration intensified as she pursued scant clues with a single-minded focus and desire. She rifled through a stack of papers on the counter, despite the loss of her team. Even though the bullet-ridden bodies on the pavement had disappeared, the remnants of a gang war still lingered. Bloodstains splattered throughout the area served as a reminder of the carnage that occurred only an hour earlier. Bullet holes ripped through the facade, nearby vehicles, and asphalt. Spent brass rounds littered the grounds. The ominous sight gripped James, but the outcome paled in comparison to the detonation of a nuke. Nonetheless, Rahman roamed the streets of America and planned something even more deadly and insidious.

"Found anything yet?" He paced back and forth.

She shook her head. "They covered their tracks."

"The cavalry will arrive in another twenty minutes. We must be gone or face countless questions and delays. If that happens, we'll never catch Rahman before he carries out his operation, whatever that might be." The DS agent sighed.

"There has to be a clue here. We just have to find it." The skilled Russian scanned left to right. "Now give me a hand," she barked naturally.

He joined her in a frenzied search. His optimism waned about finding anything useful given the small size of the room. Rummaging through the workbench table, he considered Rahman's quest for something grand. He scoured the surface, uncovering electrical wire, remnants of soldering, electrical tape, screws, and some tin foil fragments. Glancing behind the bench, he saw a partially exposed photograph and retrieved it. The photograph depicted an altimeter device.

"Keep looking Svetlana, I'll be right back."

"Where are you going?"

"I don't have time to explain, but I think it will help us discover Rahman's plans." The resolute agent marched out the door, glancing back at the Russian agent before sprinting ahead.

His confidence spiked about uncovering the Chechen's plan. His face flushed for not thinking of it sooner. Running to the side of the storage area, he discovered a ladder leading to the roof. He climbed the ladder in seconds and ran to the point where his drone hit the sniper. The drone lied lifeless on its side; its puny body and wings damaged from its collision with the terrorist. He retrieved the high-tech drone and scampered down the ladder.

Approaching the Russian agent, he tapped her on the shoulder. "It's time to go."

"We're not finished."

"I have what we need." He displayed the drone. Stopping at his car, he opened his trunk and removed a suitcase, the drone's backpack, and a laptop.

"We'll have to take your car. Mine is toast. We need to download the hard drive off this amazing little piece of technology." His posture stiffened.

"You're kidding me. What information could that little toy possibly hold?"

"This multi-million dollar toy saved your life. I used it to dive-bomb the sniper who was going to put a bullet into your pretty head. It's the latest state-of-the-art aerial surveillance equipment, using sophisticated nanotechnology. The drone's onboard camera system and expansive memory allowed me to capture incredible amounts of information. I just need to remove the memory card so I can download it to my laptop."

She leaned in closer to the American. "So you use it to spy on unsuspecting people. That's brilliant. No one would suspect a passing bird as an unmanned aerial vehicle."

"We use it to conduct surveillance on criminals, not to watch our citizens. I'm sure your government would use it to invade your people's privacy or spy on foreigners." His jaw tightened.

"What makes you so sure we don't have it already? Russia has pioneered and made enormous advances in technology, such as drones and robotics."

"Yeah, and what you haven't built, you stole. I'm aware of the UAV technology you pilfered from Canada and your recent operation using it."

"There's no way you could possibly know of our operation. It's highly classified." She shook her head.

"You're not the only one who does their research. I've read your file after our initial encounter. Should we get going?" His eyebrows rose twice.

"Let's go, but don't you think for a minute that we're through with this conversation. I've a couple more questions for you."

"I'd be surprised if you didn't." He blew out a long breath.

The two agents walked to the front of the storage facility and entered her car. She turned the car's ignition key and immediately cranked up the air conditioning. Her run in with Rahman, combined with the desert heat, caused her to perspire.

"I have a hotel room nearby. Let's go there, freshen up, and figure out Rahman's next move. I need to change out of these torn clothes." Her pupils twinkled as she eyed the American.

"Sounds good. I'm thirsty and starving." He stretched his neck.

Andropov drove out of the parking lot onto the main road and accelerated to the speed limit. She hit the brakes while swerving to avoid striking a family of prairie dogs scurrying across the road. She continued driving without batting an eye. Her driving prowess, quick reflexes, and equanimity impressed him. Within hours, she lost a good friend, battled an international terrorist, deactivated a nuke, and cheated death. She steadfastly focused on her next objective without remorse or an emotional scar from the ordeal. He could see they had a few traits in common; ones he truly admired. Even though they lived worlds apart, he realized they were much alike. Neither of them would rest until they stopped Rahman.

"That was a nice piece of driving you displayed back there." James rubbed his forehead.

She gave a playful grin. "I imagine you receive similar training to us. The FSB invests heavily in training us for our jobs. Antiterrorism driving is one of the many courses we receive. At this point, my driving is instinctive."

"I know what you mean. My government has trained me as an antiterrorist driving instructor, so I can teach our personnel overseas. I enjoyed ramming other vehicles and learning how to immobilize fleeing cars." He turned and winked at the Russian.

"It's amazing how much training we receive to defend our respective ways of life. Let's hope our training will ensure our success. If we don't stop the Chechen, then all the training in the world won't matter as life changes overnight."

James gave a flat look. "Nuclear terrorism certainly changes the stakes of the game. They can destroy an entire city or financial hub with one push of a button."

Andropov turned left and pulled into the parking lot of the Parkside Plaza Hotel. She drove to the back and parked in a spot next to the building's rear entrance. Her room selection seemed calculated, as it kept her comings and goings relatively private. Upon exiting the vehicle, she popped the trunk, retrieved her equipment, and set it on the ground. Her hand slammed the trunk shut and then her finger depressed a button on her key chain; all the doors locked simultaneously. Leading the way, she walked through a backdoor by swiping her key card. She ambled back to a main corridor and took a sharp left to her suite. Opening the door, she motioned him forward and closed the door as he entered the luxurious suite.

"The Russian government must pay you better than ours. I see they treat you pretty well." James displayed a pinched expression.

She smiled. "Make yourself at home. Mi casa es tu casa."

"You speak Spanish."

"I speak five languages, including Russian, English, Spanish, French, and German." She caressed his forearm.

He admired the woman's linguistic capabilities. "I only speak English and Spanish. I should've learned Chinese from my mother. My parents were both first-generation Americans. They insisted I speak English, even though they were bilingual."

"That's too bad. Speaking Chinese would be useful in today's world. We have our concerns with the Chinese. They're on an economic, political, and military upswing and will eclipse even your country as the dominant superpower. Speaking Chinese would've given you the competitive edge in knowing the language of your adversary."

"Then I should've learned Russian as well." He avoided eye contact.

The Russian threw her bag up onto a couch. "We're no longer your enemy. I'm going to shower and change my clothes. Help yourself to drinks in the refrigerator. I'll be back in twenty minutes."

He grabbed a Pepsi from the refrigerator, sat down at a small desk, and lifted his laptop's lid. While his computer powered up, he discovered a menu for room service in the drawer. He reviewed it and ordered a Southwest chicken salad, a bacon cheeseburger with french fries, two glasses of fresh squeezed lemonade, and two slices of apple pie. He pondered her tastes, but knew he could eat both dishes given his ravenous appetite.

Opening the hummingbird's memory enclosure, he removed the micro SD card and inserted it into his laptop's port. The icon surfaced on his monitor within seconds, so he downloaded it directly to his computer. He needed to enhance many of the images and his computer featured a tailored-made application. Running the footage, he froze the video over the storage facility, and then advanced it frame by frame. Once he arrived at the desired frame, he optimized the angle and its contrast. He then used his specialty software to magnify the image; its four-power enhancement allowed him to read many of the items plastered on the wall. It appeared the high-tech gadget would pay for itself with just one picture.

Andropov emerged from her room in a white cloth robe as he isolated each image on Rahman's wall. She approached him from behind and leaned over his shoulder; her wet hair draped on his back. "Have you uncovered anything useful yet?"

Her hair's subtle strawberry fragrance distracted him. His head swiveled, positioning his face cheek to cheek with the Russian agent. After gazing into her eyes, he turned back to his monitor. "Take a look at this screen."

"What is it?" She inched her head over his shoulder to peer at the screen.

He pointed to the screen. "You see this drawing."

"Yes, it's hard to read though."

Sharpening the image with his mouse pointer, he illuminated the container, plutonium core, and the fusing system. "The drawing clearly shows a thermal nuclear bomb; it fails to clarify the fusing system other than time delay."

His mind recalled the electrical components in the storage room. He deduced that Rahman had built a different fusing system. Time seemed the best way to escape a nuclear detonation. He speculated that Rahman had another more nefarious purpose in mind.

A sudden knock at the door interrupted his concentration. James leapt to his feet. "I got it. It's just room service."

Glancing through the door viewer, he saw a cart and a Hispanic server looking at the bill. He opened the door and requested the man to set the food and drink on the table. Paying him with cash, he gave him forty-five dollars and advised him to keep the change. Pleased by James' generosity, the waiter dashed out the door, leaving the two agents to dine alone.

James pulled out a chair and seated his Russian partner. "Thank you Matt. That was considerate of you to order. Which is mine?"

"You may have either."

"I didn't think I was hungry until now. I'd like the cheeseburger."

"Good choice. The half-pound of beef will fix your appetite."

"I hope you don't mind the salad."

"I should eat more vegetables and roughage. At least that's what my doctor says. Besides, I'll have more room for my big slice of apple pie." He scooted his chair closer to the table.

The two talked idly about their interests and her thoughts about America as they ate. He tried to elicit more information about her than she could of him. A choppy conversation ensued as neither agent yielded to the other about themselves or their parent organizations. The two rival agents' profession fostered suspicion to enhance survival, but it limited meaningful conversation.

"You don't like to talk about yourself and I'm not sure why. You're a beautiful, smart, witty, and talented woman with great reflexes and instincts."

Her head dropped slightly. "My instincts didn't serve me well today. I lost my entire team."

"You were severely outnumbered and you're still alive to fight another day. You helped deactivated a nuclear device that would've killed countless people. That's not too bad for a day's work. I'm sorry about your team. They were patriots to your country." He placed his hands on top of hers.

"Thanks Matt." She leaned forward and kissed him on the cheek.

He beamed. "What was that for? Not that I'm complaining, I just want to know how to earn another one."

She lightly held James' face with her hands and kissed him softly on his lips. "I truly appreciate your compassionate words, your thoughtfulness, and the fact that you saved my life today. It's now up to us to stop Rahman. We need to trust each other. Failure isn't an option."

"Then we need to discover Rahman's plans and fast. We know he's going to use a nuclear weapon, but we need to figure out where. I think we're forgetting something important. What did he mention back in the storage facility?" The American cupped his chin.

Her face crumpled. "He advised us that he's Chechen."

James shifted back and forth. "And he fights for his country. What else?"

"Rahman revealed he had a plane to catch. What do you suppose he meant by that?"

He fidgeted in his seat. "He mentioned his destiny awaits him. Why did he say that?"

Andropov shook her head. "No, he stated that his destiny awaits him in space."

The DS agent scratched the side of his face. "I wonder what he meant by that. Let me try a word search on my laptop."

The dogged agent conducted a web search inputting plane, Chechen, al-Qaeda, and space. Scrolling through several pages of web results yielded nothing, so he narrowed the search parameters. Eliminating first Chechen and then plane from the word search, he ran a web search with just al-Qaeda and space. After reviewing two pages of search results, he uncovered an interesting historical article; it speculated that al-Qaeda could be planning an attack against the space shuttle for symbolic reasons.

Turning to Andropov, he cringed. "I have an idea. Are you familiar with the civilian space program near Roswell, New Mexico?"

"Are you talking about the program to launch private citizens into space created by a famous entrepreneur?"

"That's the one. Now imagine terrorists hijacking it and using it to detonate a nuclear weapon high above the U.S." His neck stiffened.

Her lips pursed. "That would be catastrophic. A nuclear weapon detonated in space over the central part of the U.S. would create a devastating electro-magnetic pulse. It would blanket most of America and instantly fry all electronics, transporting America back to the Stone Age. Airplanes would fall from the sky, vehicles would stop working, and water, sewer, and electrical networks would fail. Food would rot, medical services would collapse, and transportation would become almost nonexistent. This devastation would make survival difficult and could kill millions of people while threatening their way of life."

The two agents sat transfixed on one another. They recognized the stakes and the essence of time. They both knew that if they left immediately for Roswell and the launch facility, they could arrive by nightfall.

# CHAPTER 36: DARK KNIGHT

*Thirty-Five Miles Southwest of Roswell, New Mexico*

Dusk approached as the sun descended behind the towering snowcapped mountains. Nightfall would soon overtake the light of day; the two seasoned agents forged an alliance with the darkness. They abandoned their vehicle along a dirt trail just off the main road. The two agents stood atop a small ridge and analyzed the landscape in front of them. The rocky terrain presented injury concerns; it also served as hunting grounds for venomous snakes and scorpions that lurked in the cool night breeze. The splendid pink sunset to the west was lost upon them.

Surveying the landscape through her binoculars, Andropov handed them to James for his thoughts. He appreciated the Russian agent's route selection; it provided them a blend of natural cover, traversable terrain, and a stealthy approach to the fence line. His eyes transfixed on a futuristic structure in the backdrop. The airport-space facility appeared like a scene straight from a sci-fi movie set with its low-lying, organic shape; it resembled a stingray with a severely swollen tail. He imagined Area 51 looked similar.

Descending a small rocky incline, James held Andropov's hand to aid their balance as she led their way. The Russian beauty remained resolute, disciplined, and focused. She reached the base of the hill and set her course to the fence. Trotting beside her, he tightened both straps to his backpack to reduce a jarring noise from its contents. Her pace quickened without even a notion of stress on the leggy blonde. The American agent glanced over at her, but her focus remained ahead. After fifteen minutes, they had run the two miles to the fence and squatted down next to it. Her breathing remained easy as she examined the fence. He struggled to catch his breath.

Observing bold red signs posted every fifty feet, they realized the electrified fence top presented yet another challenge. The Russian agent remained undeterred. She embraced any challenge.

"Now what?" He whispered.

Andropov set her backpack on the ground and unzipped it. Pulling out a heavy blanket, she unfolded it and then threw it over the electric fence topper.

She turned to James. "You go first. I'll give you a hand." He placed his right foot into her clasped hands. "Okay, jump and grab the blanket and the wire beneath it to hold you in place. Then pull your feet up to the underlying metal stanchion and leap over the topper."

"So you want me to be a guinea pig. If I end up barbequed, then you'll find another way in or around."

"Something like that. Now, just do it. I thought you Americans were all cowboys. Our scientists at Moscow University specifically designed this blanket for this scenario. Don't worry and trust me. The blanket acts as an insulator. We can power our computers from it later." She gave him a playful nudge.

James leapt up and vaulted over the fence in one smooth motion, landing hard on the ground; his knee buckled from the force of the impact. He staggered to his feet, bending down to rub his knee. He watched her jump up and, with one continuous motion, catapult over the fence. She landed on the ground in a standing position. Her agility, strength, and endurance impressed him.

"You sure made that look easy."

She winked. "I wasn't always an FSB agent. I was a gymnast in my early years."

"Is there anything you can't do?" He shook his head, smiling.

"We Russians can do just about anything, but let's find out. We need to get to Rahman fast."

Darkness now lingered over the plateau. A light breeze blew in from the west bringing seasonably crisp air to the desolate tract of land. The stars shimmered in the clear night sky as the moon replaced the vanishing sun. Reaching into her backpack, she removed a thermal imager. Her hand twisted a switch to power the device. Raising the viewer to her eyes, she scanned the facility, zooming in on the hanger area. Even in the Stygian night, she could see the distinguishing silhouettes of modern ingenuity; on each side of the hanger rested a futuristic carrier plane with a wingspan of one-hundred and forty feet. With separate fuselages, it appeared as two planes merged into one, fused together by a common internal wing. In the middle of the hanger sat two sixty-foot aerodynamic rockets, each identical and supporting a split-wing design. The spacecraft's pioneering design employed more curves than its predecessor design or that of the space shuttle. Its split wing gave it better flight stability; the wing's ability to pivot skyward independent of the passenger compartment permitted a slow descent. This prevented the craft from burning up while reentering the earth's atmosphere.

Noticing movement on the left side of the hanger, she swept her eyes to the left. Arcs of flickering light emanated from inside the carrier craft. She counted five armed men patrolling the floor, each equipped with a Russian assault rifle.

She handed James the imager. "This operation doesn't look right. Check out the uniformed officers assigned to protect the facility. They're carrying Russian-made weaponry."

James raised the thermal imager to his eyes. "They aren't Americans. I bet they're Rahman's men and they're planning to steal the spacecraft for their operation. We were right."

"I hate always being right." She scowled. "He's going to launch into space and detonate a nuke, causing an electromagnetic pulse that will blanket America. He'll wipe out all electronic systems. Millions will perish as airplanes plunge from the sky, cars and trains crash, and your infrastructure shuts down. And tens, perhaps hundreds of millions more will perish in the years ahead from lack of electricity."

"We've got to stop him. I should call the national security advisor to request a Special Force's team."

"There's no time for that. We need to act fast. It's up to us, so get your head into the game," she snapped back.

"How can we penetrate the facility undetected?" James looked at his ad hoc Russian partner.

"Follow me. There's a side door to the rear."

Andropov reached down and zipped up her backpack, slinging it on her shoulders in one smooth motion. Standing up, she dashed parallel to the facility. James struggled to keep up with the endurance and part-time marathon runner. She avoided running too close to the hangar to evade a sentry's watchful eye. She recognized they needed the element of surprise to triumph over the odds. Traversing the distance in about five minutes, he knew they covered another mile of ground. His heartbeat elevated, so he breathed deeply to slow its pace.

Stopping at the door, the Russian agent analyzed the lock. "This mechanism will be tough to crack." Her hand reached into the side pocket of her backpack and removed a lock-picking set. "You don't happen to have the key Matt. No, I didn't think so." She kneeled down and inserted the pick and the torque wrench into the locking mechanism.

The Russian worked the lock with the finger dexterity of a concert pianist. She conquered pin by pin until she achieved a light, barely audible click. Her hand gripped and turned the doorknob slowly, uncertain of what awaited her on the other side. She considered the uneasy silence as a good sign, so she drew her pistol and swung the door open. Glancing back, she eyed James while he finished inserting MP-5 magazines into his chest and belt pouches. Her focus on the lock prevented her from witnessing his abrupt change into his tactical attire. Her backpack held the tools for espionage while his held the gear for a counterassault. Their tactical skills complemented one another while serving as a force multiplier to battle unfavorable odds.

Entering the building, the DS agent took the lead, skulking down the corridor. Andropov followed closely behind him with her silenced pistol, periodically scanning over her shoulder to safeguard their rear. Muffled words droned louder as they approached the main hangar. The two agents recognized the voice and language; Rahman called out orders in Arabic. Their astute deduction landed them in the right place. This would be their last opportunity to stop him. The fate of America rested in their hands, and they both preferred it that way.

Preparing to breach the hangar, she noticed an unfriendly a deck up aiming his assault rifle at James. Unhesitant, she fired a single shot that found its mark, hitting the Chechen in the head. The man slumped forward over the rail; his momentum propelling him over, as he somersaulted to the floor. His impact on the cement floor echoed throughout the hanger.

James eyed the area in front of them. A barrage of bullets forced him to backpedal behind the corner. "There goes the element of surprise."

"Nothing's ever easy." She gave him a silent look.

A voice behind them broke their brief reverie. "Don't move or I'll kill you!"

Ahead of his next command, she turned toward the sentry and unleashed her kilowatt smile. Her hand sprang upward, deflecting the rifle's barrel toward the exterior wall as he squeezed the trigger; ten rounds sprayed and shattered the window. Glass rained all over the floor. She lunged forward and raked his throat with her fingertips forming a tiger claw, collapsing the man's larynx. Dropping his weapon, the sentry gasped for his last breath before falling to the floor. James admired her killing efficiency and her ability to protect his back.

Peering around the corner again, everything quieted unexpectedly. A faint commotion within the plane captured their attention. They crept forward, clinging to the wall to minimize their exposure to anyone lurking above.

Leading the way, James surveyed the large area and advanced forward as Andropov covered his rear. Even though she had proven more than capable, he would defer his edict that ladies should go first. The DS agent edged forward while his peripheral vision detected sudden movement to the left. He turned, lifted his submachine gun to acquire its sights, and fired a three-round burst. His rounds struck the Chechen rebel as he squeezed his trigger to his assault rifle. The rebel dropped to the ground lifeless, but his rounds hit James squarely in the chest. James' eyes widened as he staggered back and fell to the ground.

Andropov stepped forward to shield the downed agent while scanning the area for other hostiles. Three men converged on her from both sides and her rear; their weapons drawn and aimed at her. Realizing their advantage, she raised her hands into the air and surrendered. She could have killed one of them, but the other two would have gunned her down. Her pragmatism surfaced as she recognized the futility of her predicament in a second. Her death would not benefit anyone.

James rolled to a sitting position; his chest ached from the rounds slamming into his ballistic plate. Rahman's men greeted him with the butt of a rifle; blood trickled from his forehead. They bound his hands and then rolled him to a seated position. Andropov's eyes met the American agent's before returning her gaze to the room around them. The sound of rapidly approaching footsteps echoed throughout the large bay area; Rahman's nostrils flared as he eyed the agents.

"Agent Andropov, why can't you just die like a good Russian woman?" The Chechen shook his head, frowning. "And Agent James, the same applies to you. I can't believe you disarmed my nuclear weapon in Santa Fe. That must've taken some real ingenuity. Oh well, that was only meant for show as far as I'm concerned."

She cringed. "You're a murderous bastard. You won't get away with detonating your nuke in space and wiping out America."

"You're very fortunate Svetlana, but that's where you're wrong. There's no one to stop me now."

"How can you kill so many innocent men, women and children?" She lamented; her face reddened.

"Do you know how many innocent people your government killed in Chechnya? Don't lecture me without first asking it of your government; a government for which you willingly kill and support," Rahman sneered, jabbing his finger in her face.

Andropov shook her head rebelliously. "Why don't you just put me out of my misery? I have no fear of death."

"That would be too easy. Besides, I feel extremely generous today. I'm offering you a special deal tonight. You'll be one of the few private citizens to venture off into space. Most people have to pay a quarter of a million dollars for such a privilege." Rahman grinned. "You'll exit this earth to space for free. This journey is something that not too many of your fellow countryman have experienced. It will be more revered than burial at sea. I'm sure you'll get a star put up on a memorial wall for your sacrifice."

"That's the CIA. The FSB honors their dead in other ways. Who will honor you when I kill you?" She stated defiantly as her face flushed.

"That would be an interesting trick. Since you seem to fancy me, I'll make your life comfortable for its remaining time on earth."

The scar faced man snapped his fingers. "Put her in the spacecraft. Make sure she's bound tight and strapped in. I don't want her to miss out on the space experience and a new world order."

Walking to the spacecraft flanked by two of Rahman's men, Andropov turned to James. "I'll see you soon."

Rahman sneered at the sentiment. "Isn't that romantic? I guess the Cold War's truly over. Times have changed. It's interesting to see a Russian spy who has a crush on an American agent. That's excellent. I almost hate to separate you two lovebirds."

"You're funny Rahman. Then why separate us? I always wanted to see space before I died. This opportunity is perfect. You should give the condemned man his dying wish. There's room for six." James turned his palms upward.

"There's room for only five. I gave the nuclear weapon a seat." Rahman canted his head while contemplating the agent's request. "This occasion is monumental and I'm feeling generous. Load this infidel into the spacecraft and make sure he can't get loose. I need to oversee the insertion of the additional fuel tank in the carrier craft."

Moving toward the American, a lieutenant hit him across the temple with the butt of his rifle. James dropped to the floor like a rag doll; his limp frame dragged to the airplane by two of Rahman's cronies.

Rahman appreciated his men's handling of the DS agent. He knew the head strike had to hurt, but the American's condition did not concern him. He had other pressing work to attend to as he prepped the carrier ship for its lengthy journey. He recognized the task's difficulty and understood air-to-air and surface-to-air tactics as a former Soviet pilot. Nevertheless, like all of his plans, he had a viable path forward; one that he would execute soon and just prior to sunrise.

# CHAPTER 37: RED ALERT

*NSA Listening Site, New Mexico Desert*

Jack Dawson's stomach rumbled as his ten-hour shift neared its end. Yet, the diligent bureaucrat's day only reached its midpoint. A virulent coronavirus outbreak required him to work a double shift. He had worked for the National Security Agency for eight years; he relished the high-tech game that he ingeniously and artfully played. He had spent twenty-years in the U.S. Army mounting signals operations against America's adversaries in the far corners of the globe. He now enjoyed the hunt from the comfort of his ergonomic leather chair and array of supercomputer systems that he meticulously managed and maintained.

He preferred tracking terrorists to that of the Cold War spy. He recognized both could cause irreversible damage to U.S. national security. However, the terrorist, following the nine-eleven attacks, had become the chase of the century. The stakes had never been higher with today's terrorist determined to acquire nuclear, biological, chemical or radiological weapons. Failure to timely uncover a significant plot could mean the potential death of millions of his fellow Americans. He vowed to thwart terrorism plots on his watch and he always kept his word.

Modern advancements in fiber optics and satellite communication had changed the nature and complexity of the game. Fortunately, he had the best equipment that money could buy, courtesy of the U.S. government. He directed twenty-five state-of-the-art antennas that captured myriad signals from around the globe. The sheer power at his fingertips amazed him. Strategically positioned high power antennas would snatch conversations from the unsuspecting and rapidly relay them to a supercomputer; its colossal processing power analyzing billions of transmissions for key buzz words and phrases. His consistent work more than occupied his time. Every so often, an urgent intercept landed on his desk and spun his team into a frenzy to unravel its mysteries.

The airwave's superhighway heralded expansive riches beyond the mind's imagination. People often spoke without regard to the reaches of disparate intelligence services that could track a phone conversation in the far reaches of the earth, isolate code in seemingly unbreakable encryption, and invade the populace's privacy from the edge of space. Signals intelligence would dominate government centers, boardrooms, drug cartels, organized syndicates, and even terrorist organizations. Information ruled the game and many would pay handsomely for it. This could give the recipient a critical edge in today's competitive society or during bilateral or multilateral negotiations. The armchair spy knew the U.S. government remained the largest consumer of such information.

Punching several keys in quick succession, Dawson ran a diagnostic check of his billion-dollar computer systems. He habitually analyzed it at the beginning and end of each shift to ensure the supercomputer's operating integrity. His systems processed literally millions of conversations each day in over twenty-six distinct languages. His painstaking work had proved its worth more than one hundred-fold. In fact, the nation's government elite had a ravenous and never-ending appetite for his intelligence product. The U.S. president frequently relied on signals intelligence to ascertain critical developments in flashpoints or around the world. It often corroborated human intelligence, becoming vital because of the decaying capability of human ground assets.

Concentrating on the Middle East after several popular uprisings, Dawson combed the airways for anything of strategic value. He specifically sought information that could provide senior policymakers an advantage in the Palestinian and Israeli peace talks. The president prioritized a meaningful peace deal and felt it within his grasp, something that eluded previous administrations. Dawson recognized the problematic nature of peace in the region and its importance in America's war on terrorism. The long plight of the Palestinians often served as a rallying cry throughout the Muslim world; terrorist groups often vowed revenge for perceived atrocities and injustices against their Palestinian brothers. He focused his team's energies on Israel's Arab neighbors, the Egyptians, Syrians, and Jordanians. An alert from Russia startled him as it covered the far fringes of his collection parameters.

"Jack, you need to see this information coming in from Siberia." Lori Taylor's voice cracked.

Taylor had worked for the NSA for only three years. She had proved her worth tenfold with her linguist abilities and astute powers of deduction. Her talents routinely deciphered the intricacies of a conversation. Even with encrypted systems, many spoke in code to disguise their sensitive missions and covert operations. This precaution resonated with the Russian military, who knew the vulnerabilities of communications systems, even seemingly secure ones. Taylor's forte involved analyzing these hidden meanings. She had listened to tens of thousands of foreign conversations over the years. Not surprisingly, she always found the hidden meaning behind their exchanges.

Dawson approached Taylor's desk. "What have you got? I hope it's good." He put his hand on her shoulder.

"Do you remember the flash traffic that H-Q sent us to look for possible Russian actions? I've uncovered something of that nature." Her eyes bulged.

She tapped a few keystrokes on her computer. Her monitor displayed the conversation she had flagged moments earlier. The computer's screen flashed the transmission:

*"Roger tower. We're on a direct intercept course; we'll reach our objective in twenty minutes. The American aircraft has violated our airspace. Do I have permission to engage?"*

*"Negative Airwolf. You're only to approach and observe. We have information that this high-tech plane is defecting to Moscow."*

*"Copy that tower. We'll keep you apprised. Airwolf Out."*

"We were only able to capture this small bit of the discussion. This conversation came from the pilot of a MIG-29 and the tower. I presume he was communicating with his superiors." Taylor rubbed her face.

Dawson crossed his arms while observing her screen. "Continue your analysis. I've seen that look before. You won't stop until you have the answer."

She sighed. "The North American Aerospace Defense Command is currently tracking this purported American plane. They believe it's the Aquila, which has gone missing from the Galactic Transport Center near Roswell."

"Did you say Aquila? Aquila is the carrier plane of a carbon composite constructed aircraft capable of reaching into space. It's light, strong, resilient, and fuel-efficient. It will allow wealthy citizens the opportunity to travel into space, albeit for only about six minutes." His face tightened.

"That technology's revolutionary. Do you think the Russians are stealing the state-of-the-art aircraft?" Taylor asked, quirking an eyebrow and scowling.

"Oh my God, it can't be." Dawson turned away; his mouth fell open. He linked together the intelligence he received earlier in the day.

"What is it? What's happening?" She fidgeted in her seat and stared up at her boss.

He puckered his brow. "I can't believe it, but it's starting to make sense. First, we have the smuggling of nukes into America and the attempted detonation of one of them. We also have an infamous Chechen leader – with al-Qaeda links – who is bent on killing millions of people. He's now returning to Russia with a nuclear weapon and in an aircraft capable of reaching space."

"I don't get it. What does it all mean?" She muttered, shrugging her shoulders.

"Have you heard of an electromagnetic pulse?"

"Uh, uh, only a little bit. I know that it can zap electronics, rendering them useless." Her eyes narrowed.

"It can be a whole lot worse if a nuclear weapon is detonated at the fringe of space. On July 9, 1962, the Atomic Energy Commission and the Defense Atomic Support Agency detonated Starfish Prime. It involved a 1.4-megaton H-bomb test at an altitude of two-hundred and fifty miles, some nine-hundred miles southwest of Hawaii over the Pacific Ocean. The pulse shorted out streetlights in Oahu." His eyes darkened and intensified; his mouth supported a grim twist.

"Please, in laymen's terms?" She glanced up.

"The detonation of an atomic bomb anywhere from twenty-five to five-hundred miles high electrifies or ionizes the atmosphere about twenty-five miles up, triggering a series of electromagnetic pulses. The pulse's reach varies with the size of the bomb, the height of its blast and design. Basically, a nuclear weapon detonated in space can create an electromagnetic pulse that could blackout an entire country." He shook his head.

"Go on. This electromagnetic pulse info is fascinating and a bit scary. It sounds like a great plot for a novel." Taylor twisted her necklace as her face tightened.

"Our subject matter experts disregarded the prospect. They believed you needed a missile to take the weapon to at least twenty-five miles high. It appears the terrorists have found another way to reach the altitude without the use of a missile. It's rather ingenious." His eyes bulged as he touched his throat.

"More like diabolical." She looked away.

"So what else can you deduce from this information?" Dawson rubbed his temples. He realized it would be merely supposition on her part, but he had learned to trust her instincts. Her prescience consistently brought remarkable results. It had frequently linked innumerable intelligence bits that shaped high-level negotiation strategies.

"Given Russian war doctrine, their leaders have never trusted us. They always feared that America would strike first with nuclear weapons, minimizing their ability to fully retaliate. I imagine the Russians could see this as a first strike and order a full scale nuclear reprisal." Her eyes widened as her stomach sank.

"How sure are you?" Dawson cocked his head to the side.

"You can never be sure based on leadership profiles, but I'd estimate it's sixty to seventy percent probability." She gave a half-shrug. "We could run a computer-generated analysis to ascertain how precise. But even then, it's nothing more than an educated guess based on key characteristics and input."

"How long will it take?" He leaned in; his eyes focused.

"Just a few minutes to input the data and the supercomputer will do the rest." She glanced at her mentor.

"What are you waiting for? Run it." His lips parted slightly.

"I'm on it boss."

The analyst meticulously inputted the data within minutes into her special software program. The supercomputer's immense processing power calculated the seventy-two percent probability within minutes. "That's not bad?"

He beamed. "That's good enough for me. This analysis is excellent work. We need to get this information to Fort Meade at once. Please relay the transmission and our analysis to the command center. This intelligence needs to go all the way to the top, and fast."

Patting her on the shoulder, Dawson returned to his chair. He and his protégé had stumbled onto something big. He found capturing signal's transmissions both exhilarating and alarming. Nevertheless, nuclear weapons horrified him. He feared the mutual destruction scenario, given the loss of life.

Taylor assembled her report in ten minutes, compiling all the necessary bits of information for her superiors. She recognized that simplifying the information avoided confusion while fostering understanding. Policymakers had a limited amount of time for reading given the voluminous amounts of material they digested daily. She had learned early on that intelligence recipients often wanted the facts behind the critical revelation.

She electronically sent her report and attachments to Dawson, who reviewed them in minutes. The quality and speed of her work impressed him. His work would be so much easier, if he had others with her proven abilities. His protégé always produced, no matter the priority or time crunch.

"Lori, this work is excellent. You're the best in the business. I'm going to request that your position be upgraded because of your work's importance. I'll cite this report as an example," he stated, nodding. He realized that the people drove the mission and recognized the importance of rewarding performance. Today's leaders frequently neglected their people, instead tending to their own ambitions.

"It's always nice to know that my work is valued. That's reward enough, even though a little extra money wouldn't hurt. I'll send it now." Her lips parted slightly.

As much as Dawson knew the stakes of the doomsday scenario, he prayed that he could provide the information to the policymakers in time for them to orchestrate an interdiction and spare humanity this awful catastrophe. He redoubled his team's efforts. He wouldn't sleep until this one was over and in the books.

# CHAPTER 38: EXECUTIVE ORDERS

*Oval Office – Washington, DC*

Seated behind his desk in the Oval Office, the president thumbed through the latest economic projections when O'Reilly burst in waving the latest intelligence derived from the National Security Agency. The commander-in-chief withheld his irritation from the sudden imposition. He recognized that his unscheduled visit meant a major crisis loomed in some distant land.

"Mr. President, I apologize for interrupting your preparations for your televised speech to the American people. I know our economic recovery and soaring national debt are important issues, especially given the impact of the Coronavirus pandemic. However, you need to read this report immediately. We're about to enter World War III unless you intervene." O'Reilly laid the Top Secret folder before his boss.

"That's a bit melodramatic Pat." He looked up.

"On the contrary Mr. President, wait until you read it." O'Reilly pointed to the classified folder. His face grave as he rubbed his eyes.

"Please have a seat and make yourself comfortable while I have a quick read. There's fresh coffee over there on the counter." The president motioned to the coffee pot while glancing at a picture of his wife and kids displayed on his desk.

The president opened the folder, glancing down at the fine print. He cursorily scanned through the admonitory sourcing caveats to jump to the executive summary. After a minute, he glanced up at his longtime friend and chief confidante.

The president shook his head. "What do you think? Is this plot plausible? Do you think this Chechen terrorist is capable of such a heinous plan?"

"Mr. President, it's not only plausible, but it's happening now. The aircraft is out of our missile range and currently in Russian airspace. You need to call the Kremlin and convince the prime minister to shoot down the aircraft."

"This job isn't getting any easier. Mistrust between our countries is at an all-time high since the Cold War. Will he listen or believe that I'm giving the U.S. plausible deniability by warning him?" The president grimaced.

His chief advisor shrugged. "It's up to you to convince him. I'd recommend you place all your cards on the table. He'll no doubt want to know the facts, so you should tell him all of them. You should state that Moussa Rahman, a Chechen rebel, has stolen the Aquila and possesses a nuclear weapon. You should underscore that he intends to detonate a nuclear weapon in space and over Siberia; thereby creating an electromagnetic pulse that will destroy the majority of electronics throughout Russia."

"He's got to believe it. The facts speak for themselves." The president held his head.

O'Reilly looked away. "There's more sir. I believe DS Special Agent Matt James and FSB Agent Svetlana Andropov are onboard that aircraft. They've turned up missing. Andropov's rental car was abandoned on a dirt road near the Galactic Transport Center. By requesting the prime minister shoot down the Aquila, you're also requesting that he terminate the two agents."

"Now why did you have to tell me that? These agents just prevented a nuclear catastrophe on U.S. soil and now I'm signing their death warrants," the president bemoaned.

"There's no other choice. Both agents knew the risks. They know their lives aren't worth the risk to the world. They're simply expendable assets."

"They don't pay me enough to do this job." His shoulders curled forward. He pushed his coffee to the side.

"Mr. President, we both know you don't do it for the money. Now let's go make that urgent call." O'Reilly's posture stiffened; his lips parted slightly.

The president shook his head. "No, I want to conduct a secure video conference. I need to look at his face and read his body language and demeanor."

"I'll make it happen." O'Reilly stepped out of the Oval Office briefly to direct his staff to set up the call immediately. He returned a minute later to collect the president, who pondered the intelligence report. He had read many disturbing briefs during his tenure, but none as grave as the one before him. Conventional wars remained difficult and complex. The thought of a nuclear war turned his stomach. Nuclear proliferation and one man's determination to crush a country caused his current dilemma. He reflected fleetingly about the number of terrorists in the world with similar ambitions as Rahman. Even if he stopped the Chechen leader today, he knew his efforts would inspire other fanatics to strive to do something equally as big.

Standing behind his desk, he glanced down again at a photograph of his wife and two kids. He considered his kid's future if he failed. He quickly dismissed the counterproductive thought. The president signaled for his national security advisor to join him. Walking down the corridor, the president analyzed the report in his head. He understood intelligence all too well and knew that faulty intelligence had started past wars. Yet, the facts seemed indisputable. Logic dictated few other reasonable conclusions. He hoped the Russian prime minister would agree.

Walking into the secure conference room, the president gestured to the information specialist who worked through an interpreter to coordinate with his counterpart a half a world away and eight time zones apart. The midday sun blanketed DC, making it a little after eight o'clock in the evening in Moscow. Fortunately, the late spring months in Moscow translated to over fourteen hours of daylight. This would allow Russia's pilots the opportunity to see their target before destroying it with their missiles. It would be a routine mission, provided the prime minister gave the order for the Aquila's destruction. It fell to the president to convince him to do so and that opportunity would come in seconds.

Sitting at the end of the conference table, the president faced a seventy-two inch screen. He rubbed his face while gathering his thoughts. A voice indicated their secure connection as the Russian prime minister appeared on screen.

"Good evening, Mr. Prime Minister. I apologize for the abrupt call. I have urgent information for you."

"I hope it's good to break me away from a dinner I'm hosting for the Indian prime minister," the Russian spoke English with only a slight accent. He canted his head as his eyes enlarged.

"Unfortunately, it's very dire and I need your assistance to resolve it, and time's running out." The president's fiery eyes stared at the screen.

The prime minister held his hands out. "How can I help you my friend?"

The leader of the free world maintained his poker face. "A Chechen rebel leader named Moussa Rahman has stolen the Aquila and is flying toward northwestern Siberia. We believe he'll launch the aircraft tethered to it into space to detonate a nuclear weapon."

"This information is indeed serious." The prime minister turned to his right to receive some insight from his most senior military commander. "Mr. President, General Barkowski has advised me that we've scrambled two MIG-29s to intercept the aircraft; they will reach the Aquila in less than three minutes."

"That's good news Yuri. We officially request that you shoot down the Aquila at once to avert this plot. I must underscore that we're not responsible for this plot or violation of your airspace. This heinous act is the sole work of a Chechen terrorist with no U.S. affiliation. We want to make this absolutely clear to avoid any misunderstanding and prevent a reprisal attack on America." The president stared at the screen.

"We understand that the aircraft's occupants wish to defect. How do I know you're not fabricating this information to avoid us having this state-of-the-art spacecraft?" The Russian crossed his arms.

"With all due respect Mr. Prime Minister, what I've told you is the truth. Our intelligence reflects that you're intimately familiar with Rahman and his threats. Now if you want to risk the state of your country on the belief that I'm attempting to deceive you, then I can't be held responsible for the horrific consequences that will befall your country. We both know that a high-altitude E-M-P detonated over your country will literally throw you back into the Dark Ages. This attack will kill your infrastructure and millions of innocent men, women, and children." The president pinched the bridge of his nose while squeezing his eyes tight.

The prime minister hit the mute button while he conferred with his top brass. He studied and knew the effects of electromagnetic pulses. He even tasked his military and top scientists to produce it as a viable first-strike weapon. The prime minister recognized the catastrophic effects of an EMP and its countless casualties. It would be the perfect attack against his country and that's what bothered him. The room descended into chaos as the hard right advocated a nuclear strike on the U.S. They feared a ruse in preparation for a nuclear first strike once the E-M-P destroyed their defenses.

The prime minister restored order to the room. Consensus seemed impossible and, in the end, he would make his decision alone. The difference of opinion frustrated him as the facts warranted shooting down the invading craft at once. He could not risk an E-M-P's damage to his country.

Punching the mute button again, the prime minister eyed the man halfway around the world. "Mr. President, I apologize for the delay. I needed to consult with my staff regarding both the information and our response. I'll order our fighters to shoot down the Aquila at once; however, I first need a written request from you outlining the reasons for shooting down a civilian aircraft."

The president looked over to his national security advisor. He signaled to him with a flick of the wrist to prepare a document for his signature. Like all great advisors, he had already anticipated such a request and prepared the document ahead of time. He handed the president a folder with the official request. "Mr. Prime Minister, we'll provide you an official request in minutes. I just need time to read this document before I sign it. Can you hold for a minute?"

"By all means Alex, take your time." The Russian knocked back his glass of vodka.

The president scanned the document. He removed a gold pen from his suit jacket pocket and scribbled his signature. He held the document up. "Yuri, this official request will be faxed to you at once. I hope it meets your needs."

"I'm sure it will. Once I have it, I'll give our pilots the official order to engage; they're now approaching the Aquila." The prime minister eyed his staff.

"I appreciate your intervention, but I need to add one more detail before you shoot down the aircraft. We believe that FSB Agent Svetlana Andropov is being held hostage, along with one of our agents." The president glanced down.

"You should've told me this news at the beginning. You're asking me to sanction the death of the granddaughter of one of our great Soviet leaders. This development certainly won't sit well with her family and may hurt me politically," the prime minister lamented. "I can't afford another scandal that my opponents can use against me."

"Does it make a difference? The facts remain the same. Moussa Rahman still intends to use the Aquila to harm your country. I myself had to request you shoot down an aircraft with an American agent onboard; one that was responsible for thwarting a nuclear attack on American soil. I'm sure you would agree that the fortunes of the many outweigh the few. This decision isn't about our political fortunes. It's about doing what's right." The American politician licked his lips.

"That's easy for you to say. It's not your missiles slamming into a civilian aircraft with the granddaughter of one of our national heroes. The fallout will be huge." The prime minister clasped his hands together.

"Fair enough, but it's my signature requesting it. So I'm just as much culpable for the action as if I pulled the trigger myself." His eyes widened. "If the job was easy Yuri, then anyone could do it."

"This request is a critical and one I'll honor. I want your assurances to control the media. Remember the fallout of Korean Airlines flight 007 that we mistakenly downed in the fall of 1983. This tragic incident brought about some of the tenses' moments of the Cold War. It also resulted in the escalation of anti-Russian sentiment in the United States and around the world." He stared intently at his American counterpart.

The president clasped his hands under his chin. "Yuri, I give you my word that I'll fully explain to the American people and the world. I will state that this incident was requested by me and I'll outline the reasons for the action."

"Alex, your word has always been good enough for me. I'll order my interceptors to strike now. It will be over in a minute. I'll call you once the mission's complete."

"I must ask one last favor before you return to your engagement. I need you to recover the wreckage and the nuclear warhead. We need to identify the warhead's origin. Hence, I'd like a joint investigation on this incident. Nuclear proliferation has become a major problem and we need to work together to plug any holes." The president rubbed his chin.

"You certainly aren't shy about your requests. I'll see what I can do. We may need to conduct a joint press statement in the near future. You'll owe me big for this." The Russian exhaled while looking up.

"I didn't expect you'd do it for free. I'll talk to you soon. Let me know the outcome of the mission. Bye." The president's tense muscles now relaxed.

A flick of the switch terminated the video teleconference. The president anticipated addressing the American public about the breach in security at the borders and the intelligence failure that placed the nation in jeopardy. O'Reilly stayed one step ahead of his boss. He had convened the National Security Council who would meet in less than ten minutes. They would discuss the issue and its ramifications to the nation and the administration. It would be yet another long day in the White House.

# CHAPTER 39: UNBREAKABLE

James awoke as the carrier plane ascended to thirty-nine thousand feet. Dried blood coated the side of his face. His head throbbed as he blinked repeatedly to shake his blurred vision. Dazed and disoriented, his eyes scanned the area. He admired the spacecraft's futuristic yet retro design once his double vision subsided. The craft's twelve-foot long and eight-feet in diameter cabin held three rows of two seats. Its formfitting seats comforted its occupants while softening the G-forces during space launches and descents back to earth. The circular windows uniformly positioned throughout the cabin offered three-hundred and sixty degree views around the aircraft. Beyond the bulkhead sat two pilots who controlled the spacecraft's myriad functions. He now understood the space ride's steep price. The weary agent appreciated the marvel of American ingenuity, but Rahman's originality troubled him.

Seated to his right in the second row, he eyed Andropov struggling to escape from the ropes; its thick fibers bounded her hands and legs to the seat. Bright red burn marks lined her wrists; blood trickled from them due to the constant friction she exerted against the rope's fibers. He knew the temporary setback would not discourage her and feared she would rip her hand off if it permitted her escape.

"It's about time you woke up from your nap. There's work to do." Her voice wavered.

James vacillated. "How long have I've been out?"

"We've been airborne for roughly eight to ten hours. What's Rahman doing? He should've already launched the spacecraft. Kansas or the central part of America is only a couple hours from New Mexico. America's heartland is the perfect area to detonate the nuclear device to ensure that it fully blankets the country." She winced as the fibers cut deeper into her flesh.

The DS agent struggled to turn his left wrist inward; his arms and wrists pinned firmly to his side and thighs. He turned his wrist slightly inward to read the small black compass affixed to his watchband. It read west, so he shook and turned his wrist a bit further. The compass still pointed west.

"I don't think we're headed over the central portion of the United States. We're headed west. Are we over water or land?" His face crumpled.

"I may be able to help you there." She wiggled back and forth. The Russian agent knew that if the plane yawed right then she could see the ground even at their current elevation.

Rahman approached them from the cockpit. "You both should just sit back and enjoy the ride." He rubbed his mouth. "We'll reach our launch point in about an hour."

James' body posture straightened. "Where are we going?" It appears that we're going away from America."

"I never said I was remaining in America." Rahman chortled. "I paid an inside source at the Galactic Transport Center for information and filing a flight plan. This allowed me to comply with FAA regulations and avoid U.S. fighter jets scrambling to intercept me."

James' brows pulled in. "That's rather thorough and ingenious."

"I also told you I had a plane to catch and I'm going into space. Although I hinted I was going to Russia, I didn't tell you where. But since you asked, we're flying to northwestern Siberia. I'll then launch this spaceship to an altitude of roughly sixty miles high and detonate the nuclear weapon in front of you. This E-M-P will throw Russia back into the Dark Ages and then my forces can return to power."

"This plan is madness." Her face reddened. "You'll kill millions of innocent Russians."

"That's precisely the point. This is the ultimate hijacking and use of an aircraft as a suicide weapon. It will dwarf the casualty figures of the nine-eleven attacks. With one attack, I'll free my homeland and strike a major blow to Russia. It won't be so great when I'm finished with them." Rahman puffed out his chest while raising his chin.

"You'll never penetrate Russian airspace." Andropov's fiery eyes glared at his face. "You'll be shot down by our aircraft or ground defenses."

"You may be right. Things may go down two ways. First, we're permitted to fly straight to Moscow, as we've signaled our intention to defect. Given American greed, they're likely to speculate we're interested in selling them our latest space technology. On the other hand, they could perceive us as a genuine threat and shoot us down. Now, if I detonate this device in space, Russia may suspect it as a deceptive American first strike. It's highly likely that they would launch their nuclear-tipped missiles at the U.S. in retaliation." The Chechen's eyes glowed.

"No one wins in a nuclear war. You may survive the initial attack, but as nuclear winter settles in, nothing survives. Are you willing to risk the planet's survival for your own personal vendetta?" James' face flushed.

"I'll take my chances. There are no great gains without great sacrifice. Sit back and enjoy the ride. I've things to do." Rahman swaggered to the cockpit, leaving the two agents to contemplate his revelation.

They found Rahman's plan to start a war between the superpowers as diabolical, but feasible under the circumstances. His unwavering commitment and grandiose plans oddly impressed the two agents. They contemplated their options. None of them seemed achievable. All of them involved freeing themselves as their first step. The only question remained how, and then they still needed to improvise their next steps.

Andropov tried to leverage her ring, but the rope restricted her movement. James used his double-jointed forearms to twist and insert his thumb into his pants' outer pocket. With a quick downward tug by his thumb, he ripped his pocket open, exposing his key chain. Carefully removing it with his thumb, he flipped it into his palm; his four fingers clasped the metallic object firmly. Aiming the thin portion of the flashlight key chain toward his wrist, he depressed a button. A two-inch blade sprang out and sliced through a portion of his skin. His lack of reach and mobility prevented him from sawing the ropes. The dogged agent pierced the blade's tip into the rope a dozen times. He then rotated his forearm and curled it towards his shoulder, pitting the weakened fibers against his strength. The rope suddenly snapped; his arm shot up and hit the chair's headrest with a thump.

The DS agent eyed the closed cockpit door. Reaching over, he cut the ropes to his right side, liberating himself to free the Russian agent. He cut the ropes binding her to the seat. She stood seconds later.

The two agents crept toward the nuclear weapon. James ran his hand over a countdown timer, an altimeter, and a push button detonation switch. He contemplated the reasons for three separate activation means. Rahman must have anticipated trouble. Kneeling beside the weapon, he analyzed the altimeter; it resembled an aneroid barometer or a pressure-measuring instrument.

"This instrument is calibrated to miles. It's set to detonate at an altitude of sixty miles high," he whispered.

James observed the lead wire connected to the needle and the other to a nail driven through the dial at sixty. The weapon would detonate once the needle touched the nail. It would be a routine deactivation with the right tools. A key chain and small blade would stretch his skills. He rotated the point of the blade back and forth like a drill and pressed lightly on the faceplate to avoid jarring the mechanism.

"That's going to take too long. Step aside." The Russian agent removed her wristwatch and turned it to its side. Depressing a button, a red laser cut through the outer glass and sliced the needle in half. "That should do the trick. The wires will never touch. That's one down and two systems to go." She pressed her lips together.

The two agents examined the inactive countdown timer, contemplating the location of the triggering mechanism. The clock reflected two minutes. Using her laser from her watch, she created a rectangular opening, exposing the clock's internal mechanisms and wires.

A voice emanated from the cockpit. "Are you looking for this?" Rahman held up a remote control no bigger than a pack of cigarettes. He depressed the switch; the timer lit up and started its countdown to zero.

James stepped forward, separating Andropov from the Chechen rebel. He positioned his right foot forward in preparation to go head-to-head with the Chechen terrorist.

Shooting her laser at a red wire, Andropov stopped the countdown timer with ninety seconds remaining. "I got it." The Russian agent pulled James by the neck until they were nose to nose. "Let's take over this aircraft. Two against two is great odds for us." Her fists tightened.

"Moussa, we've got a MIG-29 on our tail. It has a missile lock on us," the copilot shouted. "We're at forty-nine thousand feet."

Rahman vaulted back into the cockpit and latched the door. He excitedly requested the carrier ship to release the spacecraft. The MIG-29 pilot fired two missiles at its twin fuselage. The missiles locked onto the carrier aircraft's twin engines as the spacecraft broke free of it. The two agents scurried to their seats, latching their seatbelts in preparation for Rahman igniting the rocket engine. The Chechen waited seconds as the missiles slammed into the larger ship, erupting into a ball of flames. The Russian pilot realigned his sights and fired the Fulcrum's 30mm cannon. Rahman ignited the spacecraft's engine, sending a flame rearward as the craft accelerated away from the area. The MIG-29 strafed the tail of the spacecraft. He gave pursuit, but the spacecraft would reach supersonic speed in only eight seconds.

Unaware of the spacecraft's specifications, the MIG-29 pilot attempted to keep pace with the blistering rocket. Rahman pulled back on the stick and sent the spacecraft into a vertical climb. The Russian fighter pilot activated his afterburners, but Rahman pulled further away with each passing second. The MIG-29 pilot locked his missiles onto the blazing target and fired, making one final effort to fulfill his mission. The missiles lost ground and burned out as the spacecraft accelerated to Mach three. The pilot relayed the situation to the tower and ultimately to the Kremlin who monitored the mission's progress. The pilot broke off pursuit to return to base as instructed.

Andropov and James felt the full effects of G-force as their bodies thrust back into their seats; blood rushed from their head and chest to their feet and lower extremities. Breathing rapidly to counter a sudden drop in oxygen levels, they both struggled to control their blurred vision as they now blazed straight up at twenty-five hundred miles per hour. They would be in space in less than ninety seconds.

# CHAPTER 40: FALLOUT

*Above Siberia*

Both James and Andropov had felt the effects of G-force while racing cars and riding roller coasters. These experiences paled in comparison to the rocket ride and the 4-Gs that now twisted their bodies. The ergonomic chairs absorbed the pressures of sudden acceleration. His mind raced through a number of scenarios. He needed to wait until the rocket engine shutdown and they reached space, which meant maneuvering at zero gravity. James had to prevent the Chechen from pushing the button affixed to the nuclear weapon. This action would be difficult in normal conditions, let alone while free-floating around the cabin. He calculated they had less than five minutes to subdue the two terrorists, deactivate the bomb, and gain control of the spacecraft before descending back to earth. He needed to accomplish these feats and then deploy the split-wing of the aircraft. This would slow the rate of descent and prevent the craft from vaporizing during reentry; the craft's design relied on aerodynamics instead of the heavy heat shields seen on the space shuttle.

With less than forty seconds before they entered the thermosphere, James glanced at Andropov who embraced the G-force while observing her ascent into space. The sky changed from cobalt blue to mauve to indigo before turning to black in a few seconds.

"I'm glad you're enjoying the ride. Once we reach space, we need to keep Rahman away from the nuke while neutralizing him and his copilot. We must put them down fast and that will be difficult in zero gravity. This will be the ultimate wrestling championship contest, so let's get ready to rumble." A slight grin emerged from his tense face.

"What's your plan? Now is a good time to share it with me?" Andropov asked, gazing alertly.

"Of course I have a plan Svetlana." He winked. "Just follow my lead."

"No problem. What do we do? How do you know so much about this aircraft and space procedures?" She raised her eyebrows and offered a questioning gaze.

He tilted back his head. "I have a private pilot's license, which forced me to learn all sorts of flight procedures and principles. I'm also a space enthusiast. I've studied this project since its inception. It's a marvel of modern ingenuity, state-of-the-art materials, and the brilliance of a visionary aircraft designer. I've even trained on a flight simulator, thanks to my uncle's contacts. He helped me gain flight time and experience in his Cessna Skyhawk."

"This is no computer game and you can't hit the replay button if you don't like the outcome." She licked her lips.

"I know, but the principles remain the same. In twenty seconds, we'll need to get quickly to the nuclear weapon to prevent Rahman from detonating it. Our movements will be slow, so we'll need to compensate. Even if we don't take control of the aircraft, we must prevent him from getting near this bomb. At worst, we can thwart the attack and burn up during reentry. At best, we can incapacitate both of them and take control of the ship. You have any questions?" The self-assured American struck a knowing grin; his eyes gleamed.

The FSB agent beamed. "If we make it out of here, I'm going to find a way to repay you for saving my life yet again. This has been the toughest and most complicated mission of my career. We've been through so much in these last few days. It's all surreal." She grabbed and caressed his hand.

"I know. Five seconds." He glanced out the round overhead window and watched as light turned to night. They had entered the front edge of space, but the gravity of the situation eclipsed the awesome sight.

James unbuckled his seatbelt as the rocket engine shutdown; mild vertigo suddenly gripped him. Relaxed and floating freely, he grabbed the chair's headrest and pulled himself toward the nuclear weapon. He now stood between it and the cockpit door. Andropov joined him seconds later at Armageddon's gateway. The peaceful and eerie quietness seemed dreamlike, if not euphoric.

The cockpit door swung open as Rahman appeared in the doorjamb. James braced his feet against the base of the seat, bent at the knees, and then vaulted forward. His momentum propelled him into the Chechen as the two collided and launched back into the cockpit. James' martial arts and wrestling training would be useful at this distance. He knew that strikes and kicks would have a limited effect given the gravitational forces at work.

Clasping Rahman's ear with his left hand, he threw a right elbow strike to the terrorist's temple. "I hope that hurt, you son-of-a-bitch." Re-cocking his elbow, he drove it into the Chechen's lower jaw, as the copilot grabbed him from behind.

Breaking free, Rahman vaulted for the door as the American struggled with the copilot who tightened his chokehold. James grabbed the pilot by his forearm as he snaked it deeper around his neck. The DS agent forcibly thrust himself backwards, driving the attacker against the wall. The copilot yelped from the force of the impact. James sprang skyward, back-flipping to break the copilot's grip while coming down behind him. He wrapped his legs around each leg of his adversary like a grapevine. Maneuvering his right arm over his opponent's shoulder and around his neck, he pulled his forearm back. Cinching it up, the agent flexed his bicep while clasping his hands together. His bicep and forearm clamped down on both sides of the pilot's neck and the carotid arteries. The pilot flailed as blood ceased feeding his brain. Six seconds later, he fell limp.

He pivoted to see Andropov fighting Rahman to keep him at bay from the nuclear warhead. Pulling himself forward by the doorjamb, he lunged at the Chechen who kicked Andropov's stomach. She floated backwards from the force of his kick. Rahman reached for the button to detonate the warhead, but felt a smooth surface. While James wrestled with the terrorists in the cockpit, Andropov had sheared off the button with her laser. Rahman now needed to strip the wires' rubber coating and splice them together to detonate the bomb. This gave the two agents time to stop him.

Nevertheless, they needed to slow their descent as they accelerated back toward earth. If they failed to deploy the spacecraft's split-wing, they would not slow enough and burn up during reentry. By raising the unique split-wing, the spacecraft would descend belly first while the tail would stabilize the craft during their 7-Gs free fall. Time was running out.

He glanced at Andropov. "Get to the cockpit and deploy the wing upward. If you can't do that in the next minute, we'll fry."

She lunged at the cockpit door; James pushed her toward it with one hand as he grappled with Rahman with the other one. He had under a minute to immobilize the terrorist and assist her with the spaceship's descent.

James blocked the terrorist's punches thrown at his head and upper torso. He parried the Chechen's right jab, stepped in, and clasped the back of Rahman's neck with both hands. Pulling his neck down while jumping up, the agent catapulted his knee into the terrorist's solar plexus. The Chechen groaned and doubled over. Releasing his clasp, he slid his arm around Rahman's neck and squeezed for ten seconds. The unresponsive Chechen wilted and floated freely. James tossed him aside. The effects of weightlessness started to wane. He had little time to find his seat before experiencing rapid acceleration in excess of 6-Gs. Vaulting toward the cockpit, he strapped himself into the pilot's chair.

"I see you found the switch to deploy the split-wing. We need to ensure that the aircraft descends with its belly down. With the split-wing deployed, it will stabilize us as we descend, just like a feather floating down to the ground. It greatly increases the drag of the aircraft. Remember there are no heat shields," he said, scanning the instrument panel.

"Something's wrong." She fixated on the orange flashing light on the control panel. "I think the craft lost electrical power as I deployed the split-wing. It's only partially deployed." She pinched the skin at her throat.

"We need to get it fully deployed or we're screwed. There should be a manual override somewhere. We just have to find it." He eyed the control panel.

"Are you sure you know what you're doing Matt." Her face turned ashen as her heart pounded. "This is it; we're not going to make it." She eyed the American.

"Svetlana, trust me. We can do this. We'll drop through the atmosphere to sixty-thousand feet and then withdraw the split-wing to glide back to earth."

"It sounds simple." Her frown faded from her face.

"The aircraft's creator is a genius. It's all about physics and aerodynamics. He kept its functioning simple in comparison to the space shuttle. That means there's far less that can go wrong."

"I hope you're right." She peered through the windshield at earth.

"There it is." James grabbed the lever and struggled with the effects of G-force and resistance; the level popped free. The unique split-wing fully deployed. He felt the stick gain added responsiveness. Approaching 7-Gs, he glanced at Andropov. Her eyes focused on the control panel and its altimeter; it clicked off numbers faster than the accumulation of the U.S. national debt. The sky quickly returned, first from the darkness to indigo to mauve, and finally cobalt blue.

The DS agent flipped the switch to the split-wing with no effect as they hit sixty-thousand feet. Instinctively compensating to overcome the problem, he dropped the nose of the craft while releasing the lever to the split-wing. Physics did the rest, as he now entered into a steep dive. He jerked back on the stick to raise the nose and allow the aerodynamics of the craft to take effect. He began the remainder of his glide. They would be on the ground in less than twenty minutes.

Glancing at the American, she smiled. "Nicely done. I think we made it."

"That was sheer luck making it through the reentry process."

"You seemed so confident."

He tapped his fingers together. "That was for your benefit. I didn't want you to think that we were going to burn up in the atmosphere. Not a good way to die, although I doubt we would've felt much."

She combed her fingers through her hair. "What do we do now?"

"We need to find a large clearing or field. The terrain looks rugged below."

She cleared her throat. "I completed survival training in Siberia. It's not very hospitable land. There are plains with hills west of the Ural Mountains, but I doubt we can get that far. The southern border has uplands and mountains. Unfortunately, there are vast coniferous forests and tundra where we're likely to land. I recommend a southwesterly tract toward Omsk. We'll face very harsh conditions. If we don't find shelter, then we're finished."

"Thanks, I appreciate your optimism. Which direction should I take to boost our survival odds?"

The Russian shrugged. "Your guess is as good as mine."

James yawed to the right and held a steady southwesterly course. The craft's responsiveness and stability amazed him; it glided effortlessly cutting through the air. The sky's crispness and clarity allowed him to see unspoiled forests and mountains for hundreds of miles. With no engines, the glide yielded a euphoric tranquility.

He could have easily landed the craft under normal conditions. This landing would be exacerbated without the proper runway or airport. He mentally prepared himself to ditch the aircraft in a lake or on an ice bed. He just needed a clearing, as he feared endless forested areas with no chance of avoiding a frontal tree impact.

He glanced over at Andropov. "Please check on Rahman. If he's alive, then you better strap him into a seat. We'll figure out what to do with him once we land."

She stood quickly and walked to the cabin area. Bending over the motionless body on the floor, she felt the side of his neck with her fingers. A slight pulse indicated his toughness, so she dragged him to the cabin's last row. Grabbing under his armpits, she jerked the weighty man onto the front edge of the seat. She jostled him back and forth in the chair. She struggled to get him firmly rested in the seat in preparation for a rough landing. She snapped the buckle and cinched the strap tight.

"You didn't choke him hard enough. He's still breathing," she said, buckling herself in.

His eyes narrowed. "My apologies, I only tried to incapacitate, not kill him."

Checking the instrumentation, he maintained his southwesterly course heading. He glanced at their altitude, which read twelve-thousand feet and descending rapidly. Gazing forward, his eyes darted to a meadow, marsh, stream, and open field just a few miles ahead of their current position. Unable to see any other viable options, he banked left and started a corkscrew descent to bleed off some of their altitude. With less than five minutes until impact, he scrutinized his altimeter. He needed to hit the mark precisely to survive the landing. If he hit too soon, it would guarantee a hard landing and fracture the craft; if he landed too late, then he would run out of open space. The trick involved precisely hitting the water and then sliding onto dirt for the last part of the landing.

Lining himself up for his final approach, he concentrated on his objective. He mentally visualized periodic positions along his chosen flight path. Nearing the field, he feared overshooting the target. He jerked back on the stick and raised the aircraft's nose. The speed of the craft decreased as he approached the water. At less than one-hundred feet, he dropped the nose and hit the marsh in the middle. The craft skipped several times across the water before it slid onto the embankment. The craft vaulted skyward from the bank's gradual incline. This jolt cracked the fuselage at the midway point; a loud pop echoed throughout the cabin and cockpit. When the aircraft hit the ground again, the force of the impact split the craft. The rear third of the cabin and tail broke off and slid into a secondary marsh. Glancing fleetingly to the rear, James saw the tail of the craft sink into the water. He had no time to worry about the Chechen. He needed to get the spacecraft stopped before the encroaching tree line.

James realized that he had little control over the aircraft's trajectory. He cinched his seatbelt as the craft bounded in excess of fifty miles per hour. The aircraft started to turn askew, which caused him concern regarding a side impact against the trees.

"This isn't good. Brace for impact!" He gritted his teeth.

Her feet gripped the floorboard. "I never thought we'd make it this far."

"I didn't think we would either." He gave a hesitating nod. "Hold on. Here it goes."

The aircraft hit a tree at the point where the wing joined it, shearing it off. The spacecraft rebounded back to its original heading. The force of the collision threw the nuclear weapon free of its binding. It bounced and clanked around the cabin. Luckily, its shell remained intact and kept the plutonium core from being exposed. Unfortunately, that now meant a frontal impact into a large conifer tree.

James considered the frame's durability, but favored the odds of the tree's survival as they slammed into it. The sheer force of the impact jolted the two agents forward and upward. The craft's nose crumpled as its rear end vaulted skyward before smashing back down on the ground. The nuclear weapon launched from the craft; it landed hard in a bed of fresh powdery snow.

Unconscious, the two agents hunched forward in their seats; their heads resting on the dashboard as blood trickled from their foreheads. Given the near-freezing temperatures, they would perish in less than an hour. The thick forest canopy blocked the sun's powerful rays from warming their shady confines. The two had beat the odds and made it back to earth, but only time would tell if they would survive.

# CHAPTER 41: LOOSE ENDS

*Damascus, Syria*

Knocking on the wooden door, Nissan glanced over his shoulder while rubbing his clammy hands on his pants. A pair of Russian MIG-29 fighters buzzed the neighborhood; their sonic booms echoed throughout the streets, setting off a symphony of car alarms. After an eerie pause, the door viewer unlatched. Nissan snapped his head around toward the door. A cold black eye scanned him from head to toe. The door sprang open; its rusty door hinges screeched while in motion. A portly man motioned him into the dwelling. Entering the house, Nissan's gaze darted around the room while his throat's dryness caused him to swallow excessively. He panned the room noticing a woman cuddling her two-year-old while three other children huddled next to her. Their collective anxiety filled the room. Stepping down the stairs, Nissan's stomach churned as he placed a hand in his pocket. He gripped his briefcase harder as his heart palpitated and his throat constricted.

Nearing the bottom of the stairs, he noticed six stoic faces; their eyes darted from one another and now turned to him. He felt their eyes burn through him; his compromised state dawned on him. He landed in no-man's-land with nowhere to go and no backup.

Nissan sat at the head of the table; his hand slowly lowered his briefcase to his feet. "Brothers, our plan failed. Oddly, there's been nothing on the news. Just the fact that we attempted this operation on U.S. soil should've caused the Administration and Congress to rethink their position on the Middle East and Afghan-Taliban peace process."

"That's enough babbling Nissan." Hassan Nidal stood. "You said this plan was fool proof. You're the fool. We look like idiots by this mission's failure. What do you have to say?" Nidal's face flushed as he clenched his fists and pounded the table.

Nissan scratched behind his ear. "It wasn't my fault that the plan was discovered." He reached down, flipped a switch on his briefcase, and glanced at his watch. "The plan was brilliant. The mission must've been compromised. One of us is leaking information." He neglected to tell them the culprit, but their facial expressions indicated they suspected him.

"Don't think we didn't notice your tardiness prior to our meeting regarding our targeting of Satan's top diplomat. Admit it; you needed to provide your handlers operational specifics. Your betrayal led to American commandos thwarting our attack in Ramallah, not to mention discovering our future plans. Try to deny this Nissan." Moustafa Yousef sneered.

Nissan shook his head. "That's preposterous." He knew otherwise. He had passed other useful information along the way. None of which seemed to matter now.

"Explain this." Kahlil Moumad held up a letter from an anonymous source. "You're reporting to the SVR Nissan. Admit it." Moumad's eyes protruded as his nostrils flared.

Nissan reached for the letter. "Let me see it. I want to read it for myself." He scanned the one-page letter written in Arabic. Although the letter lacked a signature, he recognized the writing style as belonging to Igor Chirtoff.

Why that bastard, he thought to himself. Fortunately for Nissan, the letter didn't name him specifically, but instead it alluded to him. This ambiguity gave him a fighting chance and an opportunity to raise doubt as to the letter's authenticity. He needed to act like a defense attorney, whose job involved casting doubt in the jurors' minds. These six terrorists had already decided his guilt. He needed to create some doubt, and he had limited time to do so.

"This letter doesn't point the finger at me." Nissan shook his head. "This could be any of you. This letter's another ploy by the spy to undermine our cohesiveness until he can cover his tracks."

The others started nervously glancing at each other. Nissan's optimism increased as he wanted to create further doubt to divert suspicion so he could escape.

"If you read this letter, then you would've noticed this reference to living in the West Bank. Many of us have spent time there, if only to gather intelligence to defeat our enemy." Nissan threw the letter on the table. "Go ahead. Read the damn thing. If you need more proof, I've got something in my car that will prove my innocence. I'll go get it." He stood and walked toward the stairs.

"Sit down," Nidal barked. "You're not going anywhere until I say so."

"Who put you in charge?" Faisal Akmhat stood, as a vein in his temple bulged. "This type of attitude caused my faction to splinter off. I'm not going to sit here and take this bullshit any longer. How can any of you question my loyalty? I've been at this war longer than many of you have been alive. I suggest we all reexamine the letter and think this through before we do anything." Akmhat sat and eyed his colleagues.

"I agree with the old man." Muhammad Ayud slightly clenched his fists. "No one here should question my loyalty either. I've been responsible for several of the most glorious strikes against the 'Great Satan' this decade."

"Stop bragging," Nidal snapped back. "That ego of yours will get you killed. Never underestimate your enemy."

"Good. While you're examining the letter, I'll relieve my bladder." Nissan stood again and shuffled to the bathroom. Although his chance of his escape faded, the bathroom provided distance and might shelter him from the blast. He glimpsed at his watch; only one minute and twenty-six seconds remained. Nissan shut and locked the door. His eyes scanned the room for the safest area to take cover. He flushed the toilet for effect and then washed his hands for the same reason. Splashing water on his face, he then cupped his hands under the faucet and gulped some water. The heat of the room and his current circumstances parched him. He hunched behind the sink and remained perfectly still. His mind raced to his wife and newborn son. The sudden realization of his dispensability jarred him.

His stomach churned as he pondered the briefcase Chirtoff gave him. He had rewired the bomb and changed the clock from a zero countdown to an eight-minute one. The device used the clock as a safety and triggering mechanism. Once the device activated, it would only arm when the clock reached zero. The inventor wanted the bomb to go live upon activation. With the device detonating by four different methods, it would kill Nissan and the six others. Their deaths would bury the secrets of their operation.

Only a few would know the full deception involved in killing the peace process and the strengthening of a long-term war on Islamic extremism. However, only Igor Chirtoff could take full credit for all phases.

"What are you doing in there?" Nidal yelled out. "Get out here."

"I'll be out in a second. These things take time." Nissan glanced at his watch and gritted his teeth.

The C-4 high explosive detonated on time. The blast damaged the structural integrity of the house. The floor above and the rooftop came crashing down. Flying debris from the blast landed blocks away from the scene. It had Chirtoff's desired effect, killing everyone in the house. The blast ripped the bathroom door from its hinges and shredded it. Fragments pelted Nissan hitting a major artery on his leg. Blood spilled out on to the floor and turned the carpet red in seconds. Nissan felt faint; his senses heightened as death loomed. Screams and cries emanated from the street and nearby building. He knew the device maimed and injured innocent bystanders. He prayed for forgiveness and then faded into a deep and everlasting sleep.

# CHAPTER 42: SURVIVAL INSTINCTS

*Southwestern Siberia*

The sun began to descend behind the nearby mountains as the temperature dipped below freezing. James awoke from his unconscious state; the frigid air invigorated his senses. Blood trickled from a two-inch gash above his right eye; the cockpit and its instrumentation panel splattered red from his head's impact with it. Slightly dazed with a throbbing headache, he glanced over at Andropov who was out cold. Unbuckling his seatbelt, the DS agent stood and shuffled to her side. His fingers touched the side of her neck; her pulsed pounded strong.

Astonished they survived their descent, James nudged the FSB agent, but she remained lifeless. Glancing down, he caressed her soft pale cheek. He then rummaged through the aircraft, gathered a medical kit, four water bottles, and a dozen protein bars. Throwing them into a backpack, he slung it over his shoulders. He stepped out from the open fuselage and inhaled the crisp air which made his lungs sting; his exhaled breath wafted in the frigid breeze. The agent's heart pounded as his blood pressure increased with each passing breath. Goosebumps peppered his arms as his eyes panned the dense forest. He closed his eyes and listened to the howling wind. A strong squall approached from the west.

The astute agent needed to find shelter or they would both perish; sub-zero temperatures would soon descend upon the lush valley. With only two hours of daylight remaining, he had to find refuge fast. He turned his ear to a faint chime from the southwest. Tightening the backpack's straps on his shoulders, he unbelted the Russian agent and carried her in his arms. He walked out of the craft and towards the marsh. He followed a small stream in the direction of the chime. The gusting wind permitted him to pursue the soft-pitched rings as if they were summoning him to safety.

After traversing about a quarter of a mile, James glanced across the torrent to a small cabin. It rested about thirty yards back from the stream. He waded through the hip-deep frigid water. Its powerful current and uneven rocky bottom twisted his body and challenged his feet. He wobbled and stumbled over the riverbed's jagged edges and slippery surfaces. Lifting Andropov higher to his chest, his muscles ached from fatigue. The resolute agent trudged through the powerful current; water splashed skyward and blanketed the Russian beauty. He crept across the icy stream in minutes and walked up to the front porch. His fist pounded on the door, but there was no response; he opened it and wandered over to a nearby couch in front of a large stone fireplace. He gently laid the Russian agent down on the hard, bumpy surface.

Turning toward the fireplace, a number of dried logs rested next to it. James built a fire and after several minutes, it's raging flames radiated warmth throughout the room. Removing her pants and shirt, he admired her well-sculptured and lean body. He turned his eyes away and hung her clothes next to the fireplace. Covering her with a dusty blanket, he searched the cabin for non-perishables. Its bareness, other than a five-year-old bottle of red Georgian wine, reflected the cabin's lack of use. In the corner, the agent found a fishing rod with a finely woven fly attached to the end of the line. Grabbing the fly rod, he walked out of the cabin and down to the stream. His famished condition added greater incentive to catch his dinner.

His intense eyes scanned the water and spotted an eddy behind a large boulder; it served as an ideal hole for a trout waiting to ambush its prey. James cast the fly, whipping it back and forth; the line cracked through the air. Continuing to let line out, he finally reached the front of the eddy. The artificial fly landed in the slow-moving current. He twitched it with a short jerk; the water exploded as a fish inhaled the artificial bait. His rod bent in half as the fish swam into open water in an attempt to escape the angler's prowess. The avid sportsman played the fish, letting it run for twenty yards and following it downstream. He then turned the reel's handle, pitting his skill against the mighty Siberian trout. After about fifteen minutes, he beached the five-pound fish on the shore. His hands pounced on the flopping fish. Grabbing the fish by its mouth and gills, he removed the fly's hook and eyed his catch.

Returning to the cabin, he placed his rod down and walked toward Andropov; she remained lifeless. James retrieved a knife off the counter and carried his fish outside to a large flat rock. He lopped off its head and purged the fish of its innards. Walking down to the stream, he submerged the fish into the crystal clear mountain water. His hands numbed as he vigorously waved the fish back and forth to rinse it. Taking the fish inside, he sprinkled salt on it and placed it on the fireplace's grill. Pivoting the grill above the fire, he watched its glowing flames embrace his dinner. After about ten minutes and several turns, the backyard grill master cut the fish into two portions. Finding two wine glasses, he rinsed them from the faucet which pumped water from the stream. He filled the glasses to their capacity and set them on the counter. James dragged a small wooden table to the couch. He then set both plates side by side and sipped the vintage wine. Its sweet and fruity taste appealed to his palate.

Reaching down to Andropov's shoulder, he gently nudged her. Her eyes rolled open as she glanced up at him.

"Where are we?" She stretched her arms above her head.

"Alone at last." He raised his glass of wine. "Cheers Svetlana."

She sat upright, cinching the blanket around her body and eying the room. "Dinner smells wonderful. When did you find time to make it?"

"The remnants of our spacecraft are about a quarter of a mile from here. I luckily stumbled onto this place as the temperatures plunged below freezing. As for dinner, I caught it in the stream. I scavenged the wine from here, compliments of the owner of this fine establishment." The American pushed up his sleeves.

"We should eat before it gets cold. Besides, I'm starving." The Russian beauty picked up her glass of wine. "Cheers, I'm glad we survived and landed safely back on earth. I never thought we could do it." She beamed; her eyes wide and glowing.

"Me neither, but I'm glad we did." His smile exploded across his face.

The two ate their one-course meal. They discussed an array of topics, ranging from childhood to university studies to their current aspirations. They finished their dinner and snuggled together watching the blazing fire while sipping their wine. By the time they had finished their conversation and the bottle of wine, midnight gripped the Siberian countryside. A hooting owl, howling coyote, or some other wild animal occasionally broke the silent night.

Anticipating a busy day, they decided to sleep. They both prioritized the recovery of the nuclear weapon, as the Russian military would soon descend upon the area.

The DS agent stood and walked to a chair across the room. She summoned him back to the couch. "You should stay here with me. Sleeping on the hard chair is no way to go through the night. Besides, the fire is here and I need your body to keep me warm."

James' eyes twinkled in the low light. "You won't get an argument from me. I'd much rather share our bodily warmth."

The Russian rose and invited the American to lie down first. She joined him as he lay down, planting most of her lean body on top of his. He wrapped his arms around her and pulled the Russian closer to keep her anchored on the couch. The pace of the last few days, the fresh air, and the wine's alcohol exhausted them.

Andropov pulled herself up and softly kissed his lips. "That was for saving my life." She kissed him again; her soft moist lips clamped onto his.

"And what was that for?" James leaned in.

She beamed. "That was for the excellent dinner and conversation." She cupped his face with both hands, pulling him back for another adoring kiss. "And this is because I want to."

"I feel the same about you. I've never met anyone like you." He peered into her eyes as his heart raced.

It seemed implausible that the two agents stumbled upon a cabin in the middle of the Siberian forest as their bodies melded together in the backdrop of the fire. It appeared more like a great getaway that would provide them a romantic interlude. It felt so right considering their shared experience over the last couple of days. It seemed only natural that they would find comfort in each other's arms, or so James convinced himself. Things began to heat up as he relinquished his last embrace; he could barely keep his eyes open. The two agents decided to sleep, both exhausted from their journey into space. She snuggled her head on his chest and the two drifted off into a well-needed and deserved slumber.

.   .   .   .   .

It was a little past six in the morning. The sun's rays pierced through the two windows on the front side of the log house. The window's shades did little to block the sunlight. James awoke and remained still, choosing instead to watch the silent Russian beauty rest; her angelic appearance radiated warmth within his stomach and chest. She impressed him as both a worthy adversary and an outstanding partner. He pitied the fact that they lived worlds apart and that a dated ideology separated them. The Cold War's resurrection reignited strong suspicions between the two mighty superpowers. Their ability to bridge their backgrounds with a common threat pleased him. They both battled pure evil and united to do so. Their selfless actions proved to overcome their ideological and philosophical differences. He recognized the unlikelihood that he would ever see her following their rescue. He knew Congress would demand his immediate return to Washington, DC to answer questions, while Moscow would insist on her return for the same reasons. He dreaded their inevitable separation as the woman that lay beside him had thawed his guarded heart. She appeared his equal in every respect while also embracing her femininity; a rarity in a world struck by deadlines, crisis and career aspirations that left little time for social lives.

The irony of meeting his match under such dire circumstances did not escape him. She understood the demands of the job and its potential strain on a relationship. The career had cost him several promising relationships over the past five years. He understood a woman's reluctance to commit to a relationship; it always surprised him when he encountered a willing one, despite the insurmountable odds. They always discovered the reality of the job overshadowed its theoretical basis of frequent travel, separation, and the risks of job-related injury or death.

While gazing at her, she awoke with a warm smile. She stretched her arms above her head causing her body to press firmly against his chest. He wondered if she did it intentionally, as it aroused his senses.

He kissed her cheek. "Good morning, I'm glad you slept. It's going to be a busy day. We need to find the nuclear weapon and arrange for our rescue."

"Now that it's daylight, we'll be rescued soon. We'll be separated and taken to Moscow for a debriefing. That doesn't give us much time." She beamed.

"Time for what?" He pondered her statement.

"I know you have strong feelings for me. I can see it in your eyes and by the way you look at me. I also have strong feelings for you. Can't you tell by the gleam in my eyes?" The FSB agent gave him a yearning look. Her eyes sparkled in the light.

James pulled the beauty closer to him. He kissed her passionately, causing her to reciprocate. Although the fire ceased during the night, warmth radiated as the two agents caressed and kissed one another. He enjoyed the passion with no regrets as he lived in the moment. She reignited a burning desire deep within him. He recognized his weakness for the Russian beauty and the danger in getting close to her; but for once, he gave into his heart over his brain.

The cabin's door flew open. Andropov wrapped the blanket around her body. James sat up, throwing his shirt back on. The intense backlighting only revealed a silhouette lurking in the doorway.

The unwelcome visitor broke the eerie silence and awkwardness. "Am I interrupting?" The man's laugh boomed throughout the cabin. "I see you two finally let your passions get away." The man squinted as his eyes adjusted to the darkened room.

The two agents recognized the deep and livid voice as Moussa Rahman.

Rahman dragged the nuclear weapon into the doorway. "Look what I found. It's now armed." His mouth twisted.

"That isn't going to do you much good out in this wilderness. You'll kill thousands of trees, but that's not your intention. You're after a high body count." James stroked his throat and then grimaced.

"You're quite perceptive Agent James. It's time to settle a score. She can referee. I've installed a dead man's switch on this device, which is activated. If I release it, then the nuke will detonate. Svetlana, come here and hold the switch. Agent James, I'll meet you outside."

"You got it. I'll show you no mercy this time." James gave him an intense, fevered stare.

"Good, I wouldn't have it any other way." Rahman glanced at Andropov. "My dear, you have three seconds to take possession of this trigger before I let it go."

She sprung to her feet, grabbed her shirt next to the fireplace and threw it on. "I'm coming. Don't do anything stupid."

Rahman reached for the woman's hand and gently passed her the switch; her fingers clasped the switch in its depressed position as the Chechen released it.

"It's all yours. Don't let go." He flicked his hand in front of his nose.

"Let's get to it." James sidestepped the Chechen and strolled toward the outside.

Rahman struck him in the back of his head as he passed; the agent fell to the ground. "Didn't you learn a thing about turning your back on your adversary?"

James picked himself up. "If that's all you have, then you're in trouble. I'll destroy you." The special agent clenched his fists as he put his right leg forward.

"Give it your best shot." The Chechen sneered.

The two men squared off while Andropov clenched the switch. She contemplated her choices if James lost the fight. She surveyed the cabin for something to anchor the button; the cabin held little within her reach, so she watched the two rivals face off in a death match.

Rahman's height and weight gave him an advantage. The skilled agent remained undeterred. After several punches and kicks, each man continued to assess his opponent. James' patience waned. He looked for his opening and then it appeared. He parried Rahman's jab to his face, stepped inside, and clasped his arms around the Chechen's back. He lowered his hips and twisted, flipping the terrorist into the air and slamming him to the ground. James wrapped his legs around the Chechen's, preventing him from turning off his stomach. Tasting victory, he sunk his arm around his neck. He squeezed with all his strength; Rahman's arms flailed for seconds before his eyes rolled back and his body went limp.

"Don't make the same mistake again. Kill him!" Andropov yelled. "You can't give him any more chances."

He cinched his chokehold tighter for a second before releasing it. "I can't as I'm bound by American law. I've used only that force necessary to neutralize the threat." James stood, brushed his pants off, and staggered toward Andropov. His eyes searched the cabin's porch for something that could secure the bomb's button in the down position.

James stumbled to the cabin's stairs. He hunched over and took a deep breath.

Andropov shouted, "Watch out Matt, he has a knife."

Turning to see Rahman charge at him with a knife, James prepared to defend against the sharp instrument. A shot rang out, piercing Rahman's head and splattering blood and tissue around the surrounding area. The Chechen fell lifeless to the ground. James instinctively raised his hands above his head, as he scanned the nearby wood line. Its thick brush offered plenty of concealment for the shooter.

A lone man emerged from the trees holding a high-powered sniper rifle. With Rahman's death, his mission ended abruptly. Even though the man wore a camouflage outfit, Andropov recognized him as he approached the cabin.

"Svetlana, it looks like you're in a bit of a bind. I'll leave you this toolkit, so you can disarm the fusing system. At the very least, you can tape the button down until the military team arrives to handle it." Chirtoff gave a crisp nod.

"Is everything okay?" She eyed the man.

"I've taken care of everything. I have to go now. The Russian military will be here in less than ten minutes and I need to be gone. I was never here."

"How am I supposed to explain Rahman's death by a high-powered rifle?" Andropov shrugged her shoulders.

"You'll think of something. You always do." Chirtoff winked.

Andropov shook her head. "I assume it's all over. I can go back to my regular job with the security service."

"You two did excellent work saving our countries from Rahman's revenge. If I were you agent James, I'd leave before the troops arrive. They're likely to shoot you on sight as a spy or enemy of the state. Many people erroneously think that you were trying to detonate a bomb over Russia." Chirtoff rubbed his cheek.

"We both know that's far from the truth. Besides, Svetlana will vouch for me." James looked at her.

Chirtoff shook his head. "Well, you roll the dice Agent James, but I warned you. Now Svetlana, you don't need me anymore. You're better than I was ever at this game."

"It won't be the same without you Igor." She broke eye contact and shrugged.

"I'm retiring for good. You'll only have one master from now on. The FSB will have to survive without my services. I'm going fishing. You two make a good couple." The spymaster turned and walked away.

The two agents watched the man vanished into the thick woods. She admired Chirtoff's unique ability to remain one step ahead of everything. She speculated he led a super-secret cell within the Russian Intelligence Services. She doubted she would see him again, and that suited her fine; she hated the double life. The tenacious Russian agent just wanted to serve and defend her country.

"Are you okay Matt? I knew you could beat him. Can you give me a hand with this nuke?"

"Sure, give me a second." He walked over to the Chechen and placed a small stone on the ground at his head's exit wound. He struggled to lift a nearby fifty-pound boulder over his head and then slammed it down on Rahman's head." He walked back to Andropov and winked. "Was it blunt force trauma or a sniper's bullet that killed him? It's hard to tell. Now, let's get you separated from the device." He rummaged through the kit to find a roll of electrical tape.

Andropov released the dead man's switch once James finished securing it with layers of tape. She walked back into the cabin and slipped into her pants. Sitting on the couch, she donned her shoes. She contemplated Chirtoff's advice to the American, knowing the validity of his warning.

"Matt, you need to get going. Take the backpack and go southwest. I can't bear to lose you." Her eyes narrowed.

"Quiet, I hear helicopters coming." The American looked skyward. "It's already too late. They're here."

"It's two helicopters, both killer whales. I can tell by the sound of their rotors. That means it's a twelve-person team coming to rescue us." The Russian's eyes enlarged. "Stay close to me; I'll protect you."

James watched the commandos rappel from the helicopters and fan out to surround them in under ten seconds. He would take his chances with the

Russian agent. She lifted her credentials as the squad leader entered the cabin.

"I'm Svetlana Andropov of the Federal Security Service. This American's my responsibility and my witness."

"Get out of my way," the professional soldier ordered while shoving her aside.

James braced himself for the impact of the rifle's butt against his head. Instead, the soldier motioned him to come with him. Both Andropov and James followed the soldier to a clearing where the helicopter landed. James eyed the small cabin as the killer whale lifted off; he watched the special operations team disarmed the nuclear device. He glanced over at Andropov who sat across from him. She winked and smiled thinly. Relief energized their tired bodies as the helicopter sped off over the Siberian landscape. James would remember this escapade for the years ahead. Duty meant that he would soon tell his story in its entirety.

# CHAPTER 43: POLITICAL EXPEDIENCY

*Two Weeks Later – Capitol Hill*

The committee chairman pounded his gavel; the wood knocks echoed throughout the chamber. The stir of the crowd quelled as their eyes focused on Senator John Edward Coleman of Georgia. He had served in office for more than two decades. Given his influence and savviness, many on both sides of the aisle sought his direction and guidance. A man with incredible business instincts, he became a multi-millionaire by the age of thirty. Becoming bored with stock brokering, he invested his time in politics with the same shining results. His staff used to comment, "When J.E. Coleman speaks, people listen." This assertion was an understatement. Many felt that he would be president one day.

James sat at a wooden rectangular table facing fifteen senators. It had been years since he had last testified, that being a passport and drug related case. Customs agents had been shadowing a drug trafficker who orchestrated a major shipment every year for ten years. The resourceful suspect evaded prosecution; that was until DS charged him with several counts of passport fraud.

Raising his right hand, James repeated the familiar words. He wondered how many others took the committee's oath, not paying attention to the moment's importance. He marveled at the normalcy of the proceedings as his concentration intensified. The agent would relay his story one more time, only this time for the official record. He took no pleasure in testifying about his own government's inefficiency. James recognized that his conscience would be clearer and lighter.

Coleman scanned the audience from left to right. "Our committee will come to order. This afternoon's session will conclude our hearings on nuclear, chemical and biological terrorism, along with border security. In today's final session, we'll focus on the terrorist threat posed by weapons of mass destruction."

He glanced down at his notes. "I'm pleased to welcome, as a witness to our last panel, Diplomatic Security Special Agent Matt James. We thank Agent James for taking the time to be here this afternoon on such an important issue. I certainly look forward to hearing his testimony. I expect his testimony will be a candid description of the events taking place in the West Bank, New York, DC, and New Mexico, as well as the problems and challenges our nation faces in combating the dangers posed by terrorist groups and our porous borders. Agent James was instrumental in thwarting a nuclear attack in America and Russia, which could've started World War III."

Coleman sipped his glass of water and then reseated his glasses on his nose. "There's irrefutable evidence that many state sponsors of terrorism currently possess weapons of mass destruction or W-M-Ds. And they're all too willing to assist terrorist groups as Iran did recently with the Khorasan Group. They specifically provided them nuclear weapons, safe passage, and sanctuary while obtaining plausible deniability. Even if we could eliminate the threat posed by state sponsors, terrorist groups could still obtain the necessary materials and manufacture deadly chemical gas and biological weapons. A Japanese religious cult demonstrated this when conducting their deadly Sarin attack in the Tokyo subway in 1995."

"An expert witness at an earlier hearing underscored that W-M-Ds are the greatest threat our nation faces today. Admittedly, this was also the case in the past, as the Cold War pitted Russia against America. However, both superpowers readily understood the risks of retaliation, which provided a significant deterrent. We're not as fortunate with terrorist groups and organizations. They've no notion of deterrence and feel that they'll be justly rewarded for carrying out their horrific attacks."

Coleman glanced up from his notes to assess the audience's reaction. "I've read several classified reports outlining the thwarted nuclear attack on our homeland. Both the FBI and CIA claimed that they penetrated, monitored, and tracked these terrorist groups into our country. I have yet to see any compelling proof of this claim. In reviewing myriad statements on this topic submitted before this committee, we've decided to let you hear firsthand from Agent James. His description of events surrounding the near-fatal nuclear attack on America is simply stunning. Before hearing from him, I'll ask our minority member, Forrest Nichols, if he has any remarks to convey."

Senator Nichols, Democrat from Massachusetts politely nodded to the chairman. "Thank you, Mr. Chairman. I want to commend you for holding these monumental hearings. I also would like to welcome Agent James who has served his country with dignity and honor. I want to extend to Agent James my gratitude for his courage, professionalism, and exemplary public service. Without saying any more, I'd like to allow Agent James to make his statement to the committee. Agent James, the floor is yours." Nichols looked directly at the DS special agent.

James cleared his throat, eying the exit. His mouth remained dry as he took in a calming breath. His eyes focused on the chairman. "Mr. Chairman and other distinguished committee members, it's indeed an honor for me to appear before you today to address the risks posed by weapons of mass destruction from terrorist groups and organizations. The threat is real as we recently uncovered. Had we failed to thwart the Chechen leader's plans, then there would've been a disaster of unmatched consequences. I don't intend to burden you by reading my full statement; however, I'd ask that it be entered into the record in its entirety. Instead, I'll highlight the important points."

James lifted a glass of water, taking several swigs before setting it down. "My involvement in this case dates back to my emergency deployment to the West Bank. The mission was relatively simple in theory. My team and I were to conduct surveillance detection operations in support of the secretary of state's visit. In conducting our mission, we uncovered an attack team comprised of Khorasan Group members. They wanted to assassinate the secretary with the goal of interrupting the peace process. Fortunately, we thwarted the attack."

"Excuse me Agent James. How do you know your information's correct?" The democratic senator from California interrupted.

"That's a good question Mrs. Johnson." His eyes narrowed as he fingered his collar.

"If you allow me to finish my opening remarks, I'll explain it, so it will become perfectly clear." He clenched his teeth. It was obvious that not all of the committee had read his classified brief.

"The answer to your question is that I was there. I worked closely with an FSB agent to track the Chechen leader to America. We then interrupted the Khorasan Group's plan to detonate a nuclear weapon in Santa Fe. However, we discovered his even bigger plan to hit Russia given his ideology and desire for revenge."

Senator Johnson savored the sudden opening. "The FBI accuses you of bungling the operation and allowing Rahman to escape with several other nuclear warheads. How do you answer these allegations?"

James stared steadily at the senator. "If we'd followed the FBI's instincts regarding this case, then we'd be all dead right now. They believed the original source lacked credibility. They then interfered with our efforts to pursue the case, touting jurisdiction. Finally, they tried to block us from investigating the source's information." His eyebrows lowered and pinched together as he curled his lip.

"They claim you obstructed justice and that you should be charged for your actions. They allege you interfered in a federal investigation and withheld pertinent information." Johnson pointed at the agent.

"With all due respect, 'story' is the accurate word in this case. Our federal agencies failed to share information, as they were all vying for the headline-breaking news. They should've instead safeguarded America and its people." James pursed his lips.

Johnson's face flushed as a sheen of sweat surfaced on her cheeks and forehead. "The FBI believes you deliberately and knowingly withheld information from them."

The committee chairman turned to his left. "Can you prove these allegations Senator Johnson? Let me remind you that Agent James isn't the focus of this hearing." He wanted to be clear on the facts. He already knew of the CIA's involvement and its failure to interdict the nukes before they reached America. The agency's report remained highly classified and could not be discussed in today's open forum.

"I apologize, Mr. Chairman. I've no further questions for Agent James at this time." Johnson thumbed through her notes.

James' lips pressed into a fine line, thinking about the expression, "Admit nothing, deny everything, and make counter accusations." He looked up. "I stick to my earlier response. I had no knowledge of the FBI's investigation as they concealed their full involvement in the case. Why don't you ask DS Special Agent Jack Kline what transpired? He knows."

Senator Johnson's eyes glowed as she prepared to contradict the agent's testimony. "This committee received a sworn statement from Special Agent Kline. He indicated he sent a cable to DS headquarters outlining the FBI and CIA's involvement with the case. How do you respond to that statement?"

James sat back in his seat. "I didn't see the cable."

The senator sat up in her chair. "Are you asserting that you had no knowledge of the FBI's jurisdiction and case?"

James glared back at her. "Could you please repeat the question?" He knew how to push buttons.

Senator Johnson appeared annoyed by the delaying tactic. "Yes Agent James, are you..."

The committee chairman halted her in mid-sentence. "Senator Johnson, the purpose of these hearings isn't to antagonize the witness. It's to hear his testimony, and from it and others, we'll determine the truth and make appropriate recommendations. Please, Agent James, continue with your testimony."

The agent gave a brisk nod. "Thank you, Mr. Chairman. As I noted, Rahman evaded capture during the FSB's attempted takedown in Santa Fe. Solid investigative work allowed us to pick up his tracks. He continued to the Galactic Transport Center to hijack a carrier ship and spacecraft capable of reaching space. It was an ingenious plan. Fortunately, we interdicted them at the center, but Rahman stole the aircraft and launched, despite our efforts. He took both FSB Agent Svetlana Andropov and me hostage and tied us up in the spaceship."

"Who gave the order for you to go after Rahman?" Johnson raised her voice. "You should've called the FBI to interdict Rahman. Your botched takedown almost cost hundreds of thousands of lives."

"More like millions." James folded his hands. "Senator, are you suggesting I acted inappropriately? I didn't give the order to go after Rahman. National Security Advisor O'Reilly directed me to pursue Rahman.

Why don't you ask him?" He tilted his head to the ceiling and let out a heavy sigh.

The committee chairman defused the situation, steering James' testimony to its conclusion. "Agent James, no one here's accusing you of acting inappropriately. As Senator Nichols eloquently stated, this committee appreciates your actions and professionalism. We now invite you to finish your testimony." He turned in his chair, frowning at the freshman senator for challenging the agent's testimony.

James spoke for another twenty minutes without further interruptions except to clarify his testimony. His testimony divulged nothing new that the committee could not already see in his report and opening statement. He detailed the thwarting of Rahman's nuclear attacks on the ground and in space to avoid an EMP.

He sipped his water before concluding his testimony. "We must secure our borders by smartly building an impenetrable fence in critical areas to protect our sovereignty. Our porous borders easily allowed the terrorists and nuclear weapons into the United States. In fact, your own report concluded a rogue group couldn't effectively deploy an EMP over the United States. Your report reflected that the only platform for deploying one into space was a missile. I guess Rahman proved you all wrong. A resourceful terrorist can find many ways to destroy a nation, as Rahman almost did in this case. Therefore, if you're looking to affix responsibility, there's no shortage of people to blame. I've nothing further to add." The agent leaned back in his seat and eyed the committee.

The committee chairman tapped his microphone to quell the stir of the crowd. James' straightforward testimony had surprised the majority of those present. He expected no less of a reaction from them. After all, the DS agent outlined a story that served as a wake-up call for action. Terrorists virtually succeeded in a major plot which would have decimated the American way of life. No one in the room realized how only a few dedicated individuals could wipe out the most powerful country in the world with the strategic use of a single nuclear device.

Direct and brief questions followed. None of the senators wanted to grill the heroic agent during an election year. The follow-up questions indicated the FBI told a different version of events, not a surprise given the circumstances. James noted how cleverly the FBI had interspersed embellishments with the truth, painting a different picture of their role. James remained unfazed by their depiction of events. To him, it appeared as a vintage Washington dick-dance, where bureau representatives and politicians bent the truth for their own agenda; he understood that those in attendance knew the dance all too well.

Entranced by his thoughts, he missed the cue for his closing statement. The DS legal advisor tapped him on his shoulder. "Are you okay?"

James snapped his head around. "What?"

"It's over. It's time to finish."

The DS agent glanced up at the chairman and acknowledged with a single nod. "Mr. Chairman, this isn't over. We were fortunate this time against a small cell. More bothersome is the fact that many state sponsors of terrorism, like Iran, have unknown amounts of W-M-Ds. These weapons are perhaps more dangerous than nuclear weapons because they're easy to mass-produce and hard to detect. Biological weapons could be dispersed and our government wouldn't recognize it until our people started dropping around us. It's an extremely dangerous time in our nation's history."

The committee chairman nodded in agreement. "What do you suggest Agent James?"

James welcomed the opportunity to express the answer he had preached to his colleagues for years. "It's quite simple senator. Our law enforcement and intelligence agencies need to closely cooperate to defeat this dangerous threat. Perhaps it's time to reinvent our intelligence and law enforcement apparatus to make them more efficient and effective." He raised his chin, exposing his neck. His intense and lively eyes scanned the committee.

"What do you mean?" The senator reviewed the room, as the crowd stirred.

James sipped his water and gently set the glass down on the table. "I've worked in federal law enforcement for roughly thirteen years now."

The DS director reached over and covered the microphone. "This isn't the place. Let's wrap it up and get out of here."

James frowned, grabbing the director's hand. "With all due respect, sir, I beg to differ. This may be the only time in my life that I can affect national policy and I intend on taking it." He gingerly lifted the director's hand from the microphone.

"As I was saying senator, I've been in the business for a while. I find the lack of total cooperation between the agencies disturbing. Competition and duplication undermine law enforcement efforts, effectiveness, and efficiency. The majority of agencies are constantly engaged in turf battles, only concerned about preserving their own self-interests. They easily forget they're here to serve and, more importantly, protect. The public deserves better for their tax dollars and the good of the nation."

"Can you provide this committee with specific examples?" Senator Reynolds, Democrat from New Jersey, asked with a gleam in his eyes.

The steely agent repositioned himself in his chair. "I most certainly can. DS received information regarding a top ten most wanted terrorist and energized the host nation to arrest him. We involved the DEA and other federal agencies at post. However, the bureau wanted to hold off for days to get their team into country. We couldn't risk the delay, so we swooped in and nabbed the terrorist. The bureau was furious with our actions and operation. The funny thing is that they claimed they arrested the terrorist; I suppose that is true when the host nation extradited him. I could give you countless other examples, but I would be wasting your time. This isn't the right forum for this discussion." James fiddled with his watch. "I only present this as an example of the way a lack of cohesive leadership hampers our efforts to successfully protect the American people."

"In closing I'd like to underscore you've heard the dangers posed by nuclear, chemical, and biological weapons. Nuclear weapons were almost used in America and Russia; its consequences would've been catastrophic. There are still many persons, groups, and state-sponsors of terrorism that are now capable of using these weapons of mass destruction against the U.S. and its interests. It's up to the law enforcement, security and, intelligence communities to prevent this from happening. Our citizens expect our government to protect them from harm and we can't let them down."

James took a deep breath before continuing. "In this environment of severe budget constraints and an enormous national debt, institutional change is needed in the law enforcement and security agencies to make them more cost-effective and efficient; reorganization shouldn't be a piecemeal process. The agency's survival needs shouldn't outweigh the overall objectives of providing a safe environment for our citizenry."

"What's the answer?" The chairman motioned. "You've got our attention."

James scanned the room. "The solution is simple. Examine, if you will, the law enforcement and intelligence structures of most industrialized countries. Our system is bloated by any standards. The establishment of Homeland Security was necessary to centralize efforts and a great start. Nevertheless, we still have too many agencies enforcing our federal statutes, whereas one to three may suffice. In this respect, we could eliminate the overlapping jurisdictions and unnecessary costs. The process could be streamlined and much more effective. The only way to stop future catastrophic attacks on American soil is to establish a domestic intelligence agency with worldwide reach." James made sustained and strong eye contact with the chairman.

"You make a very valid point." The republican senator from Indiana pointed out. "There are at least two major problems with this thought. One, the American public is concerned about 'Big Brother' watching them. And, son, you have to realize the magnitude of what you're suggesting. Do you truly believe that all these agencies with long-standing traditions will give up their autonomy? The FBI would argue that all relevant agencies should be absorbed into them. How do you respond to these arguments?" The senator reseated his glasses on his nose.

James cupped his chin. "Look at it from two perspectives. The public is concerned about terrorism in America. It's also concerned about the debt and getting the most for their tax dollars. Here's a chance to take a bite out of both. The 'Big Brother' fear is unfounded. All law enforcement officers are bound by statutory and procedural regulations, which govern their behavior. It doesn't matter whether it's one agency or twenty. They all must abide by these rules and regulations." James inhaled deeply to regain his thoughts.

"As for the FBI, their enormous bureaucracy stifles efficiency, and they're one of the worst offenders when it comes to interagency cooperation and information sharing. In my opinion, the FBI's own nurtured culture makes it an impossible choice to head up this agency. Perhaps more importantly, the FBI leadership has recently abused its power for political purposes to target select Americans while undermining the integrity of our government. They should stick to what they do best and that is crime fighting."

James established direct eye contact with several committee members. "One of your esteemed colleagues proposed a domestic intelligence agency years ago. It is time to move forward with either an operational arm within the Department of Homeland Security or a new domestic intelligence agency. Personally, I recommend you create a domestic intelligence agency that melds certain qualities of the Israeli Shin Bet and MI5, the British Security Service."

"How do we do that without causing chaos in our existing system and muddying the lines of authority?" The chairman scratched his face.

James raised his head, smiling. "The easiest and quickest way is to combine the Diplomatic Security Service, the U.S. Secret Service, and roughly thirty-seven hundred agents from the FBI to form the new domestic intelligence agency. This newly created domestic intelligence agency would handle all terrorism cases worldwide. The FBI would then concentrate on crime and counter-intelligence."

"This would jumpstart the new agency with roughly eight-thousand agents, if my calculations are correct," Senator Reynolds chimed in. "Both the Secret Service and the Diplomatic Security Service have a deep understanding of terrorism. They've fought terrorism at home and overseas for decades while protecting their VIPs and facilities. You add members of the FBI's National Security Division and you have a formidable force."

"It certainly would, senator." James glowed. "Homeland security truly starts overseas, and Diplomatic Security should be at the forefront of any such organization. Although DS is a small organization, it has had many major successes. Ramzi Yousef, the mastermind behind the first World Trade Center bombing, is one such success. We can't afford to fail our citizenry. We must demand more from our government agencies. The consequences of failure are far too great."

James cleared his throat. "The stakes are great in this new world of global terrorism. We prevented a nuclear nightmare this time. Will we be as fortunate next time? Are we prepared? You must ask yourself these questions. I think that in the end you would agree with me. I've nothing more to say. Before I go, I'd like to thank the committee for allowing me to speak today. It has been a privilege and an honor. I hope what I've stated today resonates with you. Thank you."

The committee chairman looked up. "On behalf of the committee, we appreciate your frank testimony and remarks. We'll take them under advisement. Let's recess for the day."

James received handshakes and praise from the committee and many in the audience as he departed the room. It was only then that he convinced himself that the result justified the means. Yes, he had been used in this deadly game of roulette, but he had also saved hundreds of millions of innocent people. Who knows, maybe he was the only one who could have stopped Moussa Rahman. After all, that is what actually mattered. He had been anxious to give his ideas about a domestic intelligence agency a platform for a longtime. All told, it was not a bad result. Strolling out of the Capitol, his step seemed a little lighter.

Perched up on the steps to the Capitol, James eyed the surrounding locale and was in awe of the splendor and history of the area. He knew he shaped history. Andropov and her doings half a world away flooded his thoughts. He took a deep breath; a sudden alert from his phone diverted his attention. He looked at his screen to review the text: "Report back to the DS Training Center immediately for an emergency deployment." James knew there would be another time to rest.

# ABOUT THE AUTHOR

Mark J. Hipp was a 29-year veteran with the Diplomatic Security Service who has served as Chief of Security in London, Baghdad, Tel Aviv, Lima, and Tirana. As a former Deputy Chief and Team Leader of the Mobile Security Division (MSD), the author has spent eight years with DSS' elite antiterrorist unit responding to exigent situations in over 70 countries on five continents, as well as wrote numerous manuals on protective tactics and emergency response. He has been featured in three documentaries, but most notably in the Discovery Channel's *MSD: The Unknown Protectors.* He has also appeared on news interviews with ABC, CBS, and CNN.

# NOTE FROM THE AUTHOR

Word-of-mouth is crucial for any author to succeed. If you enjoyed *Radioflash*, please leave a review online—anywhere you are able. Even if it's just a sentence or two. It would make all the difference and would be very much appreciated.

Thanks!
Mark

Thank you so much for reading one of our **Military Fiction** novels.
If you enjoyed the experience, please check out our recommendation
title for your next great read!

*Blown Cover* by Mark Hewitt

2018 Pencraft Award Winner

CPSIA information can be obtained
at www.ICGtesting.com
Printed in the USA
BVHW070729150820
586435BV00003B/24